Mary Higgins Clark is the author of twenty-nine worldwide bestselling suspense novels, three collections of short stories, a historical novel, and a memoir, *Kitchen Privileges*. She lives with her husband, John Conheeney, in Saddle River, NJ.

Carol Higgins Clark is the author of the bestselling Regan Reilly mysteries. She lives in New York City.

The *Christmas Collection*

MARY HIGGINS CLARK

&

CAROL HIGGINS CLARK

POCKET
BOOKS

LONDON • SYDNEY • NEW YORK • TORONTO

The Mary & Carol Higgins Clark Collection first published in Great Britain by
Pocket Books, 2006
This edition first published 2010
An imprint of Simon & Schuster UK Ltd
A CBS COMPANY

1 3 5 7 9 10 8 6 4 2

Simon & Schuster UK Ltd
1st Floor
222 Gray's Inn Road
London WC1X 8HB

www.simonandschuster.co.uk

Simon & Schuster Australia
Sydney

A CIP catalogue record for this book is available from the British Library

ISBN 978-1-84983-330-1

Printed in the UK by CPI Cox & Wyman Ltd, Reading, Berkshire RG1 8EX

*Deck
the
Halls*

In the spirit of this shared journey,
we, Mary and Carol,
are dedicating this book to each other
with love.

Thursday,
December 22nd

Regan Reilly sighed for the hundredth time as she looked down at her mother, Nora, a brand-new patient in Manhattan's Hospital for Special Surgery. "And to think I bought you that dopey crocheted rug you tripped on," she said.

"You only bought it. I caught my heel in it," the well-known mystery writer said wanly. "It wasn't your fault I was wearing those idiotic stilts."

Nora attempted to shift her body, which was anchored by a heavy plaster cast that reached from her toes to her thigh.

"I'll leave you two to assess the blame for

the broken leg," Luke Reilly, owner of three funeral homes, husband and father, observed as he hoisted his long, lean body from the low bedside armchair. "I've got a funeral to go to, a dentist's appointment, and then, since our Christmas plans are somewhat altered, I guess I'd better see about buying a tree."

He bent over and kissed his wife. "Look at it this way: you may not be gazing at the Pacific Ocean, but you've got a good view of the East River." He and Nora and their only child, thirty-one-year-old Regan, had been planning to spend the Christmas holiday on Maui.

"You're a scream," Nora told him. "Dare we hope you'll arrive home with a tree that isn't your usual Charlie Brown special?"

"That's not nice," Luke protested.

"But it's true." Nora dismissed the subject. "Luke, you look exhausted. Can't you skip Goodloe's funeral? Austin can take care of everything."

Austin Grady was Luke's right-hand man. He had handled hundreds of funerals on his own, but the one today was different. The deceased, Cuthbert Boniface Goodloe, had left the bulk of his estate to the Seed-Plant-Bloom-and-Blossom Society of the Garden State of New Jersey. His disgruntled nephew and partial namesake, Cuthbert Boniface Dingle, known as C.B., was obviously bitter about his meager inheritance. After viewing hours yesterday afternoon, C.B. had sneaked back to the casket where Luke had found him stuffing rotted bits of house plants in the sleeves of the pin-striped designer suit the fastidious Goodloe had chosen as his last outfit.

As Luke came up behind C.B., he heard him whispering, "You love plants? I'll give you plants, you senile old hypocrite. Get a whiff of these! Enjoy them from now until Resurrection Day!"

Luke had backed away, not wanting to confront C.B., who continued to vent verbal outrage at the body of his less-than-generous uncle. It was not the first time Luke had heard a mourner telling off the deceased, but the use of decaying foliage was a first. Later, Luke had quietly removed the offensive vegetation.

But today, he wanted to keep an eye on C.B. himself. Besides, he hadn't had a chance to mention the incident to Austin.

Luke considered telling Nora about the nephew's bizarre behavior, but then decided not to go into it. "Goodloe's been planning his own funeral with me for three years," he said instead. "If I didn't show up, he'd haunt me."

"I suppose you should go." Nora's voice was sleepy, and her eyes were starting to close. "Regan, why don't you let Dad drop you off at the apartment? The last painkiller they gave me is knocking me out."

"I'd rather hang around until your private nurse gets here," Regan said. "I want to make sure someone is with you."

"All right. But then go to the apartment and crash. You know you never sleep on the red-eye flight."

Regan, a private investigator who lived in Los Angeles, had been packing for the trip to Hawaii when her father phoned.

"Your mother's fine," he began. "But she's had an accident. She broke her leg."

"She broke her leg?" Regan had repeated.

"Yes. We were on our way to a black tie at the Plaza. Mom was one of the honorees. She was running a little late. I rang for the elevator . . ."

One of Dad's not very subtle ways of getting Mom to hurry up, Regan thought.

"The elevator arrived, but she didn't. I went back into the apartment and found her lying on the floor with her leg at a very peculiar angle. But you know your mother. Her first question was to ask if her gown was torn."

That would be Mom, Regan had thought affectionately.

"She was the best-dressed emergency-room patient in the history of the hospital," Luke had concluded.

Regan had dumped her Hawaii clothes out of the suitcase and replaced them with winter clothes suitable for New York. She barely made the last night flight from Los Angeles to Kennedy, and once in New York had paused only long enough to drop off her bags at her parents' apartment on Central Park South.

From the doorway of the hospital room, Luke looked back and smiled at the sight of the two women in his life, so alike in some ways with their classic features, blue eyes, and fair skin, but so different in others. From the Black Irish Reillys, Regan had inherited raven black hair, a throwback to the Spaniards who had settled in Ireland after their Armada had been destroyed in battle with the British. Nora, however, was a natural blonde, and at five feet three inches was four inches shorter than her daughter. At six feet five, Luke towered over both of them. His once-dark hair was now almost completely silver.

"Regan, I'll meet you back here at around seven," he said. "After we cheer your mother up, we'll go out and have a good dinner."

He caught Nora's expression and smiled at her. "You thrive on the urge to kill, honey. All the reviewers say so." He waved his hand. "See you girls tonight."

It was a commitment Luke would not be able to keep.

A cross town, apartment 16B at 211 Central Park South was in the process of being decorated for Christmas. "Deck the halls with boughs of holly," Alvirah Meehan sang, off-key, as she placed a miniature wreath around the framed picture of Willy and herself accepting the $40 million lottery check that had changed their lives forever.

The picture brought back vividly that magical evening three years ago, when she'd been sitting in their tiny living room in Flushing, Queens, and Willy had been half asleep in his old club chair. She had been soaking her feet in a pail of warm water after a hard day of cleaning Mrs. O'Keefe's house when Willy came home, really bushed, from repairing a burst pipe that had sent showers of rusty water on the newly pressed clothes at Spot-Free Dry Cleaners down the block. Then the announcer on television began to read the winning lottery numbers.

I sure look different now, Alvirah thought, shaking her head as she examined the picture.

The brassy red hair that for so many years she had dyed herself in the bathroom sink had been transformed by Madame Judith, to a soft golden red with subtle shadings. The purple polyester pants suit had long ago been banished by her classy friend, Baroness Min Von Schreiber. Of course, her jutting jaw was the same, a product of God's design when he molded her, but she'd gotten down from a size sixteen to a trimmer size fourteen. There was no question about it—she looked ten years younger and a thousand times better now than in the old days.

I was sixty then and looked like I was pushing seventy. Now I'm sixty-three and don't look a day over fifty-nine, she told herself happily. On the other hand, she decided, looking at the picture, even dressed in that bargain-basement blue suit and skinny little tie, Willy managed to look handsome and distinguished. With his shock of white hair and vivid blue eyes, Willy always reminded people of the late, legendary Speaker of the House of Representatives, Tip O'Neill.

Poor Willy, she sighed. What bad luck that

he feels so rotten. Nobody should be stuck with a toothache during the Christmas season. But Dr. Jay will fix him up. Our big mistake was to get involved with that other guy when Dr. Jay moved to New Jersey, Alvirah thought. He talked Willy into getting a dental implant even though it hadn't worked last time, and it's been killing him. Oh, well, it could be worse, she reminded herself. Look what happened to Nora Regan Reilly.

She had heard on the radio that the suspense author, who happened to be her favorite writer, had broken her leg the evening before in her apartment in the very next building. Her high heel had caught in the fringe of a rug, Alvirah mused—the same kind of thing that happened to Grandma. But Grandma wasn't wearing high heels. She had stepped on a wad of bubble gum in the street, and when the fringe of the rug stuck to the bottom of her orthopedic sneakers, she went sprawling.

"Hi, honey." Willy was coming down the hall from the bedroom. The right side of his face was swollen, and his expression was instant testimony to the fact that the troublesome implant was still killing him.

Alvirah knew how to cheer him up. "Willy, you know what makes me feel good?"

"Whatever it is, share it right away."

"It's knowing that Dr. Jay will get rid of that implant, and by tonight you'll be feeling much better. I mean, aren't you better off than poor Nora Regan Reilly, who'll be hobbling around on crutches for weeks?"

Willy shook his head and managed a smile. "Alvirah, can I never have an ache or a pain without you telling me how lucky I am? If I came down with the bubonic plague, you'd try to make me feel sorry for somebody else."

Alvirah laughed. "I suppose I would at that," she agreed.

"When you ordered the car, did you allow for holiday traffic? I never thought I'd be worried about missing a dentist appointment, but today I am."

"Of course I did," she assured him. "We'll be there long before three. Dr. Jay squeezed you in before he sees his last patient. He's closing early for the holiday weekend."

Willy looked at his watch. "It's only a little after ten. I wish he could see me this minute. What time is the car coming?"

"One-thirty."

"I'll start to get ready."

With a sympathetic shake of her head, Alvirah watched her husband of forty-three years disappear back into the bedroom. He'll be feeling a thousand percent better tonight, she decided. I'll make some nice vegetable soup for dinner, and we'll watch the tape of *It's a Wonderful Life*. I'm glad we delayed our cruise until February. It will be good to have a quiet, at-home Christmas this year.

Alvirah looked around the room and sniffed appreciatively. I love the smell of pine, she thought. And the tree looks gorgeous. They had placed it right in the center of the floor-to-ceiling windows overlooking Central Park. The branches were laden with the ornaments they'd accumulated over the years, some handsome, some battered, all cherished.

Alvirah pushed back her large, round glasses, walked over to the cocktail table, and grabbed the last unopened box of tinsel.

"You never can have too much tinsel on the tree," she said aloud.

Three more days until Christmas, twenty-six-year-old Rosita Gonzalez thought, as she waited for Luke Reilly behind the wheel of one of the Reilly Funeral Home limos, standing near the hospital's Seventy-first Street entrance. Mentally she reviewed the presents she had bought for her five- and six-year-old sons, Bobby and Chris. I haven't forgotten anything, she assured herself.

She so wanted them to have a good Christmas. So much had changed in the last year and a half. Their father had left—not that that was any loss—and her ailing mother had moved back to Puerto Rico. Now both boys clung to Rosita as if they were afraid *she* would somehow disappear too.

My little guys, she thought with a rush of tenderness. Together, the three of them had picked out their Christmas tree last night and would decorate it tonight. She had the next three days off, and Mr. Reilly had given her a generous Christmas bonus.

Rosita looked in the rearview mirror and straightened the driver's cap over her waterfall of dark curly hair. It sure was a stroke of luck when I got the job at the funeral home, she thought. She had started working part-time in the office, but when Luke learned that she moonlighted as a limo driver, he told her, "You can have all the extra work you want here, Rosita." Now she frequently drove for funerals.

There was a tap on the driver's window. Rosita looked up, expecting to see the face of her good-natured boss. Instead she found herself locking eyes with a vaguely familiar countenance, which, for the moment, she could not place. She opened the window a few inches and was rewarded with a belch of cigarette smoke. His head darting forward, her unexpected visitor identified himself in staccato tones: "Hi, Rosie, I'm Petey the Painter. Remember me?"

How could I forget? Rosita wondered. A mental image of the brilliant chartreuse shade he'd painted the main viewing room of the Reilly funeral home in Summit, New Jersey, flashed through her mind. She remembered Luke Reilly's reaction when he saw it. "Rosita," Luke had said, "I don't know whether to laugh, cry, or throw up."

"I'd throw up, Mr. Reilly," had been Rosita's advice.

Needless to say, Petey the Painter's services had no longer been requested nor required in any of the three Reilly funeral homes.

Petey had gratuitously added bright yellow to the moss-green paint Luke had selected, declaring that he thought the place needed a little livening. "Relatives of dead people need cheering up," he'd informed them. "That green was really depressing. I had a little extra yellow paint in my car, so I threw it in for free." On his way out, he'd asked Rosita for a date, which she'd promptly declined.

Rosita wondered if he still had flecks of paint in his hair. She looked at him, but couldn't tell. A cap with earmuffs covered every inch of his head and shaded his narrow, bony face. His wiry frame was encased in a dark-blue storm jacket. The turned-up collar of the jacket grazed the graying stubble that shaded his chin.

"Of course I remember you, Petey," she said. "What are you doing here?"

He shuffled from foot to foot. "You look great, Rosie. Too bad your most important passengers never get to feast their eyes on you."

The reference, of course, was to the fact that Rosita sometimes drove the hearse in funeral cortèges.

"You're funny, Petey. See you." She began to raise the window but was stopped by Petey's hand.

"Hey, it's freezing out. Can I sit in the car? I need to ask you something."

"Petey, Mr. Reilly will be here any minute."

"This will only take a minute," he explained.

Reluctantly, Rosita threw the lock that opened all the doors. She had expected him to go around and get in beside her in the front seat. Instead, in a lightning-fast motion, he opened the back door of the vehicle and slid in.

Thoroughly annoyed with her intruder, she swiveled her head around to face him in the back of the limo, whose tinted windows shielded anyone seated there from the view of the outside world. What she saw took her breath away. For a moment she thought it was a joke. Surely that couldn't be a gun Petey was holding?

"Nobody's going to get hurt if you do what I tell you," Petey said soothingly. "Just keep a nice, calm look on your pretty face until the King of the Stiffs gets here."

A weary and preoccupied Luke Reilly emerged from the elevator and walked the short distance to the door of the hospital, barely noticing the Christmas decorations adorning the lobby. He stepped outside into the raw, cloudy morning and was glad to see his limo waiting near the end of the driveway.

In a few strides, Luke's long legs brought him to the car. He knocked on the window of the passenger side, and a moment later was turning the handle of the back door. He was inside and had closed the door behind him before he realized that he was not alone in the backseat.

Luke's unerring memory for faces, coupled with the sight of paint-flecked boots, made him realize instantly that the man sitting opposite him with the gun in his hand was none other than the idiot who had turned his viewing room into a psychedelic nightmare.

"In case you don't remember me, I'm Petey the Painter. I worked for you last summer." Petey raised his voice. "Start driving, Rosie," he ordered. "Turn right at the corner and pull over. We're making a pickup."

"I remember you," Luke said quietly. "But I prefer seeing you with a paintbrush instead of a gun. What's this all about?"

"My friend will explain when he gets in.

Nice comfortable car you got here." Again, Petey raised his voice. "Rosie, don't try any funny stuff like running a light. We don't want no attention from the cops."

Luke had barely slept the night before, and his mind was blurry. Now he felt somehow detached from reality, as though he were dreaming or half asleep, watching a movie. He was alert enough, however, to sense that this unlikely kidnapper might never have held a gun before, which actually made him twice as dangerous. Luke knew he could not take the chance of throwing himself forward in an attempt to overpower his captor.

Rosie turned the corner. The car had not quite stopped when the front passenger door opened and another man joined them. Luke's mouth dropped: Petey the Painter's partner in crime was none other than C. B. Dingle, the disgruntled nephew of the late Cuthbert Boniface Goodloe.

Like Petey, C.B. was wearing a cap with earmuffs that fit loosely over his balding head, and a bulky, nondescript storm jacket that covered his butterball-shaped torso. C.B.'s round, pale face was half covered by a dark, bushy mustache that had not been present at his uncle's wake the day before. Wincing, he pulled off the fuzzy disguise and addressed Luke.

"Thank you for being on time," he said cordially as he patted his lip. "I don't want to be late for my uncle's funeral. But I'm afraid *you're* not going to make it, Mr. Reilly."

Where are they taking us? Rosita agonized as, following C.B.'s instructions, she turned right on Ninety-sixth Street and headed for the FDR Drive north. She had seen C.B. at the funeral parlor only yesterday, had met him a couple of times before when he came to the funeral home with his uncle, who kept changing his mind about the plans for his last farewell.

Irrationally, she almost smiled, remembering that Cuthbert Boniface Goodloe had stopped in only last month to inform Luke that the restaurant he had chosen for a reception after his funeral had been closed down by the Health Department. She had driven Mr. Reilly, Goodloe, and C.B. to the Orchard Hill Inn, which Mr. Reilly had suggested as a replacement. Mr. Reilly told her later that Goodloe had painstakingly studied the menu, eliminating the most expensive items from his guests' future selections.

That day C.B., as usual, had been practically kissing his uncle's butt, which obviously had done him no good. Yesterday afternoon the viewing room had been filled with shocked but grateful members of the Seed-Plant-Bloom-and-Blossom Society of the Garden State of New Jersey—a group commonly known as the Blossoms—whose goal to spruce up every nook and cranny of New Jersey had just received a much needed million-dollar shot in the arm. The buzz was that Goodloe's dying words to his nephew had been, "Get a job!"

Had C.B. gone crazy? Was he dangerous?

And what does he want with me and Mr. Reilly? Rosita wondered as, even inside her gloves, her fingers turned to ice.

"Head for the George Washington Bridge," C.B. ordered.

At least they were going back to New Jersey, Rosita thought. She wondered if there was any hope of appealing to C.B. to let them go.

"Mr. Dingle, you may know I have two little boys who need me," she said softly. "They're five and six years old, and their father hasn't supported or seen them in over a year."

"My father was a crumb too," C.B. snapped. "And don't call me Mr. Dingle. I hate that name."

Petey had overheard. "It's a dumb name," he agreed. "But your first and middle names are even worse. Thank God for initials. Mr. Reilly, can you believe C.B.'s mom saddled him with a name like Cuthbert Boniface, in honor of her sister's husband. And then, when the old geezer passes away, he gives just about everything to the stupid Blossoms? Maybe they'll name a new strain of poison ivy after him."

"I spent my whole life pretending to like those stupid names!" C.B. said angrily. "And what do I get for it? Career advice three seconds before he croaks."

"I'm sorry about all that, C.B.," Luke said firmly. "But your problems have nothing to do with us. Why are we here, or more precisely, why are you and Petey in my car?"

"I beg to differ—" C.B. began.

Petey interrupted: "I really like that expression. It sounds so classy."

"Shut up, Petey," C.B. snapped. "My problem has *everything* to do with you, Mr. Reilly. But your wife is going to have a million ways to make it up."

They were halfway across the George Washington Bridge.

"Petey, you tell Rosie where to turn. You know the way better than I do."

"Take the Fort Lee exit," Petey began. "We're going south."

Fifteen minutes later, the car pulled onto a narrow road that led down to the Hudson River. Rosita was on the verge of tears. They reached an empty parking area at the river's edge, facing the skyline of Manhattan. To the left they could see the towering gray span of the George Washington Bridge. The heavy stream of holiday traffic crossing back and forth on its two levels only increased Rosita's sense of isolation. She had a sudden terrible fear that C.B. and Petey might be planning to shoot them and throw their bodies into the river.

"Get out of the car," C.B. ordered. "Remember we both have guns and know how to use them."

Petey aimed his revolver at Luke's head as he and Rosita reluctantly left the familiarity of the car. He gave the weapon a quick twirl. "I watched reruns of *The Rifleman* doing this," he explained. "I'm getting real good at twirling."

Luke shuddered.

"I'll be your escort," C.B. told him. "We have to hurry. I have a funeral to make."

They were forced to walk along the shore, past a deserted marina, to where a dilapidated houseboat, its windows boarded up, was anchored at the end of a narrow dock. The boat rocked up and down, as the river lapped restlessly against its sides. It was obvious to Luke that the worn and aging craft was sitting dangerously low in the water.

"Take a look at the ice that's starting to form out there. You can't be planning to put us on that thing in this weather," Luke protested.

"In summertime it's real nice," Petey boasted. "I take care of it for the guy who owns it. He's in Arizona for the winter. His arthritis is something awful."

"This isn't July," Luke snapped.

"Sometimes you get bad weather in July too," Petey responded. "One time there was a real bad storm, and—"

"Shut up, Petey," C.B. growled irritably. "I told you, you talk too much."

"You would too if you painted rooms all by yourself twelve hours a day. When I'm with people, I like to talk."

C.B. shook his head. "He drives me nuts," he said under his breath. "Now be careful getting onto the boat," he told Rosita. "I don't want you to slip."

"You can't do this to us. I've got to go home to my boys," Rosita cried.

Luke could hear the note of hysteria in Rosita's voice. The poor kid is scared stiff, he thought. Just a few years younger than Regan and supporting two children on her own. "Help her!" he barked.

Petey used his free hand to grasp Rosita's arm as, fearfully, she stepped down onto the deck of the swaying vessel.

"You're very good at influencing people, Mr. Reilly," C.B. complimented. "Let's hope you're as successful for the next twenty-four hours."

Petey unlocked the door of the cabin and pushed it open, releasing a dank, musty smell into the cold outside air.

"Whew," Petey said. "That stink'll get you every time."

"Move it, Petey," C.B. ordered. "I told you to get an Airwick."

"How thoughtful," Rosita said sarcastically as she followed Petey inside.

Luke glanced over at the Manhattan skyline, then looked upriver to the George Washington Bridge, taking in the little red lighthouse underneath. I wonder if I'll ever get the chance to see all this again, he thought, as C.B. pressed the gun in the small of his back.

"Inside, Mr. Reilly. This isn't the time for sightseeing."

Petey turned on the dim overhead light as C.B. closed the door behind them.

On one side of the small, shabby space was a seating area consisting of a Formica dinette table surrounded by a cracked, imitation-leather banquette; directly opposite was a matching couch. The furniture was all built-in units. A small refrigerator, sink, and stove were adjacent to the table. Luke knew that the two doors to the left probably led to a bedroom and whatever passed for a bathroom.

"Oh, no," Rosita gasped.

Luke followed her stare, and with dismay realized that two sets of chains were bolted to the walls in the seating area. They were the kind of hand and ankle restraints commonly used to restrain criminal defendants in courtrooms. One set was next to the couch, the other near the banquette.

"You sit here," Petey directed Rosita. "Keep me covered, C.B., while I put her bracelets on."

"I got everybody covered," C.B said emphatically. "You're over here, Mr. Reilly."

If I were alone, I'd take my chances and try to grab his gun, Luke thought angrily, but I can't risk Rosita's life. An instant later, he was sitting on the banquette, chained, with Rosita opposite him on the couch.

"I should have asked if either one of you cares to use the facilities, but now you'll just have to wait," C.B. said cheerfully. "I don't want to be late for my uncle's funeral. After all, I *am* the chief mourner. And Petey needs to get rid of your car. When we come back, Petey'll bring stuff for your lunch. I won't be hungry, though. My uncle paid for my meal today, remember, Mr. Reilly?"

C.B. opened the door as Petey turned out the light. An instant later the door slammed shut, and Luke and Rosita could hear the grating of the key turning in the rusty lock.

Trapped in the shadowy darkness of the swaying boat, they both remained silent for a moment as the reality of their precarious situation hit both of them.

Then Rosita asked quietly, "Mr. Reilly, what's going to happen to us?"

Luke chose his words carefully. "They've already told us they're looking for money. Assuming that's all they really want, I promise it will be paid."

"All I can think about is my kids. My regular baby-sitter is away until next week, and I don't trust the girl who's filling in. Her Christmas dance is tonight. She didn't want to work at all today, but I begged her to. She expects me home by three."

"She wouldn't leave the boys alone."

"You don't know her, Mr. Reilly—she won't miss that dance," Rosita said with certainty, a catch in her voice. "I've got to get home. I've just got to get home."

Regan opened her eyes, groggily sat up, swung her legs over the edge of the bed, and yawned. Her bedroom in her parents' apartment on Central Park South was as comfortably familiar as the one in the family home in New Jersey in which she'd been raised. Today, though, she did not take time to appreciate the charming ambience of the peach-and-soft-green color scheme. She had the sensation of having slept a long time, but when she looked at the clock, she was glad to see it was only a few minutes before two. She wanted to phone the hospital and see how her mother was doing, then catch up with her father. She realized that beyond the fact that she was feeling the effects of the news about her mother's accident and the hurried red-eye flight, she was filled with undefined anxiety. A quick shower might help me clear my mind, she thought, and then I'll get moving.

She put in a call to La Parisienne, the local coffee shop, and placed her usual breakfast order: orange juice, coffee, and a toasted bagel with cream cheese. This is what I love about New York, she thought. By the time I get out of the shower, the delivery boy will be ringing the bell.

The strong spray of hot water felt good on her back and shoulders. She quickly washed her hair, stepped out of the shower, wrapped herself in a robe, and rolled a towel around her head.

Ten seconds later, her face glistening with moisturizer, she answered the door for the delivery boy. She was glad he pretended not to notice her appearance. In his job, he's seen it all, she thought. But he did produce a sunny smile when she gave him a generous tip.

Moments later, the bagel unwrapped, the coffee cup in her hand, she phoned her mother's room. She knew the nurse had to be there, but no one picked up. The ringer is probably turned off, she thought. She hung up and dialed the nurses' station on that floor.

What seemed like several minutes passed as she waited for her mother's nurse to come to the phone. It was a relief to hear the friendly, professional, and reassuring voice of Beverly Carter. She had come on duty this morning, just as Regan was leaving. Although they had spoken only briefly, Regan had instantly liked the slim, fortyish black woman, whom the doctor had introduced as one of their finest private nurses.

"Hi, Beverly. How's my mother?"

"She's been sleeping since you left."

"I've been sleeping since I left," Regan laughed. "When she wakes up, tell her I called. Have you heard from my father?"

"Not so far."

"I'm surprised. But he did have that funeral. I'll give him a call. Tell my mother she can always reach me on my cell phone."

Next, Regan dialed the funeral home. Austin Grady, the second in command at "Reilly's Remains," as Regan and her mother dubbed the funeral homes, answered. His initial greeting, as usual, was suitably subdued.

"Austin, it's Regan."

The somber tone turned jolly. "Regan, hello."

Regan was always amazed at the way Austin could switch gears so rapidly, his demeanor of the moment dictated by the demands of his job. As Luke had observed, he was perfectly suited to this line of work. Like a surgeon, he was able to disassociate himself from surrounding emotions.

"Is my father there?" she asked.

"No, I haven't spoken to him since he called early this morning to send for a car. Your poor mother," he commiserated in a most upbeat tone. "What's going to happen next? And I know your father was really looking forward to the trip to Hawaii. I understand she tripped on a new rug you bought her in Ireland."

"Yes," Regan said quickly, guilt about her purchase washing over her again. As her best friend, Kit, always said, "Guilt is the gift that keeps on giving."

"Austin, my father told us he was going to be there for a funeral you were having today. Didn't he show up at all?"

"Well, no, but the service went beautifully. The old guy had been planning it for years.

Your father probably realized he didn't really need to come." Austin chuckled. "Right now the mourners are all enjoying a free lunch across town. The deceased left the bulk of his estate to the Blossoms. They're all at the restaurant, and they look like one happy group. They inherited enough money to buy sprinkling cans for every plant in the state of New Jersey."

"Lucky them," Regan said.

"Your father has a 3:30 dentist's appointment on his schedule. I don't think he'll miss that."

"Thanks, Austin." Regan hung up and dialed Luke's cell phone. After several rings his voice mail came on. As she listened to her father's voice telling the caller to leave a message, her sense that something might be wrong deepened. Her father hadn't been heard from in hours, even to inquire about her mother. She left a message for him to call her.

She sipped her coffee and thought for a minute. I can't just sit here, she decided. She glanced at the clock. It was now 2:35. She called the dentist's office to confirm that her father had not canceled his appointment.

"Please ask him to wait for me," Regan said to the receptionist. "I'm leaving the city in a few minutes, and it shouldn't take me more than an hour to get there."

"Will do," the receptionist promised.

Regan hurriedly dressed and dried her hair. After Dad has his appointment, we can do the errands together, she thought. Then we'll drive back to the city to see Mom.

But even as she pulled on her coat and ran down to grab a cab, Regan somehow knew that that wasn't what she would be doing this afternoon.

How long had he and Rosita had been locked up in the dark, chilly houseboat? Luke had no sense of time. It seemed like hours. They could have left the light on, he thought angrily.

After C.B. and Petey the Painter took off, Luke had tried to reassure Rosita. "Trust my hunch," he told her. "When those jerks come back, they'll tell us what they want. And when they get it, they'll let us go."

"But we can identify them, Mr. Reilly. Do you really think they can be that stupid?"

"Rosita, probably nobody else could be that stupid, but I believe it of that pair. It won't be long before we're missed. Don't forget, my daughter's a private investigator, and she'll have everyone looking for us."

"Just as long as someone takes care of my kids. I'm so afraid that ditzy baby-sitter will dump them with someone they don't know. My little guy, especially, is painfully shy."

"If there's one thing I'm sure of, it's that when Regan realizes we're missing, she'll check on your kids."

They hadn't spoken for a while. It was only about ten feet across the cabin to the built-in couch where Rosita was chained. Had she dozed off? Luke wondered. The lapping of the water against the sides of the boat made it impossible to hear any sound of movement from her.

"Rosita," he said softly.

Before she could answer, a thud on the deck startled both of them. The sound of the key grating in the lock dispelled Luke's hope that whoever was outside might be a potential rescuer.

The door opened. A somber trickle of light and a blast of cold air preceded Petey and C.B. into the cabin.

"How are our campers doing?" C.B. asked jovially as Petey snapped on the overhead light. "I hope you're not vegetarians. We bought ham and cheese sandwiches." Both men were carrying grocery bags.

It was with mixed emotion that Luke noted how small the bags were. Either they were planning to have them out of here in a short time, or there would be frequent take-outs from the local fast-food outlets in Edgewater.

"Either one of you want to go to the can?" Petey asked solicitously.

Luke and Rosita both nodded.

"Ladies first," Petey said. He released Rosita's hand and ankle shackles. "You can close the door, but don't get any stupid ideas. Besides, it don't have a window."

Rosita looked at Luke. "Could you lend me a dollar for the attendant?"

When it was Luke's turn inside the tiny cubicle, he considered his options and realized he had none. Even if he could overpower Petey when he was refastening the chains, C.B. would be standing with his gun trained on Rosita. I have to play along with them, he thought.

While Luke, Rosita, and Petey ate their sandwiches, C.B. sipped coffee. "I'm full," he said, looking at Luke. "That restaurant you suggested wasn't bad. The veal parmigiana was the best I've had in ages. Although I'm surprised I could digest my meal, having to look at those nerds from the Blossom Society. It was only the thought of you two back here that got me through."

"You could have brought me back some veal parmigiana," Petey griped. "I think this rye bread is a little stale. And he didn't put enough mayo on mine." He peered over at Luke's sandwich. "Let's switch halves."

Luke grabbed the second half of his sandwich and took a big bite out of it. He laid it back down on the wax paper. "Be my guest." Luke was inordinately pleased to see the disappointed look on Petey's face.

Petey looked at Rosita. "No dessert for the boss. You can have his Twinkies."

"I'd rather choke," Rosita snapped.

"Now that we're one big happy family, let's get down to business." C.B. crushed his empty coffee cup and stuffed it into the deli bag.

"Be careful, the pickles are still in there," Petey protested.

C.B. groaned and dumped the contents of the bag on the scarred Formica table.

"Don't get mad," Petey said. "I wasn't at some fancy lunch. I feel like I've been on a bus all day. Once I dumped the car at Kennedy, I had to take a bus to the Port Authority. Then I hadda wait for another bus to Edgewater. Then I hadda wait for you at the bus stop. You were too cheap to let me take a cab. *You've* been riding in a nice warm car all day—"

"Shut up!"

But Petey wasn't finished. "I had my four dollars ready to pay when I crossed the George Washington Bridge. Then when I'm waiting in a long line to hand it over, I discover there's an E-Z Pass on the floor of the car. I stuck it back up on the windshield and switched lanes fast. Some jerk almost plowed into me. He starts honking his horn like a crazy person. Then I saved you more money when I went over the Triborough Bridge. You should have noticed that E-Z Pass when you rode up front. I'm surprised at you."

C.B.'s eyes bulged. "You used the E-Z Pass? You moron! I took it off so they wouldn't be able to track us. Now they can check and find out where it's been used."

"Really?" Petey looked awestruck. "I'll be darned. What will they think of next?" He turned to Luke and Rosita. "C.B. is so smart. He reads a lot of detective novels. I never had much chance to read. Mr. Reilly, I know he really likes your wife's novels. I think one of them is even autographed."

"When you release us, I'll get him another one. And when is that going to happen?"

Petey reached for a pickle. "Explain our plan, C.B. It's so good. In a few days we're going to be on a beach somewhere with a million dollars in our suitcase."

C.B. interrupted Petey. "I'm telling you for the last time, Petey. Keep your mouth shut!" He pulled Luke's and Rosita's cell phones from the leather pouch where he had stashed them. "Mr. Reilly, it's nearly 4:30. We're going to get in touch with your family and tell them we want a million dollars cash by tomorrow afternoon."

Rosita gasped. "A million dollars?"

Petey piped in. "He's got viewing rooms all over New Jersey, and his wife sells a lot of books. Hey, C.B., maybe we should ask for more."

C.B. ignored him.

"I can guarantee my family will pay you the money," Luke said carefully. "But it's Thursday afternoon of Christmas weekend. I don't know how they'd be able to get it by tomorrow."

"Believe me, they can," C.B. said. "If they want to."

"He read it in a book," Petey volunteered. "Banks do things for important people, like opening their doors at all hours. And you're a real important person."

"But my wife is in the hospital," Luke protested.

"We know that. Where do you think we picked you up?" C.B. asked. "Now—who do you want us to call?"

"My daughter. She just got in from California. She'll get you the money." He gave them her cell phone number: "310-555-4237."

Petey started scribbling the number on a piece of paper he had torn off the brown deli bag. "Say that again"

Luke repeated the number slowly.

C.B. turned the phone on and began dialing.

"That implant came out smooth as silk," Dr. Jay assured Alvirah. "I have Willy on oxygen now. I'd like you to wait a little while before you take him home. He's still groggy."

"That laughing gas really knocks Willy out," Alvirah commented. "But he sure was looking forward to it. He's been in such misery."

"Well, give him a couple of days, and he'll be good as new. The prescription for antibiotics should clear up his infection." Dr. Jay's pleasant, bespectacled face broke into a smile. "He'll be able to enjoy the Christmas holiday. I know *I'm* looking forward to it." He looked at his watch. "I have one more patient, and then I'm on vacation."

"Any big plans?" Alvirah queried with her usual genuine interest in the comings and goings of her fellow creatures.

"My wife and I are taking the kids skiing in Vermont."

"Nice," Alvirah said, shaking her head. "When we won the lottery, I made a list of all the things I've always wanted to do in this lifetime. Skiing was one of them. But I haven't gotten around to it yet."

She did not miss the alarmed expression on

Dr. Jay's face. "I bet you think I couldn't do it," she challenged.

"Alvirah, I've known you long enough. Nothing you do would surprise me."

Alvirah laughed. "Don't worry. I won't crash into you on the slopes just yet. If the weather reports are right about a storm, you should have some great skiing."

"If it does hit, we'll already be there. We're leaving tonight." Dr. Jay looked at the door. "He's never late," he murmured more to himself than to Alvirah, then said, "I'll check on Willy and start to wrap things up around here."

As the doctor left the waiting room, Alvirah admitted to herself that she really had been worried about Willy—more worried than she had allowed herself to realize. Willy has always been so healthy, she thought. I won't even let myself consider that something could be seriously wrong with him. She was so deep in thought that the ringing of the office bell startled her. That must be the patient Dr. Jay is waiting for, she reasoned. She jumped up to answer the door as a buzzer released the lock.

Alvirah immediately knew that the slender, dark-haired young woman who came into the waiting room was not the patient Dr. Jay was expecting. She had clearly heard him say that *"he"* was never late.

She quickly sized up the newcomer— around thirty, very attractive, wearing a handsome suede jacket, jeans, and boots; obviously preoccupied. She smiled fleetingly at Alvirah as she looked at the empty reception desk.

"Everybody except Dr. Jay has gone home already," Alvirah volunteered cheerily. "He's waiting for his last patient."

Alvirah could see that the look of concern on the young woman's face immediately deepened.

Dr. Jay appeared at the doorway. "Hi, Regan. Where's your father? He's holding up my vacation."

"I was hoping to hook up with him here," Regan said.

"Well, he should be along any minute. I expected him half an hour ago."

"It's so unlike my father to be late."

"There's a lot of traffic out there," Dr. Jay said with a wave of his hand.

The expression on Regan's face, however, remained clearly troubled.

"Is anything wrong?" he asked her.

Regan walked closer to the doctor and lowered her voice, a useless exercise, since Alvirah Meehan could hear a mouse sneeze from three rooms away. "It's been kind of crazy," she began, and briefly explained about her mother's accident.

That's who she is! Alvirah thought: Nora Regan Reilly's daughter. Of course! I thought she looked familiar. She's a private investigator, just like me. Only she has a license. Alvirah sat up straight and cocked her head, praying they didn't move into Dr. Jay's private office.

"I thought I'd help my father do some shopping this afternoon after he saw you," Regan was saying. "Because we were planning to go to Hawaii, we don't have a Christmas tree or any food in the house."

I love Hawaii, Alvirah thought.

"What worries me," Regan continued, "is

that I can't reach my father on his cell phone, and he hasn't called my mother since he left her room at the hospital this morning. And now he isn't here. None of this is like him." Her voice was forlorn.

Uh-oh, Alvirah thought. She's right. Something's wrong.

"Well, let's wait and see," Dr. Jay said reassuringly. "He'll probably be here any minute. If he isn't, with all that happened today, it must mean that he simply forgot. He's obviously got a lot on his mind. I'm sure there's a logical explanation."

He looked over at Alvirah. "Willy should be ready to go in about fifteen minutes."

"Take your time," Alvirah said, grateful that Willy wasn't ready yet to walk out the door. She watched as Regan restlessly crossed to the window, looked out at the parking area, then sat in the straight-backed chair opposite the couch.

After a moment, Alvirah leaned forward. "I just want you to know that I've read every one of your mother's books and I love them. I was so sorry to hear about her accident. I can see you're worried about your father, but take my word, when something happens to a wife, husbands are useless. They forget everything."

Regan smiled slightly. "I hope you're right. I'm going to try calling him again." She pulled out her cell phone and dialed. "No answer," she said. "I'll try the hospital."

Let him be there or have called, Alvirah prayed as Regan spoke to her mother's nurse.

Regan put down the phone. "My mother is still asleep, which is good. My father hasn't called, which isn't." She stood up and once again walked to the window.

Alvirah wanted to say something comforting, but she knew there was nothing to be said. Had something happened to Luke Reilly?

Nearly twenty minutes later he was still not there.

"Okay, Alvirah, you can collect your patient," Dr. Jay said as he came down the hall, his hand under Willy's arm.

"Hi, honey," Willy said feebly.

"Take him home and let him sleep it off," Dr. Jay instructed. "And have a great holiday." He turned to Regan: "Any word?"

"Dr. Jay, I think it's obvious my father isn't going to make it today. I'll call a cab to take me to the house. I'm sure I'll catch up with him there."

"Don't you live here in Summit?" Alvirah asked, but didn't wait for an answer. "I know you do. It says so on the book jackets. We've got a car and driver outside. We'll drop you home. Come on, Willy."

Before she could protest, Regan found herself sitting next to Alvirah in the backseat of a sleek, black limo. Willy, his legs stretched out, his eyes shut, was leaning back on the opposite seat.

"I've taken driving lessons three times in the last three years," Alvirah explained. "The instructors always found excuses to pass me off on someone else." She laughed. "I can't blame them. You wouldn't believe all the parking cones I've flattened."

Regan smiled. She instinctively liked Alvirah and realized now that she had heard her
name somewhere before. As the car pulled
onto the main road, she said, "I feel as though I
know you from somewhere. Your name is
familiar."

Alvirah beamed. "I know you're a private
investigator, and I guess you could say I'm
kind of in your business. I've accidentally been
around when the police needed help. Then
I've written about what happened for the
Globe. I'm what you might call 'a roving crime
correspondent.' "

"Roving isn't the word," Willy volunteered,
without opening his eyes. "Alvirah's always at
full throttle, looking for trouble."

Regan laughed. "My mother sent me a couple of your columns. She enjoyed them and
thought I'd be interested in the cases. She was
right." Alvirah's coat was open. Regan leaned
over. "Is that your famous pin with the hidden
microphone?"

"I never leave home without it," Alvirah
said proudly.

Regan reached into her pocket. "I'm going to try my father's office."

But there was nothing new: Austin Grady still hadn't heard from Luke.

With a sigh, Regan clicked off the phone.

For the next five minutes, Alvirah did a running commentary on the Christmas decorations of the various houses they passed. Finally Regan said, "That's our house up on the left."

"Oh, lovely," Alvirah breathed, craning her neck to get a better look. "A lot nicer than the houses I used to clean, I'll tell you that."

It was obvious that no one was home. The Reilly house, unlike its neighbors, was in total darkness.

The long driveway extended to the garages at the rear of the house. The chauffeur stopped at the walk that led to the front door.

"Let me go in with you while you check your messages, Regan," Alvirah said, a note of concern in her voice.

Regan knew what Alvirah meant. If there had been an accident, there might be a call on the machine. "I'll be fine, Alvirah. I can't thank you enough. You need to get Willy home."

Reluctantly Alvirah watched Regan go up the steps and disappear into the house. The car began to move slowly down the driveway. They were just turning back onto the street when the soft ring of a cell phone made Alvirah look around quickly. I don't have mine with me, she thought. Then she spotted it. The phone Regan had been using was on the seat next to her, its green light flashing.

I'll answer it, she thought. I bet it's her father. She picked it up and flipped it open.

"Hello," she boomed happily.

"Regan?" The voice was deep and raspy.

"I'll get her," Alvirah said, as she yelled for the driver to go back. "Is this her father?"

"It's a message from him."

"Oh, good," Alvirah shouted.

As Alvirah jumped out of the car and ran up the walk, she did not hear C.B.'s comment to Luke: "Whoever answered your daughter's phone has a voice like a foghorn."

Fred Torres hung up his uniform and closed the door of his locker with a decisive snap. "That's it for two weeks, Vince," he said to his partner. "It's anchors away for me."

"I wish I were going sailing in the Caribbean," Vince Lugano said as he pulled on a sweater. "While you're on deck with a beer in your hand, I'll be putting together a fire engine and a dollhouse."

The tiny lines around Fred's dark brown eyes crinkled when he smiled. "You love every minute of it," he said.

"I know I do," Vince agreed, looking with affection at the man who had become his best friend since they were sworn in as police officers in Hoboken, New Jersey, six years ago.

Fred was twenty-eight years old, just under six feet tall, lean and muscular. His olive complexion, dark hair, and general good looks made him the perfect target for well-meaning friends who just happened to have an available sister or cousin. He was about to begin his final

term at Seton Hall Law School after the holidays.

Vince, the same age as his partner, was two
inches taller and twenty pounds heavier, with
sandy hair and hazel eyes. He had never been
interested in anyone except his high-school
sweetheart, whom he married five years ago.

"What time do you leave?" Vince asked.

"I've got an eight o'clock flight tomorrow
morning."

"You'll be at Mike's party tonight?"

"Sure."

"See you there."

Fred had intended to drive straight home
to his apartment in a small brownstone at the
south end of town. But he impulsively
stopped when he turned the corner that led to
his street and spotted the dazzling array of
poinsettias in the flower-shop window. It
won't take that long, he assured himself as he
went in and selected a plant. He had met
Rosita Gonzalez at a party a month ago, and
they'd gone out to dinner together a couple of
times since. He had invited her to the party

tonight, but she didn't have anyone available to baby-sit.

As he got back in the car, he smiled, thinking of her and remembering the night they had met. They both had arrived at that party at the same time. He had parked behind her. She had been driving a glistening black limousine. As they walked up the steps together, he introduced himself and said, "You certainly arrive in style."

"Wait till you see what I go home in," Rosita had joked. "Among my activities, I drive a limo. One of the guys I work with will be dropping off my car and taking this one."

When the party ended, Fred had walked her out to her twelve-year-old Chevy. "Just call me Cinderella," she said with a smile.

She seemed so young, with her long, dark hair and infectious laugh, that it was hard for him to believe that she was the mother of two little boys.

"Does Cinderella have a phone number?" he asked.

And now, as he found himself driving to her house, Fred wondered if this was such a good idea. There was more traffic than he had expected, and he hadn't begun to pack for his trip. He admitted to himself that showing up at her house might be sending Rosita the wrong message. He had no intention of getting too involved with anyone at this point. For the foreseeable future, he wouldn't have enough time to devote to a relationship—especially one that involves kids, he thought.

Rosita lived in a modest garden-apartment complex not far from Summit. The shortest day of the year was yesterday, Fred thought. I can believe it. At 4:30 it was completely dark. He parked in a visitor's space, went up the path, shifted the festively wrapped plant to one hand, and rang the bell of Rosita's ground-floor unit.

Inside the apartment, seventeen-year-old Nicole Parma was in a state of near hysteria. At the sound of the chimes, she rushed to the door. "Your mother probably forgot her key," she yelled to Chris and Bobby, both of whom were sitting cross-legged in front of the television set.

Neither one of them looked up. "Mommy

never forgets her key," six-year-old Chris said matter-of-factly to his younger brother. Only eleven months apart in age, they could pass for twins.

"But Mommy said she'd be home by now," Bobby said, his voice low and troubled. "I don't like Nicole. She won't play with us like Sarah does." Sarah was their regular baby-sitter.

Forgetting all of Rosita's warnings about not opening the door until she knew who was on the other side, Nicole flung it open. Fred did not miss her look of acute disappointment when she saw him standing there.

"Is Mrs. Gonzalez home?" He took a step back, not wanting to suggest that he would make any attempt to enter unless invited.

"No, and I expected her over an hour ago!" The answer was almost a wail.

"It's Fred!" Chris shouted, jumping up.

"Fred!" Bobby echoed.

Both boys were at the door, crowding past Nicole to greet him.

"That's Mommy's friend!" Chris told her. "He's a policeman. He arrests people."

"Hello, you two." Fred looked back at Nicole. "I just wanted to drop this plant off for the boys' mother."

The boys were pulling at Fred's jacket.

"I can tell it's all right if you come in," Nicole said. "Rosita should be here any minute."

"Mommy better be here soon," Chris volunteered as Fred stepped inside. "Nicole's freaking out. She's got to get ready for her dance tonight and doesn't want to look ugly 'cause she lovvvvves her boyfriend. Ha ha ha, Nicole."

If looks could kill, Fred thought, as the young girl glared at Chris.

"You brat! I told you to hang up the phone when I was talking before."

"Kissy, kissy, see you later, I can hardly wait." Chris made a loud smacking sound with his lips.

"Kissy, kissy," Bobby repeated, mimicking his brother's sing-song tone.

"Come on, guys," Fred said. "That's enough." He saw the tears shining in Nicole's eyes. "You're running late, I guess."

"Really late," she confirmed, as her mouth

quivered and the tears began to roll down her cheeks.

"Hasn't Rosita called?"

"No. I tried her cell phone, but there was no answer."

"She must be on her way home." The same impulse that had made him stop at the flower shop elicited the next words from his mouth: "Look, I've got some time. I can wait with the kids." He started to pull out his police ID. "You can see the boys know me."

Chris ran over to an end table and picked up a framed picture. It was a group shot taken at the party where Fred and his mother had met. "There he is!" he cried, pointing at the photograph and running over to Nicole. "That's him in the back row."

Nicole barely glanced at Fred's ID or at the good-times snapshot before she was out the door, one arm already in the sleeve of her coat.

"She's a pain," Chris observed. "All she did was talk on the phone with her boyfriend. Yuck."

"She wouldn't play checkers," Bobby said quietly.

"She *wouldn't?*" Fred said, his voice suitably incredulous. "I *love* to play checkers. Let's find a place to put Mommy's plant, then we'll see if you two can beat me. Red or black?"

When Regan opened the door, Alvirah waved the cell phone at her. "The call you've been waiting for!" she said breathlessly.

Regan grabbed the phone. "Dad?"

Without hesitation, Alvirah stepped inside and closed the door. I just want to make sure everything's all right, she told herself. But an instant later, judging by the look on Regan's face, she was certain that something was very, very wrong.

Instead of the voice Regan had been expecting to hear, she was chilled by a curt command, "You'll talk to him in a minute. Get rid of whoever is with you."

This isn't the police or a hospital calling, Regan thought. She made a snap decision to let Alvirah stay. Not that she would have had much choice. Alvirah's two feet were practically glued to the marble floor. But the concern in her eyes made Regan glad for her presence. "Thank you, Alvirah," she said loudly. "I won't keep you." She reached past her and noisily opened and closed the door.

That guy doesn't want anyone else to overhear what he's telling Regan, Alvirah thought. Yanking open her coat, she quickly unhooked the sunburst pin that she always wore, turned on its tiny hidden microphone, and handed the pin to Regan.

Regan's eyes widened at first, and then she nodded, realizing what Alvirah intended. "Let me talk to my father," she said as she held the sunburst pin next to her ear and the earpiece of the phone.

"Not so fast," the gruff voice snapped. "I've got a list of demands."

In the houseboat, Petey nodded his approval. "Kind of like a top-ten list," he whispered to Luke, with a friendly punch to his manacled arm.

C.B. glared at him.

"Sorry."

C.B. continued. "You must have one million dollars in cash by tomorrow afternoon. It must be in one-hundred-dollar bills, in a duffel bag. At six o'clock on the dot, and I *mean* on the dot, be in your car driving into Central Park at the Sixth Avenue entrance. You will receive a phone call telling you where to leave the money. Do not call the police if you want to see your father and his cutie-pie chauffeur again. Once the money has been received and counted, you'll get a call about where to pick them up."

"I want to talk to my father now," Regan demanded.

C.B. walked over to Luke and held the phone to his ear. "Say hello to your little girl. And tell her she'd better do as she's told."

It was with heartsick relief that Regan heard Luke's calm voice. "Hi, Regan. We're both okay so far. Your mother will know where to get the money quickly."

Before Regan could answer, C.B. pulled the phone away. "That's enough from you. It's Rosita's turn." He was at her side. "Say hello to Regan."

The words rushed out of Rosita's mouth. "Take care of my boys."

Again C.B. didn't give Regan a chance to respond. "Okay, Regan Reilly," he said. "We've got a date. Six o'clock tomorrow. Right?"

"I'll be there," Regan said. "But I have to talk to my father and Rosita again before I drop that money." Trying to keep the mounting fury out of her voice, it was her turn to ask, "Right?"

"You've got it, Regan." The line went dead.

"Beverly, I feel like nine miles of torn-up road," Nora told her nurse as she looked into the mirror of her small compact and applied lipstick.

Beverly Carter smiled. "You look fine, Mrs. Reilly," she said reassuringly, fluffing up Nora's pillows. "I'm glad you slept so long. You seem a lot better than you did this morning."

"I certainly feel better," Nora said, glancing at her watch. "It's 6:30. Let's turn on the news and see what else has happened in the world today."

"It's me," Regan announced as she pushed open the door which had been slightly ajar.

Nora's face brightened. "You're early. That's great. Where's Dad?"

Regan hesitated. "He's been delayed."

"Mrs. Reilly, I'll be outside if you need me," the nurse said.

"Beverly, why don't you go have dinner?" Regan suggested. "We'll be visiting for a while. Take your time."

When the nurse left, Regan closed the door and slowly turned around to face her mother. Her expression was troubled.

"Regan, what is it?" Nora asked, her voice suddenly panicky. "What's wrong? Has something happened to Dad?"

"Mom, I . . ." Regan began, searching for the right words.

"He's not dead, is he?" Please God, Nora thought, not that.

"No, no—nothing like that," Regan said swiftly. "I spoke to him a couple of hours ago."

"Then what? What is it?"

"There's no simple way to tell you. He's been kidnapped, and someone called me with a ransom demand."

"Mother of God," Nora whispered. She clasped her hands against her chest as if to shield herself from another blow. "How did it happen? What do you know?"

Regan hated to see the pain on her mother's face as she related the little she knew about Luke's disappearance: her attempts to reach him; her decision to go to Dr. Jay's office; the ride to their home in Summit with Alvirah Meehan, whose articles about crime Nora had sent to her; and finally, the call on her cell phone demanding the million-dollar ransom.

"If Rosita's with him, and he didn't make it to the funeral, then the kidnapping must have happened right after he left here this morning." Nora's eyes welled with tears. She looked out the window. It was impossible to believe her husband of thirty-five years was out there somewhere in that cold, dark night, at the mercy of someone who might at any moment snuff out his life. "We can get the million dollars. But Regan, we have to let the police in on this."

"I know. Alvirah is friendly with the guy who runs the Major Case Squad here in Manhattan. He would be the right person to call. That squad handles high-profile kidnappings. Alvirah is with me. She's waiting outside."

"Bring her in," Nora said, "but wait a minute. Who else knows about this?"

"Nobody except Alvirah's husband and his sister, who's a nun. She's staying with him right now. After the dental surgery, he's pretty out of it."

"What about Rosita's children? Who's minding them?"

"I got her phone number from Dad's Rolodex," Regan replied. "When I called, I spoke to a friend of hers who said he had just relieved the baby-sitter. I only told him that Rosita had been detained, but I could tell that he suspects something is seriously wrong."

"As long as the kids are all right for the moment." Nora took a deep breath as she tried to pull herself up on the bed. Damn this leg, she thought. To be trapped like this when every fiber of her being screamed for her to take some action. "Let's get Alvirah in here," she said. "We'll get in touch with her connection in the police department and then get a million dollars together."

Regan had scarcely opened the door before Alvirah bustled into the room, walked over to the bed, and gave Nora Reilly's hand a reassuring squeeze. "We're going to get your husband and that girl back safe and sound," she promised.

There was something about Alvirah Meehan that made Nora believe she could do just that.

"Last year I lectured at John Jay College about the case of a baby whose kidnapping I solved," Alvirah told her. "The newspapers called it the baby bunting case because I found the bunting the baby had been wearing when she was abducted from the hospital."

"I remember that case," Nora said. "That one was right around Christmas too."

Alvirah nodded. "Yes, it was. We got the baby back on Christmas Eve. Jack Reilly was at my lecture that day and invited me to have lunch with him. He's the grandest fellow, and so smart. Only thirty-four years old and already in charge of the Major Case Squad with the rank of captain." She reached for the phone. "He'll know how to handle this. He works out of One Police Plaza."

"Reilly?" Nora asked.

"Can you believe that? And he spells it just like you do too. I asked him that day if you were related." Alvirah waved her hand dismissively. "You're not."

Regan smiled slightly as she sat on the edge of the bed and closed her hand over her mother's outstretched fingers. Together they listened to Alvirah's refusal to take no for an answer.

"I don't care if he's not due back until Monday, " Alvirah was saying. "Nobody else will do. I want you to page him now. Here's the message: 'It is absolutely urgent that you call Alvirah Meehan immediately at . . .' what's the phone number here, Regan?"

"Give him my cell-phone number," Regan replied. "It's 310-555-4237."

Alvirah replaced the receiver. "Knowing Jack Reilly, I'll hear from him in the next ten minutes."

Eight minutes later the cell phone rang.

Jack Reilly did not even mind the particularly impossible traffic on the East River Drive. His suitcase was in the trunk, and he was headed for his parents' house in Bedford. It was evident that the usual one-hour trip would take almost double that time tonight. The holiday exodus from Manhattan was well under way.

Of his six siblings, he hadn't seen two of his brothers and one of his sisters since August, when they'd all been at the family home on Martha's Vineyard. Counting spouses and children, there'd be nineteen of them under the same roof for the next four days. I just hope we don't end up killing each other, he thought with a grin. The weather reports were indicating a heavy storm over the weekend.

He jammed on the brake. Despite the bumper-to-bumper traffic, the car on his right had made a sudden move and cut in front of him. "You'll get there a lot faster now, won't you pal?" he muttered, looking out at the mass of red taillights that extended as far as the eye could see.

Jack Reilly had sandy hair that tended to curl, hazel eyes more green than brown, even features with a strong jaw, and a broad-shouldered, six-foot-two body. Keenly intelligent, quick-witted, and with a sharp sense of humor honed by growing up in a large family, he had undeniable charisma. Both at social gatherings and at work, his laid-back presence somehow filled the room.

His easygoing manner disappeared, however, when he was on a case. The grandson of a New York police lieutenant, after graduating from Boston College he surprised his family by making the decision to pursue a career in law enforcement. In the twelve years that followed, he had risen through the ranks from patrolman to captain and head of the Major Case Squad. Along the way he also had picked up two master's degrees. His goal was to become police commissioner of New York, and few who knew him doubted he would make it.

His pager beeped. He had taken it off and laid it in the well of the car's console. He picked it up, glanced at the number, and was not at all happy to see that it was his office trying to reach him. Now what? he thought as he pulled out his cell phone.

Fifteen minutes later he was tapping on the door of Nora's hospital room. Alvirah ran over to open it. "I'm so glad you got here so fast!" she exclaimed.

"I was right by an exit on the FDR Drive," Jack said as he greeted Alvirah with a peck on the cheek. He looked past her and recognized the face of Nora Regan Reilly. He knew the very attractive young woman standing beside her had to be her daughter. He had seen that same anguished expression on the faces of the relatives of other kidnap victims. They wanted help, not sympathy.

"I'm Jack Reilly," he said as he shook hands with both of them. "I'm terribly sorry about what's happened. I know you want to get right down to business."

"Just the facts, ma'am," Regan said with a ghost of a smile. "Yes, we do."

I like him, Nora thought as he took out a notebook. He's solid. He knows what he's doing. With a pang, she watched Jack Reilly glance around and pull up the chair Luke had occupied that very morning.

Immediately after they made the phone call to Regan Reilly, C.B. and Petey put on their coats and hats. As C.B. gratuitously explained to Luke and Rosita, it was happy hour at the bar in Edgewater at which he had met Petey some months earlier.

"Yeah," Petey brayed. "And wouldn't ya

know, Mr. Reilly, we met because of you."

"How did I manage that?" Luke asked, an edge in his voice as he flexed his fingers and shifted the handcuffs to move them past his wrist bones.

"I'll tell ya. Talk about coincidence. A couple of weeks after I painted your viewing room, I'm sitting at Elsie's Hideaway, and there's C.B., sitting at the other end of the bar, drowning his many sorrows."

"You were in a pretty sorry state yourself," C.B. interjected.

"Yeah," Petey agreed. "I gotta admit. At the time I wasn't feeling so good about life myself."

"Losers," Rosita muttered under her breath.

"Huh?" Petey asked.

"Nothing."

"Come on Petey," C.B. said impatiently. "Let's go. The cheese and crackers will be gone before we get there."

"The crowd that place attracts—vultures, every one of them," Petey said, shaking his head with disgust. Hellbent on finishing his story, he continued: "So I said to myself, I've seen that guy before. But where? Then I said to myself, wowie—I know where. It was at that lively joint of yours, Mr. Reilly. Turns out he and that old buzzard of an uncle had stopped by while I was doing the paint job."

"What a beautiful story," Rosita said sarcastically.

"Yeah. So I bring my beer over, friendly like, and we got to talking." Petey's voice changed. "And he told me you were all making jokes about that nice color I painted your room—and after I'd mixed it special for you."

C.B. opened the door to the deck. "When Uncle Cuthbert took a look at that room, he said he'd rather be waked in a fun house."

"That really hurt my feelings," Petey lamented. "But it all worked out for the best." His face brightened. "If he and his uncle hadn't poked their noses into the room, I wouldn't have met C.B. And now we're gonna start a new life with your million dollars, Mr. Reilly. We'll be on the beach, meeting gorgeous girls and everything."

"Good for you," Luke snapped. "Does that

radio over there work?" He nodded his head in the direction of the little kitchen.

Petey glanced at the top of the refrigerator where a scratched and painfully old radio was perched precariously. "Sometimes. If the batteries are working." He reached up and flipped it on. "What's your fancy? News or music?"

"News," Luke said.

"There'd better be no bulletin about your disappearance," C.B. said darkly.

"I assure you there won't be."

Petey twisted the dial until he found an all-news station. The sound was raspy and tinny, but clear enough to be understood. "Enjoy," he said as he followed C.B. out the door.

After they left, Luke and Rosita listened to the traffic and weather reports. A nor'easter was making its way up the East Coast. According to the forecast, it would be in Washington, D.C., tomorrow and was expected to hit the New York area on Christmas Eve.

"Listen up, you last-minute shoppers," the announcer cautioned. "We expect between eight and ten inches of snow, high winds, and icy road conditions. So it would be wise to get all your shopping completed by tomorrow afternoon. On Saturday the roads are going to be hazardous, so play it safe and make plans to stay home by the tree."

"I was going to put up our tree tonight, with my sons," Rosita said quietly. "Mr. Reilly, do you think we'll be home on Christmas Eve?"

"Nora and Regan will make sure that the money is paid. And I really do believe these guys intend to let us go. Or at least they'll tell someone where to find us once they have the money in their hands."

Luke did not tell Rosita what was now becoming his greatest fear. Stupid as they were, C.B. and Petey would never disclose his and Rosita's whereabouts until they were safely beyond the long arm of the law. This probably meant they'd be heading to a country that would not extradite them. If we're still here on Saturday, Luke thought, this river might be loaded with chunks of ice that could easily tear holes in this rotting tub. It had already been an unusually cold December. A storm would pull the ice that had already formed up north down the river.

Three long hours later, C.B. and Petey reappeared, this time carrying bags from McDonald's.

"Elsie put out some spread," Petey rejoiced. "Normally, she's a Scrooge, but I guess miracles happen during the holidays. Although she did get annoyed when I tried to fix a little doggie bag for you two. That's why we picked up some Big Macs."

"Set it out for them," C.B. ordered. "Then get blankets and pillows from the bedroom. As soon as they eat and get settled for the night, I'm out of here. And you get a good night's sleep too, Petey. We've got a big day tomorrow."

"We sure do," Petey said, his speech slightly slurred thanks to Elsie's eggnog. *"Who Wants to Be a Millionaire?* We do! C.B. and Petey, New Jersey's finest! But who needs Regis? We've got Luke Reilly."

The length of the chains made it possible

for them to lie back, Luke on the banquette and Rosita across the way on the couch. For hours Luke lay awake. Petey's tumultuous snoring from the tiny bedroom reverberated through the drafty cabin, but somehow it was easier to take than the sound of Rosita crying softly in her sleep.

"I think we're all agreed," Jack Reilly said, summing up the hour they had been together in Nora's room. "Mrs. Reilly . . ." he began.

"Nora," she corrected. Maybe someday Mom, she thought with a quick flash of humor. Oh God, I can just imagine what Luke would say if I told him that in the middle of his kidnapping, I'm trying, as usual, to fix Regan up. *When* I tell him, not *if,* she corrected herself. But one thing was certain: Luke would like Jack Reilly.

"Nora," he continued. "We've canceled your private nurses. You might be getting phone calls here about Luke and Rosita, and the fewer people who know about this, the better. Now I want you to try and get some rest. If you think of anyone who might hold a grudge, for whatever reason, against you or Luke, or even Regan, call me immediately."

Nora shook her head and raised her hands helplessly. "I just can't imagine."

"I understand. Of course, we'll be checking into Rosita's ex-husband as well," he said, then paused. "And then again, this could just be someone who knows that you have money."

"That's why when the lottery commission asked me and Willy to do a commercial about how happy we are with all our money, I told them to go jump in a lake," Alvirah announced. "Of course, I'd already been on plenty of shows, but enough's enough."

"You're right, Alvirah," Jack assured her. "Nora, first thing in the morning, you'll contact your broker and arrange a million-dollar loan against your stock portfolio. You're sure they won't start asking questions?"

"It's our money," she said firmly. "Nobody tells us what to do with it."

Regan was glad to see that her mother's fighting spirit was returning.

"We'll alert the Federal Reserve bank to start assembling the ransom money," Jack said. Then he turned to Regan. "You and Alvirah are going to Rosita's home now to speak with whomever is baby-sitting her sons. You'll have to use your discretion about how much to tell him. Our people should have her phone covered by now. If this baby-sitter wants to leave, we can send a social worker over."

"I have the perfect person for the job," Alvirah said triumphantly. "Sister Maeve Marie. She works with Cordelia, Willy's sister. Maeve's great with kids, and she used to be on the New York City police force. And like Sister Cordelia, she can make the Sphinx look like a blabbermouth."

Jack smiled. "Good. And Regan, after checking out Rosita's home situation, you and Alvirah are going to meet your father's assistant at his office."

Regan nodded. At Jack's request, she had phoned Austin Grady and obtained the license number of the car Rosita had been driving, as well as the E-Z Pass account number. Jack had already called this information in to his office.

They had agreed that Austin had to be fully informed, but the only thing Regan had told him so far was that there was a serious problem. "He'll be waiting there for us," she said.

"You'll bring the car you'll be driving for the ransom drop back into the city tonight," Jack confirmed.

"Yes. My mother's BMW."

"One of my guys will meet you later at your parents' apartment on Central Park South. He'll take the car downtown to be bird-dogged."

All three women knew "bird-dogging" was the slang for placing an electronic device attached by a magnet under the car so it could be tracked by a helicopter. Another tracking device would be placed with the ransom money, so that once it was transferred, the money could be followed to wherever the kidnappers were taking it.

The hope, of course, was that the kidnappers would then lead them to where the hostages were being kept.

"Alvirah, let me have the recording you made of the ransom call," Jack said.

"I want a copy of it first thing in the morning," Alvirah ordered as she unsnapped the cassette from the back of her sunburst pin.

"Another brilliant move by Alvirah," Jack said with affection, holding up the tiny cassette. "Even if he tried to disguise it, we have the kidnapper's voice on tape, and our tech guys may be able to learn something from the background sounds."

As Alvirah beamed at him, he kissed her cheek. "My team will be waiting for me down at One Police Plaza." He touched Nora's hand. "Try not to worry too much." He turned to Regan. "We'll keep each other posted."

When he left, the room suddenly felt empty. There was a momentary pause, and then it was as though the three women had the same thought at once.

There was no time to waste.

It had been a busy day for Ernest Bumbles, president and chairman of the board of the Seed-Plant-Bloom-and-Blossom Society of the Garden State of New Jersey. He awoke in the morning to the happy realization that it wasn't all just a dream. Cuthbert Boniface Goodloe had indeed left virtually his entire estate to the society.

The joyous news had reached them only hours after dear Mr. Goodloe had breathed his last. Ernest had received a call from Goodloe's lawyer with "sad news and glad news," as he put it. "Mr. Goodloe is no longer with us," he said with a sigh, "but his association with the Blossoms gave him so much pleasure for the past three years that he has left virtually his entire estate of a bit over one million dollars to your society."

Ernest had been busy mulching his thistles in the greenhouse behind his home when his wife, Dolly, had come running out with the portable phone. A sufferer of severe allergies, she covered her face with a surgical mask whenever she entered the greenhouse.

"Bumby," she cried, her voice muffled, "a call for you. He sounds smart, so it must be important. A-choo."

Even with the mask, the mulch always got to her.

The reason Mr. Withers had phoned before Goodloe had finished knocking on the pearly gates soon became clear. It had been Mr. Goodloe's express wish that the Blossoms turn out in full force for his wake, his funeral, and the luncheon to follow. Needless to say, Blossoms all across the state had dropped their shovels, ripped off their gardening gloves, and gathered to mourn their now beloved benefactor.

In the emergency board of directors meeting called by Ernest before the services, one of the members pointed out that were it not for Luke Reilly, none of this would have happened. Three years earlier, Reilly had been feted as Man of the Year at their annual banquet, in recognition of the fact that his three funeral homes were a boon to the local floral industry.

The night of the award, Cuthbert Boniface Goodloe had been his guest at one of the tables Luke had been strongly encouraged to buy.

Goodloe had been so enchanted by the society's four-minute film on the positive effects of talking to your plants that he had signed up to become a member that very night.

At the meeting after Goodloe's death, they had unanimously voted that in recognition of Luke Reilly's networking skills, he would be presented a Blossom Society Proclamation at the post-funeral luncheon. Much to their disappointment, however, Reilly did not show up. His associate, Austin Grady, had informed them of Luke's wife's unfortunate accident.

Ernest was especially disappointed. He had wanted to put the framed proclamation— enscribed on the finest parchment money could buy and surrounded by dried flowers— in Luke's hands personally. He had looked forward with great anticipation to seeing the thrilled expression on his face when he unwrapped the proclamation and read the message.

TO ALL WHO READ THESE WORDS

Greetings and Salutations.
Be It Known That Luke Reilly,
By Virtue of Bringing Our Beloved
Benefactor
Cuthbert Boniface Goodloe
Into the Fold of the Blossoms,
Is now and forever,
By the Authority and Recommendation
of the Board of Directors,
Freely and Without Reservation,
A Lifelong Member of the
Seed-Plant-Bloom-and-Blossom Society
of the Garden State of New Jersey
With all its honors, rights
and privileges thereof.
Presented on this Twenty-second Day of
December, at the dawn of the Second
Millennium,
E Pluribus Unum

When he had not appeared at the luncheon, Grady had assured Ernest that Reilly undoubtedly would drop by the funeral parlor sometime in the late afternoon. Ernest went there at five, but still there was no sign of him. Grady urged him to leave the festively wrapped gift, but that was absolutely out of the question. There are few times in one's life, Ernest thought, when you get to see pure, unadulterated joy on the face of one's fellow man. If it was humanly possible to see Luke Reilly before he and Dolly left for her mother's house on Christmas Eve and to give him that gift in person, he was going to do it.

"Bumby," Dolly said as she poured him a second cup of coffee, "if you want to stop by the funeral parlor before we go caroling with my choral group, we have to hurry."

"You're right, as usual." He gulped down the coffee and pushed back his chair.

Twenty minutes later he was back in the office of the funeral parlor inquiring about Luke Reilly's whereabouts.

"I'm afraid he's been delayed," Austin Grady said.

Bumbles thought he detected a slight irritation in the other man's voice. He was tempted to explain the contents of the package, but to do so would risk spoiling the surprise.

"I'll be back," he promised.

"We close at nine," Grady warned. "That's only a little over an hour from now."

"Tomorrow morning then," Bumbles said cheerfully as he carefully picked up the package he had rested on a chair and disappeared out the door, fragments of the proclamation running through his head. ". . . Be it known that Luke Reilly, by virtue of bringing our beloved benefactor Cuthbert Boniface Goodloe into the fold of the Blossoms . . ."

Bumbles couldn't wait until the whole world knew just what Luke Reilly had done for them.

It was 9:30 in the evening when their car pulled up to the garden apartment complex where Rosita lived. Between them, Alvirah and Regan had worked out the scenario they would follow once inside. They needed to size up the man who was with the children. If he turned out to be very close to Rosita, they would tell him what had happened. If he was simply helping out till she got home, they would tell him they had Sister Maeve Marie ready to jump in a car and drive over from New York.

Nora had told them that Rosita's mother was now living in San Juan with the rest of her family. Jack warned that it would be unwise to notify any of them yet. "They can't do anything to help," he pointed out, "and it could create a terrible problem if word of this got out."

"Be careful," the driver warned as he opened the door and offered his hand to help Alvirah out. "It's pretty slippery here."

"He's such a nice man," Alvirah said to Regan as they walked up the path. "I felt funny when I pushed the button that raised the partition in the car so he couldn't hear us."

"So did I," Regan said. "That's why I'm glad we're picking up my mother's car right after we leave here. We've got to be able to talk freely if Jack Reilly or anyone else calls."

Alvirah knew that by "anyone else," Regan meant the kidnappers.

The driver was right; there were patches of ice on the path. Regan tucked her arm under Alvirah's elbow to keep her from slipping.

At the entrance to Rosita's ground-floor apartment, they looked at each other for a moment, then Alvirah pressed her finger firmly on the bell.

Inside, Fred was sitting on the couch, a sleepy little boy on either side of him. Hearing the bell, Chris sat up. "Maybe Mommy did forget her key," he said in a tired, hopeful voice.

Bobby rubbed his eyes as he straightened up. "Is Mommy home?"

Fred felt his throat tighten. How many times in his job had he been the one to ring the bell, bearing news of an accident or worse?

Regan Reilly had been evasive on the phone. Was that what she was coming to tell them?

He experienced a fleeting instant of profound relief when he opened the door and realized there were two figures standing outside in the dark. The relief, however, was painfully short-lived. An older woman was standing next to the one he knew had to be Reilly. Perhaps a social worker, he thought with a sinking heart. If so, that means something terrible has happened to Rosita.

"Fred Torres?" the younger woman asked.

He nodded.

"I'm Regan Reilly."

"And I'm Alvirah Meehan," Alvirah said heartily.

"Come in," Fred said quietly.

Alvirah preceded Regan. She glanced around the room. Two little boys with dark hair were standing together by the couch, the expression in both sets of large brown eyes apprehensive and disappointed.

"Now which one of you is Chris and which one is Bobby?" she asked, a warm smile brightening her face. "Let me guess. Mrs. Reilly told me all about you. Chris is the oldest, so that must be you." She pointed to the taller of the two.

Chris smiled tentatively.

"I'm Bobby," the younger one said, moving closer to his brother.

"Where's Mommy?" Chris asked.

"Did you know that Mrs. Reilly broke her leg last night?" Alvirah asked, dropping her voice as though she were telling an important secret.

"Mommy told us this morning before she left," Bobby said with a yawn. "Mommy said that tonight we would make a card and send it to Mrs. Reilly."

"Well, Mrs. Reilly needs your mommy's help tonight," Alvirah said softly. "So she just wants you two to go to bed, and she'll be home as soon as she can."

"I want her to come home now," Bobby said, suddenly on the verge of tears.

"Mrs. Reilly is nice," Chris told him. "It's all right if Mommy stays with her when she's sick."

"But when do we get to decorate our tree?" Bobby asked plaintively.

"In plenty of time for Christmas," Alvirah assured them.

Regan had been watching. Alvirah knows exactly how to handle the kids, she thought. Walking over to them, she said, "I'm Mrs. Reilly's daughter, and I'm so glad your mommy is with my mother right now. Having your mommy there makes mine feel so much better."

"Then your daddy is Mr. Reilly," Chris said. "I like his cars."

"Especially the reeeealy long ones," Bobby added, yawning again.

"You know, I think both you boys look pretty tired," Alvirah observed, "and that's just the way I feel too."

Fred knew exactly what these two women were doing—they were reassuring the boys about their mother, then they wanted them out of earshot.

"Okay, guys, bedtime," he said, putting his hands around two small shoulders.

Bobby peered up at him anxiously. "You're not going to leave us, are you Fred?"

Fred bent down and looked into the two distressed faces. He hesitated, then said firmly, "Not until Mommy gets home."

While he was settling the boys in their room, Alvirah went into the tiny kitchen and put the kettle on the stove. "I need a cup of tea," she announced. "How about you, Regan?"

"Good idea. I'd love one." Regan glanced around the cozy yet slightly cluttered apartment. The brightly slipcovered couch and matching chair with their rounded arms and thick pillows looked wonderfully comfortable. A corner with shelves had been turned over to the children's videotapes and toys. But it was the sight of the Christmas tree, already in the stand, just waiting to be decorated, that clutched at her heart.

By the time the kettle began to whistle, Fred Torres had emerged from the boys' bedroom. "I promise I'll be right out here, guys," he said as he closed the door.

Alvirah poked her head out of the kitchen. "I'm making myself at home, Fred. A cup of tea?"

"Yes, thanks." He looked at Regan. "Tell me what's going on."

"What is your relationship to Rosita?" she asked.

"We've had a couple of dates." He pulled out his police ID. "I'm a cop. Rosita's in trouble. What is it?"

Alvirah came into the living room holding a tray. "I'll put it right here on the table. Why don't we all sit down?"

Fred sat straight backed on the edge of the club chair, Alvirah and Regan opposite him on the couch.

"Fred is a police officer, Alvirah," Regan said, then looked directly at him. "Rosita and my father were kidnapped sometime this morning. We believe it must have happened between ten o'clock, when my father left the hospital after visiting my mother, and twelve o'clock, when he was supposed to show up for a funeral."

She looked down at the cup she was holding. "At about 4:30, I received a ransom call demanding one million dollars by tomorrow afternoon. We've already met with the head of the Major Case Squad in New York."

Fred felt as though he had been punched in the stomach. "Kidnapped?" he said, his tone disbelieving, his face registering shock. He glanced down the hall at the closed bedroom door. "Those poor kids."

Alvirah turned to Fred and put her hand on the sunburst pin on her suit jacket; on the drive out to Rosita's apartment, she had inserted a new cassette. "Fred, do you mind if I record our conversation? Sometimes we say things that don't seem significant at the moment, but that really turn out to be significant later. In some cases I have worked on, listening to the tapes over and over has led to the break we needed."

"Go ahead," he said. Ignoring the cup of tea cooling in front of him, he listened intently while Regan and Alvirah filled him in on everything they knew.

"Do they have any idea who could have done this?" he asked.

"None at all," Regan said. "We think this is just about money, though. My father has no enemies that we know of."

"Did Rosita discuss her ex-husband with you?" Alvirah asked. "From what Nora told us, he's something of a ne'er-do-well who could probably use some money."

"I only met Rosita last month, at a party. We've been out to dinner twice. She didn't want to talk about him. Today the kids told me they hadn't seen him in a long time."

"He sounds like a real charmer," Regan said. "The police are going to be checking him out very carefully."

Fred shook his head. "I hope for the kids' sake he's not involved. Rosita didn't give any indication that she'd had any trouble with him lately. When we went to dinner, we talked about the usual things. She really likes her job." He nodded at Regan. "She said your father is the best boss anyone could have. And that he keeps his cool no matter what happens. But there was nothing she said that would indicate he was having any real problem with anyone."

Regan put down her cup. "When we leave here, Alvirah and I are going over to my father's office to meet with his associate. We're going to dig around to see if perhaps there are any business problems that could be relevant. It's possible the kidnapper is a disgruntled person, perhaps even a former employee, who has a grudge against my father."

"That's sensible, and it's almost the only thing you can do. The hardest part of a kidnapping is having to wait for the kidnappers to make the next move," Fred added angrily.

"I have to keep busy," Regan said matter-of-factly, as she and Alvirah got up.

"My sister-in-law is a nun," Alvirah told Fred as she gathered the cups. "There's a young woman in her convent, Sister Maeve Marie, who was a cop before she realized she had a vocation. Maeve is wonderful with kids; she can be here in an hour if you want to go home."

Fred thought about the party he was missing, the plane he was supposed to catch in the morning, the long-planned sail with his friends. All those things seemed so trivial now.

He thought about Rosita, her dark hair spilling on her shoulders, her warm smile as she joked. "Just call me Cinderella."

Not every kidnapping ended happily, he thought. In fact, many did not.

He shook his head. "You heard me tell the boys—I'm not leaving."

It had been said of Alvin Luck that his name didn't suit him. Fifty-two years old, with thinning brown hair, a slight frame, and an amiable but timid smile, he lived with his mother in a rent-controlled apartment on Manhattan's West Eighty-sixth Street. The author of twelve unpublished suspense novels, he eked out a living doing temporary jobs while waiting for his break in the publishing world.

Given the season, his current odd job was to don a red suit and white beard and ho-ho-ho his way through the toy section of a discount department store near Herald Square.

"Stop slouching, Alvin!" his boss screamed

at him regularly. "Santa Claus is supposed to have some authority."

You'd think I was working for F. A. O. Schwarz and not this junk shop, he often thought.

Alvin was not without spirit.

Nor was his lack of success in the publishing world due to a lack of diligent research. He had dissected every mystery and suspense novel that had appeared on the *New York Times* bestseller list in the last twenty years, and then some. He was a virtual walking encyclopedia when it came to the plots, characters, and settings used by hundreds of suspense and mystery novelists. He had filled notebooks with plotlines, and he consulted them regularly when working on his own stories. He had divided the plots into categories such as espionage, bank robberies, murder, extortion, domestic crime, hijackings, arson, courtroom drama, and kidnapping.

His only luxury was to attend writing seminars and mystery conventions, where he listened attentively to the sage advice of published writers and later tried to corner editors at the cocktail parties.

He had been getting ready for work on Thursday when he heard on the radio the news about Nora Regan Reilly's broken leg. Over the oatmeal that his mother prepared for him every morning, he had discussed it with her.

"Mark my words," he said. "Nora's next book will be set in a hospital. She'll make the best of this situation."

"Eat your oatmeal. It's getting cold," his mother admonished.

Dutifully, Alvin picked up his spoon and slurped the somewhat lumpy mixture. "I think I'll send her a card."

"Why not stick in the picture you took of that husband of hers at the last mystery-writers' dinner?"

"You're right. I did get a good shot of him," Alvin recalled. "But only one. In the other picture his head got cut off because he's so tall."

"I like tall men. Your father was a shrimp, God rest him."

"Maybe I'll put the picture in a little holiday frame and drop it off at the hospital after work. The store has some frames with nice Christmas sayings on them."

"Don't spend too much on it," his mother cautioned.

"They're on sale," Alvin said, a trace of irritation in his voice. "Nora Regan Reilly always talks to me at the cocktail parties and is so encouraging."

"Not like those editors," his mother had sighed.

Alvin went to work, looking forward to the surprise he was planning for Nora Regan Reilly. To his disappointment, most of the best Christmas frames already had been snapped up. He settled on one that said, I'LL BE HOME FOR CHRISTMAS . . . IF ONLY IN MY DREAMS. Considering how she's stuck in the hospital, it applies more to her than to her husband, he thought, but it will have to do.

To his disgust, there was no employee discount on sale items.

"What do you expect?" the salesgirl asked

as she popped her bubble gum. "They're practically giving this stuff away." She studied the frame before placing it in a bag. "Maybe that's not such a bad idea," she mumbled as Alvin carefully placed his wallet back in a deep pocket of the Santa Claus suit.

The evening-shift Santa Claus apparently had not made it down from the North Pole, and Alvin's boss told him he had to work until 8:00 P.M. That was when the sign went up that Santa was back in his workshop. By then, Alvin's ears were numb. He'd had enough of listening to the incessant demands hurled at him by an unending stream of children, all of whom seemed to take sadistic pleasure in plunking down on his boney knees.

"You don't look much like Santa," a number of the little darlings had said accusingly.

In all, it had been a long day, but that did not deter Alvin from making his planned pilgrimage to the Upper East Side. Since it was his responsibility to keep the Santa Claus suit pressed, he carried it back and forth to work. It was now neatly folded in a shopping bag, with the gift-wrapped, framed picture of Luke Reilly resting on top.

He had picked out a get-well card and written in it, "Nora, thought you'd like to have a pic of your sweetie." On a whim he signed it, "Your number-one fan."

Now he would have something to talk about with Nora Regan Reilly next time he saw her at a mystery-writers' event. He could reveal himself as the mysterious benefactor who'd sent her the nice framed picture.

Once inside the lobby of the hospital, Alvin noticed a gift shop, and in the shop window the word SALE caught his eye. Underneath the sign were perched adorable teddy bears wearing Christmas hats. He hurried in just as the shop was about to close. I won't tell Mother, he thought. But wouldn't it make it really special if a teddy bear is holding Luke Reilly's picture?

The saleswoman obligingly waited while he unwrapped the frame and stuck it in the arms of the teddy bear he had selected. She tied a huge Christmas bow around the box while Alvin counted out the exact change, which came to fourteen dollars and ninety-two cents.

Thanking her, he left the shop and went over to the reception desk. They assured him the package would go up to Mrs. Reilly immediately.

"Oh no, not until the morning," he said firmly. "I wouldn't want to disturb her. It's late."

"That's very thoughtful," the woman said pleasantly. "Have a nice holiday."

Alvin went out into the cold night air once again and walked up York Avenue to Eighty-sixth Street, to catch the crosstown bus. Glowing with Christmas spirit, he smiled cheerily at the passersby who were spilling out of restaurants and shops.

They all ignored him.

Jack Reilly's top assistant, Sgt. Keith Waters, as well as Lt. Gabe Klein, the head of TARU, the Technical Assistance Response Unit, were waiting in Reilly's office at One Police Plaza when he arrived there.

"Long time no see," Waters said laconically.

"You just can't stand being away from here, can you?" A handsome black man in his late thirties, with keen intelligent eyes, he radiated restless energy.

"It's you I miss," Jack said.

But the note of levity disappeared as they promptly got down to business.

"What have you got on the car?" Jack asked.

Gabe Klein began, "The records from E-Z Pass show that the car went through the Lincoln Tunnel into Manhattan at 9:15 A.M. That would be when the girl went in to pick up Luke Reilly at the hospital. At some point the car must have been driven back to New Jersey, because it crossed the George Washington Bridge into New York again at 11:16 A.M. Then it crossed the Triborough Bridge in a lane headed for Queens at 11:45 A.M. That was the last time the E-Z Pass registered any activity."

"That means they may have reached New Jersey before they were abducted," Jack said. "Or maybe they were abducted in New York and taken to New Jersey. Most likely the car has been dumped somewhere. Stretch limos aren't that easy to hide."

"We have a bulletin out for it," Keith responded, "but nothing's turned up so far."

"You put on a safeguard for prints?"

It was a rhetorical question. That was the first thing Keith would do in a kidnapping situation. If located, the car would not be touched until the lab technicians got there.

Now, in terse sentences, Jack filled them in on the rest of the details.

Both men made notes as they listened.

Gabe Klein, fiftyish and balding, wore glasses that perched precariously on the end of his nose, giving him a bookish, slightly vague appearance. To a casual observer, he looked like the kind of man who was unable to change a lightbulb.

It was an impression that was absolutely wrong—Gabe was a technical wizard and ran the highly sophisticated unit that had become a vital tool in the police force's crime-solving efforts.

"These are the phone lines we're covering, right?" Gabe rattled off the numbers Jack had phoned in. The Reilly home and apartment, Rosita Gonzalez's apartment, the funeral homes, Nora Reilly's hospital room.

"And if they call back on the daughter's cell phone, she knows enough to try and keep them on the line so we can pinpoint the location," Gabe confirmed.

"Regan is a private investigator in Los Angeles," Jack said. "She knows the drill."

"That's a break," Keith observed. "Then you think it's okay to have her drive the car to the ransom drop?"

"She's smart," Jack said shortly. And very attractive, he thought.

"When do we get to work on the car she'll be driving?" Gabe asked.

"She's bringing it in tonight. She knows we have to bird-dog it."

"We've alerted the Federal Reserve that we need the million by tomorrow afternoon. They're working on it," Keith informed Jack. "Does the family have any idea who might have done this?"

"Reilly's wife and daughter can't come up with anyone. Rosita Gonzalez has an ex-husband who's something of a troublemaker. His name is Ramon. Mrs. Reilly thinks he lives in Bayonne."

"We'll get on that," Keith said.

"Rosita has two little kids. Regan Reilly is going there now to check on them and to get a fix on whoever is with them. Then she's headed to her father's office to talk to his associate."

Jack looked at his watch. "It's a long story, but Regan met Alvirah Meehan today, and now she's involved as well. Remember her? She's the lottery winner who lectured at John Jay."

"Sure I do," Keith said. "She was the one who got that baby back when all the cops in New York couldn't find her."

Jack pulled the cassette from his pocket. "Well, she's still on the ball. She managed to record the ransom call."

Gabe stared at the tiny cassette. "You're kidding." He picked it up and held it in his hand. "Does she want a job? I could use her."

"She'll have my head if you don't make an extra copy for her. But first, let's hear this tape amplified. Maybe there'll be something in the background that will help us."

As the machine was being readied, Jack felt his frustration building. They could study the tape. They could put a tracking device with the money. They could bird-dog the car. They could look for logical suspects. But until they were following Regan's wired car to the point of contact with the kidnappers, they were mostly in a waiting game.

The phone on Jack's desk rang. He picked it up. "Jack Reilly." There was a pause. "Good work," he said decisively, then looked across the desk at Gabe and Keith. "They found the limo at Kennedy Airport."

At 9:30 that evening, Austin Grady locked the doors of the Reilly funeral home behind the last of the mourners of one-hundred-and-three-year-old Maude Gherkin, the local battle-ax. In his entire career as a mortician, he had never heard the expression, "It's a blessing," uttered more often or more fervently.

Four times since her hundredth birthday, Maude had been snatched from the jaws of death. During her final hospital stay, a home-made sign had appeared over her bed: DO NOT RESUSCITATE . . . NO MATTER WHAT. The doctors suspected it was the handiwork of her eighty-year-old son, who after Maude's fourth mirac-ulous return from the long white tunnel, had been heard to shout, "Aw, give me a *break!*"

Austin turned out the lights in the room where Maude was now resting. He sighed. Hard as they tried, they hadn't been able to get the sour expression off her face.

"Night, night, Maude," he muttered. But the little ritual he had with the clients at closing time did not bring a smile to his lips tonight—he was much too worried about Luke and Rosita.

Since Regan had phoned some hours ago, his suspicion that they had been kidnapped had become a near certainty. Why else would Regan have needed the limousine's license plate and the E-Z Pass account number? Why else couldn't she talk to him about it on the phone?

An hour later, when Regan arrived with Alvirah Meehan in tow, his suspicions were confirmed.

"The police have arranged to have these phones tapped," Regan said. "There's just a chance the kidnappers might call here."

They were startled by a sudden knocking on the window.

"What on earth?" Austin muttered as he recognized the face of none other than Ernest Bumbles, his nose pressed against the glass, who smilingly held up the package he had been carrying earlier and waved it at them.

Austin went over and struggled to raise the window.

"Sorry to bother you," Ernest said, clearly lying. "I saw your light was on and thought maybe Mr. Reilly was back."

This time Austin did not attempt to keep the irritation out of his voice. "He's not here! If you want to leave that package, I'll see that he gets it. Better yet, his daughter will take it home for him. There she is." He pointed at Regan.

Ernest stuck his head in through the open window. "I'm so pleased to meet you. Your father is a wonderful man."

I don't believe this, Regan thought.

Alvirah had turned toward the window so the sunburst pin wouldn't miss a word.

"I'm sorry I can't come in, but my wife, Dolly, is out in the car. She's not feeling that well. We were out singing Christmas carols tonight, and she strained her throat on the final fa la la la la la la la la of 'Deck the Halls.' "

That used to be my favorite Christmas carol, Regan thought. Not anymore.

"I'll be back tomorrow. I want to give this to your father personally. Bye now." Like a game show contestant who has failed to answer the final question, Ernest vanished.

Austin shut the window with a decisive snap. "That guy is a nut case."

"Who is he?" Regan asked.

"The head of some plant society," Austin said. "They honored your father a few years ago."

"I kind of remember that," Regan said. "He's active in so many organizations that he's always being honored."

Regan realized that she was played out. There was nothing more she could accomplish here at the moment. Austin had told her that there was absolutely no one he could think of who would want to bring harm to Luke. In his memory nothing unusual had happened at any of the three Reilly funeral homes.

"We'd better get going," Regan said. "I've made arrangements to stay in my mother's hospital room tonight, and I've got to get this car to Manhattan so the police can prepare it for tomorrow. Let's talk in the morning."

"Regan, I'll get here early and start going through the records from the last few months and see if there are any problems that I didn't know about," Austin promised. "I don't think I'll find anything, but it's worth a look."

As the three of them started to leave, Alvirah noticed the discreet sign bearing Maude Gherkin's name and an arrow pointing to the room where she lay in repose.

Alvirah crossed herself. "May she rest in peace. Did you ever hear the story of the woman who was passing Frank Campbell's funeral parlor in New York and had to go to the bathroom? She stopped in there and then felt she shouldn't leave without paying her respects to somebody. So she popped into a room where there were no visitors for the poor soul in the casket, said a quick prayer, and signed the register. Turned out it was in that guy's will that anyone who showed up at his wake got ten thousand dollars."

"Alvirah, you already won the lottery," Regan said, smiling.

"And believe me, you'd be wasting your time putting your John Hancock in Maude's book," Austin told her as they stepped outside and he shut and locked the door behind them. Hold down the fort, Maude, he thought.

Friday,

December 23rd

"Rise and shine everybody! Time to start our million-dollar day," Petey called out as he emerged from the bedroom, clad in striped pajamas, his toothbrush in hand. He switched on the overhead light. "This is sort of like camp, isn't it?"

Why doesn't that idiot just let us sleep? Luke thought. The last time he had looked at the illuminated dial of his watch, it had been 4:00 A.M. He had finally fallen asleep, and now he was being jolted awake for absolutely no reason. He squinted at his watch. It was 7:15.

He could feel the beginning of a dull headache. His muscles were aching from a combination of the damp, cold air and being forced to contort his body to fit on the narrow, short banquette. The increasing choppiness of the river was causing the boat to knock against the dock, increasing his overall sense of misery.

A hot shower, he thought longingly. Clean clothes. A toothbrush. The little things in life.

He looked across the cabin at Rosita. She had pulled herself up on one elbow. The strain she was feeling was clearly visible on her face. Her dark-brown eyes looked enormous, stark against the increasing pallor of her complexion.

But when their eyes met, she managed a smile and tossed her head in Petey's direction. "Your valet, Mr. Reilly?"

Before Luke could reply, there was a loud pounding on the door. "It's me, Petey," C.B. yelled impatiently. "Open up."

Petey ushered him in, taking the McDonald's bags out of his hands.

"And here comes the butler," Rosita announced softly.

"Did you remember to get me an Egg McMuffin with sausage?" Petey asked hopefully.

"Yes, you moron, I did. Get dressed. I can't stand looking at you like that. Who do you think you are, Hugh Hefner?"

"Hugh Hefner gets a lot of girls," Petey said admiringly. "When we get that million, I'm going to go out and buy a pair of silk pajamas, just like Hef's."

"If I left it to you, we'd never get that million," C.B. sputtered as he snapped on the radio.

He looked at Luke. "I was listening to *Imus in the Morning* on the way over. He put a call through to the hospital. Your wife is going to be on in a few minutes."

Nora was a frequent guest on the Imus program. Imus must have heard about the accident and phoned her. Luke sat up and leaned forward, desperately eager to hear her voice.

C.B. was twisting the dial, searching for the station. "Here we are," he said finally.

Nora's voice came through the static. "Hello, I-Man."

"Where are the hash browns?" Petey was poking through the bags.

Luke couldn't help himself. "Shut up!" he shouted.

"All right, already," Petey said.

"Nora, we were sorry to hear about your accident," Imus said. "I fall off a horse and you trip over a rug. What gives with us?"

Nora laughed.

Luke marveled at how at ease she sounded. He knew that she was feeling exactly as he would if the situation were reversed. But she had to keep up appearances to the rest of the world until this thing was resolved.

However it's resolved, he thought darkly.

"How's the funeral director?" Imus was asking.

"He's talking about you," Petey cried. "Whattayaknow!"

"Oh, he's just great," Nora said, laughing.

"He's yachting," Petey yelled at the radio, and slapped his knee, pleased as always with his own humor.

Imus was thanking Nora for the children's

books she had sent his young son. "He loves it when we read to him."

Luke had a moment of acute nostalgia, remembering how he and Nora had always read to Regan when she was little. When Nora said good-bye to Imus, Luke swallowed over the lump he could feel forming in his throat. Would he ever hear her voice again?

"Mrs. Reilly sent books to my boys for Christmas too," Rosita told him, her voice gentle. "She told me that Regan's favorite thing when she was a child was when you read to her."

And Regan had a favorite book, Luke thought, one book she always carried over to him. *"Read me this one again, Daddy,"* she'd say as she climbed on his lap. Oh my God, he thought, as he remembered which book that was.

Luke's mind began to race. He knew that C.B. had agreed to let Regan talk to him and Rosita this afternoon before she paid the ransom. Was there any chance he could somehow communicate to her a clue as to their whereabouts? Was there any way he could let her know that from where they were being held they could see the George Washington Bridge and the quaint red lighthouse perched beneath it?

Her favorite book had been about those two famous structures. Its title was *The Little Red Lighthouse and the Great Gray Bridge.*

"Bye, I-Man."

Nora hung up the phone.

"Good job, Mom," Regan said.

Both of them had slept fitfully through the night, Regan stretched out on a cot that the nursing staff had sent in. There were times when she awoke and heard her mother's light, even breathing, a sign that she was sleeping. Several times, though, she was immediately aware that Nora was awake, and they would talk quietly in the near darkness of the hospital room until sleep overtook one of them.

At one point during the night, Nora said,

"You know, Regan, they claim that at the moment you die, your whole life flashes before you. I have the oddest sensation that the same kind of thing is happening to me now, but in slow motion."

"Mom," Regan protested.

"Oh, I don't mean that I'm about to die, but I guess when someone you love is in grave danger, your mind becomes a kaleidoscope of memories. Moments ago I was thinking about the apartment Dad and I had when we were first married. It was tiny, but it was ours, and we were together. He'd go off to work, and I'd hit the typewriter. Even when I kept getting rejection slips, he never doubted for one minute that I was going to make it. When I finally sold that first short story, boy, did we celebrate."

Nora paused. "I can't imagine life without him."

It took a giant effort for Regan, who had spent most of the night reliving her own memories of her father, to say softly, "Then don't."

At 6:00 A.M., Regan got up, showered, and changed into the black jeans and sweater she had picked up at the apartment before returning to the hospital.

As she and Alvirah were driving back from New Jersey the night before, she had phoned Jack Reilly and learned that the limo had been found at Kennedy Airport. He told her it had been towed to the lab at the Police Academy garage on East Twentieth Street, where they were going over it with a fine-tooth comb, looking for clues to the identity of the kidnappers.

Regan knew from her own experience the kinds of painstaking tests they would undertake and the carefully defined procedures they would follow. They would check any unidentified fingerprints they might find against the millions of prints stored in the FBI computers. They would collect any traces of fibers or hair for analysis. She had been involved in many cases where a minuscule, seemingly innocuous object turned out to be the Rosetta stone that led to the solving of the puzzle.

Jack had also filled her in on what the E-Z Pass records revealed. ". . . which as you know isn't necessarily significant. They could have been switched to another car."

Regan looked at her mother's breakfast tray, which was virtually untouched. "Why don't you at least drink the tea?" she asked.

"Irish penicillin," Nora murmured, but she did pick up the cup.

News of her accident had resulted in a deluge of flowers from the Reillys' friends. After the first few bouquets had been placed around the room, Nora requested that the others be distributed throughout the hospital.

There was a tap on the door, and a smiling volunteer asked, "May I come in?"

She was holding a box tied with a bright Christmas ribbon.

"Of course," Nora said, attempting a smile.

"First delivery of the day," the woman said sweetly. "It was left for you last night, but the girl at the desk stuck a note on it saying it should be held until the morning. So here it is!"

Nora reached up to take the box. "Thanks so much."

"Don't mention it," the woman said. She turned to Regan. "Make sure she takes good care of that leg of hers."

"I will." Regan knew she sounded abrupt, but she was anxious to keep unnecessary people out of the room. If the kidnappers happened to call before the agreed-upon time, she wanted to be able to speak freely and to record the call with the sunburst pin Alvirah had lent her.

"I always keep a backup," Alvirah had explained as she thrust the tiny recording device into Regan's hands. "Even though the cops have your phone covered, with this you'll have your own tape of any calls that come in."

Nora was sliding the bow off the box.

"Bye, now," the volunteer smiled. She walked out leaving the door slightly ajar.

As Regan was closing it, she heard a gasp from her mother and spun around.

"Regan, look at this!" Nora cried, her voice panicked.

Regan hurried over and stared down at the now open package. Inside, nestled in the arms of a stocking-capped, fluffy brown teddy bear, was a picture of her father, wearing a tuxedo and smiling warmly. But it was the lettering around the tacky red-and-green frame that shot a cold chill through her body. I'LL BE HOME FOR CHRISTMAS, it read across the top. . . . IF ONLY IN MY DREAMS, completed the sentiment at the base of the frame.

There was an envelope in the box. Regan ripped it open. On an ordinary get-well card the sender had printed: "Nora, thought you'd like to have a pic of your sweetie." It was signed, "Your number-one fan."

"Let me see that." Nora took the card out of her hand. "They're threatening us, Regan!"

"I know."

"If anything goes wrong and they don't get the money . . ." Nora whispered.

Regan had already begun dialing Jack Reilly's number.

Jack had been up all night directing the frenetic activity that was the modus operandi of the Major Case Squad when involved in a breaking case.

The lab had lifted prints from the limo, and while there were many different sets to run through their computers, so far no match had been found. A few strands of polyester black hair suggested that one of the kidnappers had been wearing a disguise. The short length of the hairs indicated a fake mustache rather than a wig. The only other discovery of possibly great significance was a few tiny flecks of paint that had been found on the limousine's floor, around the brake pedal.

Suspicion for the abduction was beginning to center on Rosita's ex-husband, Ramon Gonzalez. A check with the police in Bayonne had revealed that he was well known to them. A compulsive gambler, he was rumored to be heavily in debt to local bookies and had not been spotted recently in his usual haunts.

Of potentially vital importance was the fact that Junior, his younger brother and fellow gambler, was a sometime housepainter. They shared an apartment in a run-down, two-family house. The landlord, who also lived in the building, said that he had not seen them in a couple of days and complained that they were behind in their rent.

Jack had notified the FBI and was now working in tandem with them. Besides the police helicopter, which would be tracking Regan's car, an FBI fixed-wing aircraft would be overhead, ready to follow the signals sent by the device planted in the bag with the ransom money.

Alvirah's tape recording of the call from the kidnappers had been run through an exhaustive audio analysis. The voice of the person who had made the ransom demand, as well as those of Luke and Rosita, could be heard clearly. The feeling was that the low and almost guttural tone of the caller was almost surely an attempt to alter his normal tones. Another man's voice could be detected in the background, although it was so faint that whatever he said had not yet been deciphered.

From analyzing the ambient sounds on the tape, they were able to ascertain that Luke and Rosita were being kept in a relatively cramped area near a body of water.

As Gabe Klein observed, "That really narrows it down—three quarters of the earth is covered with water."

Now, except for the intense manhunt for the Gonzalez brothers, the police were entering the waiting-game segment of the investigation.

Regan's call, however, changed that.

"I'm on the way," Jack told her.

Twenty minutes later, Jack was in Nora's room at the hospital.

"The logo on the box is from the gift shop downstairs," Regan told him.

"There's nothing in the picture that gives me a clue about where it was taken," Nora said.

"Luke and I go to a lot of black-tie affairs."

"By the time we realized what this was, our fingerprints were already on the card and the frame," Regan said.

"Don't worry about it," Jack told them. "If there are any other fingerprints, we'll get them. Do you happen to know what time the gift shop opens?"

"I already asked," Regan said. "Nine o'clock."

"How about if you go down there and speak to them?" Jack said. "See what you can find out about who might have bought this. We have to be careful not to let anyone think this is a police investigation."

"I thought I'd tell them that the person who bought the gift forgot to sign the card, and we wanted to be able to send a thank-you note."

Jack nodded. He looked at the bouquets of flowers in the room. "Nora, there's been publicity about your accident. This could, of course, be a somewhat macabre coincidence."

"I do get a lot of mail from people who

read my books," Nora acknowledged. "But isn't the sentiment on that frame too much of a coincidence?"

"Possibly," Jack admitted.

"In which case, it becomes a pretty grim threat," Nora said.

Regan was studying him. "Jack, you're leaning toward coincidence. Why?"

"Because Rosita's ex-husband is our strongest suspect, and from what I know about his type, this kind of thing is way too subtle for him. But then again . . ."

He shrugged and looked at his watch. "It's almost nine o'clock. Regan, why don't we go down to the gift shop together and see what we can find out? Then I'll take all of this downtown and give it to the lab."

He looked at Nora. "I know how upsetting this is for you. But it could be an important break for us. There may be fingerprints that will match up with some we've found in the car. If the frame wasn't bought downstairs, we'll try to trace it to where it was purchased. Perhaps someone in the gift shop will be able to give us a description of whoever bought the teddy bear."

Clearly on the verge of tears, Nora nodded. "I understand."

Jack turned to Regan. "Let's go."

Meanwhile, on the Upper West Side, barely a mile away from the hospital, Alvin Luck was bent over his bowl of oatmeal, still glowing with pleasure at the thought of the happiness his gift must be giving to Nora Regan Reilly, perhaps at this very moment.

He had wisely not broken his resolve to keep his mother in the dark about the purchase of the teddy bear. But his wisdom only went so far.

"What do you mean you didn't sign the card?" his mother badgered as she settled heavily into the chair opposite him. "Are you crazy? What were you thinking? She could help you get published. For God's sake, her editor is Michael Korda!"

"Will Mommy be home soon?"

It was the first question Chris and Bobby asked when they opened their eyes at 7:30. At least they slept well, Fred thought as he answered, "She'll be home as soon as she can."

On the shelf in Rosita's closet he had found extra sheets and a blanket and pillow, so he had bunked on the couch. It would have been more comfortable to stretch out on top of her bed, but he had found himself unable to do that. It felt almost as though it would be an invasion of her privacy.

He knew that the deeper reason was that everything in the bedroom conveyed a sense of Rosita's presence that was haunting.

A smiling picture of her with her arms around the boys dominated the top of the small dresser. There was a faint scent of perfume—a scent she had worn when he last saw her—emanating from the atomizer on her dressing table. When he had opened the closet door to find the bedding, the first thing he saw was her white silk robe and, peeking from beneath it, a pair of satin bedroom slippers.

Cinderella, he thought with a stab of pain.

Before he had settled on the couch the night before, he'd called Josh Gaspero, the friend he'd planned to meet. "Not home," he muttered to himself as Josh's machine picked up. "Figures. He's probably over at Elaine's having a Christmas drink with the regulars." The explanation he'd left had been brief. "Delayed on a special case. I can't discuss it. I'll try and catch up with you down there in a couple of days. I've got the schedule of stops."

Now he watched as Chris and Bobby went into the bathroom and reached for their toothbrushes without being told. When they began lightly splashing water on their faces, though, Fred decided to lend a hand. "As my mother used to tell me, 'You wash for a high neck,' " he said as he rubbed soap on a warm washcloth and took over.

While he made coffee, the boys got their own cereal and juice. "Please, will you make the toast in the oven?" Chris asked. "Our toaster broke, and we're not allowed to turn on the gas ourselves."

"Mommy gets really mad if we play near the stove," Bobby volunteered.

"Mommy's right," Fred replied.

Had the lab found anything significant in the limo? he wondered. By now they would have gone over it thoroughly. Alvirah Meehan had called him from her apartment last night and told him about the find. "Regan asked me to let you know. She said we'll keep you informed on anything that comes up."

As they were finishing breakfast, Sgt. Keith Waters from the Major Case Squad phoned. "Captain Reilly asked me to call you, Fred. I know what the situation is out there. Let me bring you up to date on what we have here."

He began with the results of the lab's inspection of the limo and the focus on Ramon Gonzalez and his brother.

"We're homing in on them. You're in place in Rosita's apartment. We want you to go through it carefully and see if you can find anything that would suggest that her ex was either threatening her or trying to get money from her. Keep your eye out for anything that would show where he might be hiding out now. You know the routine. We have a search warrant, of course."

Fred was aware that the boys were listening intently to his conversation, trying to figure out who was on the phone. "Will do," he said, "and if you see Rosita, tell her that the boys are being very good and are glad she's helping Mrs. Reilly."

"But tell her she has to be home for Christmas," Bobby cried out, dismayed.

"And ask her when we're going to decorate the tree." Now even Chris seemed to be about to cry.

"What are you going to tell them?" Waters asked softly.

"Sure, I'll be glad to," Fred replied heartily. He turned to the boys. "Mommy sent word that she's going to be really tired when she gets home, so she'd like it a lot if we'd decorate the tree for her today."

He saw the doubtful look on their faces. "I'm really good with the lights, and I can reach to the top. We'll save your favorite ornaments for your mom to hang when she gets home. How about that?"

"Good luck," Keith Waters said as he hung up the phone.

Willy was snoring loudly in the bedroom, and Sister Cordelia was fast asleep on the living room couch when Alvirah tiptoed into the apartment at midnight.

A newspaper was under Cordelia's hands, and her glasses were perched on the end of her nose. Alvirah had removed the glasses and newspaper, unplugged the Christmas tree, and turned out the lights, without disturbing her.

Now, over breakfast, the three of them comfortable in their bathrobes, she related everything that had taken place since she had phoned Cordelia yesterday and asked her to stay with Willy.

"The ransom drop is set for six o'clock tonight, and I intend to be in one of the unmarked cars following Regan," Alvirah declared as she spread a generous lump of butter on her English muffin.

Now that the troublesome dental implant had been mercifully extracted, Willy both sounded and looked more like his old self. "Alvirah, honey, I worry about you being in one of those cars," he began to protest, but then shaking his head, poured himself more coffee. "Useless," he muttered.

Cordelia, the eldest of Willy's six sisters, had entered the convent fifty-three years earlier, at age seventeen. Now the mother superior of a small convent on Manhattan's Upper West Side, she and the four nuns who lived with her spent their time tending to the needy in their parish.

Their many activities included running an after-school day-care center. Two years earlier, Alvirah had been the one to track down a long-missing child, who turned out to be one of the seven-year-olds in their charge.

After having been her sister-in-law for more than forty years, nothing Alvirah did could surprise Cordelia, and that included winning $40 million dollars in the lottery.

Alvirah and Willy had been most generous with their newfound wealth. As Cordelia put it, "They're the same down-to-earth people they always have been. Willy still comes running whenever any of our people need a plumber. The only difference in Alvirah is, now that she isn't cleaning houses anymore, she's turned into a first-rate amateur detective."

With her regal carriage and no-nonsense air, Cordelia inspired both trust and deference. She also had a way of getting immediately to the heart of the matter.

"Are those ransom drops usually successful?" she asked.

"More successful in fiction than in fact," Alvirah said with a sigh. "And the problem is that if something does go wrong, the kidnappers tend to panic."

Cordelia shook her head. "I'll get everybody praying. I'll just say it's for a special intention."

"We need all the prayers we can get," Alvirah said soberly. "I just feel so helpless."

"Honey, thanks to you they have the kidnapper's voice on tape. That could turn out to be a big help," Willy reminded her.

"Isn't that the truth?" Alvirah exclaimed, clearly cheered. "The detective gave me a copy of the tape last night. Let's listen to it." She got up, retrieved the cassette from her purse and reached into the mahogany cabinet in the living room for her special, highly sensitive tape player, yet another gift from her editor at the *Globe*.

She had spent many hours with her ear cocked to its speaker, listening for nuances in the countless conversations she had recorded in her relentless pursuit of justice.

Willy moved the coffeepot out of the way as she set the machine down between the empty bacon plate and the jar of imported raspberry jam.

She snapped in the cassette. "After we hear this, I'm going to get dressed and head over to the hospital. I told Regan I'd come by this morning. What a long day this is going to be for them. There's almost nothing to do now but wait until six o'clock tonight."

"I feel better today, so if there's anything they need for me to do, I'd be glad to help out," Willy offered.

"I'll call you from the hospital," Alvirah promised as she pressed the PLAY button.

The cassette made for grim listening. Willy's frown and the tightening of Cordelia's lips mirrored Alvirah's own sense of anger and concern.

"It's pretty straightforward," Cordelia said when it was over. "It especially breaks my heart to hear that young mother so worried about her boys."

"I'd like to get my hands on that guy," Willy said as he unconsciously punched his left palm with his right fist.

Alvirah was rewinding the tape. "I want to hear it again."

"Did you pick up something, honey?" Willy asked hopefully.

"I'm not sure."

She played it a second time and then again,

her eyes tightly closed. Then she turned off the machine. "There's something there that's ringing a bell, but I can't quite figure out what it is."

"Run it through once more," Willy urged.

"No, it won't make a difference right now. It will come to me later. It always does," she said. Frustrated, Alvirah got up from the table. "I can tell it's something important. *But what is it?*"

When Regan and Jack entered the gift shop in the hospital lobby, the carefully made-up fortyish woman behind the counter was yawning. Spotting them, she halfheartedly held up a carefully manicured hand to cover her open mouth.

"Excuse me," she said. "I'm so tired. All this holiday stuff has me aggravated."

"I know what you mean," Regan murmured sympathetically.

"At least you're standing here with a good-looking guy. I haven't had a decent date in months."

"Oh, we're not—" Regan began, but Jack nudged her and smiled at the saleswoman, whose name tag read "Hi. My name is LUCY."

"They told me to get a job in a hospital. You'll meet a lot of doctors. So I get myself hired here to help out for the month of December." She paused briefly as though unable to believe what she was about to report. "Not one doctor has set foot in this place since I started three weeks ago. They all go flying right through the lobby in their white coats."

"Oh dear," Regan found herself murmuring inanely. She cleared her throat. "Well, I'm sorry to bother you but . . ."

"Go ahead," Lucy said in a resigned voice as she picked up her Styrofoam coffee cup. "I'm all ears."

"We need to speak to whomever was working in here last night."

"You're looking at her. Why do you think I'm so tired?"

Regan and Jack exchanged glances. What a stroke of luck was the unspoken mutual thought.

Jack had put the teddy bear with the framed picture in a clear plastic bag he'd gotten from the nurses' station.

Regan held it up "We think this teddy bear was bought here last evening."

"Bingo."

"You remember selling it?"

"Bingo."

"Can you tell us anything about the person who bought it?"

"Please. Don't get me started. I let him in when I'm closing up, and he takes forever to pick out a teddy bear." Lucy pointed to the display of bears on the shelves. "Do you see any difference between any of them and the one you've got there? I don't.

"Then he reaches down into his shopping bag and pulls out the package that frame was wrapped in. So I stand here—after I've been on my feet all day—and wait for him to unwrap the package, just so he can use the paper again. Then he sticks the frame in the teddy bear's arms and asks me to rewrap the whole thing. So I put it in a box and tied it with a ribbon. Then he takes out his wallet and spends forever getting the exact change out of the secret compartment." She rolled her eyes.

"I can tell you one thing," Lucy concluded, "anyone who goes out with him better know the definition of Dutch treat."

"He paid in cash?" Jack asked.

She looked pained. "Isn't that what I just said?"

"How would you describe him?" Jack continued, a steely edge creeping into his voice.

She paused. "What's this all about anyway? Please don't tell me he's Bill Gates's long-lost brother."

Regan smiled reluctantly. "He left this for my mother, who's a patient upstairs, but he didn't sign the card. She wants to be able to send a thank-you note."

"That's weird," Lucy said, looking genuinely perplexed. "He seemed so pleased with himself, ya know, sticking the frame in the box with the teddy bear and all. I would have thought he'd have signed the card."

"I might be able to figure out who it is if

you give me an idea of what he looks like," Regan prodded.

Lucy scrunched up her face. "Not that great," she replied. "You know, around fifty maybe. Brown hair, not much of it, average height, a little wimpy."

"You say he was carrying a shopping bag," Jack said. "Did you happen to notice where it was from?"

She rolled her eyes again. "Oh yeah, I went shopping there once. I bought an outfit that fell apart first time I washed it."

"Where was that?" Regan asked.

"Long's. You heard their commercial? 'I'm longing for Long's.' I'll tell you one thing—I'm not longing for Long's."

"What time do you close here?" Jack asked.

"Usually 7:30. This week we stay open till 9:00. We want to get rid of all this holiday stuff. Once Christmas is over, you can't give it away."

It was obvious that there was nothing more to be learned from her. Regan and Jack crossed the lobby to the reception desk. The obliging clerk there knew who had been on duty the previous evening. "It's my friend Vanessa. Let me phone her."

Regan was dismayed to hear from Vanessa only the same vague description of the man who had left the package. "Did he by any chance mention his name or say that he was a friend of my mother's?"

"He didn't say anything except that he didn't want to disturb her last night."

Regan tried to keep her tone casual as she said, "I guess whoever left it won't receive a thank-you note."

"A mystery gift for a mystery author," Vanessa said brightly. "Tell her I hope she feels better."

Regan hung up. "She gave the same physical description, but unfortunately didn't add anything, Jack." She turned to the receptionist and thanked her for her help.

As they started to walk away from the desk, Jack pointed to the security cameras that ringed the lobby. In a low tone he said, "I'll get last night's tape. We should be able to pick him out with that big box he was carrying."

"Hello, you two." Alvirah's hearty greeting was unmistakable. Before they could respond, she spotted the object in Regan's hand. With a worried frown, she said, "There's got to be a reason you're carrying that teddy bear in a plastic bag."

"Let's go up to Nora's room," Jack suggested. "It's easier to talk up there."

Five minutes later, when they walked into her room, Nora was hanging up the phone. "I called my broker. The million dollars is being debited from our securities account and credited to Chase Manhattan. From there it will go to the Federal Reserve. I said I was making an overseas investment." She smiled wanly. "Pray God this is the best million dollars we will ever spend."

Jack nodded. "We're doing everything in our power to see that it is."

Together he and Regan told Nora and Alvirah what little they had learned about the donor of the gift. "There was nothing outstanding about him physically. He paid cash.

From what we hear, he certainly took his time, so he wasn't nervous. And he was carrying a shopping bag from Long's department store."

"Long's!" Alvirah exclaimed. "Before I won the lottery I used to 'long for Long's.' It's like most of those discount department stores. You have to wade through a ton of junk to find a bargain, but sometimes it happens. Most people see it as a challenge."

She glanced at the frame. "Yup, that looks like a Long's special. Do you want me to check it out for you, Jack?"

Jack knew that Alvirah was a master at ferreting out information. She had an almost uncanny way of getting people to open up. Why not? he thought. Later, if they could get a half-way decent image from the security cameras, he would send one of his squad out to the store to see if anyone there could ID the guy.

"I think it would be a great idea for Alvirah to go to Long's," Nora said.

For a moment, Regan considered accompanying her, then rejected the idea. The store would most likely be packed with last-minute shoppers. If the kidnappers called her on her cell phone, she'd barely be able to hear them.

There was something else. The look on her mother's face told her that she was needed here.

"I'll get started looking into the security tapes," Jack said.

"And I'm off to Long's," Alvirah announced, glad that there was finally some action she could take.

C.B. and Petey had had a busy morning. After breakfast, they left the houseboat and headed west to the isolated and rundown farm off Route 80 where Petey's cousin allowed him to keep his outboard motorboat.

As they rattled down the dirt road leading to the farmhouse, C.B. grumbled, "What a dump this place is."

Petey took offense. "It is my cousin's after all. And thanks to him, I've had a place to keep the boat that's going to collect our million dollars, Mr. Hoity-toity. Beggars can't be choosy," he admonished.

"Are you sure your cousin's away?"

"It's Christmastime, remember? Everybody's going somewhere, including us—huh, C.B.? I drove my cousin and his wife to the bus station a few days ago. They should be at my aunt's house in Tampa by now."

C.B. groaned again. "Don't talk to me about relatives."

"Do you miss your uncle?" Petey chuckled, as he jammed on the brake of his paint-stained pickup truck in front of the barn door.

C.B. did not deign to answer. If Uncle Cuthbert had done the right thing, I wouldn't have to put up with this moron, he thought. The closer they got to putting their hands on the money, the more nervous he became that something would go wrong.

He knew that the location he had chosen for the ransom drop was brilliant. It was just trusting Petey to get there in one piece that was the problem. But Petey had assured him that he could navigate the waters around Manhattan with his eyes closed—which C.B. figured was probably the way he usually did it.

They got out of the car, and Petey ran to open the barn door. "Ta-daaaah," he cried as he yanked a cracked and aging tarp from a decrepit boat, perched atop the trailer used to haul it to the water.

C.B. almost burst into tears. He hated his uncle more than ever. "Are you trying to tell me that thing *floats?*"

By now, Petey had scrambled up the side of the trailer and jumped into the boat. "If it had a sail, it could win the America's Cup," he yelled. He took off the painter's cap, which was his chapeau of choice, and waved it at C.B. "Ahoy, maties!" he cried.

"Get down here, Popeye."

Petey gave him the A-OK sign and scampered down. "This baby has really got the juice!" he bragged. "My cousin rebuilt the motor after I found it in a junkyard."

"Which is where it belongs. When was the last time that tub was in the water?"

"I went fishing that nice day in October," Petey said, scratching his neck. "Let's see, was it Columbus Day? Or was it the weekend after?"

"I bet it was Halloween," C.B. replied. "Let's hitch that wreck up to the truck and get out of here. It's freezing."

Petey started backing up his vehicle, his head stuck out the window as he urged C.B. to give him some guidance. "How much more room I got there, brother?" he yelled.

C.B. cringed. Before he could answer, Petey had clipped the side of the barn.

After several failed efforts, they finally secured the trailer and went bumping back down the road.

Petey blew his nose and dabbed at his eyes. "I may never see this place again."

"Consider yourself lucky."

C.B. pulled out his notebook, and they went over the plans for the evening. They'd lower the boat into the water in a cove Petey knew about, which was a half-mile south of the houseboat. They'd ditch the trailer there.

At precisely six o'clock, Petey would board the boat and steer it north on the Hudson, through Spuyten Duyvil around the top of Manhattan, to the seawall near the pier at East 127th Street. That was where Regan Reilly would be told to deposit the ransom money. It should take Petey about half an hour to get there.

C.B. would be stationed at the houseboat, and at six o'clock would make the first phone call to Regan Reilly, allowing her to speak briefly to her father and Rosita. He'd tell her to start driving through Central Park. Then he'd hang up before the call could be traced.

He'd rush across the George Washington Bridge and down the East Side Drive, calling Regan several more times along the way with instructions as to where she should drive next. "It's known as a delaying action," he explained to Petey. "In case she called the cops, it'll be harder for them to follow her from a distance. For all they know, we have her in sight."

The final instruction would be for Regan to cross Second Avenue at 127th Street and take the Marginal Street exit and drive onto the isolated dock. There she would be instructed to drop the duffel bag on the seawall and leave.

Once the drop was made, Petey would scramble up, grab the money, hop back on board, and then, with no time to spare, race down to 111th Street, where C.B. would be waiting in the car they had rented under a false name.

Petey would abandon the boat, which, thanks to the fact he never had bothered to register it, and that the motor had been bought in a junkyard, would be untraceable.

After that, they'd drive back to the house-boat and amuse themselves by counting their money until their flight to Brazil the following night.

"The storm they're forecasting better not screw us up," C.B. said, worried. "The sooner we get out of these parts, the better."

"*Arriba, arriba!* Cha-cha-cha," Petey sang,

tapping his hands rhythmically on the steering wheel.

C.B. decided the best way to cope with Petey was to ignore him. He pulled one of Nora Regan Reilly's early books out of his bag and turned to chapter eight, which was filled with his own notations.

"I just want to go over this again," he said, more to himself than to his partner in crime.

Austin Grady arrived at the office early Friday morning and immediately began reviewing the big appointment book on Luke's desk.

Starting with the present, he studied Luke's activities day by day, going back for two months. He found absolutely nothing that brought to mind any mention by Luke of a difficulty or problem.

The references to the lunches Luke had had with the late Cuthbert Boniface Goodloe brought an unconscious smile to Austin's lips and for a moment relieved the sickening tension that enveloped him. No bride ever planned her wedding with as much attention to detail as Goodloe had dedicated to his funeral, he thought.

Wanting to ensure a full house for his final good-byes, Goodloe had issued specific instructions. If he died on a weekend, the wake was not to be held until Tuesday. He wanted two full days and nights of viewing, with the funeral to be held on Thursday. That was exactly how it had happened.

"It takes time to notify everyone and get the obituary in the papers," he had said. God knows that plant society got plenty of notice, Austin thought—now we can't get rid of them.

The phone on his desk rang. "This had better not be that Bumbles guy," he muttered to himself. It was Regan. For an instant the sound of her voice gave him a quick hope that maybe she'd say that Luke and Rosita were safe. But, of course, that was not to be.

He told her what he had been doing. "I'm

going to keep at it," he promised. "I'm also going to ask some subtle questions around here to see if there's been a problem with any employee that didn't reach our ears."

"Thanks, Austin," Regan said quietly. "Who knows who could have done this. Right now the police are focusing on Rosita's ex-husband. Apparently he has heavy gambling debts, owed to the wrong people."

"That'd motivate you to get your hands on a million dollars any way you can."

"Of course, this could be the work of some-one who's been mad at my father for the last ten years." There was a brief hint of levity in Regan's voice. "It's like what they say about us Irish. We forget everything except the grudge."

"Don't I know it, Regan," Austin agreed, thinking of his grandmother, who never for-gave her cousin for "stealing her thunder" by scheduling her wedding two weeks before her own long-planned nuptials. Grandma went to her grave sixty years later, still griping about it, Austin thought. The fact that her cousin endured a horrible marriage did nothing to appease her.

"How's your mother doing?" he asked.

"She's hanging in there. I'll be here with her until late this afternoon."

He knew what she meant. "Give her my love, and take care of yourself, Regan."

"Will do," Regan said. "Talk to you later."

Austin had barely replaced the receiver when the phone rang again. He picked it up, the hope always in the back of his mind that it would be Luke's laconic voice saying, as he had at least a thousand times before, "What have we got going on there today, Austin?"

"Austin Grady," he said.

"Ernest Bumbles!" The voice grated through Austin like fingernails on a blackboard.

"Luke is not here," Austin told him firmly. "And no, I don't know when to expect him."

"I'll keep trying," Ernest said cheerfully. "Bye now!"

Luke and Rosita wrapped the thin blankets around themselves as best they could. Even though there was a propane heater, it did little to dispel the bone-chilling dampness of the drafty boat.

"If we get out of here, I'm taking my kids to Puerto Rico for a week," Rosita said. "It'll take me at least that long to warm up."

"When we get out of here, I'll send you all, first class," Luke promised.

Rosita smiled wryly. "You'd better watch your cash flow. Your bank account just went south a million bucks."

"You owe me half."

"You have some nerve!" This time Rosita genuinely laughed. "As C.B. keeps saying, ad nauseam, if you hadn't introduced his dear departed uncle to the Blossoms, he never would have changed his will."

"I couldn't get anybody to go to that dinner," Luke protested. "I had tables to fill!"

"Do you think Mr. Grady might make the

connection and have the cops check out our friend C.B.?" Rosita asked.

Luke decided to be honest. "I don't see why he would. C.B. kept his anger pretty well hidden at the wake, although I did catch him stuffing rotting foliage in his uncle's coffin after viewing hours."

"Are you kidding? Did you tell Mr. Grady?" she asked hopefully.

"Unfortunately, no," Luke said. "I felt kind of sorry for C.B. Over the years I've encountered a lot of understandably emotional people, acting out of character at the time of a death."

"Then he showed up at the funeral and the luncheon, and I guess behaved himself. Since you didn't make it to the funeral, they probably realize now that we were already missing. So no one would tie him to this," Rosita concluded.

Luke nodded in agreement. "They wouldn't have any reason to."

"I guess there's no way anyone would give Petey a second thought either," Rosita continued. "You being your usual unflappable self, Mr. Reilly, never even let on to him that you were less than thrilled with the job he did."

"I felt very flappable, but it was easier to pay him off and send him on his way. And you must admit, we did get a lot of laughs out of it."

"We sure did."

"That reminds me, Rosita. If you had gone out on that date with Petey, we might not be here."

"I'd rather be here."

Luke chuckled. "I'm forced to agree."

They fell silent for a few minutes; then Rosita said, "I wonder who's with my kids?"

"Regan will make sure they're well looked after."

"Oh, I know that," she said quickly. "It's just that they're probably with someone who doesn't know them, and it always takes a while for Chris and Bobby to feel comfortable with a new baby-sitter." She paused. "I'm sure they're missing me, but they're also probably mad that I haven't come home yet. They've had enough to deal with this past year and a half, with their father deserting them."

"Once you're home, things will be back to normal faster than you think," Luke said, trying to reassure her.

"What bothers me," she said hesitantly, as if she didn't want to vocalize her deepest fear, "is that it's so unbelievable that someone like C.B., who seems so ineffective, would plan and actually pull off a kidnapping. I can't help but wonder what else he's capable of doing, if he decides he doesn't want to leave witnesses."

Luke started to speak, then closed his mouth. There was always the chance the cabin was bugged. He wanted to tell Rosita about his plan to try to communicate to Regan that they were in the vicinity of the subjects of her favorite children's book, the one about the bridge and the lighthouse. He knew it was a stretch, but it was the only card he had to play.

Rosita was absolutely right. C.B. might be capable of a final act of vengeance.

Alvirah hurried past Macy's, heading for Long's department store, around the corner. The traffic had been so heavy she had gotten out of the taxi and jumped into the subway to get downtown. Despite the cold, last-minute holiday shoppers were out in force. Normally she enjoyed window-shopping, but today that was the last thing on her mind.

Alvirah knew that it would be almost impossible to track down the man who had bought the cheap picture frame, but still she was determined to try.

She barreled through the revolving door of Long's and then paused and looked around, getting her bearings. I haven't been here for a while, she thought. Truth to tell, I haven't missed it. But she remembered the layout as though it was yesterday. Men's Department first floor, just like every other store. Retailers know that men hate to shop. When you finally lasso them into the store, the clothes better be popping out at them.

Junk like the frame would definitely be in the basement. There was a line waiting to get on the down escalator. The woman ahead of Alvirah had three small children in tow and looked frazzled.

"Tommy, I warned you not to tell your brothers there's no Santa Claus," she hissed in the eldest child's ear.

"But there isn't!" he protested. "Ma, you don't think that joker in the toy department is really Santa, do you?"

"He's helping Santa out!"

"I heard somebody call him Alvin."

"Never mind," his mother said as she guided her children onto the steps of the escalator.

Precocious, Alvirah thought, amused. But then watching the mother with her children reminded her of the two boys in New Jersey, waiting for their mother to come home.

As they descended into the basement, a banner with the word SALE came into full view. The first floor had been crowded, but down here was a madhouse! Boxes of picked-over Christmas cards were now marked half price. Tables were piled with tree ornaments, Christmas lights, tinsel, and gift wrap. That frame had to come from here, Alvirah decided, when she spotted a counter straight ahead that was covered with a bewildering array of Christmas knick-knacks.

Alvirah's bargain-hunting years had left her with the ability to maneuver her body along sales counters without infuriating her fellow shoppers. It worked very well for her today. Within seconds she had found the section where boxes of frames were piled high, an example of each type open and on display. She spotted one that, at a glance, looked just like Nora's.

Excited, she reached around another shopper, lunged for the frame, and whipped out her reading glasses. JINGLE MY BELLS was scrawled across the top in gilt lettering.

"Jingle your own bells," Alvirah muttered, as with a snap of her wrist, she placed the frame facedown on the table. But when she picked up the one next to it, she smiled broadly. I'LL BE HOME FOR CHRISTMAS . . . IF ONLY IN MY DREAMS, it read. This was it!

Alvirah managed to catch the eye of the sales clerk, a good-looking boy who couldn't have been more than eighteen.

"I'll take this," she said, waving the frame at him.

"Let me see which one that is." He reached over and took it from her hands. "Oh, we've got plenty of those." He placed the sample back on the counter and took a box from the only large pile. It was stamped, "Made exclusively for Long's."

Good, Alvirah thought. That answers one question.

"I'm surprised there are any of these left," she said brightly.

He shrugged. "The others went like hotcakes. Not this one."

"Maybe you haven't had them on display long enough," Alvirah said hopefully.

"It seems like they've been there forever." He took her money and rang up the sale.

Alvirah's heart sank. This was like trying to find a needle in a haystack. "Maybe you can help me out," she said hurriedly, knowing the woman at her right elbow was starting to get impatient. "Someone dropped off one of these for my friend in the hospital last night, and the card didn't have a name on it. She feels terrible that she doesn't know who left it. You don't by any chance remember ringing up another one like this, do you?"

"You have to be kidding, lady. You know how busy we've been since Thanksgiving? I won't remember you in two minutes."

"I'll put my picture in one of these frames and send it to you," Alvirah retorted.

"Everything all right here?" a supervisor who appeared from out of the woodwork inquired.

"I was just talking to this nice young man," Alvirah said in a syrupy voice. "He was being so helpful."

"Keep longing for Long's!" the supervisor chirped and rushed off to troubleshoot elsewhere.

"I only fill in on this counter at breaks," the boy said quickly, obviously grateful Alvirah had not complained about him. "The girl who is here most of the time is off today. She'll be back tomorrow morning. We're opening at nine because it's the last day of Christmas shopping."

"What's her name?"

"Darlene."

"Darlene what?"

"Darlene Krinsky."

"She worked yesterday?"

"All day till closing."

"Thank you," Alvirah said. She'd give this information to Jack Reilly. It was the best she could do for now.

As she walked away, she heard the woman who had been at her elbow say loudly, "Thank God to get rid of Sherlock Holmes."

As the time for the ransom drop approached, the tension in the Major

Case Squad at One Police Plaza increased. Everyone who would be involved was in and out of Jack Reilly's office.

It had been a totally frustrating day. The prints they had found in the limo did not belong to anyone on record. The security-camera tapes from the hospital had proven basically useless. The man who had left the gift for Nora Reilly was of average height with slouching posture. When he had entered the hospital, he had been carrying the shopping bag cradled in his arms, virtually hiding his face. Only the back of his head was visible when he entered the gift shop, and when he exited, the huge bow on the box effectively shielded his face from the cameras.

Alvirah had reported on her trip to Long's department store. They had gotten Darlene Krinsky's address and phone number from the store's business office, but so far she hadn't been located. Not surprising, two days before Christmas, Jack thought. She's probably running around shopping, or partying. Not that he expected a talk with her would lead to anything. If that guy hadn't used a credit card for the teddy bear in the gift shop, it was doubtful that he used one for a frame that cost loss than ten dollars.

But the conversation with Alvirah did have one direct result. She was going to be riding in the backseat of his car tonight. He still wasn't quite sure how she had talked him into it, but as she pointed out, the only direct link they had to the kidnappers was the tape made because of her quick thinking. It was a fact that could not be denied.

At three o'clock, everyone involved in the ransom drop assembled in Reilly's office. Jack and his close friend, FBI agent Charlie Winslow, jointly ran the meeting.

In painstaking detail, they reviewed every aspect of what would be happening. There would be six cars in the mobile surveillance unit covering Regan Reilly as she followed the kidnappers' instructions. They would stay in touch by portable radios operating on a closed FBI frequency.

The tech unit monitoring Regan's cell phone

would immediately convey the instructions through the closed circuit to the mobile unit.

"Our agents have picked up the ransom money from the Federal Reserve," Winslow told them. "Tonight our aircraft will be overhead to track it, wherever it goes."

"You guys," Jack said, nodding to five detectives on the right side of the room, "will be eyeballing the Reillys' apartment building in case the kidnappers try anything as she's leaving the garage. Once she's on the street, you jump in your cars and join the mobile unit. Any comments?"

Dan Rodenburg, a seasoned police veteran of thirty years, shifted in his seat. "I don't like the idea of Regan Reilly driving alone in that car," he said flatly.

Neither do I, Jack thought. "We've thoroughly discussed it with her. She will not further endanger those two lives by having one of us hidden in the car. She was told to keep the police out of it. Regan knows what she's doing; she's a licensed PI of considerable note in California."

Charlie Winslow addressed the look of skepticism on Rodenburg's face. "We've made Regan Reilly an FBI special deputy for this mission. She'll be armed."

Jack continued, "Regan's car will be driven into the garage at her parents' apartment on Central Park South at approximately quarter to six. Regan will be waiting there. The duffel bag with the money will be on the front seat. She'll drive the one block to Sixth Avenue and turn onto the park drive at six o'clock.

Jack paused. "I shouldn't have to say this, but I will. It's just possible that one of you will have the chance to nail whoever makes the pickup. Don't do it. The safety of Luke Reilly and Rosita Gonzalez is what this is all about. Whoever grabs the ransom money may have a prearranged signal that if he isn't back by a certain time, get rid of the hostages. Unfortunately we've seen that happen."

He stood up. "That about wraps it up," he said. "As you know, we have an APB out for Ramon and Junior Gonzalez. Everything points to them."

Just as everyone was getting up to leave, the phone on Jack's desk rang. They all stopped, knowing that he had given orders to hold his calls except any that directly related to the case.

Jack picked up the phone. "Reilly." He listened. "Both of them? . . . Since Tuesday? . . . You checked all the phone records? . . . Big winners, huh?"

He hung up. "The Gonzalez brothers are living it up in Las Vegas, winning back the money they lost in Atlantic City. Which means . . ."

Charlie Winslow finished the thought. "Which means we haven't got any idea who we're dealing with."

Fred had managed to keep Chris and Bobby busy a good part of the morning by giving them the task of sorting the ornaments and untangling the Christmas lights. While they were absorbed in trying to beat each other at finding the most ornaments that needed new hooks, he quietly went through the apartment. It was a task he found unsettling., It was only the image of Rosita being held against her will that kept him searching for anything that would help bring her home.

It was clear that her life was an open book. The divorce papers showed that the decree had been issued almost a year ago. It granted liberal visitation to the father—something he apparently took little advantage of. The bank statements showed she lived within her means, and there were no dunning letters indicating overdue bills.

Casual questions to the boys about their activities and their mother's friends did not raise any flags.

From everything he could see, Rosita was not romantically involved with anyone and had little or no contact with her ex-husband. This confirmed his initial belief that Luke Reilly must have been the target for the kidnapping, and that Rosita simply had the hard luck to be with him.

At noon he drove with Bobby and Chris to his apartment and got a change of clothes. From there he took them to SportsWorld, an indoor amusement complex, where they had lunch and went on the rides. He kept his cell phone in his breast pocket the entire time. He knew that Keith Waters would call him immediately if there were any developments, or if anyone left a message on Rosita's phone.

They returned to the apartment late in the afternoon. Somehow it seemed to have lost its cozy, welcoming feeling. He could see the way the boys' spirits immediately began to wilt.

Tears began running down Bobby's cheeks. "I thought Mommy would be home by now."

Fred pointed to the Christmas lights and ornaments now in neat piles on the floor. "Come on, we've got to get that tree ready. We want to surprise her when she does get home."

"But we want to save some ornaments for Mommy to put up," Chris reminded him.

"Absolutely. Hey, does Mommy ever play Christmas music?"

"Oh, sure. Mommy loves Christmas music. We have lots of CDs," Chris informed him.

"I choose first." Bobby ran over to the stereo.

As the cheerful sounds of "Rudolph the Red-Nosed Reindeer" filled the room, the phone rang.

Chris raced to grab it, then, disappointment evident in his face, he said, "It's for you, Fred."

It was Keith Waters, calling to tell him that the Gonzalez brothers were no longer suspects. Not a big surprise, Fred thought as he hung up, but still a big disappointment. As the saying went, Better the devil you know. Gonzalez may be desperate for money, but he probably would not have murdered the mother of his children.

Were Rosita and Luke Reilly in the hands of sociopaths?

At 4:30, Nora said to Regan, "You'd better head over to the apartment. Give yourself plenty of time to get there."

Regan could tell how nervous her mother was getting. "I wish you weren't alone," she said.

"I'll keep busy." Nora reached into the drawer of the bedside table and took out her rosary.

"A lap around the beads," Regan smiled.

"A marathon around the beads," Nora corrected her.

Regan bent down and kissed her mother's forehead.

"Be safe, Regan." Nora's voice broke.

Unable to answer, Regan gave her a quick hug, then turned to leave. As she opened the door, she paused and looked back at her mother. "You know, Mom, there's another line that follows 'I'll be home for Christmas . . .' "

" ' . . . you can count on me,' " Nora said.

"That's the one."

Regan gave her a thumbs-up and closed the door behind her.

Luke's eyes widened in disbelief when Petey emerged from the bedroom.

Rosita murmured, "Oh my God, I don't believe it."

"Surf's up!" Petey cried. He was moving somewhat awkwardly, weighted down by a full-body wet suit.

"Don't tell me the ransom drop is at a costume party," Luke said.

Rosita nodded. "And he's going as Jacques Cousteau."

"Watch your mouths!" a high-strung C.B. snarled. "There's nothing that says I have to let them know where to find you two."

"That wouldn't be fair," Petey exclaimed, blinking his eyes. He rotated his neck and shoulders. "This thing feels weird. I shoulda gotten it a size smaller."

Always leave room to grow, Luke thought.

"Quit griping and get your goggles and whatever else belongs to that getup," C.B. ordered as he pulled on his own coat and unlocked the door. "It's time to get out of here."

"Hey, wait a minute," Luke said, alarmed that he might not get the chance to talk to Regan. "You told my daughter she could speak to us before she hands over the money. Don't think she'll give it to you if you don't keep your end of the bargain."

"Don't worry," Petey said. "C.B.'s just giving me a ride down to my boat."

"Come on!"

"Okay, okay, don't rush me. I've got a lot on my mind."

They were gone.

But not for long. Ten minutes later, Petey was back. "Forgot the keys to my boat," he said almost apologetically. "Like I told C.B., it's what happens when you rush too much."

At 5:30 Alvirah changed into a comfortable pants suit and rubber-soled shoes for her role as a passenger in Jack Reilly's car, following Regan to the ransom drop. She fastened her sunburst pin on her winter jacket, "That recorder is going to be turned on from the minute I set foot in the car," she announced.

A concerned Willy eyed her sensible shoes. "Honey, if there's a foot chase, you're not going to try to get in it, are you?" he asked anxiously.

"Oh, gosh no, Willy. I couldn't keep up. But if for any reason we get out of the car, I don't want to break my neck. It's getting icy."

"As long as you promise to stay back, no matter what happens."

They went down the hall to the living room where Cordelia was waiting for them.

When Regan had phoned twenty minutes earlier, Cordelia had answered and spoken to her quietly.

"Is your mother alone at the hospital?" she'd asked.

"Yes," Regan had said. "Which bothers me a lot, but she was very adamant about not telling anyone, even her closest friends, about what's going on. She's so afraid of a leak to the media."

"She shouldn't be by herself," Sister Cordelia said firmly. "I'd like to volunteer to go over there. And I know Willy would too."

Five minutes later, Regan called back. "I thought my mother wanted to go this alone, but she says she'd welcome your company."

They went down in the elevator together.

The doorman hailed a cab for Willy and Cordelia, then turned to Alvirah.

"A friend is picking me up," she explained.

From the front door, she could see the garage of the Reillys' apartment building. At seven minutes of six, Regan drove out in the dark green BMW. "Godspeed, Regan," Alvirah whispered, as Jack Reilly's car pulled up to the curb. She ran across the sidewalk and slid into the back seat.

"Alvirah, this is Detective Joe Azzolino," Jack said, indicating the driver. He did not take his eyes off the BMW as he spoke.

"Nice to meet you, Joe," Alvirah said crisply. No small talk at a time like this, she thought.

The long block to Sixth Avenue, as native New Yorkers still called the Avenue of the Americas, was clogged with taxis and limousines, picking up and discharging people at the upscale hotels and restaurants that lined Central Park South.

They followed Regan's inch-by-inch progress. "This traffic is perfect for the timing," Jack said with satisfaction. "She won't have to worry about delaying too long at the intersection."

At precisely six o'clock, Regan turned left into Central Park.

A voice came over the FBI closed circuit. "Her cell phone is ringing."

"Have you got it straight?" C.B. asked as he drove down the narrow track that led to the cove where they had secured Petey's boat and hidden the trailer.

"Can a duck swim? Is the Pope Catholic? Do bears—"

"Don't do this to me," C.B. begged. "Let's go through it just once more. You are going to get on that termite-infested piece of wood you call a boat. You are going to watch the time, and at precisely six o'clock turn on the engine and leave."

"Shall we synchronize our watches, me matey?"

C.B. glared at him, then continued. "You will guide that bucket through Spuyten Duyvil, around the north end of Manhattan to the Harlem River—"

"Spuyten Duyvil is Dutch," Petey volunteered. "I think it means 'in spite of the devil.' Current is reeeeeally bad up there. Yup. But no problem for an old salt like me."

"Shut up! Shut up! *Shut up!* I gave you Rosita's cell phone to use—"

"Mr. Reilly's is much newer. You could have given that one to me. But no—"

C.B. braked so violently that Petey was thrown forward. "I could have had a concussion," he said reproachfully.

"To continue, I will call you at about quarter of seven. By then you will be in place, tied to the dock at 127th Street, next to the seawall. I will speak to you briefly. *Try* to understand that the location of a cell phone can be traced in less than a minute."

Petey whistled admiringly. "That's really fast. It's all about technology today, isn't it, C.B.? Me, I like things a little simpler."

"God knows you've proven that," C.B. moaned.

Even with the traffic along River Road, it took C.B. less than ten minutes to drive the half mile from the cove to the houseboat. Every time he made the final turn off the busy thoroughfare, he was acutely aware that a passing police car might trail a car driving down a road that led to a marina closed for the winter.

When they'd hatched the plan, it was Petey who came up with the idea of taking the houseboat he looked after at Lincoln Harbor, a year-round marina in Weehawken, to the isolated pier in Edgewater.

That part of the plan has worked, C.B. grudgingly admitted to himself, as he looked nervously in the rearview mirror. *And the next time I turn onto this road, I'll have a million bucks in the backseat.*

He made the turn, but drove at a snail's pace until he was sure there was no one behind him. Then he picked up speed for the remaining stretch to the parking area. Once there, he left the car and walked down the dock to the houseboat. The wind was increasing and the temperature dropping. The weather report he had heard on the radio had indicated there was still a chance the storm would blow out to sea.

I don't care where it blows, as long as by then, I've blown out of here with the money, he thought.

The footing was tricky getting on the houseboat. The current was pulling the vessel out, then slapping it back, hard against the dock. Who could possibly want one of these torture chambers? he asked himself as he tried to hoist his out-of-shape body from the pier onto the deck. There was one frightening moment when his legs were pulled into a near-perfect split, one leg on the pier, the other headed out to sea with the boat.

"You'd have to be Gumby to do this as a steady diet," C.B. wailed aloud as he finally got both feet planted on the deck. But this night-mare is almost over, he promised himself as he unlocked the door to the cabin.

Ten minutes later, at precisely 6:00 P.M., he dialed Regan's cell phone. When she answered, in his rehearsed, guttural tone he ordered, "Keep driving north. Your father and Rosita are fine. As a matter of fact, they even listened to your mother on Imus this morning . . . Isn't that right, Luke?" He held the phone up to Luke's mouth.

"I did hear your mother this morning, Regan." Let her get what I'm trying to tell her, Luke prayed. "I can just *see* myself reading your favorite book to you when you were little."

"That's enough!" C.B. said. "Here's Rosita."

"Regan, who's with my boys?"

Before Regan could answer, C.B. pulled the phone back. "Circle the park, Regan. I'll call you back."

He broke the connection. "I'm out of here," he told Luke and Rosita. "Wish me luck."

Her father and Rosita were still alive. The kidnappers were going to collect the ransom. Regan had not realized just how desperately she had feared that something would cause them to panic, and there would be no further word from them.

Circle the park. That was what he had told her to do. There was heavy traffic on the winding park road as far as the Seventy-second Street exit, where a steady stream of cars turned onto Fifth Avenue. Many others veered left to the West Side. Far fewer continued driving north.

Not good, Regan thought. With so little traffic, it will be easier to spot that I'm being followed. Near 110th Street the road curved west, then headed back south. The caller hadn't given her a time limit for the drive through the park, but neither had he said to hurry. He's probably smart enough to know that the cops can fix a location on a cell phone if it's on for more than a minute or so, she thought. That's why he barely let them say anything to me.

Dad heard Mom on Imus this morning, she thought. They had talked about the children's books Mom had sent to Imus for his son. But why did Dad talk about reading to me as a child? He must have *known* he only had a few seconds. And he mentioned my favorite book. Which one *was* it? I can't even remember myself.

She was passing the exit to Ninety-sixth

Street on the West Side. The traffic was picking up.

Last night Mom told me she kept thinking about the days when she and Dad were just starting out. She mentioned their first apartment and selling her first short story. Dad's obviously doing that same kind of reminiscing.

Regan blinked back the tears that started to well in her eyes.

She was passing Tavern on the Green. The restaurant, always brilliantly illuminated, was particularly festive with Christmas lights. When she was little, it had been a special treat to ride the carousel near the Central Park Zoo and then have lunch there.

She was at the southern end of the park, on a strip of road running parallel to Central Park South. She had made almost a complete circle.

The cell phone rang again.

"Sailing, sailing, over the bounty Maine," a goggled Petey sang as he steered his boat north under the George Washington Bridge. But then as the cold, wet air stung his exposed cheeks, he switched to the song he remembered from his first-grade play: "Oh, it's so thrilly when it's chilly in the winter—"

Clunk!

"Iceberg alert!" Petey yelled as the boat bounced up and down. Once again he switched tunes. ". . . my heart will go onnnnn." He had seen *Titanic* three times. If I'd been steering that baby, we'd have made it, he thought.

Petey felt free as a bird. It seemed as if he had the whole river to himself, and he was making great time. He patted the side of the boat. "I'm going to miss you when I'm in Brazil. We've had a lot of fun together. I sure hope the cops find you a good home."

He was almost at the top of Manhattan. "Spuyten Duyvil, here I come," he called as he veered off to enter the narrow tidal strait that connected the Hudson and the Harlem Rivers.

"Feels like I'm in a washing machine," he muttered as the swirling currents fought to twist and turn his aging craft.

"I made it!" he said triumphantly fifteen minutes later, as he tied the boat to the seawall at 127th Street, well hidden under the Triborough Bridge.

W here do all these people think they're going? C.B. fumed as he waited in a line to pay the toll at the George Washington Bridge. They should be home wrapping their presents. Of course, I'll be unwrapping mine in a couple of hours, he mused. The thought cheered him up.

He had written out the instructions he intended to give Regan Reilly. I hope you like to zigzag, he thought, because that's what you'll be doing until seven o'clock.

He checked his watch. It was 6:20. Time to

call Regan again, but not until he was out of the vicinity of the bridge. He wanted to be sure to get a clear connection.

As soon as he reached the Harlem River Drive, C.B. pulled out the cell phone. "Time to see the pretty trees on Park Avenue, Regan," he said when she answered.

"What do you think they're up to, Jack?" Joe Azzolino asked his boss as the kidnappers' instruction to Regan to head to Park Avenue was relayed to them from the eavesdropping base at headquarters. "Eagle" was the code name assigned to the operation.

"The obvious answer would be that one of them is tailing her and is trying to spot our cars," Jack said. So why do I have a gut feeling that they've got something up their sleeves that we haven't figured out? he asked himself. They were never going to be able to pinpoint the location of the cell phone. Both calls had been much too brief.

The next call came at 6:35. Regan was told to leave Park Avenue, go up Third Avenue, pull over at 116th Street, and wait.

Jack keyed his transmitter. "Eagle one to all units. Lay back. Give her a little room, but keep her in sight."

Ensconced in the backseat, Alvirah had been remarkably quiet so far, mainly because she had been trying to figure out something that had been bothering her for the last half hour. Finally it came to her, and suddenly she knew why it had struck a chord this morning when she listened to the tape of the kidnappers' first call. One of Nora Regan Reilly's early books had dealt with a kidnapping in Manhattan. In that story, the victim's wife was told to drive up Sixth Avenue from Greenwich Village and enter the park at Central Park South. It's the coincidence of the Central Park South entrance that's been jiggling in my mind, she thought.

When she reached 116th Street, Regan pulled over and double-parked. Azzolino stopped their car at 115th Street and usurped the spot another driver was about to claim. They waited silently.

As more of the plot of Nora's book came back to her, Alvirah realized that in that story, the kidnapper had the wife driving back and forth from the East Side to the West Side. What he really had been doing, however, was maneuvering her farther and farther north, and nearer and nearer to the Harlem River, Alvirah remembered.

In the novel there was something about leaving the ransom money near the river. *Then what?* she wondered. She had read the book so long ago, it was difficult to remember the details. Alvirah frowned in concentration. I've got to put my thinking cap on. But first she thought she should at least say *something* about the similarity of what had happened in Nora Regan Reilly's novel and what was happening now.

"Don't the police have a boat unit on Randall's Island?" she asked.

"Yes, we have a Harbor Unit there," Jack said without turning his head. "Why?"

"Well, it's just that Randall's Island is right next to the Triborough Bridge. It would only take one of your boats a few minutes to travel across the river."

"That's right." There was a hint of impatience in his voice.

"You see, in one of Nora's books that I read a long time ago, the ransom drop was . . ."

At the same moment they heard, "Eagle base to all units. She's been instructed to continue north on Third."

"In Nora's book," Alvirah continued, "the victim's wife drove down a dock or a pier or something and put the money on a seawall. Somebody was waiting in a boat and reached up and grabbed it."

A trailer truck had been racing the light and was now caught in gridlock halfway across Third Avenue. Regan had just cleared the intersection before the truck crossed. Now they were blocked by the truck and could no longer see her. "Eagle one to all units," Jack snapped into the transmitter, "we're locked in. Don't lose her."

"Jack . . ."

"Alvirah, not now, please."

The trailer truck was moving slowly past. Azzolino floored the accelerator. Even running the light, they were now a full block behind Regan.

They were passing 123rd Street.

Somehow Alvirah was absolutely sure of what would happen next. Dollars to donuts, Regan would be instructed to drive on a lonely road along a dock on the Harlem River. They'll tell her to leave the money on a seawall.

"Jack, I know you'll think I'm crazy, but you've got to listen to me," she said. "Those kidnappers have read Nora's books, and they're following one of her plots. You've got to get some of your men over to the river around the Triborough Bridge right away. There's a boat there waiting to make the pickup."

We need this, Joe Azzolino thought.

"Eagle base to all units. She's been told to take a right on 127th Street."

Marginal Street, Alvirah thought. That's the road she'll be told to take.

"Jack, listen to me. You've got to get a boat on the river or you'll lose them."

"Alvirah, for God's sake—"

"Eagle base to all units. She's been told to drive east and take the exit . . ."

". . . to Marginal Street," Alvirah finished with him.

Marginal Street appeared to be not so much a road as a long, bumpy, desolate dock. Regan drove along it slowly, not sure how far to go.

The phone rang again. "Drive as far as the Triborough Bridge and stop." Again the connection was broken.

Wild with tension, C.B. phoned Petey. "She'll be there in thirty seconds!"

Petey squealed with delight, then lowered his voice until it seemed to be coming from somewhere deep in his toes. "Ready, partner."

He was proud of himself that, even in this moment of great stress, he remembered to disguise his voice.

Regan's eyes darted from one side to the other, but she saw no sign of anyone nearby. She reached the underspan of the bridge and stopped. Overhead she knew hundreds of cars were passing to and from the three boroughs, but this place felt so removed from all that activity that it might have been on another planet.

She looked to either side of her car, then in the rearview mirror. This road was so isolated that the appearance of any other vehicle would make it apparent to the kidnappers that she was being followed. *Don't come too close, Jack,* she thought, *you'll scare them off. I can handle myself.*

The cell phone rang and she grabbed it. "I'm here," she said.

"Get out of the car. Take the duffel bag to the seawall and put it down on the edge. Return to your car. Back up slowly. When all the money is safely in our hands, you will learn the whereabouts of your father and Rosita. If it is not . . ."

The phone went dead.

Regan got out of the car, walked around it, and opened the passenger door. Jack had told her the duffel bag weighed twenty-two pounds. She grabbed it by the handle, lifted it in her arms, and carried it to the seawall. As she leaned over to lay it down, she realized that there was a boat tied to the wall only a few feet away.

A boat, she thought with dismay. They're making the pickup in a boat! The mobile unit from the Major Case Squad would be useless.

But the duffel bag was bugged, and the overhead aircraft would follow it to its destination. Pray God that that was where they were keeping Dad and Rosita.

Wanting desperately to see anything that might later help her identify the kidnappers, Regan allowed herself a fleeting sideward glance toward the boat as she straightened up. The only thing she could discern was that whoever was on the vessel was wearing a wet suit.

Before she could get back in the car, she heard a voice from the boat call out, "Thank you very much, Regan."

"Eagle one to all units. Stay back. Pickup is probably by boat." They could see Regan's car roll to a halt nearly two blocks down the dock.

"She's been told to get out of the car and leave the money on the seawall," Eagle base reported.

"Hook me up to the Harbor Unit," Jack snapped.

Alvirah listened as in terse, urgent phrases, Jack told the commander there what he needed. "Follow the boat they're in . . . no running lights . . . do not apprehend . . ."

"Jack, Regan is backing up. She must have made the drop." Azzolino pointed to the BMW, which was slowly coming toward them.

Jack jumped out and was opening Regan's door before the wheels stopped rolling. "They were on a boat." It was not a question.

"There appeared to be just one of them. He was wearing a wet suit," Regan said, shaking her head. "I couldn't believe it. That weirdo called out to me by name to say thank you. It was chilling. He sounded almost like a little kid."

"He's a little kid who is very familiar with your mother's books," Jack said grimly. He looked out at the water. A Harbor Unit boat, its running lights off, could be seen heading down the river.

By now that guy's probably a mile away and ditching the boat, Jack thought. Our only hope now is the tracer in the duffel bag.

I should have listened to Alvirah.

Petey the Painter had never experienced such excitement. His head was pounding, his brain was throbbing, his ears were ringing, his hands were trembling. He had never been so deliriously happy in his life.

There was a million dollars at his feet! A million dollars for him and C.B. to have a good time with. He wished they were going to

Brazil tonight. He really deserved a vacation. The Copacabana, he thought. Beautiful girls! He heard that a lot of them went topless on the beaches down there. Woo-woo!

Inside his gloves his fingers were freezing. They'd warm up when he was counting the money.

The river's current was going north. But bucking against it didn't slow him down. The pier at 111th Street was right ahead. And so was the pedestrian bridge he would use to cross over the FDR Drive.

C.B. would be waiting there for him in the car. He would jump in with the money, and off they'd go.

He pulled up to the pier and quickly tied the boat to it. Now for the tricky part, he thought. He stood up, his feet parted, and braced himself to pick up the bag and hoist it to the pier. He reached down and cradled the bag lovingly in his arms. No mother had ever held her newborn with more tenderness.

It was time to go. Whenever God closes a door he opens a window, Petey thought sadly as he looked at his boat for the last time. Overwhelmed, he bent over to kiss the bow. As his lips touched the briny surface, a wind-whipped wave slapped against the boat. Petey felt himself toppling forward.

SPLASH!

As Petey belly-flopped into the water, his precious cargo went flying out of his hands, landing a few feet beyond his reach. The swirling current of the East River now claimed it as its own and began to whisk it northward.

Desperately, Petey began a furious dog-paddle in an effort to retrieve it but within seconds realized it was hopeless. The current was trying to suck him under. He managed to get back to the boat, which he no longer felt like kissing, and grabbed onto the side for dear life.

What can I do? What can I do?! he thought, his mind a jumble of confusion.

There was only one thing he could do, he thought, gasping for breath. Drag himself up to the pier, cross the pedestrian bridge, and meet C.B. He'll get over it, he kept telling himself. After all, it's only money, and I could have drowned.

Five minutes later, a soggy Petey was tapping on the window of C.B.'s rental car. "I've got good news and bad news," he began.

"You've done everything you can," Alvirah assured Regan as they drove from Marginal Street to the hospital. "And you said the guy in the boat sounded polite and even thanked you. That's a good sign."

"I hope so. Alvirah, I just can't believe these people got the idea for the location of the ransom drop from one of my mother's books. I read that book so long ago, I'd forgotten all about it."

"You'd have been just a kid when it came out."

Regan sighed. "My mother has written so many books, even she forgets the details of plots from twenty years ago. I'm trying to think how that one ended."

Alvirah knew. The kidnap victim had never been heard from again.

They exited the FDR Drive at Seventy-first Street and parked the car on First Avenue. Entering the hospital, they passed the gift shop on the way to the elevator. Inside they could see that Lucy was on duty. She and Regan exchanged glances, and Lucy waved.

"Still here," Lucy called out.

"She's the one you talked to this morning about the teddy bear, isn't she?" Alvirah asked.

"Yes."

In the elevator up to Nora's room, Alvirah made a mental note to drop in on Lucy on the way out. Sometimes you don't know how much you know, she told herself. Maybe if I talk to her, I can jiggle that girl's brain a bit. It's worth trying.

Regan opened the door of the room. Nora, Sister Cordelia, and Willy greeted her and Alvirah with expressions of stunned disbelief.

"What?" Regan asked through suddenly dry lips. "Did you hear something about Dad?"

"Jack just called here," Nora said. "He didn't

want to tie up your cell phone. He thinks there's a good chance you'll be getting another call very soon."

"About finding Dad and Rosita?" Regan asked, somehow knowing the answer.

"No." Nora paused. "The Harbor Police just plucked the duffel bag with the million dollars out of the East River."

"Oh my God," Regan gasped.

Nora's face was ashen. "Jack thinks it means one of two things. Either they dropped it by mistake—which would be good—or for some reason they panicked because they suspected there was a tracking device in it." Her voice rose sharply. "Regan, if we get a second chance with these people, there's going to be nothing but money in the bag."

"Mom, the only reason for using the tracking device was in the hope that they would take the money to where they're keeping Dad and Rosita. You know that."

They all knew that, but Regan could see the same fear on all the faces around her that she was sure was on her own. Whether it was a bungled ransom drop or a deliberate discarding of the money, it meant that her father and Rosita were in the hands of some very unhappy abductors.

"*You were kissing your boat good-bye?!*" C.B. howled as he drove up First Avenue. "You couldn't do it while you were waiting for Regan Reilly? You could have smothered it with kisses!"

"Would you turn up the heater? I think I caught a chill in that river." Petey sneezed. "See?"

C.B. punched the steering wheel. "You had the million dollars in your hands and you let it go."

"No use crying over spilled milk," Petey said. "I could have drowned, you know. Did you ever think about that?"

"Did you ever think about the fact we have no money, we have two hostages on our hands, and . . ."

"We should have set up a petty-cash fund for their food. I had to fork over six bucks for . . ."

"Petty-cash fund! You just lost us a million dollars!" C.B.'s throat was starting to hurt from the strain of shouting.

"We'll figure a way to get it back," Petey said optimistically.

"Just what do you suggest?" C.B. asked, his voice dropping to a dangerously low level.

"Good question."

"Do you think maybe we should call Regan Reilly and tell her what a bumbling idiot you are?"

"Uh-uh."

"Do you think we should get on that plane to Brazil with barely enough money for a week's vacation?"

"Uh-uh."

"Do you think we should release Reilly and Rosita, and then have a beer with them at Elsie's?"

"Uh-uh."

"Then what do you suggest?"

"It's hard to think when I'm cold." Petey leaned back and reached for the trash bag on the backseat. "Being that we don't need this anymore, I'm going to use it to try and get warm." He started ripping it at the seams.

"I had thought of everything," C.B. moaned. "I knew that they'd be able to come up with the million bucks. I knew that they'd probably call the cops. I knew that there'd almost certainly be a tracking device attached somewhere to the bag. I read a lot of mysteries, you know."

"Reading is important," Petey said approvingly.

". . . I would have dumped the money from the duffel bag into that trash bag, which I would now like to wrap around your neck. And that duffel bag should now be lying in the middle of 111th Street instead of floating around the East River."

Petey shifted in his seat, the trash bag crinkling around him. "Wait a minute. You think they called the cops?"

"Of course. They always call the cops."

"That irritates me. We asked her not to,

right?" Petey complained. "You should let her know that when you talk to her."

C.B. gave him a withering look, but then his eyes narrowed. The best defense is a good offense, he thought, as an idea began to form in his mind.

Shortly after 8:30, Jack Reilly joined Regan, Alvirah, Willy, and Cordelia in Nora's hospital room.

"I understand that I was a big help to my husband's kidnappers," Nora said.

"Apparently you were," Jack agreed. "I've got a little more information," he told them, "but not as much as I'd like. A boat was found tied to the pier at 111th Street. We're pretty sure it was abandoned by the kidnappers. It's on its way to the lab now. That was also probably the place where the bag with the money went into the water."

"How would you know that?" Sister Cordelia asked.

"It was at that point that the guys on the aircraft tracking the bag of money realized it had switched directions and started heading north."

"Did the boat have any markings?" Regan asked.

"None. And it's obviously a rebuilt motor, which means it probably can't be traced. We're hoping for fingerprints."

There was a moment of silence. Everyone understood that the next move was up to the kidnappers.

Sister Cordelia squeezed Nora's hand. "It's time we let you get some rest. We'll keep praying."

"I'm glad you were here," Nora said sincerely. She looked at Willy. "I can't believe you made me laugh."

He smiled at her. "I'm saving my best stories for when you feel better."

Alvirah turned to Regan. "Now keep me posted. Call at any hour. I'm going to do some homework with those tapes."

Jack had given her a cassette with all the calls from the kidnappers Eagle base had taped. "This might not be orthodox, but after what happened today, I don't care," he had said. "Alvirah, next time you try to tell me something, I swear I'll listen."

The doctor came in as Alvirah, Willy, and Cordelia were leaving. He obviously knew there was a personal problem of some kind but did not probe. "How's that leg feeling?" he asked.

"Not the best," Nora admitted, the weariness in her eyes clearly visible. Reluctantly she agreed to take a painkiller.

Regar was sure that if her mother were left alone, she'd fall asleep. "Mom, I'm going to run downstairs and get a cup of coffee. I won't be long. Can I bring you back anything?"

"No, but you should eat something."

Jack walked out with Regan. "Okay if I join you for that coffee?"

Once in the cafeteria, Jack prevailed on Regan to have a sandwich.

"We're certainly keeping you from enjoying the holidays," Regan said. "I can't believe tomorrow is Christmas Eve. You must have had plans."

"My family will still be there when I get home. My parents live in Bedford, and that's where the whole clan will be this week. There are so many of us, they won't even notice I haven't shown up yet."

Regan smiled. "Being an only child, if I don't show up it's noticeable."

Jack laughed. "If you were one of ten, it would be noticeable."

That remark would have snapped my mother awake, Regan thought, smiling. Kind of wakes me up too.

They talked about what the kidnappers might do next.

"My biggest fear is that absolutely nothing will happen next," Regan admitted.

"Regan, keep in mind that you talked to your father and Rosita less than three hours ago," Jack said.

"Those few words my father said keep running through my mind. He mentioned reading my favorite book to me when I was a little girl. I thought at the time he was just being nostalgic, like last night when my mother was remi-

niscing about when they were newlyweds."
She shook her head. "But now I'm not so sure.
I have a feeling he was trying to tell me some-
thing."

"What was your favorite book?" Jack
asked.

"For the life of me, I can't remember."
Restlessly Regan tapped her hands on the table.
"Maybe my father brought it up because my
mother and Imus talked about children's
books this morning."

"More than likely that's all it was. But you
know as well I do that kidnap victims often try
to pass messages if they possibly can."

"Oh, it's you two again!" The call came
from across the room.

They looked up to see Lucy from the gift
shop bearing down on them.

"Can't get enough of each other, huh?" Her
eyes darted around. "I always take a walk
through here before I go home. As usual, no
Dr. Kildares in sight." She shrugged. "What
are you going to do? Say, your mother must be
some stickler for writing thank-you notes. One

of her friends was just in the shop, asking about the guy who bought the teddy bear."

Regan and Jack looked at each other. "Alvirah," they said in unison.

Willy and Cordelia were waiting for Alvirah on a couch in the lobby when she emerged from the gift shop.

"Well, I did find something out," she reported.

"What did you learn, honey?" Willy asked.

"The man who sent that teddy bear with Luke Reilly's picture was carrying a Long's shopping bag."

"You knew that."

"Yes, but Lucy—that's the clerk's name— remembered something else. There was a red jacket or sweater, or at least some sort of red clothing, in the bag."

"So?" Cordelia asked.

"Oh, I know it's not much, but it's something," Alvirah said, sighing. "Maybe it will help jog the memory of the salesclerk at Long's when I talk to her tomorrow."

Cordelia was going home.

Alvirah and Willy put her in a cab, then hailed one for themselves. "Two-eleven Central Park South," Willy said.

Even though it was late and the temperature was steadily dropping, the streets were filled with people. When the cab reached the area of the Plaza Hotel, Alvirah remarked wistfully, "It always looks so festive around here during the holidays. ' 'Tis the season to be jolly,' and all that." She shook her head as she remembered the sadness in Nora's eyes.

When they got home, she changed into her favorite old robe, made a pot of tea, and settled at the dining room table. I began the day with this and I'll finish the day with this, she thought as she turned on her recorder.

She listened to all the tapes, playing them in the order they had been recorded. First, the original call from the kidnappers, then the conversation with Fred Torres at Rosita's home. She replayed that tape twice, each time stopping at one point. "Probably doesn't mean a thing, but it's worth asking him about," she said aloud as she jotted a phrase on her memo pad.

Willy joined her as she was playing the tapes of the kidnapper giving directions to Regan.

"What impression are you getting of that guy?" Alivrah asked.

"He's disguising his voice," Willy said. "He's smart enough to get off the phone fast, so his location can't be traced. He planned that ransom drop mighty carefully."

"He was smart enough to realize the plot Nora used could work for him, and it did to a point. Now listen to this one." She played the tape of the call in which Luke and Rosita spoke to Regan as she started driving into Central Park.

"Hear anything special?" she asked Willy.

"It's not as clear as the calls that came after it."

"That's right. The reception isn't as good. That's probably because of the location where they're being kept. You know, there can be a lot of interference in some areas." Alvirah played the tape again. "Did you notice any-thing about what Luke Reilly said?"

"Well, the poor guy's obviously reminiscing about his life. I did that when I was kidnapped. And . . ."

"And what?"

"He kind of puts a big emphasis on the word 'see.' It's almost like he's trying to tell her something."

"That's exactly what I was thinking,"

Willy glanced at the pad. "What's that mean?" He pointed to a notation she had made.

"It's something I want to run by Fred Torres tomorrow. Rosita told him that Luke Reilly always 'kept his cool.' I want to find out if Rosita talked about any specific situation where he had to 'keep his cool.' " She looked at her watch. "It's eleven o'clock, and still no word from Regan. That means she hasn't heard from the kidnappers."

"Maybe they're trying to figure out their next move," Willy suggested.

"Then they better figure it out soon. What worries me is that the longer Luke Reilly is missing, the more likely that word of his kidnapping will get out. If it ends up in the headlines, God knows what will happen."

C.B. did not attempt to hide the situation from Luke and Rosita. When he and Petey arrived back at the houseboat, he told them exactly what had happened.

"You can't make this stuff up," Rosita said, glaring at Petey as he went into the bedroom to change out of his wet suit.

"You actually used a scenario from my wife's book for the ransom drop?" Luke asked incredulously.

"It almost worked," Petey called from the bedroom. "Has she got any other kidnapping stories we could take a look at?" He poked his head out the door. "We can't miss our flight tomorrow night. The planes are overbooked."

"I've read all her novels," C.B. said shortly. "She doesn't have any other kidnappings."

Oh yes she does, Luke thought. The other

one had come to mind only a few weeks ago when he had business in Queens and took the wrong turn coming out of the Queens-Midtown Tunnel. He had found himself on the same route she'd used for a ransom drop in one of her early short stories. He remembered it because Nora had been pregnant with Regan when she wrote that story, and since she had been ordered to stay in bed, he had driven around and checked out the route she was planning for the kidnappers to use.

"What do you intend to do now?" he asked C.B.

"At some point I'm going to call your daughter and tell her she'd better be able to come up with another million dollars. Unless, of course, the cops have already recovered our money from the East River."

There was a note of desperation in his voice. They have to get out tomorrow night, Luke thought, and they can't go without the money. "When you put me on the phone again, I'll tell my daughter to be sure to get it for you."

"You bet you will. But first I've got to figure out a new place for her to leave it," C.B. blustered.

It's worth a shot, Luke thought. By now, Nora must have realized that they had used a ransom-drop location that was in one of her books. This time, would she think about that short story and talk to the cops about it?

It was probably crazy. A one-in-a-million shot, if not totally hopeless. But like his earlier effort to convey to Regan that they were in the vicinity of the GW Bridge and the lighthouse, it at least made him feel as if he was doing something to try and save their lives.

"You know, C.B." he began, his tone friendly, "a couple of weeks ago I had to pick up the remains of a client's grandmother from a small nursing home in Queens. When I came through the Midtown Tunnel and exited on Borden Avenue on the Queens side, I got lost. In only a few blocks, I found myself in a totally deserted area right underneath the Long Island Expressway. If I were planning a kidnapping, I think I'd use that area for a ransom drop. Check it out yourself and you'll see what I mean."

C.B.'s eyes narrowed. "Why are you being so helpful?"

"Because I want to get out of here. The sooner you have the money, the sooner you'll make the call telling them where to find us."

"I feel better," Petey announced as he emerged from the bedroom in a sweat suit. "Nothing like a dry change of clothes." He pulled a Mountain Dew out of the tiny refrigerator. "I heard what you were saying, Mr. Reilly. You're really using the old noodle. I know exactly where you're talking about. I got lost there, too, on my way to a job. I wasn't going to pick up a stiff though." He turned to C.B. "It's perfect. We'd be nice and near the airport. They get mad if you don't check in at least two hours before flight time. Sometimes they give your seat away. It happened to my cousin—"

"Petey!" C.B. shrieked.

"Oh, leave him alone," Rosita said. "I'd love to hear the rest of the story."

Luke could tell that C.B. was mulling the suggestion of the drop site over in his mind.

C.B. reached into his pocket and pulled out a

folded sheet of paper. On it he had printed the step-by-step directions he had given Regan earlier. He turned the paper over. "Okay, Mr. Reilly, fire away. Petey and I are going to take a drive tonight and see if you're as smart as your wife."

"Go back out in that cold?" Petey protested.

Luke gave C.B. the directions, then said, "Before you go, you'd better call my daughter and let her start arranging to get the money. And give her a break. She's got to be worried."

"Let her worry."

It was nearly midnight before C.B. and Petey returned to the houseboat. Rosita had dozed off, but Luke was wide awake. Over and over in his mind, he had been revising the few words he would be allowed to say to Regan when the next call was made.

When C.B. turned on the light, Rosita opened her eyes and sat up.

"Well?" Luke asked him.

"Not bad," C.B. said. "It might do."

"Scary around there!" Petey exclaimed. "I told C.B. to lock the car doors."

"I think your daughter should be plenty worried by now," C.B. said. "Do you think it's too late to call?"

"Somehow I doubt it," Luke said.

R egan was sitting by a sleeping Nora when the cell phone rang. Please let it be them, she prayed, her heart pounding. She picked it up. "Hello," she said quietly.

"Did you recover the money?"

Regan stiffened. "What do you mean?"

"I mean," C.B. said angrily, "we could tell there was a tracer in the duffel bag. Don't do that again. Have another million ready, or you'll regret it. I'll call you at four o'clock tomorrow afternoon. Here's Daddy."

"Regan, at this point, I'm seeing *red*. Do as he says and get us out of here."

The line went dead.

Saturday,

December 24th

Fred had heard from Regan shortly after midnight. She'd told him about the kidnappers' call, and how they had warned her not to have a tracking device in the next ransom delivery. She hadn't spoken to Rosita, but her father had said, "Get *us* out of here."

After the call, Fred had tossed and turned on the couch. If the next drop doesn't work, they'll give up, he thought. And they won't leave witnesses.

At 3:00 A.M., he had taken the blanket and pillow and stretched out on top of Rosita's bed. Before long, he was joined by two troubled little boys who curled up against him and fell back asleep.

"Mommy's sick, isn't she?" Bobby had asked quietly when they woke up.

"Maybe she got sick like Grandma did, and went to Puerto Rico without us," Chris suggested.

"All your mommy cares about is getting home and being with you guys," Fred said reassuringly. "But Mrs. Reilly really needs her now."

"She won't stay with Mrs. Reilly tomorrow, will she?" Bobby asked.

Tomorrow, Fred thought. Christmas Day. What could he possibly tell them if she wasn't back then? And what was he going to tell Rosita's mother when she phoned to wish them a merry Christmas, as she almost certainly would.

To help pass the time, he took the boys out to breakfast, but they turned down his offer of another trip to SportsWorld.

"We should be there in case Mommy gets home," Chris said solemnly.

rnest Bumbles woke up on Christmas Eve in what was for him a very grumpy mood. He still hadn't been able to catch up with Luke Reilly, even though he had stopped by Reilly's Funeral Home twice yesterday—once in the afternoon and again in the evening.

"A gift deferred is a gift denied," he told Dolly as he packed his suitcase for their annual trip to his mother-in-law's.

Dolly knew all about Ernest's passionate nature. When he felt something, he felt it with all his heart. When he wanted something, he let nothing stand in his way. That's why, year after year, he had been unanimously reelected president of the Seed-Plant-Bloom-and-Blossom Society. But he was also a caring man. It was no wonder he never had a plant die on him.

"Bumby," Dolly said gently. "We're not leaving until late this afternoon. Why don't we drive by Mr. Reilly's house and ring the bell on our way out of town?"

"I don't want to seem like a pest."

"Oh, hush. You never could."

Nora had awakened to hear Regan talking to Luke's abductor. When the brief conversation was abruptly terminated, Regan told her, word for word, exactly what had been said.

The bedside phone rang almost immediately.

"They can't know there was a tracer in that bag," Jack said firmly. "They're bluffing. I wouldn't be surprised if the guy on the boat accidentally dropped it into the water."

"I wouldn't be surprised by that either," Regan said, "but my mother is adamant that there be no tracer in the bag this time."

"I understand," Jack said. "Regan, remind your mother that it's a good sign you talked to your father again. When he spoke to you, he said, 'I'm seeing red.' Is that an expression he uses when he's angry?"

"I've never heard him say that in my life," Regan said. "Neither has my mother."

"Then he's definitely trying to tell you something," Jack said. "See if you or your mother can make the connection."

Regan and Jack agreed to talk in the morning, then Regan had phoned Alvirah and Fred.

It was another near-sleepless night for her and Nora as they tried to make sense of what Luke had said and to remember what Regan's favorite book had been as a child.

Nora said, "Regan, when your father came home from work, you always ran to him with a book in your hand. I just can't remember what your favorite one would have been. Could it have been one of the fairy tales? 'Snow White,' or 'Sleeping Beauty,' or maybe 'Rumplestiltskin'?"

"No," Regan said. "It wasn't any one of them."

Around dawn, they both dropped off into a light, uneasy sleep.

Neither one of them had wanted breakfast. Then at eight o'clock, Nora was taken for X rays. When she returned to the room at 9:00, Regan went down to the cafeteria and brought back containers of hot coffee.

"Regan, while I was waiting to be x-rayed, something came to me that I think is important," Nora said after she took the first sip.

Regan waited.

"It is absolutely weird that a scenario from one of my early books was used for the ransom drop yesterday. That card with your father's picture was signed 'Your number-one fan.' If that person is the kidnapper, it's possible he's familiar with all my work."

"That's very possible," Regan agreed. "In which case we're dealing with an obsession. But what are you saying?"

"As I lay there, it came to me that I wrote another kidnapping story, a long time ago."

"You did? I never read it."

"I wrote it when I was pregnant with you," Nora recalled. "It was a short story, not a book, but it described in detail a ransom drop in Queens." She bit her lip. "My doctor had ordered bed rest when I was working on it, and I remember that Dad came up with the suggestion for the location of the drop. He drove out there, took pictures, and drew a map, even to the point of marking the best place to leave the suitcase of money. I was paid all of one hundred dollars for the story when it was published, and Dad joked that I should give him half."

Regan smiled briefly. "That sounds like Dad." Despite the stab of pain that hit her heart, she felt a surge of hope. "Mom, suppose you're right and the kidnapper *is* a pathological fan who's acting out your plots. It's very possible he's somehow gotten his hands on that story and will use that plot for the drop tomorrow. If we knew ahead of time the kind of directions he's likely to give me, the police can stake out the route beforehand without being visible. Where in Queens was the ransom drop?"

"God, Regan, it was so long ago, and as I said, Dad researched it for me. All I remember is that it was near the Midtown Tunnel."

"You must have a copy of the story."

"It's home somewhere in the attic."

"What about the magazine it was in?"

"It bit the dust a long time ago."

There was a tap at the door. The doctor breezed into the room, a holiday smile on his face, a batch of X rays under his arm. "Morning, ladies," he said. "How's my favorite patient?"

"Pretty good," Nora said.

"Good enough to go home?"

Nora looked at him, surprised. "You were pretty insistent on my staying for at least three days."

"You had a nasty fracture, but the swelling is going down nicely. The X rays look okay. You must be anxious to get out of here. Just be sure to keep that leg elevated." He turned to Regan. "Maybe next year, you and your parents will make it to Maui for Christmas."

"I hope so," Regan said. More than you can imagine, she thought.

When he left the room, Nora and Regan looked at each other.

"Regan," Nora said, "run and get the car. I'll get checked out of here. There are an awful lot of boxes in that attic."

At five of nine, Alvirah was in the forefront of the throng of last-minute shoppers waiting for Long's department store to open its doors. Unlike the others, she did not have a list of gifts to buy, most of which would probably be returned forty-eight hours later. She had already phoned Fred to ask about why Rosita had told him Luke "always kept his cool." He assured her that Rosita was only referring to humorous situations.

At 9:01, she was on the down escalator, headed for the basement. Fast as she was, there were already shoppers at the counter where the Christmas knickknacks had been further reduced to almost giveaway prices. They must have slept in the aisles last night, she thought, as with mounting impatience she waited to get the only salesgirl's attention.

The customer ahead of her, a thin, white-haired septuagenarian, was crossing names off her shopping list as she handed one picture frame after another to the clerk. "Let's see.

That takes care of Aggie and Margieand Kitty and May. Should I get one for Lillian? . . . Nah, she didn't give me anything lastyear." She picked up one of the "Jingle My Bells" frames. "Disgraceful," she proclaimed. "That'll be all."

"Are you Darlene Krinsky?" Alvirah asked the young saleswoman when she finally got her attention.

"Yes." Her voice was wary.

Alvirah knew she had to make it fast. She took out the frame she had purchased the day before. "My friend is in the hospital." That might get her sympathy, she thought. "Someone left one of these frames for her on Thursday night and didn't sign his name. We think he may have bought it when he was on the way to the hospital, because we know he was carrying a Long's shopping bag with some red clothing in it. He's a man of medium height, with thinning brown hair, and about fifty years old."

Krinsky shook her head. "I wish I could help you." With her eyes she indicated a group of teenagers who were waving the knickknacks they had selected, anxious to get her attention. "You can see how crazy it is around here."

"He was carrying an old wallet and may have counted the change out very carefully," Alvirah persisted.

"I'm sorry, I'd really like to help, but . . ." She trailed off. "I hope your friend feels better." She took a Santa Claus music box out of the hands of one of the teenagers.

It's hopeless, Alvirah thought dejectedly as she turned away from the counter.

"Wait a minute," the clerk said softly to herself as she started to ring up the music box.

As Alvirah reached the escalator, she felt a tap on her shoulder. "The clerk at that counter is calling you," a young man said.

Alvirah rushed back.

"You say he had a bag with red clothing in it? I know who it might be. One of the guys who plays Santa Claus was down here the other night. I'm sure that was the frame he bought. He tried to get an employee discount."

That's got to be him, Alvirah thought. "Can you tell me his name?"

"No. But he might even be upstairs now. The toy department is on the third floor."

"You must be talking about Alvin Luck," the manager of the toy department, a pinched-faced man in his late fifties, said to Alvirah. "He was working here Thursday evening, and no doubt was carrying his uniform home to press. We insist that our Santas set a good example for the children."

"Is he due in soon?"

"He doesn't work here anymore."

"He doesn't?" Alvirah asked, dismayed.

"No. He turned in his uniform yesterday. When we hired him, he made it very clear he couldn't work on Christmas Eve."

"Was he here last night?"

"No. He left at four o'clock."

"Would you have his address or phone number?"

The manager looked sternly at Alvirah.

"Madam, we have total respect for our employees' privacy. That information is strictly confidential."

Jack can get it in a minute, Alvirah thought, as she thanked the man and rushed to a telephone. And anyhow, he'll take over from here. If Alvin Luck *is* involved in the kidnapping, Jack will find out fast.

Alvin Luck and his mother handed their tickets to the usher at the door of Radio City Music Hall. Since he was a child, it had been their tradition to take in the Christmas Spectacular on Christmas Eve, and then treat themselves to a special lunch. In the old days they had dined at Schrafft's, and they both agreed that things weren't the same since that venerable purveyor of chicken à la king had closed its doors.

After lunch, weather permitting, they would take in the sights of Fifth Avenue.

Today they thoroughly enjoyed the show,

lingered over lunch, and then prevailed on a security guard to take their annual picture in front of the tree in Rockefeller Center. All the while they were blissfully unaware that half the police department in New York City was on the lookout for them.

It was nearly 11:30 when Regan, with Nora sitting sideways in the backseat of the car, her injured leg across the seat, pulled into their driveway in Summit, New Jersey. Alvirah and Willy were in a car right behind them.

Alvirah had phoned Regan as soon as she hung up with Jack and told her about Alvin Luck. "Jack will call you the minute they find him," she promised. Then, on learning about Nora's short story, she had instantly volunteered to help in the search through the boxes in the attic.

Leaning on her crutches, with Willy on one side and Regan on the other, Nora made her careful way along the walk and into the house.

"When I left here Wednesday evening, I never dreamed I'd come back this way. Or without Luke," she added, her tone flat.

The house seemed dark and somber. Regan quickly moved around, turning on lights. "Mom, where do you think you'd be most comfortable?" she asked.

"Oh, inside." She gestured toward the family room.

Alvirah took in every detail of the place as they followed Nora past the living room to the back of the house. The large kitchen spilled into the high-ceilinged family room, inviting with its generous couches, big windows, and open-hearth fireplace. "This is lovely," she said admiringly.

Nora hobbled over to the wing chair. Regan took her crutches, and when Nora was settled, helped lift the leg with its heavy cast onto the hassock. "Whew," Nora said with a sigh as she leaned back. "This is going to take some getting used to." The tiny beads of perspiration on her forehead were a testimony to the effort it had taken just to navigate the short distance from the car.

A few minutes later, after Willy and Regan had brought a half-dozen boxes down from the attic, they were all busy looking for the manuscript or magazine copy of the short story Nora remembered being titled "Deadline to Paradise."

"I thought I'd kept every piece of research, every version of every manuscript, every outline, even every rejection slip from the early days, " Nora commented. "So where is it?"

As the four of them sifted through the stacks of papers, Alvirah told them about tracking down Alvin Luck. "I can't believe that anyone who's been working as a department store Santa Claus could be part of all this," Nora said. Then they all fell silent. Half an hour later, Willy and Regan went back up to the attic to bring down more boxes. But it was a fruitless effort. At three o'clock, Nora said dispiritedly, "I may as well admit it. If a copy of that story still exists, it isn't in this house." Then she looked at Regan. "Why don't you call Rosita's and see how her boys are doing? I'm worried about them."

From Fred's tone, Regan could tell immediately that it was not going well. "They're worried that their mother is sick," he told her. "All I'm trying to do at this point is keep them distracted. I even opened the package of books your mother sent them for Christmas and read to them. Those, at least, they really enjoyed."

"I'm glad they liked the books," Nora said after Regan reported what Fred had told her. "I had Charlotte in the children's section of the bookstore put them together and send them over for me." She paused. "Wait a minute. She also sent me videos of some of the hot new movies for kids. I was going to give them to Mona." Nora gestured toward the neighboring house. "Her grandchildren are coming for a visit next week."

She looked at Regan. "Why don't you take them to Chris and Bobby? Then if you get a chance to talk to Rosita at four o'clock, you can tell her you just saw the boys."

Regan looked at her watch. She was supposed to receive the next phone call at four. It wasn't much more than a fifteen-minute drive to Rosita's. That gave her over an hour to get there and back. She knew her mother wanted her to be home when the next call from the kidnappers came. She said that just knowing her husband was on the other end of the phone made the nightmare seem a little less hopeless.

Alvin Luck and his mother could not have spent a better day together. That is, until they got home and found two detectives waiting for them.

"May we speak to you inside?" they asked.

"Sure, fellows, come on in," Alvin invited. With the security that comes from having led an absolutely blameless life, he was thrilled that real-life detectives had come to talk to him. Maybe something had happened at Long's, and they needed his help.

His mother did not share his excitement. When the detectives asked permission to look around the apartment, she glared at Alvin for granting it.

Sal Bonaventure, the detective who went into Alvin's bedroom, whistled softly when he saw the accumulation of crime literature that was stacked floor to ceiling. Piles of manuscripts crowded the shelves over the long table that served as a desk. In addition to a computer and printer, the table held dozens of books and magazines, most of them clearly very old. A stack of novels by Nora Regan Reilly, many of them lying open, was near the computer. Bonaventure saw that the pages were heavily annotated.

Sal and his partner had contacted Jack Reilly as soon as Alvin and his mother stepped into the entryway. He had told them to hold off on questioning until he got there.

Santa Claus may be the key to breaking this case wide open, Sal thought optimistically.

The snowstorm, predicted to hit earlier, finally had started—and with a vengeance—by the time Regan parked in front of Rosita's apartment. Fred Torres had been watching for her. "I told Chris and Bobby that you have some great new movies for them," he said heartily as he opened the door.

The boys were sitting on the floor, a dozen marbles scattered between them. They looked at Regan with some distrust. "When is your mommy going to be better so our mommy can come home?" Chris asked.

He's trying to be polite, poor kid, Regan thought, but he wants an answer. "Very soon," she told him as she held out the gaily wrapped package of tapes. "This is for both of you . . ."

Her voice trailed off; she did not notice when they took the present from her hands. She was staring down at the cover of one of the books lying on the coffee table. The title *The Little Red Lighthouse and the Great Gray Bridge* had caught her eye and evoked a flood of memories.

Daddy, read this one again, just once more, please.

The cover illustration was of a jaunty red lighthouse. She opened the book. The frontispiece depicted the unmistakable George Washington Bridge, with the tiny lighthouse tucked below it.

Your favorite book . . . I'm seeing red . . .

This was what Dad was trying to tell me, Regan realized with mounting excitement. From wherever he is, he can see the lighthouse.

"Regan, what is it?" Fred asked urgently.

Regan shook her head. "I hope you guys enjoy the movies. I'll see you later." She turned to Fred.

"I'll walk you outside," he said.

The tension emanating from C.B. had accelerated to an explosive level. Luke and Rosita silently observed his grim countenance as the time for making the phone call drew near. He knows this is it, Luke thought. He knows that if they don't get the money tonight, they never will. He could hear the winds building up outside. The boat was banging against the pier with ever-increasing force. If this storm keeps up, who knows when and if their flight will take off.

"Hey, C.B.," Petey said, "I gotta run home. I left my passport in the apartment."

No you didn't, Luke thought. I saw you looking at it a little while ago. What was Petey up to now? he wondered.

"You what?" C B. stared at him.

"I wanted to be sure it was in a nice safe place. I don't have much room here. You've been sleeping home these couple of nights, I notice. What's the difference? It's a five-minute walk. Pick me up at the apartment."

C.B. looked at his watch. "Be waiting outside at precisely ten minutes after four."

"Gotcha." Petey looked from Luke to Rosita. "We may not ever meet again, but I'd like to wish you all the luck in the world." With a snappy salute, he was gone.

Luke knew why his feet were feeling cold and damp. There was a trickle of water on the floor. The ice, he thought. This tub is beginning to leak.

Jack Reilly's immediate gut feeling was that Alvin Luck was no threat to mankind. He was a mystery buff, not a kidnapper. Nora Regan Reilly was just one of many writers he collected.

Any question he or the detectives asked Alvin was answered promptly and without hesitation. He acknowledged that he had taken the picture of Luke at a mystery-writers' dinner. He had bought the frame after he heard about Nora's accident.

"Didn't she like it?" he asked as they stood in his cluttered bedroom.

"I know why they're asking you all these questions," his mother butted in. "You didn't sign your name to the card." She shook her head vigorously. "They don't like that kind of stuff. They think it means you have something to hide."

"Mrs. Reilly was just surprised to receive an unsigned gift," Jack said soothingly. "You did buy the teddy bear in the gift shop yourself?"

"*What* teddy bear?" his mother asked. "Alvin, you didn't say word one about any teddy bear."

"I see you've written a lot of notes in the margins of Mrs. Reilly's books." Jack picked up one of them and flipped through the pages.

"Oh, yes," Alvin said excitedly. "I've studied hundreds of mystery writers to see how they plot. It's a great learning tool. I file my notes under categories like murder, arson, burglary, embezzlement. When I read about true cases in the newspapers, I clip them out for my files too."

"Is that why you have these notes on Nora Regan Reilly?"

"Of course."

"Any chance you ever read 'Deadline to Paradise?'"

"That was one of her earliest stories. I filed it under kidnapping." He walked around the bed to a file cabinet and pulled open the bottom drawer. "Here it is." He handed Jack a thirty-one-year-old magazine.

Regan drove as swiftly as she dared over roads that were rapidly becoming snow covered. *Dad and Rosita can see the little red lighthouse,* she thought with a glimmer of hope. They're somewhere around the George Washington Bridge. Jack had said that background sounds on the tapes indicated that they were near water.

She dialed Jack's number.

"I just spoke to your mother and told her that Alvin Luck has been eliminated as a suspect. But he might turn out to be a big help— he had a copy of her story."

"What?"

"He's a serious mystery collector. If by any wild chance the kidnappers follow the route used in the story, it'll be a lot easier to cover them."

"I have something to tell you too." Regan relayed to him what had just happened at Rosita's.

"Regan, this probably means they're being kept in New Jersey."

"Why?"

"Think about it," Jack said. "Your father left the hospital a little after ten. The car obviously was driven to New Jersey, because it came back across the George Washington Bridge into New York at 11:16. Then it crossed the Triborough Bridge into Queens at 11:45, which is just about how long it would normally take to travel that distance without stopping. If they didn't stop right after crossing the bridge into Manhattan, there's no way they could still see the lighthouse beyond that."

"For some reason, that makes me feel good," Regan said. The net is tightening, she thought.

Petey nursed a tequila sunrise at Elsie's Hideaway, where the annual Christmas Eve party was in full swing. The whole gang of regulars was there. I'll just have *one* of these, he promised himself. I've got to have my wits about me for the big night.

If C.B. knew I'd stopped in here, he'd kill me. But I couldn't leave the U.S. of A. forever without one last visit to this joint, where, like the song says, "everybody knows your name." I've gone fishing with some of these guys, he thought. Lotta laughs.

"Petey, you look down in the dumps." Matt, Elsie's longtime bartender, replaced his empty tequila glass. "Elsie says 'Merry Christmas.' "

"Aw, that's nice."

"I hear you're going away on vacation. Where to?"

"Going fishing."

"Where?"

"Down south," Petey said vaguely.

Matt was already with the next customer.

Petey checked his watch. It was time to go. He slid off the bar stool, looked at the free tequila sunrise, and with uncharacteristic resolve, left it untouched.

"Petey, do you feel all right?" Matt looked concerned as he poured cocktail peanuts into an empty dish.

"I feel great," Petey assured him. "Like a million bucks."

"Glad to hear it. Have a good time on your trip. Send us a postcard."

"Say, do you have any more of those Elsie's postcards?" Petey asked.

Matt reached under the bar. "We've got one left. Be my guest."

With a wave, Petey left Elsie's for the last time.

Regan had kept Austin Grady up to date with everything that had been happening. For the last two days, he had been fielding calls from friends of the Reillys who had heard about

Nora's accident and couldn't reach her or Luke.

When Nora phoned Austin at 3:15, he asked if he could stop by the house on his way home. Nora quickly responded, "I'd like to see you, Austin. You're the only one of our friends who knows what's going on."

Austin had been there only a few moments when Regan came in and told them about seeing the book about the red lighthouse.

"The Little Red Lighthouse and the Great Gray Bridge," Nora said. "Of course! You loved it."

"They've got to be in view of that lighthouse," Alvirah said emphatically. "There's no doubt that on those tapes he emphasized the words, 'I'm seeing red.' "

"Well, Jack thinks they're on the New Jersey side of the bridge," Regan said, and then explained why.

"If we only had some idea who did this," Nora said hopelessly. "But we have nothing else to go on, and they're calling in less than half an hour. Once they get the money, can we trust them to keep their end of the deal?" She gestured toward the window. "Look at the weather. If they did drop that bag by mistake yesterday, think of how much could go wrong today."

They all jumped when the doorbell rang.

"Regan, we can't have anyone else here. Say I'm sleeping . . ."

"I know, Mom." Regan hurried down the hall to the front door. Standing outside was the plant society president who had knocked on the window of Austin's office two nights ago. He was wearing a stocking cap, the top of which was slowly piling up with snow.

"Hi, Regan!" he chirped "Remember me? I met you the other night. Ernest Bumbles."

He was carrying a gift-wrapped package under his arm.

"Hello, Mr. Bumbles," Regan said hurriedly.

"Is your dad here?" he asked.

"I'm afraid not," Regan said. "He was delayed in New York."

"Oh, what a shame. My wife and I are on our way to visit her mother in Boston. Although with this weather, no one should be out driving! Anyway, I have this gift I have so been wanting to give to your dad. It breaks my heart that I keep missing him. But I want him to have it for Christmas."

"Let me take it then," Regan said, anxious to end the conversation and get back to the others.

"Could you do me a favor?" Ernest asked with a pleading look.

"What's that?"

"Could you please open my gift to your father now and let me take a picture of you with it?"

Regan felt like strangling him. She invited him to step inside, then quickly ripped off the ribbon and opened the box to find the framed proclamation.

"What's this for?" she asked as she read it.

Ernest beamed. "Your father has done so much for the Blossoms. He introduced Cuthbert Boniface Goodloe to our society. The poor man died just this week, but he left us a million dollars in his will. We can never thank your father enough."

"A million dollars?" Regan said.

Ernest looked misty eyed. "A million dol-

lars. Virtually his entire estate! What a generous man. And it's *all* because of your father.
We also have one of these citations to present to
Mr. Goodloe's nephew, in honor of his wonderful uncle, but he's never home either! Now
let me take your picture."

At Nora's request, Austin came down the
hall from the family room to see what was
going on. Oh my God, he said to himself when
he spotted Bumbles. This guy never quits.

He caught Regan's eye but was stopped
from brushing Bumbles off by the slight shake
of her head.

Regan held up the citation. "Austin, look at
this," she said with a forced bright smile. "My
dad's the reason Mr. Bumbles' society received
a million dollars this week from a Cuthbert
Boniface Goodloe. Did you know my dad was
directly responsible for that?"

Austin shook his head. "I had no idea."

"I was so sorry your dad had to miss our
benefactor's funeral," Bumbles continued.
"But the Blossoms showed up in full force."

"It's good you were there," Austin said.

Regan has the patience of a saint, he thought. "His nephew is his only family."

"He is?" Regan said. She looked at Ernest and asked jokingly, "How did he feel about his uncle leaving such a big gift to the Blossoms?"

Ernest put his finger to his cheek. "I couldn't say. But why wouldn't he be happy for us? We're a wonderful society. And he'll be thrilled to receive one of these citations, I'm sure. That is, if I can ever reach him."

"Where does he live?" Regan asked.

"Fort Lee."

Regan swallowed hard. The New Jersey side of the George Washington Bridge was in Fort Lee. Was it possible? "I know my father will love this."

"Well, I'm just glad you're home to receive it. I'm keeping the other one in the trunk of my car so I can drop it by when I reach that nephew."

"Give it to me," Regan said. "I mean, I'm going to be in the vicinity of Fort Lee tonight, and I'll drop it at his house so he'll have it for Christmas too."

"That would be wonderful!" Ernest cried. "But I don't have his address."

"I'll call the office," Austin said. "I'm sure we have it on file."

"I'll be right back," Ernest said as he turned, went outside, and half slid down the path to his car, where Dolly was patiently waiting. When he returned, he handed Austin the other gift. "Hold this, please." He turned to Regan as he readied his camera. "Now say cheese."

"Cheese."

"Got it."

"What's the nephew's name anyway?"

Austin and Ernest answered in unison. "C.B. Dingle."

"I win," Bobby said halfheartedly. "Now let's put in the tape."

"First we've got to collect all these marbles," Fred told him.

The three of them crawled on their hands and knees and gathered the marbles that were scattered all over the living room. "I think I saw one go under the couch," Fred said. He lifted the skirt of the slipcover and ran his hand around in the narrow space between the couch and the rug. His groping fingers closed over the marble, but he could tell that it was resting on a smooth paper surface, not the carpeting. Sliding the paper out, he realized that it was a postcard addressed to Rosita.

The scrawled message was surrounded by dabs of colorful paint. It read:

Hope we can have dinner here soon!!!!!!
                                    Petey

Chris was standing beside Fred. He looked at the postcard. "Mommy was so funny when she got that card. She said that guy's elevator doesn't go to the top."

Fred smiled. "Did you ever meet him?"

Chris looked at Fred as though surprised he would ask such a dumb question. "Noooo! Mommy met him at work."

"He works for Mr. Reilly?"

"Just once. He painted something there. They hated the color."

Fred turned the card over. ELSIE'S HIDEAWAY. EDGEWATER, NEW JERSEY. His heart skipped a beat. Flecks of paint in the abandoned limo. A guy who had worked for Luke Reilly and had been turned down by Rosita. A guy who obviously frequents a bar in the area of the George Washington Bridge.

"Start the tape," he told the boys. "I have to go in the bedroom to make a phone call."

Having bid farewell to Mr. Bumbles, Regan and Austin carried the gifts back to the family room.

"Well, this certainly supplies motive," Nora said as she read the proclamation. "But it could be another Alvin Luck situation."

"I wish we had more time," Regan said urgently. "I'd love to go up there and check him out. But the call is coming in ten minutes, and I probably will have to leave right away for

New York. Jack is going to meet me with the second batch of money."

The ring of the phone went through the room with the impact of a gunshot.

"They wouldn't call on this line, would they?" Regan asked as she ran to the phone.

It was Fred.

She listened. "Hold on, Fred." She turned to Austin. "Fred just found a postcard from a guy named Petey, who apparently did some painting at the funeral home. He had asked Rosita out. Do you know who I'm talking about?"

Austin nodded. "We only had him work there one day. He completely messed up the job." Austin paused for a moment and then exclaimed, "But wait a minute! He showed up the other night at the wake for Goodloe. He's a big buddy of C.B. Dingle."

Nora gasped. "He's a painter, and there were flecks of paint in the limo."

"And the postcard he sent Rosita is of a bar in Edgewater," Regan said. "That's just south of Fort Lee and still within view of the lighthouse."

Regan told Fred what they had learned about C.B. Dingle.

"What's Petey's last name?" Fred almost barked into the phone.

"Austin, do you know Petey's last name?"

He shook his head. "But hold on. I'll get it for you." He picked up his cell phone and called the office. "They're checking the files." A moment later he said, "His name is Peter Commet. He lives in Edgewater." Austin wrote down the address and handed it to Regan.

"Fred, here it is," she said and gave him the information. "They're calling me in two minutes. I'll get back to you as soon as I speak to them."

"Regan, I'm going looking for this guy," Fred said.

"I wish I could go with you."

At exactly four o'clock, her cell phone rang.

"Be at the Manhattan end of the Midtown Tunnel at 5:30."

"The Manhattan end of the Midtown Tunnel," she repeated, and looked at Nora.

"They're using my story," Nora breathed.

"I just brought my mother home from the hospital," Regan said rapidly. "I'm in New Jersey. I need more time than that."

"You can't have more time."

Austin put his hand on Regan's arm. "Let me go," he mouthed.

Regan nodded gratefully. "I'm not a good driver in this weather," she explained. "Is it okay if my father's associate, Austin Grady, delivers the money? He'll drive my car and use my phone. It won't do you any good if I have an accident."

There was a pause. Then she heard a reluctant, "All right. But for your father's and Rosita's sake, you better not be trying anything. Yell hello, you two."

For a brief instant she heard their voices in the background. *We're getting closer to you,* she wanted to shout. The phone clicked off.

She dialed Fred.

"I'm going up to Edgewater," Fred said.

"And Alvirah and I are going to Fort Lee."

"Can I drop the kids with your mother?"

Regan hesitated. "Don't they think . . ."

"I'll tell them Rosita's doing an errand with your dad. By tomorrow they're going to have to be told the truth anyhow."

Regan gave him directions to the house. "Give me your cell-phone number. Take down my mother's. It's the one I'll have with me. Austin will be using mine."

"We'll keep in touch," Fred said. "Be careful."

"Weather's pretty bad out there," C.B. told Luke as he clicked off the phone. "Your daughter's too nervous to drive in it, so she's sending that guy Grady."

Regan can drive in any weather, Luke thought. Is Nora all right? Is something else up?

There was an air of finality in the way C.B. looked around the cabin. He took the keys to their chains from his pocket and laid them on top of the stove, well beyond their reach.

"When we get the money, you get to go home. Once we're safely away, we'll let them know where you are."

"Unless you want to kill us, you'd better do it soon," Luke said, indicating the floor of the boat. The storm outside had intensified, and the boat was rocking with ever-increasing force. The thumping, scraping sound of ice chunks hitting its sides was becoming more frequent. The floor was completely wet.

"We'll call from the airport. As soon as we land."

"That's too long," Rosita cried. "You might not get out until tomorrow."

"You'll just have to pray that we do," C.B. said. The door slammed behind him.

At ten minutes of five, Regan and Alvirah parked in front of C.B.'s high-rise apartment building. "Here we go," Regan said as they got out.

The doorman rang to announce them.

Moments later he shook his head. "No answer. He must be out."

"His uncle died this week," Regan said.

"I heard."

"My father owns the funeral parlor that handled the arrangements and has to get in touch with Mr. Dingle. It's very important. Is there any way I could find out when he's expected?"

"The superintendent's wife cleans his apartment. I could call her," the doorman offered. "That's the best I can do."

"Thank you," Regan said. "That's very nice of you." She and Alvirah exchanged glances.

"Hey, happy to help," he said with a shrug. "It's Christmas."

A minute later he turned back to them. "Dolores said to go up to her place. She's in 2B."

Dolores's apartment was a cheerful reminder of the holiday season. The tree was lit, Christmas music was playing, the smell of roast chicken was in the air.

"We won't keep you," Regan said hurriedly, "but we do need to be in touch with Mr. Dingle."

Dolores, a woman in her late fifties, sounded sympathetic as she said, "Poor fellow. He told me he's taking a trip to make himself feel better. He was packing when I went up there this morning."

"You were up there this morning?" Alvirah asked.

"Not for long. I brought him some Christmas cookies. He invited me in for just a minute, but he seemed nervous and upset, like he was under a lot of stress. It'll do him good to get away."

"I'm sure it will," Regan said. Could they be hidden in a bedroom up there? she wondered.

"This building is lovely," Alvirah commented as she looked past her. "You have a wonderful view of the river. Is Mr. Dingle lucky enough to have one like this?"

"Oh no," Dolores said, smiling with a hint of superiority. "He has one of the small studios that face the street."

At quarter after five, snow swirling around him, Fred Torres was standing on the stoop of the shabby, two-family frame house in which Petey lived. Regan had called him after leaving C.B.'s building, saying that the only thing she had learned for sure was that he had left with his suitcases this morning, supposedly for a vacation. Luke and Rosita had almost certainly not been in his apartment.

Could they be here? Fred wondered as he rang the doorbell a second time. He had already tried the separate entrance to Petey's basement apartment, but it was dark inside, and no one answered.

Someone's upstairs, he thought. Lights were on, and he could hear the sound of a television.

The door was opened by a sleepy-looking man who appeared to be in his sixties. He was wearing rumpled jeans, an open flannel shirt, and bedroom slippers. He looked as though the bell had just awakened him. He did not seem pleased at the interruption.

"Are you the landlord of this building?" Fred asked.

"Yeah. Why?"

"I'm looking for Petey Commet."

"He left on vacation this morning."

"Do you know where he was going?"

"He didn't say, and it's none of my business." The landlord started to close the door.

Fred pulled out his police ID. "I need to talk to you about him."

The sleepy look vanished. "He in trouble?"

"I don't know yet," Fred replied. "How long has he been living here?"

"Three years."

"Ever had any problem with him?"

"Except for being late with the rent, not really. I know he'll come up with it eventually."

"Just a couple more questions and I'll let you go," Fred said. "Does he have any close friends around here?"

"If you count that gang at Elsie's Hideaway,

he's got lots of them. It's right around the corner. Hey, I'm getting cold."

"One more thing. Have you been down in his apartment in the last couple of days?"

"Yeah, I checked the thermostat after he left this morning. If he isn't going to be here, no use burning fuel—not at today's prices."

This time Fred did not stop him from closing the door. As he got in his car, Regan and Alvirah were pulling up alongside him.

"No luck here either. But follow me to Elsie's Hideaway."

Because time was tight, Jack Reilly made the transfer of money to Regan's car a few blocks from the Queens-Midtown Tunnel. "We'll be following you," he told Austin Grady, "but if he directs you the way we expect, our mobile unit will have to drop back. It's just too easy for them to be seen. We've got agents deployed in the buildings along the route. They'll track you. Good luck."

At 5:30 the call came in. "Drive through the tunnel. Stay to the right. Take the Borden Avenue exit immediately after the toll booth."

"That's what we wanted to hear," Jack said exultantly when Eagle base passed on the message.

His cell phone rang. It was Regan. "Both the nephew and the painter left with their suitcases today. They told people they were going on vacation."

Jack felt a rush of adrenaline. "Regan, I'll bet you anything that they're our guys. If they have suitcases with them, that means they're not going back to where they left your father and Rosita. After they pick up the money, they're probably headed to the airport."

"If they get away, we may never hear from them again."

"We'll keep them in sight, just in case they do go back to where they have your dad and Rosita, but the minute they hit either of the airports, we have no choice but to close in on them."

"Alvirah and I are heading to the bar in

Edgewater where the painter hangs out. Fred Torres is with us. Maybe somebody there will be able to tell us something."

"Regan," Jack said quietly. "Please be careful."

There was a crash followed by a startling lurch as the boat listed to a twenty-degree angle. Rosita and Luke were thrown to the side. Rosita cried out, and Luke winced as the manacles dug into his hands and ankles.

"Mr. Reilly, this boat is sinking! We're going to drown," Rosita sobbed.

"No we're not," Luke insisted. "I think one of the mooring lines gave way."

Less than a minute later, the boat was savagely hurled against the dock again.

Luke heard a gurgling sound, and water began to bubble from somewhere near the door. As the boat swayed once more, the ring of keys C.B. had left on the stove slid off and dropped to the floor. Desperately, Luke bent as far as the chains would allow and leaned forward. His finger touched the edge of one of the keys, but before he could attempt to grasp it, the boat pitched again, and the keys slid well beyond his reach.

Up until that moment, Luke had believed they had a chance, but not anymore. Even if C.B. made that call from wherever he was going, it would be too late. The water was rising steadily. Rosita was right—they were going to drown. Their bodies would be found chained like trapped animals, if they were found at all. This tub would be driftwood before much longer.

I had wanted a lot more years, he thought, as the faces and voices of Nora and Regan permeated his soul.

From across the cabin, he could hear Rosita whisper, "Hail Mary, full of grace . . ."

He finished the prayer with her. ". . . at the hour of our death, Amen."

Inside Elsie's Hideaway, things were hopping. Regan, Fred, and Alvirah took only a moment to orient themselves, then headed straight to the bar.

Matt the bartender came over to them. "What can I get for you?"

"A couple of answers." Fred pulled out his police ID. "You know Petey Commet?"

"Sure I do. He was sitting right where you are less than two hours ago."

"According to his landlord, he left with his suitcases this morning," Fred said.

"Maybe he did, but he was here this afternoon. He did say he was going on vacation."

"Do you know where? It's important."

"I'd like to help you, but to tell you the truth, he was kind of vague about it. Said he was going fishing down south." Matt paused. "I don't know if this means anything, but Petey didn't seem like Petey today. I asked him about it, but he said he felt like a million bucks."

Regan's blood ran cold. "Can you tell us

anyplace where he might have been hanging out between leaving his apartment this morning and coming in here a few hours ago?"

Matt shrugged. "He takes care of somebody's boat at the year-round marina in Weehawken. Maybe he decided to check it out before he takes off. He hangs out there sometimes."

"I know that place." Fred flipped open his cell phone. "Get me the number of Lincoln Harbor in Weehawken," he snapped.

A moment later he was speaking with the marina office. Regan could see the muscles in his face tighten. Whatever they're telling him, it isn't good news, she thought.

Fred finished the call and turned to Regan and Alvirah. "He took the houseboat out Wednesday afternoon and never came back. The woman I spoke to said he must be nuts. The ice is coming down the river. No boats should be out in these conditions, especially an old tub like that."

Alvirah put a comforting hand on Regan's arm as Fred put in a call to the Harbor Unit.

Matt, who had been busy making drinks, came back. "I've got an idea. Most of these people know Petey, and a lot of them work around here. Maybe they know something."

He jumped up on the bar and whistled. The crowd roared its approval. "Free drinks for everyone," someone yelled.

Matt waved his hands at them. "You already got free food tonight. Now this is important. Did anybody see Petey Commet around town today before he came in here?"

Please, God, Regan thought. She watched as people glanced at each other and shook their heads. Then someone called, "When I got off work, I drove straight here. I saw Petey coming up that path next to the Slocum Marina."

"That marina's closed for the winter. Why would he go there?" a customer near Regan mumbled.

Regan turned to him. "Where exactly is this marina?" she demanded.

"Go outside and make a left. It's a few blocks down on the right. You'll see the sign at the turn."

Fred, Regan, and Alvirah raced outside to Fred's car. He roared out of the parking lot, skidding on the snow-covered pavement.

"If they're on an old boat in this weather . . ." Regan didn't complete the thought.

"You just passed the turn!" Alvirah cried.

Fred did a U-turn and barreled down the steep, deserted road that led to the river. The wind-whipped snow reduced visibility to near zero. The road ended in a deserted parking lot. The headlights of the car penetrated the pall of snow enough for them to tell that the marina was empty. There was no boat in sight.

Fred grabbed a flashlight from the glove compartment and jumped out of the car. Followed by Regan and Alvirah, he hurried past the closed marina office. From somewhere off to the left they could hear a thumping, banging noise. Slipping and sliding in the wet snow, they rounded the corner and began to run. The powerful beam of the flashlight revealed a listing houseboat, slamming back and forth against the dock where it was moored. It looked as though it was about to sink.

"Oh my God," Regan screamed. "They're in there, I know it." She and Fred raced along the dock, Alvirah puffing behind them.

The line securing the boat to the dock was uncoiling from the cleat to which it was attached, and Fred grabbed and rewrapped it as best he could. "Alvirah, don't let this come loose."

"Dad!" Regan screamed as she made the dangerous jump onto the lopsided boat. "Rosita!" She began kicking the padlocked door.

At the sound of Regan's voice, Luke and Rosita thought they were dreaming. They were trying to keep their legs out of the icy water that was swirling along the floor. The bubbling leak had widened to a steady, gushing stream.

"Regan!" Luke shouted.

"Hurry!" Rosita screamed.

"We're coming," Fred shouted back. He was beside Regan.

Together they kicked the door repeatedly. The wood panel finally splintered, then separated. They tugged and yanked at the loose wood until they managed to make an opening big enough to step through.

Fred went inside first, shining the flashlight into the pitch-black cabin. Regan followed him, wading into the deepening water, horrified at the sight of her father and Rosita chained to the walls.

"The keys were on the floor under the stove," Luke said urgently.

Fred and Regan bent over, frantically feeling around in the freezing water, which continued to rise steadily.

Please, please, Regan prayed. *Please!* Near the refrigerator, something metallic hit her hand but then was gone. "I felt them," she said. "Right around here"

Fred directed the beam of the flashlight at the base of the refrigerator.

"There they are!" Regan screamed as she lunged for them. Now the water was up to her knees. She snapped open the key ring and gave one key to Fred. She waded to Luke and grabbed his wrist. The key did not fit.

Fred turned away from Rosita, and they made the switch.

This time the keys worked.

Within seconds, both sets of chains were dangling. Supported by Regan, Luke stood up. Fred lifted Rosita to her feet.

"This boat won't last another thirty seconds," Fred said. "Let's get out of here."

The four of them sloshed through the water and stumbled through the shattered door.

Outside on the dock, a fervently praying Alvirah was hanging on to a rope that could no longer bear the strain of a sinking houseboat. As the boat slammed against the dock one final time, she braced herself. Summoning the strength she had used to move pianos in her cleaning-woman days, Alvirah held the rope taut until all four were safely beside her.

Then beaming, she watched as Regan and her father embraced, and Fred wrapped Rosita in his arms.

I knew he liked her, Alvirah thought happily.

Austin Grady followed the kidnappers' instructions to continue east on Borden Avenue and then make a left turn on to Twenty-fifth Street.

"Then pull over and wait," he was told.

Austin drove slowly on the icy roads. The windshield wipers were barely able to keep up with the falling snow.

Twenty-fifth Street was dark and desolate, lined with old factory buildings that obviously had been closed for years. The phone rang again.

"Drive one block to Fifty-first Avenue and turn right. Go to the end of the street and pull over again. Leave the bag on the corner."

This is it, Austin thought. At the end of Fifty-first Avenue, he stopped the car, took out the bag with the million dollars, and placed it on the sidewalk. He got back in the car.

The cell phone rang again. "It's there," Austin said.

"Keep going. Make your left and get lost."

Jack was stationed four blocks away. His cell phone rang. It was Regan.

In a voice that was both tremulous and ecstatic, she said, *"We've got them!* We're on our way home."

Eagle base came on the radio. "Subjects picking up bag."

Jack keyed his transmitter. "Let's nail them."

Chris and Bobby were playing cards with Willy in the family room. Nora was sitting silently, staring into the fire. Numb with fear and anticipation, she jumped when the phone rang on the table next to her. She picked it up, terrified of what she might be about to hear.

"How's that leg of yours?" Luke asked.

Tears of relief coursed down her cheeks. "Oh, Luke," she whispered.

"We're all on our way." Luke's voice was husky with emotion. "See you in half an hour."

Nora hung up the phone. Chris and Bobby were looking at her expectantly. "Mommy's coming home," she managed to say.

C.B. and Petey, both of them handcuffed, were seated side by side in the back of the police car.

"It's not all my fault," Petey protested. "It was your uncle that died."

C.B. suddenly had the incongruous thought

that maybe jail was preferable to a lifetime in Brazil with Petey.

Jack Reilly was dropped off at his apartment in Tribeca. He went directly to his car; his suitcases and presents were still locked safely in the trunk. Home for Christmas, he thought. All's well that ends well.

On the snowy, nearly deserted streets of Manhattan, he resumed the drive he had begun two nights before. He headed east, toward the FDR Drive. Then, as though of its own volition, the car made a U-turn.

Fred and Rosita followed Regan, Luke, and Alvirah as they pulled into the driveway. The cars had not yet stopped when the door of the house was flung open and two little boys came racing out, wearing neither coats nor shoes.

"Mommy! Mommy!" they screamed, slipping and sliding as they ran down the walk.

Rosita threw off the blanket she'd been wrapped in, stumbled from the car, and scooped up in her arms the children she thought she would never see again.

"I *knew* you'd be home in time for Christmas," Chris whispered.

Bobby looked at her, his expression suddenly stricken. "Mommy, is it all right? We already decorated the Christmas tree. But we saved some of the ornaments for you to put on."

"We'll hang them on the tree together," Rosita assured him happily, as she hugged them to her.

Fred had stood back, but now he came over. "Which one of you guys do I get to carry inside?"

Luke and Regan and Alvirah opened their car doors. "Why isn't your mother running out to greet me?" Luke asked.

"Something about a rug I sent her."

They walked up the path together.

Willy was standing at the front door, waiting for Alvirah.

When Luke stepped inside his home, it was as though he were seeing it for the first time.

"Home sweet home," he said fervently, then hurried back to the family room where Nora was waiting, Alvirah close at his heels. Willy grabbed her arm. "Give them a minute alone, honey."

"You're right, Willy. It's just that I'm a hopeless romantic."

Forty minutes later, warmed by hot showers and changed into dry clothes, the captives and their rescuers were back in the family room.

The spread Nora ordered from the local gourmet deli had just arrived. Regan, Alvirah, and Willy began setting up a buffet. Austin had called, proud to have played a part in saving his friend's life.

"I'll drop by with the family tomorrow," he said.

Nora, a glass of wine in her hand, announced, "We're going to throw a big celebratory party next week—and I'm inviting Alvin Luck."

"Isn't he the guy who sent you a present when my back was turned?" Luke asked.

Rosita was sitting on the couch with Fred,

the boys at her feet. She turned to him. "Will you be back in time?"

He looked at her and smiled. "Do you really think that after tonight I want to get on another boat?"

Rosita's smile was brilliant as he said, "I'm not going anywhere, Cinderella."

The doorbell rang.

"I bet it's that Ernest Bumbles," Alvirah said jovially.

"I'm having a citation made especially for him!" Nora declared. "Put his name on the party list, Luke."

Regan walked slowly to answer the door, the sounds of laughter spilling from the room behind her. She felt overwhelmed with gratitude, peace, exhaustion . . . And something else in her heart.

She opened the door. The man she had met only two nights ago in her mother's hospital room was smiling down at her.

"Have you got room for another Reilly around here?" asked Jack.

*The
Christmas
Thief*

In joyful memory of our dear friend
Buddy Lynch
He was the best of the best—
a truly great guy.

I think that I shall never see
A poem lovely as a tree.

—*Joyce Kilmer*

acky Noonan carefully placed an **x** on the calendar he had pinned to the wall of his cell in the federal prison located near Philadelphia, the City of Brotherly Love. Packy was overflowing with love for his fellow man. He had been a guest of the United States Government for twelve years, four months, and two days. But because he had served over 85 percent of his sentence and been a model prisoner, the parole board had reluctantly granted Packy his freedom as of November 12, which was only two weeks away.

Packy, whose full name was Patrick Coogan Noonan, was a world-class scam artist whose offense had been to cheat trusting investors out of nearly $100 million in the seemingly legitimate company he had founded. When the house of cards collapsed, after deducting the money he had spent on homes, cars, jewelry, bribes, and shady ladies, most of the rest, nearly $80 million, could not be accounted for.

In the years of his incarceration, Packy's story never changed. He insisted that his two missing associates had run off with the rest of the money and that, like his victims, he, too, had been the victim of his own trusting nature.

Fifty years old, narrow-faced, with a hawklike nose, close-set eyes, thinning brown hair, and a smile that inspired trust, Packy had stoically endured his years of confinement. He knew that when the day of deliverance came, his nest egg of $80 million would sufficiently compensate him for his discomfort.

He was ready to assume a new identity once he picked up his loot; a private plane would whisk him to Brazil, and a skillful plastic surgeon there had already been engaged to rearrange the sharp features that might have served as the blueprint for the working of his brain.

All the arrangements had been made by his missing associates, who were now residing in Brazil and had been living on $10 million of the missing funds. The remaining fortune Packy had managed to hide before he was arrested, which was why he knew he could count on the continued cooperation of his cronies.

The long-standing plan was that upon his release Packy would go to the halfway house in New York, as required by the terms of his parole, dutifully follow regulations for about a day, then shake off anyone following him, meet his partners in crime, and drive to Stowe, Vermont. There they were to have rented a farmhouse, a flatbed trailer, a barn to hide it in, and whatever equipment it took to cut down a very large tree.

"Why Vermont?" Giuseppe Como, better known as Jo-Jo, wanted to know. "You told us you hid the loot in New Jersey. Were you lying to us, Packy?"

"Would I lie to you?" Packy had asked, wounded. "Maybe I don't want you talking in your sleep."

Jo-Jo and Benny, forty-two-year-old fraternal twins, had been in on the scam from the beginning, but both humbly acknowledged that neither one of them had the fertile mind needed to concoct grandiose schemes. They recognized their roles as foot soldiers of Packy and willingly accepted the droppings from his table since, after all, they were lucrative droppings.

"O Christmas tree, *my* Christmas tree," Packy whispered to himself as he contemplated finding the special branch of one particular tree in Vermont and retrieving the flask of priceless diamonds that had been nestling there for over thirteen years.

2

ven though the mid-November afternoon was brisk, Alvirah and Willy Meehan decided to walk from the meeting of the Lottery Winners Support Group to their Central Park South apartment. Alvirah had started the group when she and Willy won $40 million in the lottery and had heard from a number of people who e-mailed them to warn that they, too, had won pots of money but had gone through it in no time flat. This month they had moved the meeting up a few days because they were leaving for Stowe, Vermont, to spend a long weekend at The Trapp Family Lodge with their good friend, private investigator Regan Reilly, her fiancé, Jack Reilly, head of the Major Case Squad of the NYPD, and Regan's parents, Luke and Nora. Nora was a well-known mystery writer, and Luke was a funeral director. Even though business was brisk, he said no dead body was going to keep *him* away from the vacation.

Married forty years and in their early sixties, Alvirah and Willy had been living in Flushing, Queens, on that fateful evening when the little balls started dropping, one after the other, with a magic number on each of them. They fell in the exact sequence the Meehans had been playing for years, a combination of their birthdays and anniversary. Alvirah had been sitting in the living room, soaking her feet after a hard day of cleaning for her Friday lady, Mrs. O'Keefe, who was a born slob. Willy, a self-employed plumber, had just gotten back from fixing a broken toilet in the old apartment building next to theirs. After that first moment of being absolutely stunned, Alvirah had jumped up, spilling the pail of water. Her bare feet dripping, she had danced around the room with Willy, both of them half-laughing, half-crying.

From day one she and Willy had been sensible. Their sole extravagance was to buy a three-room apartment with a terrace overlooking Central Park. Even in that they were cautious. They kept their apartment in Flushing, just in case New York State went belly up and couldn't afford to continue making the payments to them. They saved half of the money they received each year and invested it wisely.

The color of Alvirah's flaming orange-red hair, now coiffed by Antonio, the hairdresser to the stars, was changed to a golden red shade. Her friend Baroness Min von Schreiber had selected the handsome tweed pantsuit she was wearing. Min begged her never to go shopping alone, pointing out that Alvirah was natural prey for salespeople trying to unload the buyer's mistakes.

Although she had retired her mop and pail, in her newfound life Alvirah was busier than ever. Her penchant for finding trouble and solving problems had turned her into an amateur detective. To aid in catching wrongdoers she had a microphone hidden in her large sunburst lapel pin and turned it on when she sensed someone she was talking to had something to hide. In the three years of being a multi-millionaire, she had solved a dozen crimes and wrote about them for *The New York Globe,* a weekly newspaper. Her adventures were enjoyed so much by the readership that she now had a biweekly column even when she didn't have a crime to report on.

Willy had closed his one-man company but was working harder than ever, devoting his plumbing skills to bettering the lives of the elderly poor on the West Side, under the direction of his eldest sibling, Sister Cordelia, a formidable Dominican nun.

Today the Lottery Winners Support Group had met in a lavish apartment in Trump Tower that had been purchased by Herman Hicks, a recent lottery winner, who, a worried Alvirah now said to Willy, "was going through his money too fast."

They were about to cross Fifth Avenue in front of the Plaza Hotel. "The light's turning yellow," Willy said. "With this traffic I don't want us to get caught in the middle of the street. Somebody'll mow us down."

Alvirah was all set to double the pace. She hated to miss a light, but Willy was cautious. That's the difference between us, she thought indulgently. I'm a risk taker.

"I think Herman will be okay," Willy said reassuringly. "As he said, it always was his dream to live in Trump Tower, and real estate is a good investment. He bought the furniture from the people who were moving; the price seemed fair, and except for buying a wardrobe at Paul Stuart, he hasn't been extravagant."

"Well, a seventy-year-old childless widower with twenty million dollars after taxes is going to have plenty of ladies making tuna casseroles for him," Alvirah noted with concern. "I only wish he'd realize what a wonderful person Opal is."

Opal Fogarty had been a member of the Lottery Winners Support Group since its founding. She had joined after she read about it in Alvirah's column in *The New York Globe* because, as she pointed out, "I'm the lottery winner turned big loser, and I'd like to warn new winners not to get taken in by a glib-talking crook."

Today, because there were two more new members, Opal had told her story about investing in a shipping company whose founder had shipped nothing but money from her bank to his pocket. "I won six million dollars in the lottery," she explained. "After taxes I had just about three million. A guy named Patrick Noonan persuaded me to invest in his phony company. I've always been devoted to Saint Patrick, and I thought that anyone with that name had to be honest. I didn't know then that everyone called that crook Packy. Now he's getting out of prison next week," she explained. "I just wish I could be invisible and follow him around, because I know perfectly well that he's hidden lots of money away."

Opal's blue eyes had welled with tears of frustration at the thought that Packy Noonan would manage to get his hands on the money he had stolen from her.

"Did you lose *all* the money?" Herman had asked solicitously.

It was the kindness in his voice that had set Alvirah's always matchmaking mind on red alert.

"In all they recovered about eight hundred thousand dollars, but the law firm appointed by the court to find the money for us ran up bills of nearly a million dollars, so after they paid themselves, none of us got anything back."

It wasn't unusual for Alvirah to be thinking about something and have Willy comment on it. "Opal's story really made an impression on that young couple who won six hundred thousand on the scratch-a-number," Willy said now. "But that doesn't help her. I mean, she's sixty-seven years old and still working as a waitress in a diner. Those trays are heavy for her to carry."

"She has a vacation coming up soon," Alvirah mused, "but I bet she can't afford to go anywhere. Oh, Willy, we've been so blessed." She gave a quick smile to Willy, thinking for the tenth time that day that he was such a good-looking man. With his shock of white hair, ruddy complexion, keen blue eyes, and big frame, many people commented that

Willy was the image of the late Tip O'Neill, the legendary Speaker of the House of Representatives.

The light turned green. They crossed Fifth Avenue and walked along Central Park South to their apartment just past Seventh Avenue. Alvirah pointed to a young couple who were getting into a horse-drawn carriage for a ride through the park. "I wonder if he's going to propose to her," she commented. "Remember that's where you proposed to me?"

"Sure I remember," Willy said, "and the whole time I was hoping I had enough money to pay for the ride. In the restaurant I meant to tip the headwaiter five bucks, and like a dope I gave him fifty. Didn't realize it until I reached for the ring to put on your finger. Anyhow, I'm glad we decided to go to Vermont with the Reillys. Maybe we'll take a ride on one of the horse-drawn sleighs up there."

"Well, for sure I won't go downhill skiing," Alvirah said. "That's why I hesitated when Regan suggested we go. She and Jack and Nora and Luke are all great skiers. But we can go cross-country skiing, I've got books I want to read, and there are walking paths. One way or another we'll find plenty to do."

Fifteen minutes later, in their comfortable living room with its sweeping view of Central Park, she was opening the package the doorman had given her. "Willy, I don't believe it," she said. "Not even Thanksgiving, yet, and Molloy, McDermott, McFadden, and Markey are sending us a Christmas present." The Four M's, as the brokerage firm was known on Wall Street, was the one Alvirah and Willy had selected to handle the money they allocated to buying government bonds or stock in rock-solid companies.

"What'd they send us?" Willy called from the kitchen as he prepared manhattans, their favorite five o'clock cocktail.

"I haven't opened it yet," Alvirah called back. "You know all that plastic they put on everything. But I think it's a bottle or a jar. The card says 'Happy Holidays.' Boy are they rushing the season. It's not even Thanksgiving yet."

"Whatever it is, don't ruin your nails," Willy warned. "I'll get it for you."

Don't ruin your nails. Alvirah smiled to herself remembering the years when it would have been a waste of time to put even a dab of polish on her nails because all the bleaches and harsh soaps she used cleaning houses would have made short work of it.

Willy came into the living room carrying a tray with two cocktail glasses and a plate of cheese and crackers. Herman's idea of nourishment at the meeting had been Twinkies and instant coffee, both of which Willy and Alvirah had refused.

He put the tray on the coffee table and picked up the bubble-wrapped package. With a firm thrust he pulled apart the adhesive seals and unwound the wrapping. His expression of anticipation changed to surprise and then amazement.

"How much money have we got invested with the Four M's?" he asked.

Alvirah told him.

"Honey, take a look. They sent us a jar of maple syrup. That's their idea of a Christmas present?"

"They've got to be kidding," Alvirah exclaimed, shaking her head as she took the jar from him. Then she read the label. "Willy, look," she exclaimed. "They didn't give us just a jar of syrup. They gave us a *tree!* It says so right here. *'This syrup comes from the tree reserved for Willy and Alvirah Meehan. Please come and tap your tree to refill this jar when it is empty.'* I wonder where the tree is."

Willy began rummaging through the gift-wrapped box that had contained the jar. "Here's a paper. No, it's a map." He studied it and began to laugh. "Honey, here's something else we can do when we're in Stowe. We can look up our tree. From the way it looks here, it's right near the Trapp family property."

The phone rang. It was Regan Reilly calling from Los Angeles. "All set for Vermont?" she asked. "No backing out now, promise?"

"Not a chance, Regan," Alvirah assured her. "I've got business in Stowe. I'm going to look up a tree."

3

egan, you must be exhausted," Nora Regan Reilly said with concern, as she looked fondly across the breakfast table at her only child. To others, beautiful raven-haired Regan might be a superb private investigator, but to Nora, her thirty-one-year-old daughter was still the little girl she would give her life to protect.

"She looks okay to me," Luke Reilly observed as he set down his coffee cup with the decisive gesture that said he was on his way. His lanky six-foot-five frame was encased in a midnight blue suit, white shirt, and black tie, one of the half-dozen such outfits in his possession. Luke was the owner of three funeral homes in northern New Jersey, which was the reason for his need for subdued clothing. His handsome head of silver hair complemented his lean face, which could look suitably somber but always broke into a ready smile outside his viewing rooms. Now that smile encompassed both his wife and his daughter.

They were at the breakfast table in the Reilly home in

Summit, New Jersey, the home in which Regan had grown up and where Luke and Nora still lived. It was also the place where Nora Regan Reilly wrote the suspense novels that had made her famous. Now she got up to kiss her husband good-bye. Ever since he'd been kidnapped a year ago, he never walked out the door without her worrying that something might happen to him.

Like Regan, Nora had classic features, blue eyes, and fair skin. Unlike Regan, she was a natural blond. At five feet three, she was four inches shorter than her daughter and towered over by her husband.

"Don't get kidnapped," she said only half-jokingly. "We want to leave for Vermont no later than two o'clock."

"Getting kidnapped once in a lifetime is about average," Regan volunteered. "I looked up the statistics last week."

"And don't forget," Luke reminded Nora for the hundredth time, "if it wasn't for my pain and suffering in that little predicament, Regan would never have met Jack and you wouldn't be planning a wedding."

Jack Reilly, head of the Major Case Squad of the New York Police Department and now Regan's fiancé, had worked on the case when Luke and his young driver vanished. He not only caught the kidnappers and retrieved the ransom, but in the process had captured Regan's heart.

"I can't believe I haven't seen Jack in two weeks," Regan said with a sigh as she buttered a roll. "He wanted to pick me up at Newark Airport this morning, but I told him I'd take a cab. He had to go into the office to wrap up a few things but he'll be here by two." Regan started to yawn. "Those overnight flights make me a little spacey."

"On second thought, I would suggest that your mother is right," Luke said. "You do look as if a couple of hours of sleep would be useful." He returned Nora's kiss, rumpled Regan's hair, and was gone.

Regan laughed. "I swear he still thinks I'm six years old."

"It's because you're getting married soon. He's starting to talk about how he's looking forward to grandchildren."

"Oh, my God. That thought makes me even more tired. I think I will go upstairs and lie down."

Left alone at the table, Nora refilled her own cup and opened *The New York Times*. The car was already packed for the trip. This morning she intended to work at her desk because she wanted to make notes on the new book she was starting. She hadn't quite decided whether Celia, her protagonist, would be an interior designer or a lawyer. Two different kinds of people, she acknowledged, but as an interior designer it was feasible that Celia would have met her first husband in the process of decorating his Manhattan apartment. On the other hand, if she was a lawyer, it gave a different dynamic to the story.

Read the paper, she told herself. First lesson of writing: Put the subconscious on power-save until you start staring at the computer. She glanced out the window. The breakfast room looked out onto the now snow-covered lawn and the garden that led to the pool and tennis court. I love it here, she thought. I get so mad at the people who knock New Jersey. Oh, well, as Dad used to say, "When they know better, they'll do better."

Wrapped in her quilted satin bathrobe, Nora felt warm and content. Instead of chasing crooks in Los Angeles, Regan was home and going away with them. She had gotten engaged in a hot air balloon, of all places, just a few weeks ago. Over Las Vegas. Nora didn't care where or how it happened, she was just thrilled to finally be planning Regan's wedding. And there couldn't be a more perfect man for her than wonderful Jack Reilly.

In a few hours they would be leaving for the beautiful Trapp Family Lodge and would be joined there by their dear friends Alvirah and Willy Meehan. What's not to like? Nora thought as she flipped to the Metro section of the newspaper.

Her eye immediately went to the front-page picture of a handsome woman dressed in a long skirt, blouse, and vest and standing in a forest. The caption was "Rockefeller Center Selects Tree."

The woman in that picture looks familiar, Nora thought as she skimmed the story.

An 80-foot blue spruce in Stowe, Vermont, is about to take its place as the world's most famous Christmas tree this year. It was chosen for its majestic beauty, but as it turned out, it was planted nearly fifty years ago in a forest adjacent to the property owned by the legendary Von Trapp family. Maria von Trapp happened to be walking through the forest when the sapling was planted, and her picture was taken standing next to it. Since the fortieth anniversary of the world's most successful musical film, *The Sound of Music*, is about to occur, and since the film emphasizes family values and courage in the face of adversity, a special reception has been planned for the tree on its arrival in New York.

It will be cut down on Monday morning and then taken on a flatbed to a barge near New Haven and floated down Long Island Sound to Manhattan. Upon its arrival at Rockefeller Center it will be greeted by a choir of hundreds of schoolchildren from all over the city who will sing a medley of songs from *The Sound of Music*.

"Well, for heaven's sake," Nora said aloud. "They'll be cutting down the tree while we're there. What fun it will be to watch." She began to hum: " 'The hills are alive . . . ' "

4

On that same morning a scant hundred miles away, Packy Noonan woke up with a happy smile plastered on his face.

"It's your big day, huh, Packy?" C.R., the racketeer in the next cell, asked sourly.

Packy could understand the reason for his sullen manner. C.R. was in only the second year of a fourteen-year stretch, and he had not yet adjusted to life behind bars.

"It's my big day," Packy agreed amiably as he packed his few possessions: toiletries, underwear, socks, and a picture of his long-dead mother. He always referred to her lovingly and with tears in his eyes when he spoke in the chapel in his role as a counselor to his fellow inmates. He explained to them that she had always seen the good in him even when he had gone astray, and on her deathbed she told him that she knew he'd turn out to be an upstanding citizen.

In fact, he hadn't seen his mother for twenty years before she died. Nor did he see fit to share with his fellow inmates the fact that in her will, after leaving her meager possessions to the Sisters of Charity, she had written, "And to my son, Patrick, unfortunately known as Packy, I leave one dollar and his high chair because the only time he ever gave me any happiness was when he was small enough to sit in it."

Ma had a way with words, Packy thought fondly. I guess I got the gift of gab from her. The woman on the parole board had almost been in tears when he had explained at his hearing that he prayed to his mother every night. Not that it had done him any good. He had served every last day of his minimum sentence plus another two years. The bleeding heart had been overruled by the rest of the board, six to one.

The jacket and slacks he had worn when he arrived at the prison were out of fashion, of course, but it felt great to put them on. And thanks to the money he swindled, they had been custom-made by Armani. As far as he was concerned, he still looked pretty sharp in them—not that they would be in his closet for thirty seconds after he got to Brazil.

His lawyer, Thoris Twinning, was picking him up at ten o'clock to escort him to the halfway house known as The Castle on the Upper West Side in Manhattan. Packy loved the story that in its long history The Castle had twice been an academy for Catholic high school girls. Ma should know that, he thought. She'd think I was defiling the place.

He was scheduled to stay there for two weeks to reintroduce himself to the world where people actually worked for a living. He understood that there would be group sessions in which the rules about signing in and signing out and the importance of reporting to his parole officer would be explained. He was assured that at The Castle they would be able to find him permanent housing. He could predict that it would be in a crummy rooming house in Staten Island or the Bronx. The counselors would also help him get a job immediately.

Packy could hardly wait. He knew that the receiver appointed by the Bureau of Securities to try to find the money lost by the investors would probably have him tailed. There was nothing he looked forward to more than the fun of losing that tail. Unlike thirteen years ago when detectives were swarming all over Manhattan looking for him. He was just leaving for Vermont to retrieve the loot and get out of the country when he was arrested. That wasn't going to happen again.

It had already been explained to him that as of Sunday he would be allowed to leave The Castle in the morning but had to be back and signed in by dinner time. And he had already figured out exactly how he would shake the nincompoop who was supposed to be following him.

At ten-forty on Sunday morning, Benny and Jo-Jo would be waiting on Madison and Fifty-first in a van with a ski rack. Then they'd be on their way to Vermont. Following his instructions, Benny and Jo-Jo had rented a farm near Stowe six months ago. The only virtue of the farm was that it had a large if decrepit barn where a flatbed would be housed.

In the farmhouse the twins had installed an acquaintance, a guy without a record who was incredibly naive and was happy to be paid to house sit for them.

That way, just in case there were any slips, when the cops were searching for a flatbed with a tree on it, they wouldn't start looking in places where people lived. There were enough farms with barns that were owned by out-of-town skiers for them to investigate. The skiers usually didn't arrive until after Thanksgiving.

I wired the flask of diamonds onto the branch thirteen and a half years ago, Packy thought. A spruce grows about one and a half feet a year. The branch I marked was about twenty feet high at the time. I was standing at the top of the twenty foot ladder. Now that branch should be about forty feet high. Trouble is no regular ladder goes that high.

That's why we have to take the whole tree, and if someone with nothing better to do than mind other people's business asks questions, we can say it's going to be decorated for the Christmas pageant in Hackensack, New Jersey. Jo-Jo has a fake permit to cut the tree and a phony letter from the mayor of Hackensack, thanking Pickens for the tree, so that should take care of that.

Packy's agile brain leaped about to find any flaw in his reasoning but came up dry. Satisfied, he continued to review the plan: Then we get the flatbed into the barn, find the branch where the loot is hidden, and then we're off to Brazil, cha, cha, cha.

All of the above was racing through Packy's mind as he ate his final breakfast at the Federal Correctional Institution and, when it was over, bid a fond farewell to his fellow inmates.

"Good luck, Packy," Lightfingered Tom said solemnly.

"Don't give up preaching," a grizzled long-timer urged. "Keep that promise to your mother that you'd set a good example for the young."

Ed, the lawyer who had vacated his clients' trust funds of millions, grinned and gave a lazy wave of his hand. "I give you three months before you're back," he predicted.

Packy didn't show how much that got under his skin. "I'll send you a card, Ed," he said. "From Brazil," he muttered under his breath as he followed the guard to the warden's office where Thoris Twinning, his court-appointed lawyer, was waiting.

Thoris was beaming. "A happy day," he gushed. "A happy, happy day. And I have wonderful news. I've been in touch with your parole officer, and he has a job for you. As of a week from Monday you will be working at the salad bar in the Palace-Plus diner on Broadway and Ninety-seventh Street."

As of a week from Monday a bunch of lackeys will be dropping grapes into my mouth, Packy thought, but he turned on the mesmerizing smile that had enchanted Opal

Fogarty and some two hundred other investors in the Patrick Noonan Shipping and Handling Company. "My mama's prayers have been answered," he said joyfully. His eyes raised to heaven and a blissful expression on his sharp-featured face, he sighed, "An honest job with an honest day's pay. Just what Mama always wanted for me."

5

My, my, this is such a beautiful car," Opal Fogarty commented from the back seat of Alvirah and Willy's Mercedes. "When I was growing up we had a pickup truck. My father said it made him feel like a cowboy. My mother used to tell him it rode like a bucking steer, so she could understand why he felt like a cowboy. He bought it without telling her, and boy was she mad! But I have to say this: It lasted for fourteen years before it stopped dead on the Triborough Bridge during rush hour. Even my father admitted it was time to give up on the truck, and this time my mother went car shopping with him." She laughed. "She got to pick out the car. It was a Dodge. Daddy made her mad by asking the salesman if a taxi meter was an option."

Alvirah turned to look at Opal. "Why did he ask that?"

"Honey, it's because Dodge made so many taxis," Willy explained. "That was funny, Opal."

"Dad *was* pretty funny," Opal agreed. "He never had two nickels to rub together, but he did his best. He inherited two thousand dollars when I was about eight years old, and some-body convinced him to put it in parachute stock. They said that with all the commercial flying people would be doing, all the passengers would have to wear parachutes. I guess being gullible is genetic."

Alvirah was glad to hear Opal laugh. It was two o'clock, and they were on route 91 heading for Vermont. At ten o'clock she and Willy had been packing for the trip and half-watching the television in the bedroom when a news flash caught their attention. It showed Packy Noonan leaving fed-eral prison in his lawyer's car. At the gate he got out of the car and spoke to the reporters. "I regret the harm I have caused the investors in my company," he said. Tears welled in his eyes and his lip trembled as he went on. "I understand that I will be working at the salad bar at the Palace-Plus diner, and I will ask that ten percent of my wages be taken to start to repay the people who lost their savings in the Patrick Noo-nan Shipping and Handling Company."

"Ten percent of a minimum wage job!" Willy had snorted. "He's got to be kidding."

Alvirah had rushed to the phone and dialed Opal. "Turn on channel twenty-four!" she ordered. Then she was sorry she had made the call because when Opal saw Packy, she began to cry.

"Oh, Alvirah, it just makes me sick to think that terrible cheat is as free as a daisy while I'm sitting here thrilled to get a week's vacation because I'm so tired. Mark my words, he'll end up joining his pals on the Riviera or wherever they are with my money in their pockets."

That was when Alvirah insisted that Opal join them for the long weekend in Vermont. "We have two big bedrooms and baths in our villa," she said, "and it will do you good to get away. You can help us follow the map and find my tree. There won't be any syrup coming from it now, but I packed the jar that the stockbrokers sent me. We have a little kitchen so maybe I'll make pancakes for everyone and see how good the syrup tastes. And I read in the paper that they'll be cutting down the tree for Rockefeller Center right near where we're staying. That would be fun to watch, wouldn't it?"

It didn't take much to persuade Opal. And she was already perking up. On the trip to Vermont she made only one comment about Packy Noonan: "I can just see him working at a salad bar in a diner. He'll probably be sneaking the croutons into his pocket."

6

Sometimes Milo Brosky wished he had never met the Como twins. He had run into them by chance in Greenwich Village twenty years ago when he attended a poets' meeting in the back room of Eddie's Aurora. Benny and Jo-Jo were hanging out in the bar.

I was feeling pretty good, Milo thought as he sipped a beer in the shabby parlor of a rundown farmhouse in Stowe, Vermont. I'd just read my narrative poem about a peach who falls in love with a fruit fly, and our workshop thought it was wonderful. They saw deep meaning and tenderness that never verged on sentimentality in my poem. I felt so good I decided to have a beer on the way home, and that's when I met the twins.

Milo took another sip of beer. I should have bought back my introduction to them, he thought glumly. Not that they weren't good to me. They knew that I hadn't had my big breakthrough as a poet and that I'd take any kind of job to keep a roof over my head. But this roof feels as though it could fall in on me. They're up to something.

Milo frowned. Forty-two years old, with shoulder-length hair and a wispy beard, he could have been an extra in a film about Woodstock '69. His bony arms dangled from his long frame. His guileless gray eyes had a perpetually benevolent expression. His voice with its singsong pitch made his listeners think of adjectives like "kind" and "gentle."

Milo knew that a dozen years ago the Como Brothers had been obliged to skip town in a hurry because of their involvement with the Packy Noonan scam. He hadn't heard from them in years. Then six months ago he had received a phone call from Jo-Jo. He wouldn't say where he was, but he asked Milo if he would be interested in making a lot of money without any risk. All Milo had to do was find a farmhouse for rent in Stowe, Vermont. It had to have a large barn, at least ninety feet long. Until the first of the year Milo was to spend at least long weekends there. He was to get to know the locals, explain that he was a poet and, like J. D. Salinger and Aleksandr Solzhenitsyn, needed a retreat in New England where he could write in solitude.

It had been clear to Milo that Jo-Jo was reading both names and that he had no idea who either Salinger or Solzhenitsyn was, but the offer had come at a perfect time. His part-time jobs were drying up. The lease on his attic apartment was expiring, and his landlady had flatly refused to renew it. She simply couldn't understand why it was imperative for him to write late at night even though he explained that was when his thoughts transcended the everyday world and that rap music played loud gave wings to his poetry.

He quickly found the farmhouse in Stowe and had been living in it full-time. Even though the regular deposits to his checking account had been a lifesaver, they were not enough to support another apartment in New York. The prices were astronomical there, and Milo rued the day he had told his landlady that he needed to keep the music blasting at night so it would drown out her snoring. In short, Milo was not happy. He was sick of the country life and longed for the bustle and activity of Greenwich Village. He liked people, and even though he regularly invited some of the Stowe locals to his poetry readings, after the first couple of evenings no one came back. Jo-Jo had promised that by the end of the year he would receive a $50,000 bonus. But Milo was beginning to suspect that the farmhouse and his presence in it had something to do with Packy Noonan getting out of prison.

"I don't want to get in trouble," he warned Jo-Jo during one of his phone calls.

"Trouble? What are you talking about?" Jo-Jo had asked sadly. "Would I get my good friend in trouble? What'd you do? Rent a farmhouse? That's a crime?"

A pounding on the farmhouse door interrupted Milo's

reverie. He rushed to open it and then stood frozen at the sight of his visitors—two short, portly men in ski outfits standing in front of a flatbed with a couple of stragglylooking evergreen trees on it. At first he didn't recognize them, but then he bellowed, "Jo-Jo! Benny!" Even as he threw his arms around them he was aware of how much they had changed.

Jo-Jo had always been hefty, but he had put on at least twenty pounds and looked like an overweight tomcat, with tanned skin and balding head. Benny was the same height, about five-six, but he'd always been so thin you could slip him under the door. He'd gained weight, too, and although he was only half the size of Jo-Jo, he was starting to look more like him.

Jo-Jo did not waste time. "You got a padlock on the barn door, Milo. That was smart. Open it up."

"Right away, right away." Milo loped into the kitchen where the key to the padlock was hanging on a nail. Jo-Jo had been so specific on the phone about the size of the barn that he had always suspected it was the main reason he had been hired. He hoped they wouldn't mind that the barn had a lot of stalls in it. The owner of the farm had gone broke trying to raise a racehorse that would pay off. Instead, according to local gossip, when he went to claiming races, he invariably managed to select hopeless plugs, all of which ate to the bursting point and sat down at the starting gate.

"Hurry up, Milo," Benny was yelling even though Milo

hadn't taken more than half a minute to get the key. "We don't want no local yokel to come to one of your poetry recitals and see the flatbed."

Why not? Milo wondered, but without taking the time to either grab a coat or answer his own question, he raced outside and down the field to undo the padlock and pull open the wide doors of the barn.

The early evening was very cold, and he shivered. In the fading light Milo could see that there was another vehicle behind the flatbed, a van with a ski rack on the roof. They must have taken up skiing, he thought. Funny, he would never have considered them athletes.

Benny helped him pull back the doors. Milo switched on the light and was able to see the dismay on Jo-Jo's face.

"What's with all the stalls?" Jo-Jo demanded.

"They used to raise horses here." Milo did not know why he was suddenly nervous. I've done everything they want, he reasoned, so what's with the angst? "It's the right size barn," he defended himself, his voice never wavering from its singsong gentleness, "and there aren't many that big."

"Yeah, right. Get out of the way." With an imperious sweep of his arm, Jo-Jo signaled to Benny to drive the flatbed into the barn.

Benny inched the vehicle through the doors, and then a splintering crash confirmed the fact that he had sideswiped the first stall. The sound continued intermittently until the flatbed was fully inside the barn. The space was so tight that Benny could exit only by moving from the driver's seat to the passenger seat, opening the door just enough to squeeze out, and then flattening himself against the walls and gates of the stalls as he inched past them.

His first words when he reached Milo and Jo-Jo at the door were "I need a beer. Maybe two or three beers. You got anything to eat, Milo?"

For lack of something to do when he wasn't writing a poem, Milo had taught himself to cook in his six months of babysitting the farm. Now he was glad that fresh spaghetti sauce was in the refrigerator. He remembered that the Como twins loved pasta.

Fifteen minutes later they were sipping beer around the kitchen table while Milo heated his sauce and boiled water for the pasta. To Milo's dread, listening to the brothers talk as he bustled around the kitchen, he heard the name "Packy" whispered and realized that the farmhouse indeed had something to do with Packy Noonan's release.

But *what*? And where did *he* fit in? He waited until he put the steaming dishes of pasta in front of the twins before he said point-blank: "If this has something to do with Packy Noonan, I'm out of here now."

Jo-Jo smiled. "Be reasonable, Milo. You rented a place for us when you knew we were on the lam. You've been getting money deposited in your bank account for six months. All you have to do is sit here and write poetry, and in a couple of days you get fifty thousand bucks in cash and you're home free."

"In a couple of days?" Milo asked, incredulous, his mind conjuring up the happiness that $50,000 could buy: A decent place to rent in the Village. No worry about part-time jobs for at least a couple of years. No one could make a buck last as long as he could.

Jo-Jo was studying him. Now he nodded with satisfaction. "Like I said, all you need to do is sit here and write poetry. Write a nice poem about a tree."

"What tree?"

"We're just as much in the dark as you are, but we'll all find out real soon."

7

can't believe I'm sitting here having dinner with not only Alvirah and Willy but Nora Regan Reilly, the famous writer, and her family, Opal thought. This morning after watching that miserable Packy Noonan on television, I felt like turning my face to the wall and never getting out of bed again. Shows how much everything can change.

And they were all so nice to her. Over dinner they had told her about Luke being kidnapped and held hostage on a leaky houseboat in the Hudson River with his driver, who was a single mother with two little boys, and how they would have drowned if Alvirah and Regan hadn't rescued them.

"Alvirah and I make a good team," Regan Reilly said. "I wish we could put our heads together and find your money for you, Opal. You do think that Packy Noonan has it hidden somewhere, don't you?"

"Sure he does," Jack Reilly said emphatically. "That case was in the federal court, so we didn't handle it, but my guess is that guy has a stash somewhere. When you add up what the feds knew Packy spent, there's still between seventy and eighty million dollars missing. He probably has it in a numbered account in Switzerland or in a bank in the Cayman Islands."

Jack was sipping coffee. His left arm was around the back of Regan's chair. The way he kept looking at her made Opal wish that somewhere along the way she had met a special guy. He's so handsome, she thought, and Regan is so pretty. Jack had sandy hair that tended to curl, his hazel eyes were more green than brown, and his even features were enhanced by a strong jaw. When he and Regan walked into the dining room together, they were holding hands. Regan was tall, but Jack was considerably taller and had broad shoulders to match.

Even though it was only the second week in November, an early heavy snowfall had meant there was real powder on the slopes and on the ground. Tomorrow the Reillys were going to downhill ski. It was funny that Jack's name was Reilly too, Opal thought. She and Alvirah and Willy were going to take a walk in the woods and find Alvirah's tree. Then in the afternoon they were going to take lessons in cross-country skiing. Alvirah told her that she and Willy had done cross-country skiing a couple of times, and it wasn't that hard to keep your balance—and it was fun.

Opal wasn't sure how much fun it would be, but she was willing to give it a try. Years ago in school, she had always been a good athlete, and she almost always walked the mile back and forth to work to keep trim.

"You have that blank look in your eyes that says you're doing some deep thinking," Luke observed to Nora.

Nora was sipping a cappuccino. "I'm remembering how much I enjoyed the story of the Von Trapp family. I read Maria's book long before I saw the film. It's so interesting to be here now and realize that a tree she watched being planted has been chosen for Rockefeller Center this year. With all the worries in the world, it's comforting to know that New York schoolchildren will welcome that tree. It makes it so special."

"Well, the tree is only down the road enjoying its last weekend in Vermont," Luke said drily. "Monday morning before we leave, we can all go over, watch it being cut down, and kiss it good-bye."

"On the car radio I heard that they'll take it off the barge in Manhattan on Wednesday morning," Alvirah volunteered. "I think it would be exciting to be there when the tree arrives at Rockefeller Center. I know I'd like to see the choirs of schoolchildren and hear them sing."

But even as the words were coming from her mouth, Alvirah began to have a funny feeling that something would go wrong. She looked around the cozy dining room. People were lingering over dinner, smiling and chatting. Why did a cold certainty fill her that trouble was brewing and Opal would be caught up in it? I shouldn't have asked her to come, Alvirah worried. For some reason she's in danger here.

8

Packy's first night in the halfway house known as The Castle was not much better, in his opinion, than a step up from the federal penitentiary. He was signed in, given a bed, and once again had the rules explained to him. He immediately reconfirmed his ability to leave The Castle on Sunday morning by piously explaining that as a good Catholic he never missed Mass. He threw in for good measure the fact that it was the anniversary of his mother's death. Packy had long since forgotten exactly when his mother died, but the easy tear that rushed to his eye on cue and the roguish smile that accompanied his confession— "God bless her. She never gave up on me"—made the counselor on duty hasten to reassure him that on Sunday he could certainly attend Mass on his own.

The next day and a half passed in a blur. He dutifully sat in on the lectures warning him that he could be sent back to prison to complete his sentence if he did not follow strictly the terms of his parole. He sat at meals visualizing the feasts that he would soon be eating at fine restaurants in Brazil, sporting his new face. On Friday and Saturday night he closed his eyes in the room he was sharing with two other recently released convicts and drifted into sleep, dreaming of Egyptian cotton sheets, silk pajamas, and finally getting his hands on his flask of diamonds.

Sunday morning dawned crisp and clear. The first snowfall had occurred two weeks ago, much earlier than usual, and the forecast was that another one was on the way. It looked as if an old-fashioned winter was looming, and that was fine with Packy. He wasn't planning to share it with his fellow Americans.

Over the years of his incarceration he had managed to keep in contact with the Como twins by paying a number of carefully chosen visitors to other convicts to mail letters from him and then bring the Comos' letters to him. Only last week Jo-Jo had confirmed the arrangement to meet behind Saint Patrick's Cathedral by writing to urge him to attend the 10:15 Mass at the cathedral and then take a walk on Madison Avenue.

So Benny and Jo-Jo would be there. Why wouldn't they? Packy asked himself. At eight o'clock he closed the door of The Castle and stepped out onto the street. He had decided to walk the one hundred blocks, not because he wanted the exercise, but because he knew he would be followed and wanted his pursuer to have a good workout.

He could hear the instructions received by the guy who had been assigned to tail him: "Don't take your eyes off him. Sooner or later he'll lead us to the money he's hidden away."

No, I won't, Packy thought as he walked rapidly down Broadway. Several times, when stopped by a red light, he looked around casually as though enchanted by the world he had been missing for so long. The second time he was able to pick out his pursuer, a beefy guy dressed like a jogger.

Some jogger, Packy thought. He'll be lucky if he hasn't lost me before Saint Pat's.

On Sunday mornings the 10:15 Mass always drew the biggest crowds. That was when the full choir sang, and on many Sundays the Cardinal was the celebrant. Packy knew just where he was going to sit—on the right side, near the front. He would wait until Holy Communion was being given out and get on line with everyone else. Then, just before he received, he would cut across to the left of the altar to the corridor that led to the Madison Avenue townhouse that served as an office for the archdiocese. He remembered that when he was in high school, the kids in his class had assembled in the office and marched into the cathedral from there.

Jo-Jo and Benny would be parked in the van at the Madison Avenue entrance of the townhouse, and before the beefy guy had a chance to follow, they would be gone.

Packy got to the cathedral with time to spare and lit a candle in front of the statue of Saint Anthony. I know if I pray to you when I've lost something, you'll help me find it, he reminded the saint, but the stuff I want is *hidden*, not lost. So I don't need to pray for anything that I want to find. What I want from *you* is a little help in losing Fatso the Jogger.

His hands were cupped in prayer, which enabled him to conceal a small mirror in his palms. With it he was able to keep track of the jogger who was kneeling in a nearby pew.

At 10:15 Packy waited until the processional was about to start from the back of the church. Then he scurried up the aisle and squeezed into an end seat six rows from the front. With the mirror he was able to ascertain that four rows behind him the jogger was unable to get an end seat and had to move past two old ladies before he found space.

Love the old ladies, Packy thought. They always want to sit at the end. Afraid they'll miss something if they move over and make room for someone else.

But the problem was that there was lots of security in the cathedral. He hadn't counted on that. Even a two-year-old could see that some of those guys in wine-colored jackets weren't just ushers. Besides that, there were a few cops in uniform stationed inside. They would be all over him if he set foot on the altar.

Worried for the first time and his confidence shaken, Packy surveyed the scene more carefully. Beads of perspiration dampened his forehead as he realized his options were few. The side door on the right was his best shot. The time to move was when the Gospel was read. Everybody would be standing, and he could slip out without the jogger noticing he was gone. Then he would turn left and run the half block to Madison Avenue and up Madison to the van. "Be there, Jo-Jo. Be there, Benny," he whispered to himself. But if they were not and even if he was followed, it wasn't a parole violation to leave church early.

Packy began to feel better. With the help of the mirror he was able to ascertain that one more person had squeezed into the jogger's pew. True to form, the old ladies had stepped into the aisle to let him in, and now the jogger was cheek by jowl with a muscular kid who would not be easy to push aside.

"Let us reflect on our own lives, what we have done and what we have failed to do," the celebrant, a monsignor, was saying.

That was the last thing Packy wanted to reflect on. The epistle was read. Packy didn't hear it. He was concentrating on making his escape.

"Alleluia," the choir sang.

The congregation got to its feet. Before the last man was standing, Packy was at the side door of the cathedral that opened onto Fiftieth Street. Before the second alleluia was chanted, he was on Madison Avenue. Before the third prolonged al-le-lu-ia, he had spotted the van, opened the door, leaped into it, and it was gone.

Inside the cathedral the husky teenager had become openly belligerent. "Listen, mister," he told the jogger. "I might have knocked over these ladies if I let you shoot past me. Cool it, man."

9

On Sunday afternoon Alvirah said admiringly, "You're a natural on skis, Opal."

Opal's gentle face brightened at the praise. "I really used to be a good athlete in school," she said. "Softball was my specialty. I guess I'm just naturally coordinated or something. When I put on those cross-country skis, I felt as if I was dancing on air right away."

"Well, you certainly left Alvirah and me at the starting gate," Willy observed. "You took off as if you'd been born on skis."

It was five o'clock. The fire was blazing in their rented villa at the Trapp Family Lodge, and they were enjoying a glass of wine. Their plans to find Alvirah's tree had been postponed. Instead, on Saturday, when they learned that the afternoon cross-country lessons were all booked up, they quickly signed up for the morning instructor. Then, following lunch on Saturday, a vacancy had opened in the afternoon group, and Opal had gone off with them.

On Sunday, after Mass at Blessed Sacrament Church and an hour of skiing, Alvirah and Willy had had enough and were happy to go back to their cabin for a cup of tea and a nap. The shadows were lengthening when Opal returned. Alvirah had just started to worry about her when she glided up to the cabin, her cheeks rosy, her light brown eyes sparkling.

"Oh, Alvirah," she sighed as she stepped out of the skis, "I haven't enjoyed myself this much since—" She stopped, and the smile that had been playing around her lips vanished.

Alvirah knew perfectly well what Opal had been about to say: "I haven't had this much fun since the day I won the lottery."

But Opal's smile had been quick to come back. "I've had a wonderful day," she finished. "I can't thank you enough for inviting me to be with you."

The Reillys—Nora, Luke, Regan, and Regan's fiancé, Jack "no relation" Reilly—had spent another long day of downhill skiing. They had arranged with Alvirah to meet at seven for dinner in the main dining room of the lodge. There Regan entertained them with the story of one of her favorite cases: a ninety-three-year-old woman who became engaged to her financial planner and was to marry him three days later. She secretly planned to give $2 million each to her four stepnieces and -nephews if they *all* showed up at the wedding.

"Actually, it was her fifth wedding," Regan explained. "The family got wind of her plan and was dropping everything to be there. Who wouldn't? But one of the nieces is an actress who had taken off on a 'Go with the Flow' weekend. She shut off her cell phone, and nobody knew where she was. It was my job to find her and get her to the wedding so the family could collect their money."

"Brings tears to your eyes, doesn't it?" Luke commented.

"For two million dollars I would have been a bridesmaid," Jack said, laughing.

"My mother used to listen to a radio program called 'Mr. Keen, Tracer of Lost Persons,'" Opal recalled. "Sounds like you're the new Mr. Keen, Regan."

"I've located a few missing people in my time," Regan acknowledged.

"And some of them would have been better off if she hadn't tracked them down," Jack said with a smile. "They ended up in the clink."

Once again it was a very pleasant dinner, Opal thought. Nice people, good conversation, beautiful surroundings—and now her newfound sport. She felt a million miles away from the Village Eatery where she had been working for the last twenty years, except for the few months when she had the lottery money in the bank. Not that the Village Eatery was such a bad place to work, she assured herself, and it's kind of an upscale diner because it has a liquor license and a separate bar. But the trays were heavy and the clientele was mostly college students, who claimed to be on tight budgets. That, Opal had come to believe, was nothing but an excuse for leaving cheap tips.

Seeing the way Alvirah and Willy lived since they won the lottery, and the way Herman Hicks had been able to use some of his lottery winnings to buy that beautiful apartment, made Opal realize all the more keenly how foolish she had been to trust that smooth-talking liar, Packy Noonan, and lose her chance for a little ease and luxury. What made it even harder was that Nora was so excited when she talked about the wedding she was planning for Regan and Jack. Opal's niece, her favorite relative, was saving for her wedding.

"I've got to keep it small, Aunt Opal," Kristy had told her. "Teachers don't make much money. Mom and Dad can't afford to help, and you wouldn't believe how much even a small wedding costs."

Kristy, the child of Opal's younger brother, lived in Boston. She had gone through college on a scholarship with the understanding that she would teach in an inner city school for three years after she graduated, and that's what she was doing now. Tim Cavanaugh, the young man she was marrying, was going to school at night for his master's degree in accounting. They were such fine young people and had so many friends. I'd love to plan a beautiful wedding for them, Opal thought, and help them furnish their first home. If only . . .

Woulda, shoulda, coulda, hada, oughta, she chided herself. Get over it. Think about something else.

The "something else" that jumped to mind was the fact that the group of six people she skied with on Saturday afternoon had passed an isolated farmhouse about two miles away. A man had been standing in the driveway loading skis on top of a van. She had had only a glimpse of him, but for some crazy reason he seemed familiar, as if she had run into him recently. He was short and stocky, but so were half the people who came into the diner, she reminded herself. He's a type, nothing more than a type; that's the long and short of it. That's why I thought I should know who he is. Still, it haunted her.

"Is that okay with you, Opal?" Willy asked.

Startled, Opal realized that this was the second time Willy had asked that question. What had he been talking about? Oh, yes. He had suggested that they have an early breakfast tomorrow, then head over to watch the Rockefeller Center tree being cut down. After that they could find Alvirah's tree, come back to the lodge, have lunch, and pack for the trip home.

"Fine with me," Opal answered hurriedly. "I want to buy a camera and take some pictures."

"Opal, I have a camera. I intend to take a picture of

Alvirah's tree and send it to our broker." Nora laughed. "The only thing we ever got from him for Christmas was a fruit-cake."

"A jar of maple syrup and a tree to tap hundreds of miles from where you live isn't what I call splurging," Alvirah exclaimed. "The people whose houses I cleaned used to get big bottles of champagne from their brokers."

"Those days went the way of pull-chain toilets," Willy said with a wave of his hand. "Today you're lucky if someone sends a gift in your name to his favorite charity which (a) you never heard of, and (b) you haven't a clue how much he sent."

"Luckily in my profession people never want to hear from us, especially during the holidays," Luke drawled.

Regan laughed. "This is getting ridiculous. I can't wait to watch the Rockefeller Center tree being cut down. Just think of all the people who are going to see that tree over the Christmas season. After that it would be fun to see how swift we are following the map to Alvirah's tree."

Regan couldn't possibly know that their lighthearted outing would turn deadly serious tomorrow when Opal skied off alone to check out the short, stocky man she had glimpsed at the farmhouse—the farmhouse where Packy Noonan had just arrived.

IO

I feel like I'm at the Waltons, Milo thought as he raised the lid of the big pot and sniffed the beef stew that was simmering on the stove. It was early Sunday evening, and the farmhouse actually felt cozy with the aroma of his cooking. Through the window he could see that it had started to snow. Despite the heartwarming scene he couldn't wait for this job to be finished so he could get back to Greenwich Village. He needed the stimulation of attending readings and being around other poets. They listened respectfully to his poems and clapped and sometimes told him how moved they were. Even if they didn't mean it, they were good fakers. They give me the encouragement I need, he thought.

The Como twins had told Milo that they expected to be back at the farmhouse anytime after six on Sunday evening and to be sure to have dinner ready. They had left on Saturday afternoon, and if they'd seemed nervous when they arrived with the flatbed, it didn't compare to how they acted when they took off in the van. He had innocently asked them where they were going, and Jo-Jo had snapped back, "None of your business."

I told him to take a chill pill, Milo remembered, and he almost blew a gasket. Then Jo-Jo screamed at Benny to take the skis off the roof of the van and load them back again properly. He said one ski looked loose, and it would be just like Benny to load a ski that would fall off on the highway and hit a patrol car. "All we need are state troopers on our case, pawing our phony licenses."

Then fifteen minutes later he had yelled at Benny to come back inside because a bunch of cross-country skiers were passing across the field. "One of them skidding around out there could be an eagle-eyed cop," he snapped. "Your picture was on TV when they did the story on Packy, wasn't it? Maybe you want to take his bunk in the pen?"

They're scared out of their minds—that had been Milo's assessment. On the other hand, so was he. It was clear to him that wherever the twins were going involved risk. He worried that if they were arrested and talked about him, he could at the very least be accused of harboring fugitives. He shouldn't be doing business with people on the lam, and he was already sure that their little excursion had to do with Packy Noonan getting out of the can. Would anyone believe that thirteen years ago he didn't know that the twins had disappeared at the exact time Packy was arrested and that he had had nothing to do with them since? Until now, of course, he corrected himself.

No, he decided. No one would believe it.

The twins had eluded capture for years, and from the well fed look of the two of them and their new bright choppers that didn't even look fake, they had been living well. So they certainly had at least *some* of the money that the investors had lost in the scam. Why did they risk coming back? he wondered.

Packy had paid his debt to society, Milo thought, but he's still on parole. But from the way the twins were talking when they didn't think I could overhear them, it's obvious they're all planning to skip the U. S. of A. in the next few days. To where? With what?

Milo forked a chunk of beef from the stew and popped it in his mouth. Jo-Jo and Benny had stayed with him for less than twenty-four hours, but in that short time all the years they hadn't laid eyes on each other melted away. Before Jo-Jo got crabby, they had had a few laughs about the old days. And after Benny had downed a couple of beers, he had even invited him to come visit them in Bra—

At that memory Milo smiled. Benny had started to say "Bra—" and Jo-Jo had shut him up. So instead of saying "Brazil," which he clearly meant to say, Benny had said, "Bra-bra, I mean, Bora-Bora."

Benny had never been all that swift on the uptake, Milo remembered.

He began to set the table. If by chance the twins showed up with Packy Noonan, would Packy enjoy the stew, or had he gotten his fill of stew in prison? Even if he did, it wouldn't be anything like the way *I* make it, Milo assured himself. And, besides, if anyone doesn't like stew, I have plenty of spaghetti sauce. From all the stories he had heard, Packy could get pretty mean when things didn't go exactly his way. I wouldn't mind making his acquaintance, though, he admitted to himself. There is no denying that he has what they call charisma. That is one of the reasons his trial got so much coverage—people can't resist criminals with charisma.

A green salad with slivers of Parmesan cheese, home-made biscuits, and ice cream would complete the meal that would satisfy the queen of England if she happened to show up on her skis, Milo congratulated himself. These mismatched chipped dishes aren't fit for royalty, he thought, but they didn't matter. God knows it shouldn't matter to the twins. No matter how much money they got their hands on, they'd still be the same goons they always were. As Mama used to say, "Milo, honey, you can't buy class." And, boy, was she right about *that!*

There was nothing more he could do until they returned. He walked to the front door and opened it. He glanced at the barn and once again asked himself the question: What's with the flatbed? If they are headed back to Bra Bra Brazil, they sure can't be traveling there by way of a flatbed. There had been a couple of scrawny-looking spruces on the flatbed when they arrived, but yesterday Benny threw them into one of the stalls.

Maybe I should write a poem about a tree, Milo mused as he closed the door and walked over to the battered old desk in the parlor that the renting agent had the nerve to call an antique. He sat down and closed his eyes.

A scrawny tree that nobody wants, he thought sadly. It gets thrown into a horse stall, and there's a broken-down nag that is headed for the glue factory. They are both scared. The tree knows its next stop is the fireplace.

At first the tree and the nag don't get along, but because misery loves company and they can't avoid each other, they become best friends. The tree tells the nag how he never grew tall, and everyone called him Stumpy. That's why he has been plopped here in the stall. The nag tells how in the one race he could have won he sat down on the track after the first turn because he was tired. Stumpy and the nag comfort each other and plan their escape. The nag grabs Stumpy by a branch, flings him over his back, breaks out of the stall, and races to the forest where they live happily ever after.

With tears in his eyes, Milo shook his head. "Sometimes beautiful poetry comes to me full-blown," he said aloud. He sniffled as he pulled out a sheet of paper and began to write.

II

*F*rom the first moment he spotted the van on Madison Avenue, Packy Noonan realized that in thirteen years the combined brain power of the Como twins had not increased one iota. As he leaped into the backseat and slammed the door behind him, he fumed. "What's with the skis? Why not put up a sign reading Packy's Getaway Car?"

"Huh?" Benny grunted in bewilderment.

Jo-Jo was behind the wheel and stepped on the gas. He was a fraction too late to make the traffic light and decided not to risk it, especially with a cop standing at the corner. Even though the cop wasn't actually facing them, running a light was not a good idea.

"I said you should bring skis so that we could put them on after you picked me up," Packy snapped. "That way if someone noticed me hightailing it down the block, they'd say I got in a van. Then we pull over somewhere and put the skis on top. They're looking for any old van, not a van with skis.

You're so dopey. You might as well plaster "Honk if You Love Jesus" stickers all over the van, for God's sake."

Jo-Jo spun his head. "We risked our necks to get you, Packy. We didn't have to, you know."

"Get moving!" Packy shrieked. "The light's green. You want a special invitation to step on the gas?"

The traffic was heavier than usual for a Sunday morning. The van moved slowly up the long block to Fifty-second Street, and then Jo-Jo turned east. Precisely the moment they were out of view, the man Packy had dubbed Fatso came running up Madison Avenue. *"Help!-Help!* Did anybody see some guy running?" he began to yell.

The cop, who had not noticed Packy either running or getting in the van, hurried over to the jogger, clearly believing he had a nut case on his hands. New Yorkers and tourists, united for the moment in a bit of excitement, stopped to see what was going on.

The jogger raised his voice and shouted, "Anybody see where a guy went who was running around here a minute ago?"

"Keep it down, buddy," the cop ordered. "I could arrest you for disturbing the peace."

A four-year-old who had been standing across the street next to his mother while she answered a call on her cell phone tugged at her skirt. "A man who was running got into a van with skis on it," he said matter of factly.

"Mind your business, Jason," she said crisply. "You don't

need to be a witness to a crime. Whoever they're looking for is probably a pickpocket. Let them find him. That's what they're paid to do." She resumed her conversation as she took his hand and started walking down the street. "Jeannie, you're my sister, and I have your best interests at heart. *Drop that creep.*"

Less than two blocks away the van was moving slowly through the traffic. In the backseat Packy willed the vehicle forward: Park, Lexington, Third, Second, First.

At First Avenue, Jo-Jo put on the turn signal. Ten more blocks to the FDR Drive, Packy fretted. He began to bite his nails, a long-forgotten habit he had overcome when he was nine. I'm not doing anything wrong until I don't show up at The Castle tonight, he reasoned. But if I'm caught with the twins, it's all over. Associating with known felons means instant parole revocation. I should have had them leave the van parked somewhere for me. But even if I was alone and got stopped, how would I explain the van? That I won it in a raffle?

He moaned.

Benny turned his head. "I got a good feeling, Packy," he said soothingly. "We're gonna make it."

But Packy observed that sweat was rolling down Benny's face. And Jo-Jo was driving so slowly that they might as well be walking. I know he doesn't want to get caught in an intersection, but this is nuts! Overhead, a thumping sound indicated that one of the skis was coming loose. "Pull over," Packy screamed. Two minutes later, between First and Second Avenues, he yanked the skis off the roof of the van and tossed them in through the back door. Then he waved Jo-Jo over to the passenger seat. "Is this the way they taught you to drive in Brazil? You, Benny, get in the back."

For the next twenty minutes they sat in dead silence as they traveled north. Benny, easily intimidated, cowered in the backseat. He had forgotten that Packy goes nuts when he's worried. So what's going on? he wondered. In those letters he told us to find somebody we could trust to rent a farmhouse with a big barn in Stowe. We did that. And then he sends word to get a two-handled saw, a hatchet, and rope, and then the flatbed. We did that. He told us to pick him up today. We did that. So what's it all about? Packy swore that he had left the rest of the loot in New Jersey, so why are we going to Vermont? I never heard of going to New Jersey by way of Vermont.

Sitting in the front seat, Jo-Jo was thinking in the same vein. Benny and I had ten million bucks with us when we took off for Brazil. We lived nice there, very, very nice, but not over the top. Packy tells us that he has another seventy or eighty million he can get his hands on once he's out of jail. But he never said how much Benny and me get in the split. If it goes sour, Benny and me could end up with Packy in the slammer. We should've stayed in Brazil and let him slave away for a few weeks at that dumpy diner where they got him a job. Then when we came to rescue him, maybe he'd appreciate us a little more. In fact, he'd be kissing our feet.

When they saw the "Welcome to Connecticut" sign, Packy let go of the wheel and clapped his hands. "One state closer to Vermont," he chortled. With a broad grin he turned to Jo-Jo. "But we're not gonna be there long. We'll take care of business and be on our way to sunny Brazil."

God willing, Jo-Jo thought piously. But something tells me that Benny and I should have made do with ten million bucks. His stomach gurgled as he made a feeble attempt to return Packy's smile.

12

At a quarter of eight Milo heard the sound of a vehicle coming up the driveway. With nervous anticipation he rushed to open the front door. He watched as Jo-Jo got out of the front passenger door of the van and Benny emerged from the door behind him.

So who's driving? he wondered. But then the question was answered as the driver's door opened and a figure appeared. The faint light from the living room window was all Milo needed to confirm his hunch that Packy Noonan was the mystery guest.

Benny and Jo-Jo waited for Packy to precede them up the porch steps. Milo jumped back to open the door as wide as possible. He felt as if he should salute, but Packy extended his hand. "So you're Milo the poet," he said. "Thanks for holding down the fort for me."

If I had known I was holding it down for you, I wouldn't be here, Milo thought, but he found himself smiling back. "It's a pleasure, Mr. Noonan," he said.

"Packy," Packy corrected him gently as his glance darted around the room. He sniffed. "Something smells real good."

"It's my beef stew," Milo told him, the words tumbling from his mouth. "I hope you enjoy beef stew, Mr.—I mean, Packy."

"My favorite. My mama made it for me every Friday—or maybe it was Saturday." Packy was starting to enjoy himself. Milo the poet was as transparent as a teenager. I *do* have a natural way of impressing people, he thought. How else would I have gotten all those dopey investors to keep pouring money into my sinkhole?

Jo-Jo and Benny were coming into the house. Packy decided this was the moment to make sure that Milo joined their team for good. "Jo-Jo, you brought that money like I told you?"

"Yeah, Packy, sure."

"Peel off fifty of the big ones and give them to our friend Milo." Packy put his arm around Milo's shoulders. "Milo," he said, "this isn't what we owe you. This is a bonus for being a swell guy."

Fifty hundred-dollar bills? Milo thought. But he said *the big ones*. He couldn't mean fifty *thousand*, could he? *Another* fifty thousand? Milo's brain couldn't handle the thought of that much money being handed to him in cold, hard cash.

Two minutes later he could not keep his mouth closed as a grumpy-looking Jo-Jo counted out fifty stacks of bills from a large suitcase filled with money. "There are ten C-notes in each of these here piles," he said. "Count them when you're finished writing your next poem."

"By any chance have you got anything smaller?" Milo asked hesitantly. "Hundred-dollar bills are hard to change."

"Chase the Good Humor wagon down the block," Jo-Jo snapped. "What I hear, the driver carries lots of change."

"Milo," Packy said gently. "Hundred-dollar bills aren't hard to change anymore. Now let me explain our plans. We'll be out of here by Tuesday at the latest. Which means all *you* have to do is go about your business and ignore our comings and goings until we leave. And when we leave, you will be given the other fifty thousand dollars. Are you agreeable to that situation?"

"Oh, yes, Mr. Noonan—I mean, Packy. I surely am, sir." Milo could taste and feel Greenwich Village as though he were already there.

"If somebody happened to ring the bell and ask if you'd seen a flatbed around here, you'd forget that there is indeed one on the premises, wouldn't you, Milo?"

Milo nodded.

Packy looked directly into his eyes and was satisfied. "Very good. We understand each other. Now how about some dinner? We hit a lot of traffic, and your stew smells great."

13

They're not hungry, they're *starving*, Milo thought as he refilled Packy's and the twins' plates for the third time. With satisfaction he watched as his biscuits disappeared and his salad vanished. He had done so much tasting and sampling that he had hardly any appetite, which was just as well since he kept getting up and down to open yet another bottle of wine. Packy, Jo-Jo, and Benny seemed to be in a contest to see who could drink the fastest.

But the more they drank, the more they mellowed. The skis wobbling on the roof of the van suddenly seemed hilarious. The fact that four cars had rear-ended one another on route 91, causing a massive traffic jam and forcing them to drive slowly past an army of cops, sparked another round of belly laughs.

By eleven o'clock the twins' eyes were at half-mast. Packy had a buzz on. Milo had limited himself to a couple of glasses of wine. He didn't want to wake up tomorrow and forget anything that had been said. He also intended to stay sober until his money was safely under a mattress in Greenwich Village.

Jo-Jo pushed back his chair, stood up, and yawned. "I'm going to bed. Hey, Milo, that extra fifty thousand means you do the dishes." He started to laugh, but Packy thumped on the table and ordered him to sit back down.

"We're all tired, you idiot. But we have to talk business."

With a burp he didn't try to stifle, Jo-Jo slumped back into his chair. "I beg your pardon," he mumbled.

"If we don't get this right, you may be begging the governor for a pardon," Packy shot across the table.

A nervous tremor ran through Milo's body. He simply didn't know what to expect next.

"Tomorrow we're getting up real early. We'll have some coffee, which Milo will have ready."

Milo nodded.

"Then we back the flatbed out of the barn, drive to a tree a few miles from here that happens to be located on the property of a guy I worked for when I was a kid, and cut down this very special tree."

"Cut down a *tree?*" Milo interrupted. "You're not the only one cutting down a tree tomorrow," he said excitedly. He ran over to the pile of newspapers by the back door. "Here it is, right on top!" he crowed. "Tomorrow at ten A.M. the blue spruce that was selected as this year's Rockefeller Center

Christmas tree is being cut down. They've been preparing it all week! Half the town will be there, and there'll be lots of media—television, radio, you name it!"

"Where's this tree?" Packy asked, his voice dangerously quiet.

"Hmmmm." Milo searched the article. "I could really use a pair of reading glasses," he observed. "Oh, here it is. The tree is on the Pickens property. Guess there's good pickins on the Pickens property." He laughed.

Packy jumped out of his seat. "Give me that!" he yelled. He grabbed the paper out of Milo's hands. When he laid eyes on the picture of the tree—alone and majestic in a clearing—that was about to be sent to New York City, he let out a scream. "That's my tree! *That's my tree!*"

"There are a lot of nice trees around here we could cut down instead," Milo suggested, trying to be helpful.

"*Roll out the flatbed!*" Packy ordered. "*We're cutting down my tree tonight!*"

14

At eleven o'clock, just before she got into bed, Alvirah stood at the window and looked out. Most of the villas were already in darkness. In the distance she could see the silhouette of the mountains. They're so silent and still, she thought, sighing.

Willy was already in bed. "Is anything wrong, honey?"

"No, not at all. It's just that I'm such a New Yorker, it's hard to get used to so much quiet. At home the sounds of traffic and police sirens and trucks rumbling kind of blend into a lullaby."

"Uh-huh. Come to bed, Alvirah."

"But here it's so peaceful," Alvirah continued. "I bet if you walked along any of these paths right now, you wouldn't hear a sound other than a little animal scampering through the snow or a tree rustling or maybe an owl hooting. It's so different, isn't it? In New York right now there's probably a line of cars at Columbus Circle, honking their horns because the light just changed and somebody didn't step on the gas fast enough. In Stowe you don't hear a sound on the road. By midnight all the lights will be out. Everyone will be dreaming. I love it."

A gentle snore from the bed told her that Willy had fallen fast asleep.

"Let's see what's going on in the world," Nora suggested as Luke unlocked the door to their cabin. "I like to catch the news before I go to sleep."

"That's not always the best idea," Luke commented drily. "The bedtime stories on the news aren't always catalysts for sweet dreams."

"If I can't sleep in the middle of the night, I always turn on the news," Regan said. "It helps me fall back asleep—unless, of course, there's something big going on."

Jack picked up the remote and pressed the TV button. The screen filled with the anchor desk of the Flash News Network. The coanchors were not flashing their usual sunny smiles. A tape rolled showing Packy Noonan leaving prison. "Look at this!" Jack exclaimed.

The anchor reported solemnly: "Packy Noonan, recently released from prison after serving twelve and a half years for cheating investors in his fake shipping company, left his halfway house this morning to attend Mass at Saint Patrick's Cathedral. He was being followed by a private investigator hired by the law firm that was appointed to recover the money Packy stole. But Noonan slipped out of the cathedral during the service and was seen running down Madison Avenue. When he did not return to the halfway house this evening, he officially broke his parole. We have been receiving phone calls and e-mails from outraged investors who heard this story earlier on Flash News. They have always believed that Noonan had squirreled away their money and is on his way to collect their fortunes right now. There is a $10,000 reward for information that helps lead to Noonan's capture. If you have any information, please contact the number on your screen below."

"That guy is taking a big risk," Jack said. "He served his time, and now if he's caught he'll be thrown back in jail for breaking parole. He must have that money stashed away somewhere and doesn't want to wait the two or three years he'd spend on parole to get his millions. My guess is that he'll be out of the country in no time flat."

"Poor Opal," Nora sighed. "That's all she needs to hear. She always said the money was hidden somewhere, and if she got her hands on Packy, she'd wring his neck."

Regan shook her head. "It makes me sick to think how many investors like Opal were cheated out of money that really would have made a difference in their lives. At least when Packy was in prison, they knew he was miserable. Now they have to wonder if he's going to be living high on the hog on their dime, just thumbing his nose at them."

"I told you," Luke said. "Now everybody's worked up before it's time to go to sleep."

In spite of the situation, they all laughed. "You're terrible," Nora chided. "I just hope Opal didn't watch the news tonight. She'd never close an eye."

A few doors down, in the villa she shared with Alvirah and Willy, Opal had fallen into a dead sleep as soon as her head hit the pillow. Even though she had not heard the news about Packy's disappearance, when she began to dream, it was of him. The gates of a dreary stone prison were bursting open. Packy came running out clutching fat pillowcases in his arms. She knew they were stuffed with money—*her* money. Her lottery money. She began to chase him, but her legs wouldn't move. In her dream she became increasingly agitated. "Why won't my legs move?" she thought frantically. "I have to catch up with him." Packy disappeared down the road. Gasping for breath as she struggled to move forward, Opal woke with a start.

"Oh, my God," she thought as she felt her heart pounding. Another nightmare about that stupid Packy Noonan. As she calmed down, she thought there was something more that her subconscious was working to bring to the surface. It's going to come to me, she thought as she closed her eyes again. I know it is.

ll my plans," Packy moaned. "Twelve and a half stinking years doing time, and every single minute I'm dreaming of getting my hands on my tree. Now this!"

From the backseat Benny leaned forward. He stuck his head between Packy and Jo-Jo. "What's so special about getting your hands on that tree?" he asked. "Are you supposed to make a wish or something?"

It was pitch dark. The van was the only vehicle on the quiet country road. Packy, Jo-Jo, and Benny were on their way to case the situation on the Pickens property. As Packy had exclaimed bitterly, "For all we know the Rockefeller Center people left a guard overnight watching the tree. Before we go lumbering over there in the flatbed, we gotta see what's going on."

"Benny, figure it out," Jo-Jo snarled. "Packy must've hid something in the tree and is worried he won't be able to get it out. It has to be our money stuck in there, Packy. Right?"

"Bingo," Packy snapped. "You should apply to be a member of the Mensa Society. You'd be a shoo-in."

"What's the Mensa Society?" Benny asked.

"It's a kind of club. You take a test. If you pass, you get to go to meetings with other people who passed, and you congratulate one another on how smart you all are. One of them was in my cell block. He was so smart that when he passed a note to the bank teller to fork over money, he wrote it on his own deposit slip."

Packy knew he was ranting as though he was out of his mind. Sometimes it was like that when he got rattled. Get your cool back, he told himself. Breathe deep. Think beautiful thoughts. He thought about money.

Outside the temperature was dropping. He could feel the slight slip of the tires as the van hit a patch of ice.

"So answer me, Packy," Jo-Jo insisted. "Our money's in that tree. You were in the can over twelve years. So why didn't you stash it in a numbered account in Switzerland or in a safe deposit box? What turned you into a squirrel?"

Packy could not prevent his voice from becoming shrill. "Let me explain. And listen real good so I don't have to repeat 'cause we're almost there." He floored the brake as he spotted a deer emerging from the bushes at the side of the road. "Get lost, Bambi," he muttered. As though it had heard him, the deer turned and disappeared.

The road was bending sharply to the right. Packy picked

up speed again but more cautiously. Suppose the tree was being guarded? What then?

"So, Packy, I wanna know what's going on," Jo-Jo said impatiently.

Jo-Jo and Benny had a right to know what they were up against, Packy admitted to himself. "You two were in on the shipping scam up to your necks. The difference is that you got away with big bucks and got to spend the last twelve years in Brazil while I shared a cell with a whacko."

"We only got ten million," Benny corrected, sounding injured. "You held on to at least seventy million."

"It didn't do me any good when I was in jail. The whole time the lamebrains were giving us money to invest I was buying diamonds, unset stones, some of them worth two million each."

"Why didn't you ask us to mind them while you were in jail?" Benny asked.

"Because I'd still be waiting on Madison Avenue for you to pick me up."

"That's not nice," Benny said, shaking his head. "So I guess the diamonds are in your tree somewhere, huh? Good thing Milo mentioned the tree's going to be cut down tomorrow morning. To think we could have been a day late and a dollar short."

"You're not helping matters, Benny," Jo-Jo interrupted his brother. "Now, Packy, why did you pick this tree way up here in Vermont? You know, Jersey has a lot of nice trees, and it's much closer to the City."

"I used to work for the people who owned this property!" Packy snapped at them. "When I was sixteen, my dear old Ma got the court to send me up here on some kind of 'save-the-troubled-kid' experiment."

"What kind of job did you have up here?" Jo-Jo asked.

"Cutting down trees, mostly for the Christmas market. I was pretty good at it. I even learned how to use a crane to get the big ones that were bought for the centers of towns all over the country. Anyway, when I was afraid that the auditors were catching on to us, I took the diamonds from the safe deposit box, put them in a metal flask, and stowed them up here. I didn't think it would be thirteen years before I'd be back for them. The people who own this property planted the tree on their wedding day fifty years ago. They swore they'd never cut it down."

"That would have been bad," Benny agreed. "With all the developments these days, it just could have happened. Ya know, in our old neighborhood, the ball field—"

"I don't want to hear about your old neighborhood!" Packy shouted. "Now here's the turn into the clearing. Keep your fingers crossed. I'll pull over, and we'll walk the rest of the way."

"Suppose there's a guard there."

"Maybe he'll have to spend the rest of the night watching us cut down a tree. Jo-Jo, give me the flashlight."

Packy opened the door of the van and got out. His blood was racing so rapidly through his veins that he didn't notice the sharp difference between the cold night air and the warmth of the van. Keeping to the side of the path, he was ready to merge into the shadows if he caught sight of anyone near the tree. Slowly he edged around the final turn, the twins following. He couldn't believe what he saw. The light snowfall allowed enough visibility to vaguely outline the scene. Packy turned on the flashlight and kept it pointed at the ground.

Next to the tree, his tree, was a flatbed. A crane was already in place, its cables looped near the top to guide the tree onto the flatbed after it was cut down. There didn't seem to be anyone around guarding it.

Jo-Jo and Benny knew enough not to say a word.

Slowly, tentatively, Packy approached the cab of the flatbed and peered inside. There was no one there. He tried the handle of the driver's door, but it was locked. Under the bumper, he thought. Nine out of ten truck drivers leave another set of keys under the bumper.

He found them and began to laugh. "This is a gift," he told the twins. "The flatbed and the crane just *waiting* for us. We're on our way to a flask full of millions of dollars' worth of diamonds, hidden somewhere in that tree. But we have to go back to the farmhouse to get the two-handled saw. Too bad one of you imbeciles didn't think to throw it in the back of the van."

"There's a power saw on the flatbed," Benny pointed out. "Why can't we use that?"

"Are you crazy? That thing would wake the dead. You guys can cut down the tree in no time while I handle the crane."

"I've got a bad back," Benny protested.

"Listen!" Packy exploded. "Your share of eighty million dollars will pay for plenty of chiropractors and masseuses. Come on, we're wasting time!"

16

Two hundred acres away, in the eighteenth-century farm-house in the center of his property, Lemuel Pickens was finding it hard to get to sleep. Normally he and his wife, Vidya, got into bed promptly at nine-thirty and passed out. But tonight, because of the tree, they had been reminiscing about the old days, and then they dug out the album and looked at the picture of the two of them planting the tree the day they were married, fifty years ago.

We weren't spring chickens, either. Lemuel chuckled to himself. Vidya was thirty-two, and I was thirty-five. That was old in our day. But as she always said, "Lemmy, we had responsibilities. I had my mother to take care of, and you had your father. When we'd see each other in church on Sundays, I could tell you were sweet on me, and I liked that." Then Viddy's mother died. Two weeks later Pa was feeling poorly, and before you could say "Jiminy Cricket," he had passed over, too, Lemuel remembered as he gave Viddy a poke. That woman can sure snore up a storm, he thought as she turned on her side and the rumbling stopped.

We never were blessed with children, but that tree has been almost like a child to us. Lemuel's eyes moistened. Watching it grow, the branches always so even and perfect, and the touch of blue that comes out in the sunlight. It sure is the prettiest tree I've ever seen. Even the way it stands alone in the clearing. We never wanted to plant anything near it. Over the years we've put mulch around it. Babied it. It's been fun.

He turned on his side. When those people rang the door and asked if we'd let them cut down the tree for Rockefeller Center, I almost took a gun to them. But then I heard that after I turned them down they hightailed over to Wayne Covel's place and were considering his big blue spruce. Boy, did that get my goat.

Viddy and I took about two minutes to talk it over. We're not going to be here much longer to take care of our tree. Even if we have it in our will that no one can cut it down, it won't be the same after we're gone. It won't be special to any-one, but if it goes to Rockefeller Center, it will make thou-sands and thousands of people happy. And when it gets to New York, the schoolkids and those cute Rockettes will greet our tree and sing the songs from Maria von Trapp's movie. Funny that she came along just as we were planting it. She knew it was our wedding day, and she sang an Austrian wedding song for us and took our picture next to the tree. Then we took her picture standing in the same spot.

Lemuel sighed. Viddy is looking forward so much to going to New York City and seeing our tree come ablaze with lights. It'll be on television all over the country, and everyone will know it's our fiftieth anniversary. They even want to interview us on the *Today Show*. Viddy's so excited, she's planning to have her hair washed and set at one of those fancy salons in New York. When I heard how much it was gonna cost, I almost dropped my teeth. But as Viddy reminded me, she's only had it done twice in all these years.

I just wish I could see the expression on Wayne Covel's face when we're on the TV talking to Katie or Matt. He's as sour as a wet hen because when we went running over and said we'd let them have our tree, they dropped *his* like a hot potato.

Lemuel gave Vidya another poke. She makes more noise than a tree crashing in the forest, he thought.

17

Twenty feet up, Wayne Covel could not believe his ears. He had been standing on the ladder behind Lemuel Pickens's prize blue spruce, machete in hand, about to start hacking off branches. His intention was to make such a mess of the tree that the men sent by Rockefeller Center would come running back to him. He still hadn't decided whether or not to play hard to get, but in the end he would let them have his beautiful tree.

The *Today Show* here I come, he thought.

But then from the other side of the tree he heard footsteps approaching and realized that subconsciously he had been aware of the faint sound of a car engine a few minutes earlier. It was too late for him to climb down the ladder and escape, so he did the only thing possible: He jammed the machete into the tool belt around his waist and stood perfectly still. Maybe they'll go away quickly, he hoped. Please don't let it be guards who'll stay here all night.

What do I do? he wondered frantically. I'm a trespasser.

Lem Pickens would know exactly what I was up to. My goose would be cooked.

Wayne could hear several men walking around, then moving on the far side of the tree. They were talking about diamonds hidden in the tree—millions of dollars' worth of diamonds! He almost fell off the ladder, he was concentrating so hard in his attempt to make out every word they were saying.

They had to be kidding! But they weren't—he knew it. There were diamonds hidden in a metal flask somewhere in the tree, and these guys were going to steal the tree to find the jewels.

Wayne was terrified. These weren't good guys, obviously. Could he get out of here without them seeing him? If they discovered him, they'd know he heard what they were saying. Then what? He didn't want to think about the possibilities.

"We have to go back to the farmhouse to get the two-handled saw," one of them was saying in a grouchy tone. "Too bad one of you imbeciles didn't think to throw it in the back of the van."

Thank you, God! Wayne wanted to shout. They're leaving. That'll give me time to climb down and call the cops. Maybe there'll be a reward! I'll be a hero. These guys wouldn't have hid diamonds in the tree if they got them honestly, that much he knew for sure.

He waited until he could no longer hear the sound of their car, then reached into his belt, pulled out his flashlight, and turned it on. Where could they have hidden a flask of diamonds? It had to be attached to a branch or to the trunk. The branches weren't thick enough to hold a flask inside. And if anyone had drilled a hole in the trunk, the nutrients wouldn't get through, and the tree would die.

Wayne leaned forward, lifted a few of the branches with his thick protective gloves, and shined the flashlight all around. What a joke, he thought. Talk about a needle in a haystack. But maybe I'll get lucky and spot the flask. Sure—and maybe Boston will finally win the World Series.

Even so, he descended the ladder one step at a time, carefully parting the branches and shining the flashlight between them. Three steps down, the beam of light caught on something resting on a branch above, about halfway between the trunk and the ladder.

It couldn't be—or could it?

Wayne grabbed the machete from his belt and leaned into the tree. The needles scratched his face and became embedded in his handlebar mustache, but he didn't feel them. He couldn't reach the machete far enough to cut the branch off past the object, or could he?

Wayne was on his tiptoes leaning into the tree when, with one strike, he cut the branch in half, pulled off the severed end, and scampered down the ladder. At the bottom his flashlight revealed a metal flask held tight to the branch with the kind of thin wire used in electric fences. Wayne's whole body quivered with excitement.

With a sweep of the machete Wayne cut the branch again so that the section holding the flask was only a foot long. He stifled the impulse to let out a whoop of triumph, as he did whenever the Red Sox scored a run against the Yankees, and began to run. In his haste he did not realize that the machete with his name on the handle had slid out of his belt and fallen to the ground.

All thoughts of calling the cops had vanished.

God works in strange ways, he thought as he ran around the perimeter of Lem Pickens's property. If my tree had been picked, I would have had my fifteen minutes of fame, but then it would have been over. This way, if this flask really is full of diamonds, I'm rich—and that pain in the neck Lem misses his chance to be a star.

He only wished he had the nerve to show up the next morning and see Lem's face when he visits his tree for the last time and finds nothing but a stump. Wayne was delirious with joy. And how about seeing the faces on the guys when they discover that the branch with the flask is half gone? But he wished them luck. They were doing his job for him. If they really succeeded at cutting down Lem's tree, then his might be on its way to Rockefeller Center.

Wayne ran faster through the night. I should check my horoscope, he thought. My planets must be all lined up. They just gotta be.

ack at the farmhouse Milo was roused from his nap on the couch and ordered into the kitchen for a briefing from Packy.

"I don't want to get in this any deeper," Milo protested.

"You're in it up to your neck," Packy barked. "Now we've got to get this right. We can't fit two flatbeds in the barn, and we can't leave one out in sight."

"There are plenty of lonely roads around here," Benny noted. "Why don't we leave ours on one of them? Although it's a shame—it was a good buy. Right after you sent word from prison to buy an old flatbed, Jo-Jo and I came across that one at an auction. Paid cash for it, too. We were so proud of ourselves."

"Benny, please!" Packy yelled. "When we get back here with my tree, you'll pull our flatbed out of the barn, drive north on route 100 for about ten miles, and lose it some-where. No. Wait a minute! Milo, you drive the flatbed. They know you around here. There's no law against driving a flatbed. Benny, you follow in the van and drive him back."

This is more than I bargained for, Milo thought. I don't think I'll ever get to spend that money. But he decided not to protest. He was already in too deep, and he had never felt more miserable in his life.

"Okay, that's decided," Packy said briskly. "Milo, don't look so worried. We'll be out of your life soon enough." He glanced at the twins. "Come on, you two. We don't have that much time."

When they got back to the site, the light snowfall had ended and a few stars were visible through the clouds. In a way Packy was glad to see them. It meant that he didn't need more than the lowest setting of the flashlight to guide Jo-Jo and Benny when they were sawing the tree.

The Rockefeller Center crane was in place to receive the tree when it fell. The cables of the crane were already attached to the tree to keep it from falling away from the flatbed.

I was nuts to think I could cut anything this big and count on its landing on our flatbed, Packy admitted to himself. I was nuts to forget that the bottom branches of a tree this big had to be wrapped. Let's face it, I was nuts to hide the diamonds in a tree in the first place. But the boys hired by Rockefeller Center took care of everything for me, he consoled himself. What pals.

Jo-Jo and Benny took their places on either side of the tree. They were each holding one end of the saw.

"All right," Packy directed. "This is the way you do it. Benny, you push while Jo-Jo pulls. Then, Jo-Jo, you push while Benny pulls."

"Then I push while Jo-Jo pulls," Benny confirmed. "And Jo-Jo pushes and I pull. Is that right, Packy?"

Packy wanted to scream. "Yes, that's right. Just start. Do it! Hurry up!"

Even though it was a manual saw, the sound seemed to reverberate through the woods. Seated on the crane, Packy pointed the beam of the flashlight on the base of the tree. For an instant he pointed it at the tree's back where he knew that somewhere the flask was hidden. He could see a ladder that hadn't been visible to him before and then noticed that a length of branch was lying on the ground. An uneasy feeling stirred inside him. He pointed the light back at the twins pushing and pulling.

Ten minutes passed. Fifteen.

"Hurry up," Packy urged them. "Hurry up."

"We're pushing and pulling as fast as we can," Benny panted. "We're almost done. We're almost—Timber!" he yelled.

They had severed the tree at the base of the trunk. For a moment it wavered and then, guided by Packy at the crane, the large tree was held in the air by cables and lowered in a straight line onto the flatbed. Sweat was pouring down

Packy's face. How did I ever remember to do that right? he wondered. He released the cables, scrambled down from the crane, and rushed into the driver's seat of the cab of the flatbed. "Benny, you get in with me. Jo-Jo, follow in the van, like you're escorting us. Now if our luck holds . . ."

With agonizing slowness he drove the flatbed out of the clearing and onto the dirt road. He passed the east side of Lem Pickens's property, pulled on to route 108, and finally drove up Mountain Road.

A few cars passed them on 108, their occupants hopefully too tired or too indifferent to wonder what was going on. "Sometimes they transport big trees like this at night to avoid causing a traffic jam," Packy explained, more to himself than to Benny. "That's what these birds probably think we're doing if they think at all."

There was more that he was worried about than getting back to the barn undetected—that branch lying on the ground, right below the area where the flask was hidden. That side of the tree was now exposed on the top of the flatbed. He couldn't wait to start looking for his flask.

It was exactly 3 A.M. when they reached the farmhouse. Benny jumped out, ran to the barn, and opened the door. He backed out their flatbed, making an ear-splitting racket as the remaining horse stalls broke into splinters. Milo came rushing out of the house and took over the driver's seat of the flatbed from Benny. As Benny drove the van past Packy, he waved, smiled, and gave a light tap of the horn. Packy grunted while driving the stolen flatbed into the barn. As he climbed out, Jo-Jo was shutting the barn door.

"Now I look for the red line I painted around the trunk at the spot where the branch with the flask is, and we're halfway to Brazil. The way I figure it, now it should be about forty feet up."

Jo-Jo pulled out the tape measure Packy had ordered him to bring, and together they started to measure the tree from its base. Packy's throat went dry when he saw a broken branch about twenty feet up. Could this be where that piece of branch on the ground came from? he wondered. Ignoring the sharpness of the needles, he pulled the remaining branch back and then yelled as a piece of jagged wire cut his finger. His flashlight was pointed at the trunk and the red circle around the base of the broken branch.

There was no sign of a flask, only the remnants of the wire with which he had so carefully secured his treasure.

"What?" he screamed. "I don't get it! I thought my branch would be higher by now. We've got to go back! That flask must be stuck to the branch I saw lying on the ground by the ladder."

"We can't drive the flatbed out again! We gotta wait till Benny and Milo get back with the van," Jo-Jo pointed out.

"What about Milo's heap?" Packy screamed.

"He keeps those keys in his coat pocket," Jo-Jo answered. I should have stayed in Brazil and let Packy make salads at that dumpy diner, he thought for the third time that day.

19

Lem Pickens kept waking up. He was having bad dreams. He didn't know why, but he kept worrying that something would go wrong, that maybe he had made a mistake after all about giving up the tree.

Just natural, he told himself. Just natural. He had read in a book somewhere that any cataclysmic event in our lives brings fear and anxiety. It certainly doesn't seem to bother Viddy, he thought as she continued to make the depth of her slumber known to him. Right now the noise she's making is somewhere between a jackhammer and a chainsaw.

Lem tried thinking pleasant thoughts to ease his anxiety. Think of when they flip the switch and our tree is lit up in Rockefeller Center with over thirty thousand colored lights on it. Just think about *that*!

He knew why he was worried. It would be hard to watch the tree actually being cut down. He wondered if the tree was scared. At that moment he made a decision: I'll wake up Viddy extra early, and after we have a cup of coffee, we'll walk over and sit by our tree and say a proper good-bye to it.

That settled, and feeling somewhat content, Lem closed his eyes and drifted back to sleep. A few minutes later the racket from his side of the bed was still no competition for Viddy, an Olympic snorer if there ever was one.

As they slept, a tearful Packy Noonan was sitting on the stump of their beloved tree holding a machete in his hand, the beam of his flashlight pointing to the name visible on the handle: *Wayne Covel.*

20

Wayne Covel was panting when he reached his back door, the piece of Lem's branch with the crooks' flask wired to it clutched in his hand. He laid the branch on the table in his messy kitchen, poured a tall glass of whiskey to calm his nerves, and then dug the wire cutters out of his tool belt. With trembling fingers he cut the wire that held the flask to the branch and freed it.

Flasks hold only good things, he thought as he took a sip of the whiskey. This one had been just about sealed shut, there was so much sediment around it, and he tried to unscrew it. He walked over to the sink and turned on the faucet. A groaning sound was followed by a slight trickle of water that eventually turned hot. He held the flask under it until most of the sediment was washed off. It still took three powerful twists with his hands before the cap loosened.

He grabbed a greasy dish towel and rushed over to spread it on the table. He sat down and slowly, reverently, began to shake the contents of the flask onto the crowing rooster that marked the center of the raggy towel. His eyes bugged at the sight of the treasure unfolding in front of him. They weren't kidding—diamonds as big as an owl's eye, some of them the prettiest golden color, some of them with a bluish tint, one he'd swear was as big as a robin's egg. That one he had to give an extra shake to get through the mouth of the flask. His heart was beating so fast, he needed another long swig of whiskey. It was hard to believe this was happening.

I'm lucky Lorna dumped me last year, he thought. She said eight years of me was enough. Well, eight years of her was enough. Nag, nag, nag. I was just too nice to kick her butt out. She moved forty-five minutes away to Burlington. He heard she was doing some of that Internet dating. Good luck at finding that sensitive man you're after, honey, he thought.

He picked up a handful of diamonds, still not believing his luck. Maybe when I figure out how to unload some of this fancy stuff, I'll take a first-class trip and send Lorna a postcard telling her what a good time I'm having—and that I don't wish she was there.

Pleased at the thought of one-upping Lorna, Wayne got down to the business at hand. The minute Lem finds out that tree is gone, he'll be yelling that I was behind it. I know my face got scratched, so I have to figure out an excuse for how that happened. I could always say I was pruning one of my trees and lost my balance, he decided. The one thing he did well was take care of the trees on the property that he hadn't yet sold off.

The next problem was where to hide the diamonds. He began to put them back in the flask. I'm going to be under suspicion for cutting down the tree, so I gotta be real careful. I can't keep them in the house. If the cops decide to search the place, with my luck they'll find the flask.

Why don't I just do what those crooks out by the tree did? he thought. Why not hide it in one of my own trees until everything blows over and I can make a trip to the big city?

Wayne wrapped the flask with brown masking tape and then fished around in one after another of the cluttered kitchen drawers until he found the picture-hanging wire Lorna had bought in a forlorn attempt to beautify the house. Five minutes later he was climbing the old elm tree in his front yard and, using the crooks' fine example, he returned the flask of diamonds to the protection of Mother Nature.

21

After her nightmare about Packy, Opal could barely sleep. She woke up again and again during the night, glancing at the clock at 2:00 A.M., at 3:30, and then an hour later.

The nightmare had really been upsetting and had brought to the surface all the anger and resentment she felt toward Packy Noonan and his accomplices. She had tried to make a joke of it, but it was just so *insulting* for Packy to say that he would give 10 percent of his earnings in the diner to pay back his victims!

He's making fools of us again, she thought.

The television coverage of his release kept running through her mind. On one of the stations they had done a quick review of the scam and showed Packy with those idiots Benjamin and Giuseppe Como, better known as Benny and Jo-Jo, at their indictments. Opal remembered sitting across a conference table from the three of them when they were urging her to invest more money. Benny had gotten up to help himself to more coffee. He moved like such a shlump—as though he had a load in his pants, as my mother used to say.

That was it! Opal thought. She quickly sat up in bed and turned on the light. She had suddenly realized that the man she had spotted putting skis on the rack of the van in front of a farmhouse when she was cross-country skiing the other day reminded her of Benny.

The group of skiers she was with on Saturday afternoon had been following the instructor, but the trail they were on had such a large group of slowpokes ahead of them that the instructor had said, "Let's try going around them this way." They ended up skiing through the woods near a shabby old farmhouse.

My shoelace broke, Opal remembered, so I sat on a rock, still in the woods but closer to the house. In front of it a man was putting skis on top of a van. He seemed familiar, but then somebody called him and he moved away. Even though he was hurrying, he seemed to shlump back into the house.

He was short and stocky. He shlumped. I'd swear now it was Benny Como!

But that's impossible, Opal told herself, her mind racing. What would he be doing up here? The district attorney who was going to prosecute the Comos at their trial said he was sure that Benny and Jo-Jo had skipped the country when they were out on bail. Why would Benny be in Vermont?

There was no staying in bed. Opal got up, put on her

robe, and went downstairs. The great room was one open space with a beamed ceiling, stone fireplace, and large windows that looked out on the mountains. The kitchen area was two steps up from the rest of the room and defined by a breakfast bar. Opal made a pot of coffee, poured herself a cup, and stood at the window sipping the special Vermont brew. But she barely tasted it. As she looked out at the beautiful landscape, she wondered if Benny could possibly still be out there at that farmhouse.

Alvirah and Willy won't be up for a couple of hours, she thought. I could ski over to the farmhouse now. If that van is outside, I'll copy down the license plate number. I'm sure Jack Reilly could check it out for me.

Otherwise we'll just go watch the Rockefeller Center tree being cut down, visit Alvirah's maple syrup tree, and then go home. And I'll always wonder if that man was Benny and I missed a chance to get him locked up.

I'm not going to let that happen, Opal decided. She went upstairs and dressed quickly, putting on a heavy sweater under the ski jacket she had bought at the gift shop in the lodge. When she stepped outside, she saw that the sky was overcast and felt a damp chill in the air. More snow on the way, she thought—all the diehard skiers must be in seventh heaven to have snow this early in the season.

I have a pretty good sense of direction, she told herself as she stepped into her skis and mentally reviewed the way to the farmhouse. I won't have any trouble finding it.

She pushed off with her poles and began to ski across the field. It's so quiet and peaceful, she thought. Even though she had barely slept, Opal felt awake and alert. This might be crazy, she admitted to herself, but I need to feel as if I haven't overlooked a chance to catch those thieves and see them in handcuffs.

Leg irons, too, she added. That would be a sight to behold.

She was moving uphill at a steady pace. I'm pretty darn good on these, she thought proudly. Wait till we're having breakfast and I tell Alvirah what I was doing this morning! She'll be mad as heck at me for not waking her up.

Half an hour later Opal was in the wooded area across from the farmhouse. I have to be careful. People get up early in the country, she reminded herself—not like some of her neighbors in the city whose drawn shades were never snapped up before the crack of noon.

But there was no activity at all around the farmhouse. The van was parked directly at the front door. Any closer, and whoever was driving would have gotten out in the living room, Opal thought. She waited for twenty minutes. There wasn't a sign of anyone getting up to milk cows or feed chickens. I wonder if they have animals in the barn, she thought. It really is big. It looks as if it would hold all the animals on Noah's ark.

She skied to the left to try to get a look at the license plate on the van. It was a Vermont plate, but from where she was standing, it was impossible to make out the numbers on it. It would be taking a risk, but she had to get closer.

Opal took a deep breath, skied out of the woods and into the clearing, and didn't stop until she was a few feet from the van. *I've got to make this fast and get out of here,* she thought. Now very nervous, she whispered the numbers on the green and white plate. "BEM 360. BEM 360," she repeated. "I'll write it down when I'm out of sight."

Inside the farmhouse, at the very table where only hours before conviviality had reigned, three hungover, tired, and angry crooks were trying to figure out how to recover the flask of diamonds that had been their ticket to lifelong easy living. The machete with Wayne Covel's name engraved on the handle was in the center of the table. The local phone book was open to the page where Covel's name and phone number had been circled by Packy. Covel's address was not listed.

Milo had already made two pots of coffee and two batches of pancakes with bacon and sausage. Packy and the twins had devoured the breakfast but now ignored his cheerful suggestion: "One more batch of pancakes for growing boys?"

All three were casting malevolent stares at Covel's machete.

Might as well rustle them up, Milo thought, as he began to spoon batter into the pan. Their bad fortune had obviously not affected their appetites.

"Milo, forget the Magic Chef routine," Packy ordered. "Sit down. I've got plans for you."

Milo obeyed. Intending to turn off the pancakes, he instead flipped the flame under the frying pan that was brimming with bacon grease.

"You're sure you know where this crook Covel lives?" Packy asked accusingly.

"Yes, I do," Milo confirmed proudly. "It's in the second page of that article I showed you about the tree. It said how unusual it was to find two trees worthy of Rockefeller Center in the same state, never mind on neighboring property. Everybody knows where Lem Pickens lives, and Covel's right next door."

Benny wrinkled his nose. "What's burning?"

They all looked over at the stove. Flames and smoke were rising from the ancient cast-iron frying pan full of grease. Next to it the pancakes were rapidly turning black.

"You trying to kill us?" Packy screamed. "This place stinks!" He jumped up. "I get asthma from smoke!" He ran to the front door, yanked it open, and hurried out onto the front porch.

Standing only a few feet away, a woman on cross-country skis was staring at the license plate on the back of the van.

Her head jerked around, and their eyes locked. Even though over twelve years had passed, there was instant recognition on both their parts.

Opal turned and in a futile effort to escape pushed down

hard on her poles, but in her haste she slipped and fell. Instantly, Packy was on her, his hand firmly covering her mouth, his knee on her back, holding her down. A moment later, dazed and terrified, she felt other hands grab her roughly and drag her into the house.

lvirah awakened at 7:15 with a sense of anticipation. "It feels like the beginning of the holiday season, doesn't it, Willy?" she asked. "I mean, to be seeing the Rockefeller Center Christmas tree here in its natural setting, before it's all lit up in New York."

After forty years of marriage, Willy had long since become used to Alvirah's early-morning observances and had learned to grunt approval of them even as he savored the last few minutes of drowsy near sleep.

Alvirah studied him. His eyes were closed, and his head was buried in the pillow. "Willy, the world has just come to an end, and you and I are dead," she said.

"Uh-huh," Willy agreed. "That's great."

No use rousing him yet, Alvirah decided.

She showered and dressed in dark gray wool slacks and a gray and white cardigan sweater set, another of Baroness Min's selections for her. She checked her appearance in the full-length mirror on the closet door. I look okay, she decided matter-of-factly. In the old days I'd be wearing purple slacks and an orange and green sweatshirt. Inside, I'm still wearing them, I guess. Willy and I haven't changed. We both like to help out other folks. He does it by fixing leaky pipes for people who can't afford plumbers. I do it by trying to straighten out situations when people are overwhelmed with problems.

She walked over to the dresser and picked up her sunburst pin with the microphone in the center and clasped it on her sweater. I want to record what people have to say when the tree is cut down, she decided. It will make a nice little story for my column.

"Honey."

Alvirah turned. Willy was sitting up in bed. "Did you say something about the end of the world?"

"Yes, and I told you we were both dead. But don't worry. We're still alive, and they called off the end of the world."

Willy grinned sheepishly. "I'm awake now, honey."

"I'll start packing while you shower and dress," Alvirah said. "We're meeting the others in the dining room for breakfast at eight-thirty. Funny, I haven't heard a sound from Opal's room. I'd better wake her up."

She and Willy were in the master bedroom suite on the main floor of the villa; Opal was upstairs in another large bedroom. Alvirah walked into the great room, caught the aroma of coffee, and spotted Opal's note on the breakfast bar.

Why would Opal be up and out already? she wondered as she hurried to read the note.

Dear Alvirah and Willy,

I left early to do some cross-country skiing. There's something I have to check out. I'll meet you for breakfast at the lodge at 8:30.

Love,
Opal

With growing concern, Alvirah reread the note. Opal's a good cross-country skier, but she doesn't know all these trails, she told herself. They can go into pretty remote areas. She shouldn't be out there alone. What was so important that she had to leave so early to check it out? she wondered.

Alvirah went over to the coffeepot and poured herself a cup. It had a slightly bitter taste, like coffee that had been sitting on the burner for a couple of hours. She must have left *very* early, Alvirah thought.

While she waited for Willy to dress, she found herself staring out at the mountains. Heavy clouds were forming. It was a gray day. There are so many trails out there, she thought. It would be so easy for Opal to get lost.

It was a quarter after eight. Opal had promised to meet

them at eight-thirty. It's silly to worry, Alvirah decided. We'll all be eating a nice breakfast together in a few minutes.

Willy emerged from the bedroom wearing one of the Austrian sweaters he had bought at the gift shop. "Do you think I should learn how to yodel?" he asked, then looked around. "Where's Opal?"

"We're meeting her at the lodge," Alvirah answered. I only hope we are, she thought.

23

Regan, Jack, Nora, and Luke left their cabin at 8:20 and headed toward the lodge.

"This is so lovely," Nora sighed. "Why is it that just when you really start to relax it's time to go home?"

"Well, if you didn't agree to speak at so many luncheons, you could be as relaxed as my dearly departed clients," Luke observed drily.

"I can't believe you said that," Regan protested. "But then again, I can."

"It's hard to say no when I can help raise money for a charity," Nora defended herself. "The event tomorrow is particularly worthwhile."

"Of course it is, dear."

Jack had listened to the exchange with amusement. Luke and Nora have so much fun together, he thought. This is the way Regan and I will be when we've been married a long time. As he put his arm around her, she smiled up at him and rolled her eyes. "This is an ongoing dialogue," she commented.

"Let's see what you two end up talking about in thirty years," Luke said. "I guarantee you it won't be fascinating. Couples do tend to return to the same few favorite topics of conversation."

"We'll do our best to keep it interesting, Luke," Jack promised with a smile. "But I hardly think that there's anything dull about the two of you."

"Sometimes dull is preferable," Nora commented as Luke opened the door of the lodge. "Especially when I know that Regan is in potential danger because of the case she's working on."

"It's a concern I very much share," Jack said.

"That's why I'm so glad you're getting married," Nora said. "Even when you're not together, I have the feeling that you're watching out for her."

"You bet I am," Jack answered.

"Thanks, guys," Regan said. "It's nice to know I have a team of worriers behind me."

They walked through the lobby and into the dining room. A breakfast buffet was set up on a long table at one end of the room.

The hostess greeted them cheerfully. "I have your table ready. Your friends aren't here yet." She picked up menus and led them to the table. As they sat down, she said, "I understand you're leaving us today."

"Unfortunately, yes," Nora said, "but first we're going over to watch the Rockefeller Center tree being cut down."

"Too late."

"What?"

"You're too late."

"Did they do it earlier than expected?" Nora asked.

"I'll say. Lem Pickens went over to say good-bye to his tree at six o'clock this morning, and *he* was too late. It was gone. Someone cut it down in the middle of the night, and they even stole the flatbed that was supposed to take the tree to New York. Everybody's talking about it. One of the guests just said she was watching Imus on MSNBC, and he's onto the story."

"I can only imagine what Imus has to say about this," Regan commented.

"Imus said it must have been done by a bunch of drunks," the hostess reported as she handed out the menus. "He wondered who else would bother."

"It's the sort of stunt kids would pull," Jack said.

"What are they going to do now?" Nora asked the hostess.

"If they can't find the tree today, they'll probably go back to the guy who lives next door to Pickens. His tree was their second choice."

"*There's* a motive," Jack suggested, only partly in jest.

"You better believe it," the hostess replied, her eyes wide with excitement. "Lem Pickens was already on the local news this morning, screaming that he thought his neighbor was responsible."

"He could get sued for that," Regan noted.

"I don't think he cares. Oh, look, here are your friends."

Alvirah and Willy had spotted them and were heading toward the table. Regan had the immediate impression that even though Alvirah was smiling, she seemed anxious. That feeling was confirmed when, after a quick "good morning," Alvirah asked, "Isn't Opal here yet?"

"No, Alvirah," Regan answered. "Wasn't she with you?"

"She left this morning to go cross-country skiing and said she'd meet us at breakfast."

"Alvirah, sit down. I'm sure she'll be along in a few minutes," Nora said comfortingly. "Besides, you wouldn't believe the news around here."

"What news?" Alvirah asked eagerly.

As Alvirah and Willy sat down, Regan could see that Alvirah perked up with the prospect of hearing some dirt.

"Someone cut down the Rockefeller Center tree in the middle of the night and disappeared with it."

"*What?*"

"Nobody took Alvirah's tree, did they?" Willy asked. "Then they'd really be in trouble."

Alvirah ignored him. "Why on earth would anyone go to all that trouble to steal a tree? And where could they possibly take it?"

Quickly Regan filled them in on the fact that not only were the tree and the flatbed missing, but the owner of the tree, Lem Pickens, was accusing his neighbor of theft.

"As soon as we eat breakfast, I want to get over there and see for myself what's going on," Alvirah announced. She glanced at the doorway of the dining room. "I do wish Opal would hurry up and get here," she said.

Jack took a sip of the coffee that the waitress had just poured for him. "Do you know if Opal heard the news about Packy Noonan?"

"What news?" Alvirah and Willy asked in unison.

"He didn't go back to his halfway house last night, which means he's already broken his parole."

"Opal has always sworn that he had plenty of money hidden somewhere. He's probably on his way out of the country with that loot right now." Alvirah shook her head. "It's disgusting." She reached for the bread basket, examined it carefully, and decided on an apple strudel. "I shouldn't," she murmured, "but they're so good."

Alvirah's purse was on the floor beside her feet. The sudden ring of her cell phone made her jump. "I forgot to turn this off before I came into the dining room," she noted as she dove for her purse and fumbled for the phone. "Men have it so much easier. They just hook these things onto their belt and answer on the first ring—unless, of course, they're up to no good. . . . Hello . . . oh, hi, Charley."

"It's Charley Evans, her editor at *The New York Globe*," Willy informed the others. "Dollars to doughnuts he knows about the missing tree. He's always on top of everything before it happens."

"Yes, we've heard about the tree," Alvirah was saying. "As soon as I finish breakfast, I'm going to run right over there, Charley. It's good human interest to talk to the locals. It has turned into a crime story, hasn't it?" She laughed. "I sure wish I could solve it. Yes, Willy and I can stay for an extra day or two to see what happens. I'll report back to you in a few hours. Oh! By the way, what's the latest on Packy Noonan? I just heard a minute ago that he didn't show up at his halfway house last night. My friend who lost money in his scam is up here with me."

As the others watched, Alvirah's expression became incredulous. "He was seen getting into a van with Vermont license plates on Madison Avenue?"

The others looked at each other. "Vermont license plates!" Regan repeated.

"Maybe he's the one who cut down the tree," Luke suggested. "Either it was Packy Noonan or George Washington." His voice deepened. "Father, I cannot tell a lie. I did chop down the cherry tree."

"Our local historian strikes again," Regan said to Jack. "The difference between Packy Noonan and George Washington is that Packy wouldn't admit it even if he was caught with the ax in his hand."

"George Washington never said that anyhow," Nora protested. "Those silly stories were made up about him after he died."

"Well, I bet whoever cut down that tree will never become president of the United States," Willy remarked.

"Don't count on it," Luke mumbled.

Alvirah snapped closed her cell phone. "I'll turn the ringer off and put it on vibrate. Maybe Opal will call if she's running late." Placing the phone on the table, she continued, "A priest at Saint Patrick's noticed a van with Vermont license plates standing in front of the rectory on Madison Avenue. Then a mother called in and said her little boy claimed he saw a man run up the block and get into that van. Of course Packy had just been at Mass at Saint Patrick's. The detective who was following him said he even lit a candle in front of the statue of Saint Anthony."

"Maybe the detective should light a candle there himself to help him find Packy," Willy suggested. "My mother was always praying to Saint Anthony. She was always losing her glasses, and my father could never find the car keys."

"Saint Anthony would have made a great detective," Regan commented in the same dry tone that was Luke's trademark. "I should have a picture of him in my office."

"We'd better eat," Nora suggested.

All through breakfast Alvirah kept glancing at the door, but there was no sign of Opal. The phone vibrated in Alvirah's hand as they were walking out of the dining room. It was her editor again.

"Alvirah, we just dug up some background on Packy Noonan. When he was about sixteen, he worked in a troubled youth program in Stowe, Vermont, cutting down Christmas trees for Lem Pickens. There might be no connection, but as I just told you, he *was* seen leaving New York in a van with Vermont plates. I can't imagine why he'd be bothered cutting down a tree, but keep this in mind when you're talking to people."

Alvirah's heart sank. Opal was an hour late, and there was a chance that Packy Noonan was in the area. Opal had gone to check something out. The sixth sense Alvirah could always rely on told her that there was a connection.

And it wasn't a good one.

24

arlier that morning, as the sun was coming over the mountain, Lem and Viddy, hand in hand, were trudging across their property in their snowshoes in anticipation of one last look at their beloved tree before it belonged to the world.

"I know it's hard, Viddy," Lem said. As he spoke, his breath was visible in the early morning chill. "But let's just think of all the fun we're going to have in New York. And the tree isn't gone forever, Viddy. I hear that after they take it down, they sometimes use these trees to make chips for the Appalachian Trail."

As Viddy teetered along, she replied with tears in her voice, "Well, that's nice, Lem, but I'm not up for a hike on the Appalachian Trail. Those days are long since gone."

"Sometimes they use the tree trunks to make horse jumps for the U.S. Equestrian Center."

"I don't want any horses jumping over my tree. Where is the Equestrian Center, anyway?"

"Someplace in New Jersey."

"Forget it. This trip to New York will be the last time I pack a suitcase. When we get back from New York, you can give my bags to Goodwill and take a deduction."

They turned the bend into the clearing, and their mouths dropped. Where their beloved tree had been growing and thriving for fifty years, there was only a ragged foot-high stump. The ladder the workmen had used in preparing the tree for the trip to New York City was lying on its side, and the angle of the crane was different from the night before.

"They sneaked in early and cut down our tree," Lem raged. "Wait till I get my hands on those New York people. It was our tree until ten A.M. this morning. They didn't have the right to cut it down a minute before."

Viddy, always the quicker of the two to process information, pointed to the crane. "But, Lemmy, why would they do this when they knew there were going to be a lot of reporters and television cameras? Everybody in New York loves publicity. Remember we read about that?" Shocked out of her earlier sentimental state, she declared, "This just doesn't make sense."

As they moved closer to the stump, they heard the sound of a vehicle approaching.

"Maybe they're coming back for the crane," Lem said as they stood protectively on either side of the stump. "I'm going to give those folks a piece of my mind."

A man in his thirties whom Lem had met yesterday when they were tying up the bottom branches of the tree was coming toward them. Phil something was his name, Lem remembered. They watched as a shocked expression came over his face. *"What happened to the tree?"* he yelled.

"You don't *know?!"* Lem exploded.

"Of course I don't know! I woke up early and decided to come on over. The others will be here by eight o'clock. And where's our flatbed?"

Viddy exclaimed, "Lem, I told you it didn't make sense for those Rockefeller Center people to cut our tree down early. But who else would have done it?"

Next to her, her husband straightened up to his full height, which had shrunk to six feet one, pointed through the woods with an accusatory finger, and bellowed, "That no good skunk Wayne Covel did this!"

Almost four hours later, when the Meehans and the Reillys arrived on the scene, Lem was still sputtering that accusation for all the world to hear. Because word had already gone out that somebody had managed to make off with a three-ton tree, the expected crowd of one hundred had grown to three hundred and counting. The woods were swarming with reporters, television cameras, and stringers from the major networks. To the delight of the assembled media, what had begun as a feel-good piece of Americana had turned into a major news story.

The Meehans and Reillys made their way to the police captain at what appeared to be the command post at the edge of the clearing. Alvirah was scanning the crowd in the hope that Opal might have gone directly there if she was running late.

Jack introduced himself and the others and told the captain that Alvirah was writing a story for a New York newspaper. "Can you bring us up to date, Chief?"

"Well, this tree that was supposed to end up in your neck of the woods got swiped. We found a flatbed abandoned on route 100, near Morristown, which I think may have been involved in the crime. They're tracing the registration. The Rockefeller Center people have offered a $10,000 reward for the tree if it's still in good condition. With all this coverage," he pointed to the cameras, "you're going to have a lot of people on the lookout for that tree."

"Do you think it might be kids who did this?" Alvirah asked.

"They would have to be darn smart kids," the Chief said skeptically. "You don't just go and chop down a tree that size. Cut it at the wrong angle, and it could fall on you. But who knows? It could turn up on a college campus full of tinsel, I suppose. I doubt it, though."

Lem Pickens was finally calming down. He had not left the spot for nearly four hours, except for his rushed trip with the police to bang on Wayne Covel's door at twenty of seven. Even Lem's righteous wrath could not keep him warm any longer. Viddy had gone back and forth to the house a couple of times to get a cup of coffee and warm up. Now, as they walked past the police chief, they stopped.

"Chief, has anyone spoken to that low-down tree-napper Wayne Covel again?"

"Lem," the Chief began wearily, "you know that there's nothing to ask him now. We routed him out of bed this morning. He denies knowing anything. Just because you think he's responsible doesn't *make* him responsible."

"Well, who else would do this?" Lem demanded. By now it was a rhetorical question.

Alvirah seized the moment. "Mr. Pickens, I'm a reporter for *The New York Globe*. Could I possibly ask you about someone who worked for you years ago?"

Lem and Viddy turned and focused on the group.

"Who did you say you were?" he asked.

"We're all from New York, and you'd be interested to know that between us all, we've solved a lot of crimes." Alvirah introduced the group to the Pickenses.

"I read your books, Nora!" Viddy exclaimed. "Why don't you all come up to the house for a cup of hot chocolate, and we'll talk."

Wonderful, Alvirah thought. We'll be able to ask about Packy Noonan without interruption.

"Yeah, come on," Lem said gruffly, confirming the invitation with a wave of his sinewy hand.

Alvirah turned to the police chief. "My friend went out

cross-country skiing early this morning and was supposed to meet us for breakfast. I'm getting concerned."

Willy interrupted. "Honey, I'm sure she's fine. I'll wait here. She's bound to come along. We'll catch up with you or meet you back here."

"Do you mind?"

"No. There's a lot of action going on around here. Maybe you should give me your pin to wear."

Alvirah smiled. "That'll be the day." She fell in step with the others as they followed the Pickenses to the family homestead.

25

Opal had fainted as she was dragged into the house. The men laid her on a lumpy couch in the living room. She came to immediately, then realized it was better to act as if she was still unconscious until she could figure out what to do. The house smelled of burning grease, the windows and doors were open in an obvious attempt to get rid of the odor, and a cold draft made Opal shiver. Through narrowed eyes she could see that Benny and Jo-Jo must have been the ones to help Packy drag her inside.

Those three crooks all together again! Moe, Larry, and Curly, she thought disdainfully. God didn't bless those twins with good looks, that's for sure, she thought. I remembered Benny shlumped, and now here I am. I should have told Alvirah where I was going and why. And then she had a chillier thought: What are they going to do to me?

"You can close the windows now," Packy barked. "It's freezing in here." He came over to the couch and looked down at Opal. He started to pat her on the face. "Come on, come on. You're all right."

Repulsed by his touch, Opal's eyes flew open. "Get your hands off me, Packy Noonan! You miserable thief!"

"It seems like you've come to your senses," Packy grunted. "Jo-Jo, Benny, bring her into the kitchen and tie her to a chair. I don't want her making a dash for it."

Opal's cross-country skis were on the floor. The twins hustled her into the kitchen, where a nervous Milo was making another pot of coffee and wondering what the penalty for kidnapping was. The windows in the kitchen were still open. The smell of bacon grease and charred pancakes combined with the cold air made everything seem so much worse to Opal.

She looked at Milo. "Are you the short-order cook around here? If so, it looks as if you could use a few lessons."

"I'm a poet," Milo answered unhappily.

Benny and Jo-Jo wrapped a rope around Opal's legs and torso.

"Leave my hands free," she snapped. "You might want me to write another check. And I'd like a cup of coffee."

"She's a stand-up comedienne," Jo-Jo grunted.

"No, Jo-Jo," Benny smiled. "She's a sit-down comedienne." He started to laugh.

"Shut up, Benny," Packy ordered as he came into the kitchen. "I don't see anybody else out there. She must have come alone." He sat down across the table from Opal. "How did you know we were here?"

"Give me my coffee first." Shock and then anger had been Opal's initial reactions to what had happened. She read the desperation in Packy's face and realized that he was supposed to be at the halfway house in New York. She was sure he didn't get a weekend pass to Vermont. Was he up here to get his hands on the money she had always suspected he had hidden, and then get out of the country fast? Was the money up here somewhere? Why else would he and the Como twins have come to Vermont? Certainly not to ski.

"Milk and sugar in your coffee?" Milo asked politely. "We have two percent or skim."

"Skim and no sugar." She looked at the twins. "It wouldn't hurt you two to take your coffee that way." In a crazy way Opal was beginning to feel a sense of satisfaction at getting the chance to hurl insults at these men who had caused her so much misery. I should be more afraid, she thought. But I feel as if they've already done the worst to me.

"I've been trying to diet," Benny said, "but it's hard when you're under stress."

"You've been under stress for four days. Try twelve and a half years in the can," Packy shot back.

Milo placed a mug of coffee in front of Opal. "Enjoy," he whispered kindly.

"Now talk, Opal," Packy demanded.

Opal had been silently debating how much information she should give him. If she told him that someone would surely come looking here for her, would they leave her or take her with them? She decided to stay close to the truth. "When I was cross-country skiing the other day, I saw a man in the yard here putting skis on the roof of the van. He seemed familiar. I couldn't get it off my mind, and this morning I realized he reminded me of Benny so I decided to check the license plate. That's it."

"Benny strikes again," Packy growled. "Who'd you tell?"

"No one. But the people I'm with are going to start wondering why I haven't come back." She decided not to say that the friends she was with included the head of the NYPD's Major Case Squad, a licensed private investigator, and the best amateur detective on this side of the Atlantic.

Packy stared at her. "Turn on the television, Benny," he ordered. There was a ten-inch set on the kitchen counter. "Let's see if they've discovered the stump in the woods yet."

His timing was perfect. The camera zoomed in on an agitated and furious Lem Pickens pointing at the stump on the ground and swearing that his neighbor Wayne Covel had done this to him. Packy picked up the machete on the table with Wayne's name on it.

"Yup. He's our guy," Packy said flatly. "Benny, Jo-Jo, I need to speak to you inside." He jerked his head toward Milo. "Keep an eye on her. Recite a poem or something."

"Someone cut down the Rockefeller Center tree!" Opal exclaimed as the three of them filed into the living room and huddled in the corner, out of earshot.

Milo pointed to the living room. "*They* did. Can you believe it?"

"Jo-Jo," Packy said, "did you get the sleeping pills for the flight back to Brazil?"

"Sure, Packy."

"Where are they?"

"In my bag."

"Bring me the bottle right now."

Benny looked bothered. "Packy, I know we didn't get any sleep last night. I know you're nervous and upset. But I don't think you should take a pill right now."

"*You* are an idiot," Packy said through clenched teeth.

Jo-Jo hurried upstairs and returned a moment later with the bottle of sleeping pills in his hand. He looked at Packy questioningly as he handed it to him.

"We gotta somehow get into Wayne Covel's place and find the diamonds. Even if we tie her up, there's a chance she could get away. Or if someone finds her here, she could talk. We gotta make sure she's out of it until we board the plane and are well on our way. A couple of these will keep her quiet for at least eighteen hours."

"I thought Milo was going to stay here."

"He is. He'll be sleeping right next to her." Packy shook four pills out of the bottle.

"How are you going to make them swallow those babies?" Benny whispered.

"You pour Milo a fresh cup of coffee. Drop two of these into it and stir. He'll drink it. I'm surprised he can sit still long enough to write a poem with all the coffee he inhales. I'll be nice and fix another cup for Miss Moneybags. If she doesn't drink it, we'll move to Plan B."

"What's Plan B?"

"Shove it down her throat."

Wordlessly, they all went back into the kitchen where Opal was giving Milo a laundry list of all the people who had lost money in the scam.

"One couple invested their retirement money," she said. "And they had to sell their sweet little house in Florida. Now they're supplementing their Social Security doing odd jobs. And then there was the woman who—"

"The woman who blah, blah, blah," Packy interrupted. "It's not my fault you were all so stupid. I'd like another cup of coffee."

Milo jumped up.

"Don't bother, Milo. I'll pour it," Benny offered.

"Oh, look at this!" Packy said, pointing to the television as he took Opal's cup and walked over to the stove.

On the screen they could see the chief of police and Lem Pickens knocking at the door of a rundown farmhouse. A reporter's voice was informing the viewers that about an hour ago the police chief insisted on accompanying an outraged Lem Pickens to Wayne Covel's home. "Pickens has been feuding on and off over the years with Covel, and Covel's prized tree was almost picked for Rockefeller Center," the reporter explained.

"I remember seeing that dump when I was a kid," Packy said as he put Opal's cup back down next to her. "It looks even worse now."

The door opened, and a rumpled-looking man wearing a red nightshirt appeared. A heated dialogue ensued between him and Lem. Wayne Covel's face appeared in closeup. It was not a pretty sight.

"Take a look at those scratches," Packy snarled. "They're fresh. He got them from poking around the tree and stealing our flask."

"I hear you cut down that tree," Opal accused Packy. "What did you have hidden in it? Anything of mine?"

Packy looked her straight in the eye. "*Diamonds*," he said with a sneer. "A flask of diamonds worth a fortune. One of them is worth three million bucks. That's the one I named after you." He pointed to the television. "Scratchy stole them. But we're getting them back. I'll think of you when we're living it up on your money."

"You'll never pull this off," Opal spat.

"Yes, we will." He looked at her half-empty coffee cup and smiled. He looked over at Milo's, which was still three-quarters full. He sat down. "Now everyone be quiet. I want to watch the news."

They sat through several commercials, then the local weather report came on.

"It's gray and cold out there. It looks like more storm clouds will be moving in on us today," the weatherman warned.

Packy and Jo-Jo looked at each other. They had called their pilot in the middle of the night and told him to get to the airstrip just outside Stowe and wait. Now with a possible storm coming, their getaway could be delayed. Packy was about to jump out of his skin, but he knew he had to sit still until the sleeping pills started to do their magic. He could feel the window of opportunity for his escape to Brazil rapidly closing on him.

When the weatherman finished his report, there was more rehashing about the stolen tree. Finally, a new segment was being introduced. "Packy Noonan, a convicted scam artist who broke parole, was seen yesterday getting into a van in Manhattan. The van had skis on the roof and Vermont license plates." Packy's mug shot flashed on the screen. "So maybe he's heading our way," the anchor suggested.

"Let's hope not," his coanchor trilled. "It's amazing that he conned so many people. He doesn't look that smart."

"He isn't," Opal said drowsily.

Packy ignored her as he jumped up to lower the volume. "Great. We can't use the van, and now my mug has been seen by people all over town."

"And nobody forgets a pretty face," Opal said. Her eyes felt so heavy.

Benny began to yawn. He looked down at the mug of coffee he was holding in his hand, and a horrified look came over his face. He turned and saw that Packy and Jo-Jo were staring at him, equally horrified. Even Benny knew better than to say anything.

Jo-Jo mouthed the words "You dope" and hurried upstairs to fetch two more sleeping pills. He came down and refilled Milo's cup.

Within twenty minutes there were three comatose figures in the farmhouse kitchen. All their heads were resting on the old wooden table.

"I'm sorry my brother Benny got distracted by the news story," Jo-Jo apologized. "Sometimes it's hard for him to focus on more than one thing at a time."

"I *know* what happened," Packy snarled. "Let's drag the poet and the mouth upstairs and tie them to the beds. Benny we'll stick in the trunk of Milo's car. As soon as we get those diamonds, we're out of town fast."

"Maybe we should leave Benny a note and come back and pick him up," Jo-Jo suggested.

"I'm not running a car pool! He'll be fine in the trunk. I just hope we don't have to carry him onto the plane. Now let's move it!"

26

The four Reillys and Alvirah sat in the parlor of Lem and Viddy's farmhouse. Over the fireplace, in identical frames, were a picture of Lem and Viddy on their wedding day planting the now missing blue spruce and another of a smiling Maria von Trapp pointing to the sapling.

Lem carried in a tray laden with cups of steaming hot chocolate. Viddy was following with a platter of homemade cookies in the shape of Christmas trees. "I just learned how to make these. I was going to give them out today when they cut the tree down, and if they went over big, I was going to make a batch to bring to New York." She frowned. "Now I can just throw away the recipe."

"Hold your horses, Viddy," Lem ordered. "We're getting that tree back even if I have to shoot Wayne Covel in the toes, one by one, until he tells us where he hid it."

Oh, boy, Regan thought. This guy means business.

Lem began to pass around the cups to the guests. Then he sat down on the high-backed old rocker across from the couch. That rocker looks as though it's part of him, Regan thought. She accepted one of the cookies from Viddy with a murmured thanks. Clearly Lem was ready to get down to business.

"Now, Alvirah, is that what you said your name was?"

"Yes."

"Where'd you get a name like that?"

"Same place you got a name like Lemuel."

"Fair enough. Now who did you want to ask me about?" He took a sip of his hot chocolate which was followed by a "hahhhhhhh." He looked around. "You'd better blow before you take a taste. It'll burn your tongue off."

Alvirah laughed. "My mother had a friend who used to pour her hot tea into a saucer. Her husband used to ask, 'Why not fan it with your hat?'"

"I have to admit that would have bugged me."

Alvirah laughed. "I guess he got used to it. They were married for sixty-two years. Now what I needed to ask you," she continued, "is if you remember someone named Packy Noonan who worked up here years ago in the late fall in a troubled youth program."

"Packy Noonan!" Viddy exclaimed. "He's the only one from that group who ever came back to pay a visit. The rest were a bunch of ingrates. Although, to be honest, for years I wondered if he'd been the kid who swiped the cameo pin off my dresser."

"We never had children of our own," Lem explained, "so

we used to take part in that program during the busy season when people were coming up here and selecting their own trees. It did a lot of those troubled kids good. Made them feel good about themselves. Helped straighten them out."

"It didn't work for Packy Noonan," Alvirah said flatly.

"What do you mean?"

"He just got out of prison after serving more than twelve years for scamming people out of a lot of money. He broke his parole yesterday in New York City and was seen getting into a van with Vermont license plates. I was just wondering if you'd had any contact with him at all over these years."

"He went to prison twelve years ago?" Lem exclaimed.

"I can't believe it!" Viddy said. "Maybe he *did* take my pin! But he was so nice when he came back to say hello. I was thinking how well he had turned out. He was all spiffed up. When he was a kid he looked like a bum, but that day he looked like a million dollars."

"Somebody else's million," Luke said under his breath.

"Viddy, when was it that he knocked on our door?" Lem asked.

Viddy closed her eyes. "Now let me see. My memory is not as good as it used to be, but it's still pretty darn good."

They all waited.

Her eyes still shut, Viddy fumbled for her cup of hot chocolate, picked it up, blew on it, and took a dainty sip. "I remember it was springtime, and I was making pies for the bake sale we were having at church to raise money for the senior citizens center after the basement flooded. All the bingo cards were ruined. I can tell you that that was exactly thirteen and a half years ago. It was right after the big Mother's Day storm. Everyone got drenched coming out of church, and their corsages were ruined. Anyway, that week Packy showed up at the door. I invited him in, and he was so charming. He had a piece of my pie and a glass of milk. He said it reminded him of sitting with his mother, and he told me how much he missed her. He even had tears in his eyes. I asked what he was doing with himself, and he said he was in finance."

"I'll say he was in finance," Alvirah exclaimed. "Did you see him that day, Lem?"

"Lem was back in the woods doing some tree trimming," Viddy answered. "I blew the whistle I keep by the back door, and Lem came in 'cause he knew I never blow it unless it's important."

"I got down off the ladder and came in. Boy, was I surprised to see Packy."

"Why did he say he was here?" Alvirah asked.

"He told us he was passing through on business and wanted to come over and just thank us for all we had done for him. Then he saw the picture of the tree over the fireplace and asked if it was still our baby. I said, 'You betcha. Come out back with me and take a look.' And he did. He said it looked great. Then he helped me carry the ladder back to the barn. I invited him to stay for supper. He said he had to get going but would be in touch. Never heard from him again. Now I know why. The only calls you can make from prison are collect."

"I hope he doesn't pay us another visit. Next time I'll slam the door in his face," Viddy promised.

Regan and Alvirah exchanged glances.

"And that was thirteen and a half years ago?" Alvirah asked.

"Yes, it was," Viddy confirmed, her eyes now wide open.

"I can't understand why Packy Noonan would come back here," Lem wondered aloud. "What happened to the money he stole?"

"Nobody knows," Regan said. "But everyone seems to think that wherever he is right now, he's headed for the money he managed to hide."

"He didn't hit you up to invest in his phony shipping company that day?" Alvirah asked. "That was at the very time when his scam was operating at full steam."

"He didn't ask us for one red cent," Lem exclaimed. "He knew better than to try and pull one over on Lemuel Pickens!"

Alvirah shook her head. "He pulled one over on a lot of smart people. I have a friend who lost money in his scam at that very time. Even up to the day before Packy was arrested he was trying to get her to suggest some of her friends who might want to make an investment. It's surprising that he didn't try to get you to write a check. He must have been up here for something else. This friend I mentioned was supposed to meet us for breakfast this morning and never showed up. Just the thought of Packy possibly coming to Vermont and maybe even to this area has me terribly nervous."

"The only criminal you have to worry about around here," Lem bellowed, "is the one who lives next store. Wayne Covel. He cut down my tree, and he's going to pay for it!"

"Lem, hush," Viddy scolded. "Alvirah is worried about her friend."

"Would this Wayne Covel know Packy from when Packy was up here years ago?" Alvirah asked.

Lem shrugged. "Maybe. They're about the same age."

"Maybe I'll see if he'll talk to me."

"He won't talk to me!" Lem cried.

Viddy felt the need to change the subject. When Lem got worked up, it took a lot to calm him down. "Nora," she said quickly. "I just love to read. I even tried writing poetry. There's a new fellow in town here who got a few people together for poetry readings at the old farmhouse where he's staying. But he was dreadful, so I never went back. He read one of his old poems about a peach that falls in love with a fruit fly. Can you imagine?"

"He's Milo, that really weird guy with the long hair and short beard, right, Viddy?" Lem asked.

"Honey, he's not that weird."

"Yes, he is. He comes up to Vermont. Doesn't ski. Doesn't

ice skate. Sits in that junky old farmhouse all day writing poetry. There's something weird there. Right, Nora?"

"Oh, well," Nora began, "sometimes it's good for a writer to get away and work in peace and quiet."

"Work? Writing about peaches and fruit flies is not work! I don't know how long he can keep that up. How does he pay the bills?"

Alvirah felt restless. She wanted to get out and see if there was any sign of Opal. "As you know, I'm working on a story for my paper about your tree. Is it all right if I call you later? Maybe by then the police will have some leads. I can't believe that an eighty-foot Christmas tree could vanish into thin air."

"Neither can I," Lem said. "And I'm going to organize a posse to find it!"

"More hot chocolate anyone?" Viddy asked.

27

Wayne Covel tried to get some sleep after he hid the flask of diamonds in the elm tree in his front yard.

But it was no use. He realized that hiding the diamonds in the tree was a dumb idea. If those Rockefeller Center people came swarming onto his property begging him to let them have his blue spruce, who knew what might happen? The tree in which he had hidden the flask wasn't far from it. Suppose some photographer got the notion to climb the elm and get a good picture of them cutting it down?

Having the flask out of his sight gave Wayne the willies.

Just before dawn he opened the door, went outside, climbed the elm, and retrieved the flask. He brought it back to bed with him, unscrewed the cap, took a quick peek at the diamonds, and then drifted off to sleep, cuddling the flask like a baby with a bottle.

When Lem Pickens came banging on the door with the police chief, Wayne jumped up and the flask went flying out of his hands. The cap went sailing through the air as the flask hit the uneven wooden floor with a thud. Diamonds scattered randomly around the atrociously untidy room and settled among the piles of dirty clothes on the floor.

Wayne answered the door in his red nightshirt and was appalled to find an array of television cameras waiting for him. His first thought was the terrifying possibility that the police chief had that search warrant he was worried about. When he realized they had only come a-calling so Lem could scream at him, Wayne screamed back and slammed the door in their faces. A man's home is his castle, he told himself. He didn't have to take that guff from anyone. He bolted the door and raced back to his room to retrieve the diamonds. After he had sorted through his dirty clothes and was satisfied that he had all the diamonds back in the flask, he was uncharacteristically motivated to do a wash. I wish I'd thought to count my diamonds last night, but the flask looks full, he mused.

Grabbing one of the heaps of laundry, he walked to the door in the kitchen that led to the basement, pulled it open, flicked on the light, and made his way down the creaky steps, carefully avoiding the bottom step that was broken. No wonder I don't come down here much, he thought as he breathed the dank sour smell of the musty cellar. I should get around to cleaning up this place someday, he thought, but now I can *hire* somebody to do it. First thing I ought to do is get rid of that coal bin. Pop switched to oil heat after World War II, but he never got around to getting rid of it. He just closed it off, put a door on it, and made it into a little workroom he never used.

I sure haven't used it either, Wayne thought. It would probably be easier to burn this place down and start from scratch than to clean it up. He dropped the pile of clothes on the floor in front of the washing machine, reached up to the shelf, grabbed the nearly empty box of detergent, and shook its remains into the machine. He scooped up half of the clothes, dropped them around the agitator, closed the lid, turned the dial, and went back upstairs.

His television set was on the kitchen counter next to his laptop computer. He put on a pot of coffee, flipped on the TV, and moved his computer to the table. For the rest of the morning he kept the television on, nervously flipping among the news stations, all of which seemed to be covering the story of the missing tree. He also heard over and over that Packy Noonan, a swindler who had just been paroled, had been seen getting into a van with Vermont plates and had worked in Stowe in a troubled youth program.

Packy Noonan, Wayne thought. Packy Noonan. It sounds familiar. I kind of remember that name.

At the same time Wayne was trying to educate himself on what was going on in the diamond world by visiting different Web sites. I've got to figure out where I can sell these, he thought. He came across a number of ads for appraisals. "We buy at the highest prices and sell at the lowest" seemed to be the slogan for most of the places that traded and sold diamonds. Yeah, right, Wayne thought. And yeah, I know diamonds are forever. They're a girl's best friend. They show you care. Give me a break! He smiled. Lorna would be salivating if she were here right now and got a look at these babies.

As if he had ESP or, better yet, she had ESP, he heard the click that meant a new e-mail had popped up in his box. Expecting it might be from someone who wanted him to do an odd job, he was surprised to see it was from the ex instead.

Wayne

I see you still haven't gotten rid of that red nightshirt and you're still feuding with Lem Pickens. And I hear that if they can't find his tree, yours might be cut down for Rockefeller Center. I know you'd never steal his tree — it would be too much work! Maybe you'd take that machete I gave you for Christmas and hack off a branch or two, but that would be it. If they pick your tree and you want some company to go with you to New York, give me a call.

xoxo
Lorna

P.S. What's with the scratches on your face? It looks as though you have a lively new girlfriend — or maybe you were poking around that tree!

Wayne stared at the e-mail with disgust. Xoxo, hugs and kisses, he thought disdainfully — she's just looking for a free trip to New York. Wants to get in on the act. If she only knew what the really big news was around the Covel household, she'd come flying back on her broom.

It gave him a laugh that she made a point of reminding him about the machete she gave him for Christmas. When he had opened it, she made a big deal about getting his name engraved on it. You'd have thought it was a hunk of gold. Then, slowly but surely, a troubling possibility occurred to him.

Machete.

His tool belt had felt light when he strapped it on this morning to get the flask. When he took it off, he had tossed it on the other kitchen chair. Now he dove for it and, hoping against hope, held it up.

The machete was missing!

Did I drop it near Lem's tree last night? I was out of my bird when I found the flask, so I might not have noticed if I dropped it. What did she have to put my name on it for?

Lem couldn't have found it yet, or he would have been waving it at me this morning.

Those crooks who cut the tree—maybe *they* found it. Maybe they're on the way here. Maybe they'll kill me for taking the loot.

I don't want to be here all by myself, he thought. On the other hand, if I just take off, everyone will think I cut down the tree.

The phone rang. Eager to hear the sound of another voice, Wayne grabbed it. "Hello."

Whoever was at the other end of the phone said nothing.

"Hello," Wayne repeated nervously. "Is anybody there?"

The response was a click in his ear.

28

"He definitely has the flask," Packy reported as he closed his cell phone.

"How do you know?" Jo-Jo asked.

"I just know. Call it criminal instinct."

"It takes one to know one, huh, Packy?"

They were getting a late start. It was 10 A.M., and Packy and Jo-Jo were sitting in the decrepit brown sedan that the owner of the farm had originally kept around for his handyman and then had willingly sold to Milo. Fifteen years old, with dents in all the fenders, a rear bumper held on by ropes, and replacement parts that had been salvaged from a junkyard, it was a spectacular example of a vehicle that only a person as blissfully impractical as Milo would buy.

Between them Packy and Jo-Jo had hauled Milo and Opal to the upstairs bedrooms and tied them to the bedposts. They had tried to revive Benny by dunking and dunking his head in a sink full of cold water. Finally, they gave up, dragged Benny outside, and hoisted him into the trunk of the car. In a burst of brotherly love, Jo-Jo ran back inside and grabbed a pillow to place under Benny's head and a quilt to cover him. Then he closed Benny's hand over a flashlight and pinned a note to his jacket just in case he woke up and wondered what was going on.

"I wrote that he should stay put and keep quiet until we got back," Jo-Jo explained.

"Why don't you read him a bedtime story?" Packy growled.

Packy knew there was no way they could use the van even though Jo-Jo warned him that Milo complained the car wasn't too reliable.

"Maybe you can't hear what they're saying on television," Packy yelled. "They're all talking about me getting in a van with a ski rack and Vermont plates. They're saying I worked up here in Stowe when I was a kid. Every cop in Vermont, especially in this area, is taking a long, hard look at a van with ski racks. We go out in the van, and we might as well turn ourselves in and collect the reward for finding me."

"We go out in that heap, and we're lucky if we get as far as the barn," Jo-Jo retorted.

"Maybe we should go in the flatbed with the tree on it."

Packy and Jo-Jo glared at each other. Then Packy said, "Jo-Jo, we've got to get our diamonds. That guy Covel has to have them. Nobody's looking for us in this heap. Let's go."

Packy was behind the wheel. He put on his dark glasses. "Give me one of the ski hats," he snapped.

"Do you want the blue with the orange stripe or the green with the—"

"Just give me a hat!"

Packy turned on the ignition. It sputtered and died. He pumped the gas. "Come on! Come on!"

"Maybe I should put a hat on Benny," Jo-Jo suggested. "There's no heat in the trunk. His hair is still damp."

"What's the matter with you?" Packy screamed. "The minute Benny falls asleep, you act dopier than Benny when Benny's at his dopiest."

Jo-Jo had the door open. "I'm putting his hat on," he said stubbornly. "Besides, his blood is thin after being in Brazil so long."

In an effort to preserve his sanity, Packy began to consider his problems and his options. Nobody will pay attention to this car, he assured himself. The poet's been tooling around in it long enough. We have to take the chance that it won't break down. At least we know Covel is home. We have to get inside that dump he lives in and make him give us the flask. It's only ten miles to the airstrip, and the pilot is waiting for us there.

Jo-Jo got back in the car.

"Hurry up," Packy barked. "We've gotta get out of here before somebody shows up looking for Sherlock Holmes."

"Who's Sherlock Holmes?" Jo-Jo asked.

"Opal Fogarty, you idiot! *The investor!*"

"Oh, *her*. That one has a temper. I don't want to be around when she wakes up and finds herself hog-tied."

Packy did not dignify that observation with a comment. He stepped on the gas and with a roar the car took off with its three occupants, two of whom were determined to recover their diamonds and the third who, if awake, would have shared that determination.

Inside the securely locked farmhouse, the burner that Jo-Jo thought he had completely turned off under the coffeepot was flickering slightly. Before the car had left the yard, the flame went out. A moment later a noxious odor slowly began to drift from the stove, an odor that warned of escaping gas.

29

The minute Alvirah saw Willy standing off by himself near the stump of Lem and Viddy's tree, her heart sank. She charged through the crowd of gawking onlookers and rushed to him. "No Opal?" she asked.

Knowing how upset Alvirah was becoming, Willy hedged. "Well, she's not here, honey, but I bet anything she's back at our villa right now, probably packing to go home and fretting about missing us at breakfast."

"She would have called my cell phone. I left a message at the villa for her. Willy, we both know that something's happened to her."

The Reillys caught up with them. From the look on Alvirah's face, Regan could tell that Opal was still among the missing. "Why don't we head to your place?" Regan suggested. "Maybe Opal got lost when she was cross-country skiing and is just getting back to the lodge."

Alvirah nodded. "Oh, how I wish. Let's keep our fingers crossed."

They walked rapidly from the clearing, which was still filled with television cameras and reporters. Before they reached the area where they had parked their cars, Alvirah's cell phone rang. Everyone held their breath while Alvirah pulled the phone out quickly to answer it.

It was Charley Evans, Alvirah's editor. "Alvirah, the story's getting bigger by the minute. It's on every one of the cable news stations. People from all over the country are sending in e-mails expressing their disgust at whoever stole the tree. The viewers say the tree represents a piece of Americana, and they want it back."

"That's good," Alvirah said halfheartedly. All she could think about was Opal. But Charley's next statement sent chills through her.

"And as for Packy Noonan, wait till you hear this. One of his roommates at the halfway house was watching the news about the tree stolen from Stowe and Packy being seen getting into a van with Vermont plates. He called the cops and told them that Packy was talking in his sleep the other night. First he kept mumbling, 'Gotta get the flask.' "

" 'Gotta get the flask,' " Alvirah repeated. "Well, I guess he hasn't had a drink in thirteen years. He's probably been dreaming of a cocktail or two all this time."

"But it's what else he was mumbling that is really interesting," Charley continued.

"What was that?"

"He kept saying 'Stowe.' The roommate didn't think of the town until he connected Stowe with the Vermont plates this morning."

"Oh, my God," Alvirah cried. "The friend I told you about who lost money in his scam and who came up here with us is missing."

"She's *missing!*"

Alvirah could tell that Charley's antennae for a good news story had just shot up. "She never came back this morning after an early cross-country ski run. She was supposed to meet us hours ago."

"If she ran into Packy Noonan, would she recognize him?" Charley asked.

"Like the nose on her face."

"I can tell how worried you are, Alvirah. I hope she turns up soon," Charley said. "But keep me posted," he added hastily.

Alvirah told the others about Packy's nocturnal mumblings.

" 'Gotta get the flask'?" Regan questioned. "If he wanted a drink, he didn't need to use a flask. It has to mean something else."

"A lot of people use flasks to hide their liquor," Nora suggested, "so they can have a quick nip when no one is looking."

"Remember, your uncle Terry used to do that, Nora,"

Luke said. "No one was better at sneaking a slug than he was."

"Dad, could you wait until after I'm married to share those heartwarming family stories?" Regan asked.

"Wait till you meet the rest of my relatives," Jack said to Regan with a smile. Then he turned serious. "I do wonder what would make Packy Noonan dream about a flask."

"I'd love to know the significance of the flask for Packy," Alvirah said quickly, "but right now what really concerns me is that he was talking about *Stowe* in his sleep."

Opal was not at the villa, nor had she been there to pack her bags. Everything was the same as when Alvirah and Willy had left hours before. Alvirah's note to Opal was still on the counter.

They hurried to the lodge and inquired at the desk.

"Our friend Opal Fogarty seems to be missing," Alvirah said. "Have there been any reports of anyone injured out on the cross-country trails?"

The girl at the desk looked concerned. She shook her head. "No, but I can assure you we patrol the trails all the time. I'll notify the people at the Sports Shop to go out and start looking for Miss Fogarty. How long has she been gone?"

"She left our villa early this morning and had planned to meet us for breakfast at eight-thirty. That was almost three hours ago," Alvirah said anxiously.

"They'll get the snowmobiles out right away. If she doesn't show up soon, we'll call the Stowe Rescue Center."

Stowe Rescue Center. The very name sounded ominous to Alvirah. "Opal went out cross-country skiing the last couple of days," she told the clerk. "Would you know if the instructors she was with on Saturday afternoon and Sunday afternoon are around? We only skied with her in the morning."

"Let me find out for you." The clerk picked up the phone, called the Sports Shop, and began to ask questions. A few moments later she hung up. "The instructor Miss Fogarty skied with yesterday said nothing unusual happened when they were on the trails. The instructor from Saturday afternoon is off today, but she certainly didn't make any reports of trouble on the trails when they came in."

"Thank you," Alvirah said. She gave her cell phone number to the clerk and asked her to please call immediately if she received any word about Opal. Then she turned to the group, all of whom were wearing somber expressions. "I certainly have no interest in visiting my maple syrup tree at this point, and I know you all have to get going. So go ahead. I'll call you as soon as Willy and I hear anything."

Regan looked at Jack. "I don't have to get back. I'll stay and help Alvirah and Willy look for Opal."

"I'm staying, too," Jack said decisively.

Nora looked frustrated. "I wish we could stay, but I have

to catch a plane first thing in the morning." She shook her head. "I can't back out of this luncheon."

"Nora, don't worry," Alvirah said. "And, Regan, you and Jack don't have to stay."

"We're staying," Regan said with finality.

"Don't look so worried, honey," Willy said to Alvirah. "It's going to be all right."

"But, Willy," she cried, "there is a chance that Packy Noonan is around here somewhere. He's broken parole, and Opal is missing. If Opal and Packy crossed paths, I don't know what he'd do to her. He knows she hates his guts and would be happy to see him back in jail. By breaking parole that's just where he'd end up."

"Alvirah, do you have a picture of Opal with you?" Regan asked.

"I don't even have a picture of Willy."

"Was Opal's picture in the newspaper when she won the lottery?" Regan asked.

"Yes. That's how that idiot Packy Noonan found out she had money and decided to go after her."

"We can get her picture off the computer then and make copies to show people and ask if they've seen her," Regan said.

"Regan and I will take care of that," Jack volunteered. "Luke and Nora, I know you have to pack up and go. Alvirah and Willy, why don't we meet you back at your villa in half an hour? Then we'll start spreading Opal's face around town."

"I have such a bad feeling," Alvirah confided. "I blame myself for inviting her up here. From the minute we arrived I had a feeling something would go wrong."

It was almost as if she could smell the gas that was already seeping through the farmhouse where Opal and Milo were lying in a drug-induced sleep.

30

fter the Reillys and Alvirah left the farmhouse, Viddy began to collect the empty hot chocolate cups. Lem helped her carry them to the kitchen, and it was there that the reality of what had happened hit Viddy full blast. The shock at finding her tree gone hadn't really sunk in when the police and the media were swarming around. Being on television with Lem had been exciting, and then meeting up with those nice people, the Meehans and the Reillys, had been a good distraction—particularly since Nora Regan Reilly was her favorite mystery writer.

But now all she could think about was her tree, how she and Lem had planted it on their wedding day and how Maria von Trapp had happened to come walking along the footpath, stopped to congratulate them, and agreed to have her picture taken. And then I had the nerve to ask her if she would sing that beautiful Austrian wedding song that I had heard her sing at the lodge. She was so kind, and the song was magical. I remember thinking that we'd never plant any other tree too close so that our children would be able to play in the clearing around our wedding tree.

Viddy's eyes were welling with tears as she put the cups she was holding in the sink. We were never blessed with children, and maybe it's foolish, but how we babied that tree! We measured its height every year even though somebody else had to do it for us for the last ten years because I wouldn't let Lem get up that high on the ladder anymore.

When her unexpected company came to the house, Viddy had rushed to the breakfront and taken out the cups and saucers from her cherished set of good china. She never used them except on Thanksgiving and Christmas, and then she had her heart in her mouth for fear someone would break something. Lem's nephew's wife, Sandy, was a good enough soul, but she piled dishes one on top of the other helter-skelter when she helped to clear the table. In spite of that unwanted assistance, Viddy had somehow managed to keep her china intact all these years. A few chips here and there, but nothing to get too upset about.

Knowing Viddy's feelings about her china, Lem carefully placed the cups he was carrying on top of the drainboard. Viddy went to pick them up and put them in the sink, but suddenly her eyes flooded with tears. In an involuntary gesture to brush them away, she dropped one of the cups. But before it fell into the sink where it would certainly have landed on another cup, Lem's big hand swooped under it and saved it.

"I got it, Viddy," Lem exulted. "You still have all your fancy china."

Viddy's response was to run from the kitchen into the bedroom. Then she hurried back into the parlor with their photo album. "I don't even care about my china anymore," she cried. "I know perfectly well that the minute I close my eyes for good and Sandy gets my china, she'll use it when she makes bologna sandwiches for the kids."

With trembling fingers Viddy opened the photo album and pointed to the last picture they had taken of the tree. "Our tree! Oh, Lem, I just wanted to see the expressions on people's faces when they saw it in New York City all ablaze with lights. I wanted the tree to be like a work of art with everybody admiring it and oohing and aahing over it. I wanted to have a great big beautiful picture to put right between them."

She gestured to the two photos over the fireplace. "I wanted to have a recording of the schoolchildren singing songs when our tree arrived at Rockefeller Center. Lem, we're old now. Each year when spring comes around, I wonder if I'll see another one. I know we're not going to go out in any burst of glory, but our tree was somehow going to do it for us. It was going to make us special."

"There, there, Viddy," Lem said awkwardly. "Calm down now."

Viddy ignored him, pulled a tissue out of her housedress, blew her nose, and continued. "At Rockefeller Center they keep a history of all the trees—how tall they were and how wide they were and how old they were and who donated them and whatever was special about them. A few years ago the tree was given by a convent, and they have a picture of the nun who planted it, and another picture of her fifty years later, on the day it was cut down. That's history, Lem. Our history with our tree was going to always be there for people to read about. And now our tree has probably been thrown in the woods somewhere where it will begin to rot, and *I CAN'T BEAR IT!*"

With a wail Viddy threw down the album, collapsed onto the couch, and buried her face in her hands.

Lem stared at her, dumbfounded. In fifty years he had never heard quiet, retiring Viddy say so much or show so much emotion. I never realized how deep she is, he thought. I can't say I like it.

Forget the posse.

He leaned down and took her face in his hands.

"Leave me alone, Lem. Just leave me alone."

"I'll leave you alone, Viddy, but first I'm going to tell you something. Listen to me. You listening?"

She nodded.

He looked into her eyes. "You stop that crying right now because I'm making you a promise. I saved your cup, didn't I?"

Sniffling, she nodded.

"Alrighty. I say that snake Covel cut down our tree. But you heard the Rockefeller Center people say that whoever took it must have used the crane to get it onto their flatbed. So that means it should be in good shape. Now maybe that skunk managed to take the tree, but he couldn't have gotten far with it. He was still in his nightshirt early this morning when I banged on his door. He could have hidden a tree by dumping it in the woods, but he can't hide no flatbed. Our tree is around here somewhere, and I'm going to find it. I'm going to cover every inch of this town. I'm going to walk across any property that has a big backyard and peek in every barn that's big enough to hold a flatbed, and *I'm going to find our tree!*"

Lem straightened up. "As sure as my name is Lemuel Abner Pickens, I'm not coming back till I come back with our tree. Do you believe me, Vidya?"

Viddy scrunched up her face. She looked unconvinced.

"Do you believe me, Vidya?" Lem asked again, sternly.

"I want to. Just don't get yourself arrested trespassing on other people's property."

But Lem was already out the door.

"Or get yourself shot," she called after him.

Lem did not hear her.

Like Don Quixote, he was a man with a mission.

31

"Will you look at all these cars?" Jo-Jo snarled. "You'd think they were giving away diamonds."

"Why do you always know just the right thing to say?" Packy snapped. "They're all here gawking at that stump we left in the ground."

There was a solid line of traffic both coming and going on the road to Lem Pickens's farm. People were pulling over, parking their cars on the rough shoulder, and walking the rest of the way into the forest. It had the feeling of opening day of football season.

"I'm surprised they're not tailgating," Packy growled. "What's the big deal about that tree anyway? If they knew the real story behind it . . ."

"If they knew the real story behind it, there'd be a lot more traffic," Jo-Jo said practically.

The road was gradually curving. As they got closer to the turnoff at the dirt road, cars were parked in a solid line.

"This may be a break for us," Packy muttered as they passed the spot where they had pulled in last night.

The road continued to curve as they went another thousand feet to a wire fence that defined the property line between Lem Pickens's and Wayne Covel's acreage. A television truck was in the driveway of the ramshackle house they had seen on television when Lem Pickens had so rudely banged on Wayne Covel's door and begun shouting accusations. A group of reporters was standing around a huge tree in Covel's front yard.

"That must be the runner-up in the beauty contest," Packy stated. "If I had time, I'd chop it down."

"Too bad it didn't win," Jo-Jo said. "Then Covel wouldn't have been nosing around our tree. Look, there he is."

The front door had opened, and Wayne Covel was standing there, grinning as the cameras were turned on him.

"This works for us," Packy said quickly. "Everyone seems to be out front. We'll go in the back way."

He drove around the bend. There were a few more cars parked there. He chose a space between two cars and parallel-parked Milo's heap where it would be less noticeable than if it stood alone.

Pulling his ski hat down over his forehead as far as it would go, Packy opened the door and got out of the car. He leaned back in and picked up the paper bag that contained Wayne Covel's engraved machete. Thank God for engravers, he thought, or else we'd be whistling in the dark for the crook who made off with our flask. But why would you bother to get a machete engraved? What a loser.

With a nervous glance in the direction of the trunk, Jo-Jo got out of the car and fell in step behind Packy who darted into the woods. They made their way to the back of Wayne's farmhouse. Peering out from the protection of the trees, they could see a small barn. The door was open, and a pickup truck was parked inside it.

"What now, Packy?" Jo-Jo whispered. "You think we can get in those cellar doors?" He pointed to the rusty metal doors that slanted up from the ground and obviously led to the basement.

"First I want to disable his car in case he decides to take off before we get the diamonds. I'm gonna yank a couple of wires in that truck."

"That's a good idea, Packy," Jo-Jo said admiringly. "It's like what the nuns did in *The Sound of Music*. Remember when the nuns said to the mother superior that they had sinned?"

"Shut up, Jo-Jo. Wait here. I'll signal you when I'm finished, and we'll cut across to the basement doors."

Packy ran across the twenty feet of open field to the barn, praying to his dead mother the whole time that no one would see him. Within two minutes he had pulled up the hood, cut a few wires with Covel's machete, and closed the hood with the intense satisfaction that Covel's machete was working for him now. That thought was followed by the realization that the last time the machete had been used was to free his flask from the branch where it had been hidden for over thirteen years. He waited at the door of the barn until he was as sure as he could be that the coast was clear. He raced diagonally across the open field to the cellar doors. A padlock that looked as though it had been in place for many years came apart easily with one blow of the machete. Holding his breath, Packy leaned over and lifted one of the doors. The creak of the rusty hinges made his blood freeze. He pulled it up enough to allow him to lower himself onto the steps. Then he signaled to Jo-Jo to make a run for it.

As Packy watched in agony, Jo-Jo lumbered across the yard. Packy held the door up as Jo-Jo began to step down, but then Jo-Jo stopped. "Should I pick up the padlock?" he asked in what to him was a whisper. "I mean, if someone takes a walk around the back and sees it, they might say to themselves, 'Hey! What's this all about?' "

"Grab it and get in here!"

Packy lowered the door above Jo-Jo, and for a moment they couldn't see anything.

"This place stinks," Jo-Jo said.

"No worse than a gym, which you obviously haven't seen the inside of lately."

"I like the beach."

When their eyes adjusted, they could see one window thick with grime that offered the only light. Packy flicked on his flashlight and looked around as he carefully navigated his way across the cluttered cement floor. The washing machine was clattering.

"Who does wash at a time like this?" Jo-Jo asked. "Maybe he's cleaning the clothes he wore when he cut off the branch. Destroying the evidence, you know, Packy? That's what they do in the movies."

"I didn't know you were such a film buff," Packy snapped.

Next to the washing machine was a crudely put together walled-off section with a door. Packy opened the door and looked inside. "Here's where we hide until we're sure Covel is alone." The tiny room had a workbench and some tools lying around.

The door from upstairs opened, and a lightbulb hanging from a wire over the stairs was flicked on. Packy and Jo-Jo practically dove into the workroom as a load of dirty clothes came flying down the steps. The light flicked off, and the door was slammed shut.

Jo-Jo peered out at the laundry all over the basement floor. "That guy is some slob. And he didn't need to scare us like that."

Packy's heart was thumping. "This isn't going to be easy. We've gotta figure out whether he's alone."

They stepped out of the work area, and Packy ran the

flashlight over the new load of dirty clothes that were scattered around the base of the stairs. The washing machine began to spin with the force of a tornado.

"That thing sounds like it's going to take off," Jo-Jo noted in amazement.

The door from the upstairs opened again, shocking them both. This time in their haste to get back to the protection of the workroom, Jo-Jo tripped over one of Wayne Covel's tattered flannel shirts. He threw out his palms to soften the impact of his contact with the rough cement floor. His right hand grazed what felt like a sharp stone. With a stifled yelp he yanked up his hand and glanced down. The stone glittered. He grabbed it and, holding it tightly, scampered on his hands and knees into the workroom.

Another load of laundry had come flying down the stairs, and the door was once again slammed shut.

"I scraped my hands," Jo-Jo complained, trying to catch his breath. "But I think it might have been worth it." He opened his hand and held it up. "Take a look." Packy leaned over and shined the flashlight on Jo-Jo's chubby palm.

Packy picked up the uncut diamond he hadn't laid eyes on in nearly thirteen years and kissed it. "I'm back," Packy mumbled.

"You sure that's one of yours?" Jo-Jo asked. "I mean *ours*."

"Yes, I'm sure! It's one of the yellow ones. You might not realize it, but you're looking at two million bucks. But what did that nut case do with the rest of them?"

"Maybe we should go through the laundry," Jo-Jo suggested. "As distasteful as I find that task, it might be worth it."

"Good idea. Get started," Packy ordered. He picked up the machete. "I'll sneak up the stairs to see what I can hear. If he's alone, we're going for him now."

rmed with photocopies of Opal's radiantly happy face as she held up her lottery check, Regan and Jack went back to Alvirah and Willy's villa. Under Opal's picture they had printed the information that she was missing and requested anyone who had seen her or had any leads to call either Alvirah's number or the local police.

"We posted a few of these at the lodge," Regan said. "Jack and I found out what trails her group went on yesterday. We're going to walk those trails and put up her picture on trees along the way, and where there are homes nearby, we'll ring doorbells."

"And we'll be looking out for a white van with a ski rack," Jack said. "I called my office and asked them to keep me updated on anything they learn about Packy Noonan or any breaks in that case. They can't believe I was up here when the Rockefeller Center tree was stolen. I told one of my guys to keep an eye on that case as well and to keep me posted."

They were sitting in the living room of the villa, which had somehow lost its cheery warmth. Alvirah's sense that Opal was in imminent danger strengthened with every passing minute. "Opal could be anywhere," she said, the tension in her voice obvious. "She could have been forced into a car with someone. She left so early that not many people would have been outside. Willy and I will go into town and post some pictures and show them to people. We've got to get moving before it's too late. I know I said it before, but I have a feeling that Opal is in real danger and that every second counts."

"Let's check in with each other in an hour," Regan suggested. "Jack and I both have our cell phones, and you have yours."

They left the villa together. Willy and Alvirah got into their car. Jack and Regan walked to the trail where Opal had skied with her Sunday group and followed it into the woods. Today there was no one in sight. As they walked along, Regan asked, "Jack, what do you think the chances are that Opal ran into Packy Noonan?"

"She went to check something out this morning and never came back. If she saw something suspicious and Packy Noonan is in this area . . ." He raised his hands. "Who knows, Regan?"

The snow crunched under their feet as they walked side by side, shoulders touching. Their eyes darted in and out of the woods on either side of them.

"Maybe he has a friend in this area who is hiding him," Regan said. "But why? He just spent over twelve years in prison. He's paid his debt to society for that swindle. As you said last night, he's risking a lot by breaking parole. You know, Jack, it really is odd that Packy Noonan worked for Lem Pickens and Lem's tree was cut down less than twenty-four hours after Packy broke parole and was seen getting into a van with Vermont plates. I don't know why he'd bother cutting down a tree, but it really is a little *too* coincidental, don't you think?"

Jack nodded. Deep in thought, they continued to walk along the trail, and every thousand feet or so they posted Opal's likeness on a tree. They knocked at the doors of the occasional farmhouse they passed along the way. No one recognized Opal's picture or had seen any unusual occurrence. Anyone who was home had the television on and was watching the news about Lem Pickens's missing tree.

"Those two never did get along," one woman crisply observed. "But if you want to know my opinion, Wayne Covel would never have the energy to cut down that tree then haul it out of there. Forget it! I hired him once to do some odd jobs here, and it took forever and a day for him to get them done." She invited them in for coffee, but Regan and Jack declined.

As they walked down her path and back to the cross-country trail, Regan said, "It's been just about an hour. I'll give Alvirah a call." But from Alvirah's discouraged tone it was clear even before she told them that she and Willy were having no success in finding anyone who could help.

Regan had barely closed her phone when Jack's began to ring. It was his office. Regan watched his expression change as he listened. When he closed his cell phone, he looked at Regan. "They traced the registration on the flatbed that was abandoned. It was registered to a guy who knew nothing about the tree, but it turns out his cousins, Benny and Jo-Jo Como, were part of Packy Noonan's shipping scam. And here's the kicker: They lifted Benny's fingerprints from the steering wheel."

"Oh, my God," Regan said quietly. "Maybe Opal had a run-in with him."

"Everyone thought those guys had fled the country," Jack said. "Maybe not."

"Maybe Benny's the one who picked up Packy in the van," Regan speculated. "But a flatbed? Could Packy Noonan really have been involved in the theft of the tree? Why?"

"He paid a visit to the Pickens house less than a year before he was arrested. Maybe he was looking for a hiding place for his loot. As we both know, a lot of crooks don't trust the banks or safe deposit boxes or even accounts in places like the Cayman Islands."

"He made off with millions and millions of dollars," Regan said. "It can't all be in cash. That's a lot of cash to try to hide."

"Thieves put their money in other things such as jewelry

and precious stones," Jack stated. "They can be harder to trace."

"But if he hid jewelry in Lem Pickens's tree, why would he have to go to all the trouble to cut the tree down to get it?" Regan asked. "It doesn't make sense. Well, we'd better let Alvirah know. I'm sure it will be all over the news in a few minutes. Maybe her editor has called her already." Regan re-dialed Alvirah's number.

Alvirah had just heard the news from Charley. "Regan, we're going back to the lodge," she said. "I feel as though we're wasting our time in town. I want to talk to the desk clerk again and find out who was actually in Opal's ski group. I just hope they all aren't gone by now. And I want to try again to reach the ski instructor who's off today."

"We'll meet you back there. We're just about at the end of this trail."

A dead-end trail, Regan thought as she hung up the phone.

33

Lem jumped in his pickup truck and roared down the driveway. The only comfort he felt was in knowing that there was a reward for his tree, which meant that a lot of people were looking for it. He didn't care if somebody else found it first and ended up with $10,000 of Rockefeller Center's money. All he wanted was his and Viddy's tree, still pretty as a picture, on its way to its glory time in New York City. He could just see the look on Viddy's face when they pulled the switch at the big ceremony and its branches lit up with thousands of lights.

Lem turned at the end of his driveway and stepped on the gas. His plan was to drive first past Wayne Covel's house and see what was going on. From there he would go from one barn to another and up some of the dead-end roads on the outskirts of town, where skiers had built homes. A lot of those people didn't start coming around until after Thanksgiving. Covel could have driven the Rockefeller Center flatbed up any one of those roads and just left it there. No one would see it for days unless they were looking for it.

He flipped on the radio. The local station was buzzing with the news about the tree.

"If I were Wayne Covel and I had nothing to do with the disappearance of that tree, I'd sue Lem Pickens for everything he's worth—every tree he has left on his property, every chicken in his barn, all the gold in his teeth," the host was saying. "In this country you can't publicly slander people and expect to get away with it. Now we have our legal expert here—"

Faintly uneasy, Lem shut off the radio. "You people don't know anything about justice," he said, spitting out the words. "Sometimes a man just has to take things into his own hands. Viddy needs her tree. I can't be bothered waiting around for the cops to find it. And they'd probably need something stupid like a search warrant just to take a peek in somebody's barn."

He drove slowly past Wayne Covel's house. The sight of Wayne's big tree made his blood boil. If that tree ends up in Rockefeller Center instead of mine, it'll do Viddy in, he thought. Reporters were camped on Covel's driveway. He noticed that many of the people he knew from town were standing around, admiring Covel's tree. He knew some of them couldn't stand Covel but just wanted to get their faces on TV. It was a disgrace.

Around the bend he spotted the poet's car. You couldn't

miss it, with that bumper tied on. He had a mind to take the air out of the tires. How dare he waste an evening of Viddy's life boring her to death with his god-awful poems? He'd even had the nerve to hand out copies of his poem about the fruit fly. Viddy said he likes to share it with anyone and everyone.

Lem kept driving. Maybe I'll go to the outskirts of town first, he decided. Even Covel wouldn't be dumb enough to leave the tree too close to his house.

For the next hour and a half Lem trespassed on property all over Stowe. He wandered into barns, opened doors, and climbed up and looked into windows if that was the only way he could check out a structure large enough to contain a flatbed. He was chased away by clucking chickens, neighing horses, and a barnyard dog that yapped at his heels as he made his escape.

By now Lem had worked up an appetite but couldn't go home. He did not want to face Viddy until he returned with the tree. He got back in his truck and turned on the radio to see if there were any updates about its whereabouts. That was when he got the news about Benny Como's fingerprints in the flatbed. He hit the steering wheel with his hand.

"Packy Noonan did this!" he cried. I knew in my gut he was up to no good when he happened to stop by thirteen years ago, he thought. But I wanted to believe that he had mended his ways. Huh! And Viddy always said she thought he swiped her cameo pin. I just hope Packy's in on this with Wayne Covel. If Covel's innocent, I'm in big trouble. Not only will Viddy be without her tree, but she won't have a roof over her head. He decided not to let himself think about it.

Lem abandoned his plan to stop for a quick lunch at the diner. I've just got to find my tree, he thought frantically.

First things first.

34

acky crouched near the top of the basement steps, fully aware that at any moment Wayne Covel might have a third burst of domesticity and send another load of wash flying into the basement. Which means I catch it in the face, Packy thought. But we can't wait much longer, he decided.

His knees and back were aching. He had already been there forty minutes.

First Dennis Dolan, a reporter from some town in Vermont, had rung the bell and been invited by Wayne to come in and have a cup of coffee or a beer. Dolan explained that he wanted to do a human interest story on Wayne in case his tree ended up in Rockefeller Center.

Packy had had to endure the story of Wayne's life, including the fact that his last girlfriend, Lorna, had sent him an e-mail just this morning.

When Dolan had finally asked his last inane question and departed, Wayne went back to the kitchen and turned up the sound of the television. Machete in hand and Jo-Jo behind him armed with masking tape and rope, Packy had been about to throw open the door and pounce on Covel when a sharp rap at the front door torpedoed that plan. Covel left the kitchen to answer it, then heartily greeted someone. From the conversation, it was a drinking buddy, Jake, who had stopped by to offer moral support to him about Lem Pickens's accusation. With the door from the basement to the kitchen open a slit, Packy was privileged to hear their exchange.

"Wayne, old boy, I told those reporters that Lem's out of his bird. He just doesn't like you no how and never did. Couldn't wait to lay something like this on you, could he? I get the idea if his tree don't show up, they'll be begging you for yours. Just a little tip. In case they ask you to be on television standing next to it when it's cut down, maybe you better run off to the barber and get a haircut. I'm on my way to him now. How about you jump in the car with me?"

At that suggestion Packy almost cried in frustration. But Wayne refused the friendly overture.

"Maybe you'll skip the haircut, but if I were you, I'd trim your mustache and get a nice close shave, though with all those scratches on your face, that might get a little messy," Jake continued. "Well, I'll be on my way."

The mention of the scratches on Wayne's face made Packy tighten his grip on the machete. You got them stealing my flask, he thought.

Wayne opened the front door as he thanked his buddy for stopping by. Then, to his despair, Packy heard another voice.

"Mr. Covel, may I introduce myself? I am Trooper Keddle, an attorney specializing in litigation. May I come in?"

No, Packy agonized. No!

He felt a tug on his leg. Jo-Jo whispered, "We can't wait around here like wallflowers hoping someone will ask us for a dance, Packy. You can't see much out of that window, but I can see enough to tell that it's getting real cloudy."

"I don't need the weather report," Packy snapped. "Shut up."

The lawyer was following Wayne into the kitchen. "Sit down," Covel told him. "Get out your notebook and write this down. If you think Lem Pickens can send you over to scare me, you're nuts, and he is, too. I didn't take his tree, and he's not suing me, neither. Got that, Troopy?"

"No, no, no, no, no, Mr. Covel," Keddle soothed. "We're talking about *you* suing *him*. He's made slanderous accusations. You see, he didn't use the word *alleged*. In the legal world you can accuse somebody of just about any crime as long as you say you *allege* that someone did something. In no uncertain terms and on national television Mr. Pickens has accused you of committing a crime. Oh, dear Mr. Covel, it is the ambition of our legal firm to see you fully compensated for this insult to your integrity. You *deserve* that, Mr. Covel. Your family deserves that."

"I'm not married, and I don't like my cousins," Wayne responded. "But are you telling me that what I heard them say on the radio is right? You mean I can sue Lem for badmouthing me?" At the thought he leaned back in his chair and laughed heartily.

"You can sue him for damaging your reputation, for causing grievous pain and emotional suffering that will undoubtedly diminish your ability to adhere to your normal work schedule, for throwing your back out when you rushed out of bed to respond to his hammering at your door, for—"

"I get the picture," Wayne said. "Sounds good to me."

"Not one penny do you have to lay out. My firm first and foremost cares about justice. 'Justice for the Victim' is inscribed over the desk of all our associates."

"How many people you got in your place, Troopy?"

"Two. My mother and myself."

I never once carried a gun, Packy thought. I never had to. I'm a white-collar crook. But I'd give anything to have one now. Still, Jo-Jo's a powerhouse. He can hold Covel down. I'll swing this machete around like I'm going to use it on him, and we'll have our diamonds in two seconds flat. Covel won't take the chance that I don't mean it. But we can't take on the ambulance chaser, too. From what I can see, he's pretty hefty, and there may still be some people in the front yard. If someone hears one yell, we're cooked.

Jo-Jo was tugging on his pants again. "You say the diamond

we found is worth two million?" he whispered. "Maybe we oughta settle for that."

Packy shook his head so violently that he banged it on the door.

"That door to the basement sure creaks," Wayne explained to Trooper Keddle as he pocketed Keddle's business card and got up. "Maybe with Lem's money I can get me a new one." The suggestion elicited another guffaw, which Keddle did his best to match.

But at last Keddle, with a final sales pitch about his ability to redress the wrong Wayne had suffered, was gone.

This is it, Packy thought. No more delays. He nodded to Jo-Jo. A moment later, as Wayne passed the door to the basement on his way back to the table, it flew open, and before he could do more than grunt, he was on the floor. Packy slapped tape over his mouth, and Jo-Jo yanked first his arms and then his legs back and tied them together.

"Pull down the shades in the front room, Jo-Jo," Packy ordered. "Lock the front door. Let anyone still out there get the idea that this guy's had enough company." He laid the machete down on the floor an inch from Covel's face. "You recognize it?" he asked. "I bet you do. Maybe it'll help you remember what you did with my diamonds."

He tapped Wayne on the head. "Don't even think of trying to make a noise, or you'll be eating your name off the handle. Get it?"

Wayne nodded and kept nodding.

Packy got up and hurried to the kitchen window. Standing to the side he pulled down the shade, which ended up draped over his arm. It had been tied to the roller with twine. Some handyman, he thought, and with a contemptuous glance at Wayne, he grabbed the masking tape, pulled a chair over to the window, stood on it, and began to wrap the shade around the roller with one hand and tape it with the other.

Jo-Jo had better luck pulling down the shades in the bedroom and living room, but as he was heading for the front door to lock it, the handle turned and it opened. "Wayneeeeee, sweeteeeee," Lorna trilled as she stepped inside. "Surprise! Surprise!"

35

O pal felt the way she had when she was under the anesthesia during her appendix operation. She remembered hearing someone say, "She's coming out of it, give her more."

Someone else said: "She's had enough to knock out an elephant."

She felt the way then that she did now—as if she were in a fog or under water and trying to swim to the surface. Way back when, during the appendix operation, she remembered trying to tell them, "I'm tough. You can't knock me out easily."

That's what she was thinking *now*. When she went to the dentist, it took practically a tank of nitrous oxide to get through having her wisdom teeth extracted. She kept telling Dr. Ajong to turn up the dial, that she was still as sober as a judge.

Where do I get such high tolerance? she asked herself,

vaguely aware that for some reason she couldn't move her arms. I guess they strap you down when they're operating on you, she thought as she fell back asleep.

Some time later she began to swim up to the surface again. What the heck's the matter with me? she asked herself. You'd think I'd downed five vodkas. Why do I feel this way? The possibility came to her that she was at her cousin Ruby's wedding again. The wine they had served had been so cheap that after only a couple of glasses she ended up with a hangover.

My cousin's Ruby. . . . I'm Opal. . . . Ruby's daughter is Jade. . . . All jewels, she thought drowsily. I don't feel like an opal. Right now I feel like a pebble. The Flintstones. Somebody won a prize for suggesting they call the baby Pebbles. When I told Daddy I thought Opal was a dumb name, he said, "Talk to your mother; it was her idea." Mama said that Grandpa was the one who called us his jewels and suggested the names. *Jewels*.

Opal fell asleep again.

When she opened her eyes again, she tried to move her arms and immediately knew something was wrong. Where am I? she thought. Why can't I move? I know—Packy Noonan! He saw me looking at the license plate. Those other two. They tied me up. I was sitting at the kitchen table. They bought diamonds with the money they stole from me. They stole the Christmas tree. But they don't *have* the diamonds, not yet.

The man on TV, the one with the scratches on his face, has them. What was his name? Wayne . . . I was sitting at the kitchen table. What happened? The coffee tasted funny. I didn't finish it. She fell back to sleep.

Just before she woke again, she slipped into a dream in which she had forgotten to turn off a jet on the stove. In the dream she was smelling gas. As she woke, she whispered aloud, "It's not a dream. I *am* smelling gas."

36

lvirah and Willy reached the lodge before Regan and Jack.

"The ski patrol has covered all the trails at least once," the clerk at the front desk told them. "There is no sign of her, but everyone is on the alert."

Opal's picture was prominently displayed on top of the desk. "Have a lot of people been checking out?" Alvirah asked.

"Oh, yes," the clerk said. "As you can understand, we get a lot of weekend guests. We've pointed out the picture to everyone, but unfortunately nobody so far has had any information. A few people said they remember seeing Miss Fogarty in the dining room, but that's about it."

Regan and Jack came into the lobby.

"Oh, Regan," Alvirah said. "I just *know* that Packy Noonan and Benny Como have their hands on Opal. I called the police to see if anyone reported anything, but of course no one has. They certainly would have contacted me."

Willy voiced the thought that was on all their minds. "What next?"

Alvirah turned to the clerk. "I know you left a message for the ski instructor who was working Saturday afternoon. Could you try her again?"

"Of course I can. We left several messages, on her home phone and on her cell phone, but I'll try her again. I know she's a late sleeper on her days off. Or she could be out downhill skiing. I don't think she has her cell phone with her all the time."

"Late sleeper?" Alvirah exclaimed. "It's past noon."

"She's only twenty," the clerk said with a slight smile and began to dial.

As the clerk once again started to leave a message, Alvirah commented, "I guess we're not having any luck there."

"You mentioned trying to talk to the people who were in Opal's ski group on Saturday," Jack said. "They probably have a list of those names somewhere in the computer."

"We do. I can pull that up," the clerk told him. "Give me a minute." She darted into the office around the corner from the desk.

They stood together silently as they waited. When the clerk came back out, she was holding a list with six names on it. "I know I checked out some of these people this morning, but let me look in the computer to see if any of the rest of them are still here."

The lobby door was fired open. A redheaded boy who

looked to be about ten years old charged into the lobby. His remarks to his weary-looking parents who were right behind him could not be missed by anyone on the first floor of the hotel.

"I can't *believe* someone cut down that tree! I mean, how did they *do* it? Mom, can we have the pictures developed today so I can show the kids at school tomorrow? Wait until they see that stump! I want to go to New York to see whatever tree they get with all the lights on it. Can we go there during Christmas vacation? I want to take a picture of it so I can put it next to the picture of the stump."

He only stopped talking when he noticed the picture of Opal posted by the front desk. "There's that lady who was in my cross-country ski group Saturday afternoon!" Bursting with energy, he was bouncing around as he looked at the picture.

"You know this lady?" Alvirah asked. "You went skiing with her?"

"I did. She was really cool. She told me her name was Opal, and this was her first time on skis. She was really good—a lot better than another old lady who kept crossing the tips of her skis."

Alvirah decided to ignore the "old lady" remark.

"Bobby, I *told* you," the boy's father said. "Say 'elderly woman,' not 'old lady.' "

"But what's wrong with 'old lady'?" Bobby asked. "That's what that lead singer Screwy Louie calls his wife."

"When did you ski with Opal?" Alvirah asked quickly.

"Saturday afternoon."

Alvirah turned to the parents. "Were you in that group?"

They both looked embarrassed. "No," the mother said. "I'm Janice Granger. My husband, Bill, and I skied all morning with Bobby. After lunch he wanted to go out again. The instructor knows him very well and was keeping an eye on him."

"Keeping an eye on me? I was keeping an eye on Opal." He pointed to her picture.

"What do you mean, keeping an eye on her?" Alvirah asked.

"The instructor had taken us on a different trail because there was a bunch of really slow skiers ahead of us driving us all crazy. Opal had to stop and sit down to fix her shoelace because it broke. I waited for her. I had to tell her to hurry up because she kept staring at a farmhouse."

"She was staring at a farmhouse?"

"Well, some guy was putting skis on the rack on top of his van. She was watching him. I asked her if she knew him. She said no, but he seemed familiar."

"What color was the van?" Alvirah asked quickly.

He raised his eyes, bit his lip, and looked around. "I'm pretty sure it was white."

Regan, Jack, Willy, and Alvirah, now absolutely sure that the person Opal had seen was either Packy Noonan or Benny Como, were all fearing the worst.

"Where was this farmhouse?" Jack asked quickly.

"Has somebody got a map around here?" Bobby asked.

"I've got one right here," the clerk answered.

"We've been coming up here since Bobby was born," the boy's father said. "He knows his way around here better than anybody."

The clerk placed the map of the trails on the front desk. Bobby studied it. He pointed to one trail. "This is a really cool place to ski," he said.

"The farmhouse?" Alvirah asked. "Bobby, where is that farmhouse?"

He pointed to a spot on the map. "This is where the slow-pokes were. We kind of looped around them this way. And right over here is where the elderly woman, Opal, stopped to knot the lace on her shoe."

"And the farmhouse was right there?" Regan asked him.

"Yeah. And there's a really big barn on the side of it."

"I have an idea where that is," Bill Granger volunteered.

"Can you show us the way?" Jack asked. "We can't waste any time. This is an emergency."

"Of course."

"I'm coming, too," Bobby said emphatically, his eyes wide with excitement.

"No, you're not," Janice Granger said.

"No fair! I'm the only one who knows what the farmhouse looks like for sure," Bobby insisted.

"He's absolutely right," Alvirah said firmly.

"I don't want Bobby near any trouble," Janice said.

"Could you all just lead us there then?" Jack asked. "Please. This is terribly urgent."

Bobby's parents exchanged glances. "Our car's right outside," his father said.

"Yipppeeee," Bobby cried as he ran out the lobby door ahead of them.

They all raced out to the parking lot. Jack got behind the wheel of Alvirah and Willy's car. They followed the Grangers down The Trapp Family Lodge's long winding hill on their way to the gas-filled farmhouse where a sleepy Opal was struggling to regain consciousness.

37

Resolve was one thing. Success was something else. Lem was racing everywhere but getting nowhere. His promise to Viddy to recapture their tree was looking to be as much a possibility as jumping over the moon.

Lem was now driving down Main Street. When he saw the sign for his favorite diner, he hesitated and then pulled over. His stomach was growling so loud, he couldn't think straight. A man can't think when he's hungry, Lem quickly decided. He justified his sabbatical from his quest by reminding himself that he hadn't even had breakfast. I never got back to the house till we went there with those city folk, and, good as it is, Viddy's hot chocolate can sustain a man just so far.

He got out of the truck, and a picture of a woman tacked to a lamppost caught his eye. Lem took a quick moment to study the photo of a lady holding up her winning lottery ticket. It reminded him of the time that he could have won the Vermont lottery but forgot to buy a ticket. The numbers he and Viddy always played came up that week.

Viddy was mighty cool to me for a spell, he remembered. Thank goodness it wasn't one of those real big wins. I told Viddy the taxes they take out would knock your socks off, and then the phony salesmen would start coming around bugging us about buying things we didn't need, like land in Florida that is probably nothing but a swamp filled with alligators.

There was something mulish in Viddy's makeup. She just didn't agree.

Lem's eyes narrowed. The numbers you were supposed to call if you knew anything about that Opal woman were either the police or Alvirah Meehan's.

Alvirah was at the house today. Fancy that. We're both looking for something real important to us.

Lem went into the diner and sat at the counter. Danny was working the day shift. "Lem, sorry about your tree."

"Thanks. I've got to make this fast. I'm gonna find that tree if it kills me."

"What'll you have?"

"Ham, bacon, two fried eggs, hash browns, O.J., and two slices of white toast. No butter. I'm staying away from butter."

Danny poured him a cup of coffee. Over his head and to the right, the television set was on, but the volume was low.

Lem glanced at it. A reporter was pointing to a flatbed.

Lem's hearing was starting to fail him a bit. Like in the morning, if Viddy asked if he wanted more orange juice, he was likely to answer her by asking her, "What's loose?"

"Turn that sound up, Danny," Lem yelped.

Danny grabbed the remote control and hit the volume button.

"—the abandoned flatbed where the prints of Benny Como were found was a mess. But our inside sources tell us that among the potato chip bags, gum wrappers, and fast-food boxes, investigators found something quite odd, considering who was driving that truck."

Lem leaned forward.

"A copy of a poem entitled 'Ode to a Fruit Fly' was found above the visor. The poet is unknown. His signature is impossible to decipher."

Lem jumped up as though he had touched an electric wire. "That's Milo's poem!" he cried. "And it stinks! I am some dope!" He ran out of the diner and rushed across the street to his truck.

As he started the car and jerked out of the parking space, he got madder and madder at himself. *I'm a dope!* he thought again. *It was as plain as the nose on my face, but did I see it? No. The guy that owns the dump Milo rents made his barn bigger years ago. Thought those mules he calls racehorses would win the Kentucky Derby. But the barn! It's big enough to hold my tree!*

38

"Where is my flask?" Packy asked quietly. "Where are my diamonds?"

It was a question impossible to answer since Wayne's mouth was taped shut. Wayne and Lorna were sitting on the kitchen chairs. Like Wayne, Lorna's hands and legs were tied. After Packy warned her that one squeal would be her last, he had not bothered to tape her mouth. He figured that she was too frightened to yell, and he was right. He also figured, in case Wayne the crook started playing games, that she might know where he was likely to have hidden the diamonds.

"Wayne," Packy said, "you took the flask out of Pickens's tree. That wasn't nice. It was my flask, not yours. I'm going to take that tape off your mouth, and if you start to yell, I'm not going to be very happy. Understand?"

Wayne nodded.

"He understands," Lorna quavered. "He really does. He

may not look smart, but he really is. I always say he could have amounted to a lot if he wasn't so lazy."

"I've heard his life story," Packy interrupted. "He told it to a reporter. He even mentioned you."

Lorna spun her head. "What did you say?" she asked Wayne.

"Packy, we've got to hurry," Jo-Jo urged.

Packy glared at Jo-Jo. He had seen the fear begin to fade from Covel's eyes. The girlfriend was right. Covel wasn't dumb. Right now the brains inside his skull were working overtime, trying to figure out how to keep the diamonds. With a quick movement Packy ripped the tape off Wayne's mouth, bringing with it some of the longer hairs of his mustache.

"Ewwwwwww," Wayne moaned.

"Don't be such a baby. Millions of women pay to get that done every month. It's called waxing." Packy leaned across the table. "The flask. The diamonds. Now."

"He hasn't any diamonds," Lorna protested. "In fact, he doesn't have two nickels to rub together. If you don't believe me, look in that cigar box next to the sink. It's full of bills. Most of them are marked 'overdue.' "

"Lady," Packy said, "shut up! Covel, we want the diamonds."

"I don't have—"

"Yes, you do!" Packy growled. From his pocket he pulled out the yellow diamond they had found on the basement floor. He waved it under Covel's nose and placed it on the kitchen table.

"This was mixed up with the dirty rags you threw downstairs."

"Somebody must have dropped it. There were a lot of people in and out of here today." Covel's voice was high-pitched.

"That diamond is gorgeous!" Lorna squealed.

He's scared, but not scared enough yet not to waste our time, Packy thought. He leaned across the table until his face was only an inch from Wayne's.

"I could let Jo-Jo get rough with you. And if he does, you'll talk. But I'm kind. I'm fair." He picked up the diamond and dropped it in the chest pocket of Wayne's shirt. "That little number next to your heart is worth two million dollars. It's yours if you give us the flask with the rest of them right now."

"I'm telling you, I don't know anything about them."

He's playing for time, Packy thought. Maybe he knows someone is coming back here. He picked up the machete and looked at it thoughtfully. "I guess we're out of patience, right, Jo-Jo?"

"We're out of patience," Jo-Jo confirmed grimly.

Packy raised the machete over his head and aimed it at the kitchen table. With a loud thwack it embedded itself in the wood of the table. He pulled it free.

"That's the nice machete I gave you for Christmas, Wayne," Lorna yelled accusingly.

"That's what got us into this mess," Wayne snarled. He turned to Packy. "All right, all right, I'll tell you. But only if you give me one more diamond—the one that looks like a robin's egg. You still have plenty more."

"If you have a lot of diamonds, I'd like one, too," Lorna said. "It could be a small one."

"There are no small ones," Packy snapped. "Covel, you want the robin's egg, and your lady friend wants a little one. You two ought to stick together. You're a real team. *Where's the flask?*"

"Have we got a deal?" Wayne asked. "I get the two diamonds. Don't worry about her."

"*The flask?*"

"But you still haven't promised."

"*I promise! I cross my heart and hope to die!*"

Wayne hesitated, shut his eyes, and opened them slowly. "I'm going to trust you. The flask is in the bottom drawer of the stove, inside a big pot with a missing handle."

In an instant Jo-Jo was on his knees, yanking open the drawer and tossing out pots, pans, and a rusty cookie sheet. The big pot was wedged in the drawer. Jo-Jo yanked at it so hard that the whole drawer came clattering out, sending him back on his heels. The big pot remained clutched in his hands. He opened it, looked inside, and reached in.

"This is it, huh, Packy?" He held up the flask.

Packy grabbed it from him, unscrewed the top, peeked inside, shook some of the diamonds into his hand, and cradled them lovingly as he sighed with relief. "Okay, it looks pretty full. Guess the one we found was the only one missing."

"The robin's egg?" Wayne reminded him.

"Oh, yeah, right." Carefully, Packy shook out more diamonds. "There it is—so big it can hardly get out. But that doesn't matter." He poured the diamonds back into the flask. Then he turned and his hand shot out. As he scooped the yellow diamond from Wayne's pocket, Wayne bit his finger.

"Ow!" Packy cried. "I'd better not get rabies."

"Wayne, I knew you shouldn't trust him!" Lorna cried. "You never get anything right."

An instant later Jo-Jo had taped their mouths. Packy dangled the flask in front of Covel's eyes. "You think you're smart," he said. "Your girlfriend thinks she's smart. Too bad I don't have time to sell you both the Brooklyn Bridge. Anyone who believes a crook keeps his word shouldn't take up room in this world."

He and Jo-Jo started for the back door.

39

The Grangers turned down the dirt road marked "Dead End" and were forced to drive carefully because of the snow-covered ruts and crevices they were encountering. Behind them, Alvirah, Willy, Regan, and Jack agonized at the need to slow down. But then the Grangers stopped in front of a farmhouse, and their back door flew open.

"There it is!" Bobby cried, pointing.

"Get back in the car!" his mother ordered.

Jack pulled the Meehans' car onto the field in front of the house and stopped.

"This place looks deserted," Willy said as he looked from the house to the big barn.

They walked rapidly toward the house. "Look," Jack said, pointing to the side of the barn. "There's a white van with a ski rack."

Alvirah and Regan rushed to the porch and began peering in the windows. Alvirah grabbed Regan's arm. "There are cross-country skis on the floor there."

"Alvirah, they could be anybody's," Regan said.

"They're not anybody's," Alvirah said emphatically. "That's Opal's hat on the floor next to them! We've got to go in!"

"You're right, Alvirah," Willy agreed. He tried the front door and found it was locked. He picked up a chair on the porch and tossed it through the window. At their surprised reaction he said, "If we're wrong, I'll pay for the window, but I trust Alvirah's instincts."

The overpowering smell of gas hit them.

"Oh, my God," Alvirah cried. "If Opal's in there somewhere . . ."

In a moment Jack kicked out the rest of the glass, climbed in, and opened the door. His eyes were already watering from the effect of the gas.

"Opal!" Alvirah started screaming.

They ran through the downstairs floor, but there was no sign of anyone. In the kitchen Willy hurried to the stove and turned off a burner. "This is where the gas is coming from!"

Regan and Jack raced upstairs, Alvirah behind them. There were three bedrooms. The doors of all of them were closed.

"The gas isn't as strong up here," Regan said, coughing.

The first bedroom was empty. In the second one they could see a man tied to the bed. Alvirah threw open the third bedroom door and gasped. Opal was lying motionless, also tied to the bed.

"Oh, no!" Alvirah whispered. She ran to the bed, leaned down, and saw that Opal's lips were moving and her eyes were fluttering. "She's alive!"

Jack was next to her, quickly cutting the ropes with his pocket knife. Regan was putting one arm under Opal and lifting her up.

"If the bedroom doors hadn't been closed, these two would be dead by now," Jack said grimly. "Can you two handle Opal?"

"You bet we can," Alvirah said.

As Jack hurried into the other room, Regan and Alvirah draped Opal's arms over their shoulders and rushed her down the hall.

Jack and Willy were behind them, carrying a totally comatose long-haired man.

Within seconds they were out the front door, off the porch, and hurrying to get a safe distance from the house.

"If we had rung that bell, we might have blown the whole place up," Jack said. "The way that downstairs was filled with gas, the electric discharge could have set off an explosion."

As they crossed the field, they heard a vehicle approaching. A pickup truck was barreling onto the property. Before the thought could even occur to them that it might be Opal's abductors returning, they saw Lem Pickens at the wheel. Without appearing to notice them, he whizzed past and came to a screeching halt next to the barn. As they watched, he raced to the doors, flung them open, and began to jump up and down.

"Our tree!" he yelled. "Our tree! I found our tree!" He rushed inside the barn to examine it.

"Their tree is here!" Regan exclaimed.

Opal was still draped over her and Alvirah's shoulders.

"Packy," Opal mumbled. "Diamonds. My money."

"Do you know where Packy is?" Alvirah asked her.

Lem came running out of the barn and raced over to them. "Our tree's fine. Just one branch broken!" He finally noticed what was going on in front of him. "What's the matter with these two?" he asked.

"They must have been drugged," Alvirah said. "And Packy Noonan is behind this."

"And so is this so-called poet," Lem declared, pointing at the sleeping Milo, still being supported by Willy and Jack.

"Wayne . . . has . . . diamonds. . . . Packy went there," Opal was mumbling.

"Where?" Regan asked her.

"Wayne's house. . . ."

"I knew Wayne Covel was in on this up to his ears!" Lem cried gleefully.

Regan turned to him. "Lem, you know the way to Wayne Covel's house. Ride with us there. Please! We can't waste a minute!"

Jack was on his cell phone, alerting the local police.

Lem looked back at the barn. "No way!" he shouted. "I can't let our tree out of my sight!"

Bobby Granger had escaped from his parents and came running toward them. "I'll mind your tree, mister," he called. "I won't let anybody touch it!"

"The police are on their way here and to Covel's house. Your tree will be fine," Jack said crisply. "Mr. Pickens, we really need your help. You know your way around this town."

The Grangers had caught up with their son. "We'll guard your tree," Bill Granger assured Lem.

"Well, all right," Lem said. "But tell them I have the keys to the flatbed in my pocket. I'm the one who'll drive it home to Viddy. But I'm not getting in any car with that poet."

"We'll mind him, too," Bill Granger said.

Alvirah got into the backseat of the Meehans' car. Then Jack lifted Opal in. Willy followed, to prop her up. Regan, Jack, and Lem jumped into the front seat. Jack turned on the ignition and drove as fast as he dared off the property and onto the bumpy dirt road.

"Turn left up here," Lem ordered. "I knew Wayne Covel, Packy Noonan, and that so-called poet were all tarred with the same brush. If you're looking for stolen goods, I wouldn't be surprised at all to find the loot in Wayne Covel's house. Now turn right."

Milo's beat-up car was on the other side of the road, heading in the opposite direction.

"There's the poet's car!" Lem cried. "But we know he's not driving!"

As it passed them, Alvirah shrieked, "It's Packy Noonan driving!"

Jack did a U-turn and was caught behind a delivery truck. The road was too narrow and winding for him to pass. "Come on!" he said. "Come on!"

When they came to an intersection, Milo's battered heap was no longer in sight.

"They went thataway!" Lem pointed to the left.

"How do you know?" Jack asked.

"Look! The bumper is in the middle of the road there. It finally fell off that heap."

Regan had dialed the local police. She told them rapidly that they had spotted Packy Noonan and described the car to them and the direction it was headed. Next to her, Opal was mumbling, "Get him. Please. . . . All my money."

"We will, Opal," Regan promised. "Too bad you're not wide awake for this."

Around a bend they caught up with Milo's car, which was chugging along. Smiling broadly, Jack followed the old jalopy, speeding up when necessary to prevent another car from getting in between. In the distance they could see a police car speeding toward them, its lights flashing. Jack stopped to allow the police car to make a U-turn and get right behind Packy. A moment later the sound of a policeman's voice on the bullhorn could be heard even through the closed windows.

"Pull over, Packy. Don't get in any more trouble than you're in already."

A second police car went past Jack, and two more were coming from the opposite direction. Inside Milo's heap, Packy picked up the flask and handed it to Jo-Jo. "Get rid of it!" he ordered.

Jo-Jo opened the window, lowered his hand, and tossed it. The flask of diamonds rolled down the embankment.

"All that work swindling those dopey investors down the drain," Packy lamented wryly as he watched the flask disappear. He stopped the car and turned off the ignition.

"Come out with your hands up" came the command over the bullhorn as policemen poured from several patrol cars.

Jack stopped the car, and they all jumped out, except for Opal who slumped down on the backseat. Regan ran to the side of the road and backtracked about one hundred feet. Then, sliding and slipping, she made her way down the embankment. In the snow a metal flask was resting beneath a large evergreen tree. Regan picked it up, shook it, and heard a faint rattle. Smiling, she opened the cap. "My God," she murmured as she caught the first glimpse of the contents. She poured a few of the diamonds into her hand. "These have to be worth a fortune," she said to herself. "Wait till Opal sees this."

With infinite care she dropped the diamonds back into the flask and climbed up the embankment. She ran up to Packy Noonan who was now in handcuffs. "Is this the flask in your dreams, Packy?" she asked sarcastically. "The people who lost all their money in your shipping company are going to be mighty happy to see it."

A banging from the trunk of Milo's car startled them all. Guns drawn, two policemen threw the catch and stood back as the trunk swung up. Benny sat up, Jo-Jo's note still pinned to his jacket, and took in the whole scene. "I knew we shouldn't have gotten greedy," he said yawning. "Wake me up when we get to the police station." He lay back down and closed his eyes.

Regan turned to Alvirah. "Before we have to turn these over, let's show them to Opal."

They hurried back to their car, propped Opal into a sitting position, and wrapped her hands around the flask. "Opal, honey, look," Alvirah urged. "Stay awake long enough to look."

Regan unscrewed the cap.

"What?" Opal asked drowsily.

"These diamonds represent your lottery money. Now you'll get at least some of it back," Alvirah told her.

Drowsy as Opal was, the meaning of Alvirah's words penetrated her drugged brain, and she began to cry.

An hour later Lem Pickens was driving the flatbed through town, honking the horn incessantly. Beside him, Bobby Granger was waving to the cheering crowd that had gathered along the way. Finally, they were heading up the hill to Lem's home.

Alvirah, Willy, Regan, Jack, the Grangers, and a now more alert Opal were standing with Viddy on the Pickenses' front porch. The word of the recovered tree had spread like wildfire. Media crews had hastily set up in the front yard to capture the moment when, still honking the horn, Lem Pickens triumphantly drove the Rockefeller Center flatbed onto his property. The look on Viddy's face when she saw her beloved blue spruce reminded Alvirah of the dazed joy she had seen on Opal's face, and like Opal, Viddy began to cry.

Epilogue

By the time the day of the Christmas tree lighting arrived, Lem and Viddy were practically seasoned New Yorkers. Two days after Lem recovered their tree, they were in Rockefeller Center watching its ceremonious arrival and listening to the choir of schoolchildren sing a medley of songs as the tree was raised into place. The selections from *The Sound of Music* especially delighted Viddy.

Edelweiss, she thought. Our blue spruce is my edelweiss.

They had been invited back for the party that Opal's fellow investors in the Patrick Noonan Shipping and Handling Company had thrown for her. The diamonds were valued at over seventy million dollars, so the investors would all recover at least two-thirds of their lost money.

Packy Noonan, Jo-Jo, and Benny were in prison awaiting trial and wouldn't set foot on a beach in Brazil or anywhere else for a long, long time. Milo had escaped with a slap on the wrist because of all the incriminating evidence he promised to offer and Opal's strong testimony that he had clearly been an unwilling participant who became entangled in a criminal web of deceit. Milo was now back in Greenwich Village, writing poems about betrayal. The $50,000 bonus the police found at the farmhouse was counterfeit. But he'd already won an award for a poem he wrote about a flatbed.

When the police had found Wayne Covel and his girl-friend Lorna tied up, Wayne tried to pretend he had no idea why Packy Noonan had done that to him. His testimony was shot down by the combined stories of Opal, Milo, Packy, Jo-Jo, and Benny. But as Wayne Covel then put it, "If it weren't for me, Packy Noonan would be in Brazil now with all the investors' money." He pleaded guilty to destroying the branch of the tree and claimed that he was trying to figure out how to return the diamonds without admitting how he got them. That story raised a few eyebrows, but in his plea bargain he was sentenced to only twelve hours of community service. Some community service they'll get out of that one, Viddy thought. His ex-girlfriend was back in Burlington, once again computer dating and looking for a kind and sensitive man. Lots of luck, Viddy thought.

The hardest pill Packy had to swallow was that he didn't know blue spruces grew from the top. He needn't have cut down the tree. His flask was the same distance from the ground as it had been when he tied it there. If he had known that, he and the twins could have just gone around to the back of the tree, found Wayne standing on the ladder, forced him off it, and cut the branch that held the flask.

Now Lem and Viddy were in the reserved section waiting for the tree to be lighted. Alvirah, Willy, Regan, Jack, Nora, Luke, Opal, Opal's friend Herman Hicks, who Alvirah had told her was a recent lottery winner, and the three Grangers were with them. They'd all be heading back to Herman's apartment after the ceremony. It was a beautiful cool night. Rockefeller Center was overflowing with people, and the streets surrounding it were all blocked off.

"Viddy, you and Lem did a great job on the *Today Show* this morning," Regan said. "You're both naturals."

"You think so, Regan? Did my hair look all right?"

"It better have looked all right, with what it cost!" Lem observed.

"I loved having my makeup done," Viddy admitted. "I told Lem I want to have it done again when we come back for your wedding."

"Lord, help me," Lem mumbled.

Opal and Bobby were sitting next to each other. He turned to her. "I'm really glad I was in that ski group with you," he said.

"I am, too," Opal said.

"'Cause otherwise I wouldn't be here."

Opal laughed. "I wouldn't be here or anywhere else!"

Herman took her hand. "Please don't say that, Opal."

"This is so beautiful," Alvirah sighed as she admired the whole spectacle.

Willy nodded and smiled. "Something tells me we'll be stopping by every night for the next month."

"Alvirah, we never did get a look at your maple syrup tree," Nora reminded her.

"Honey, we missed a lot of the excitement," Luke drawled.

"I don't need any more of that kind of excitement!" Opal protestd. "And believe me, from now on my money stays in a piggy bank. No more Packy Noonans in my life—the creep."

Christmas carols were being sung. It was one minute to the moment.

It's magical, Regan thought. Jack put his arm around her. That's magical, too, she thought with a smile.

The crowd started the countdown. "Ten, nine, eight . . ."

Lem and Viddy held their breaths and entwined their hands. They watched as in a brilliant and breathtaking moment the tree they had loved for fifty years was suddenly ablaze with thousands of colored lights, and everyone in the gathered throng began to cheer.

*He Sees You
When
You're Sleeping*

*We dedicate this book to the victims of the
September 11, 2001, tragedy,
to the families and friends who loved them,
and to the rescuers who risked their
own lives to help them.*

$\mathcal{T}$here's nothing worse than listening to the sounds of preparations for a great party, knowing that you're not invited. It's even worse when the party is located in heaven, Sterling Brooks thought to himself. He had been detained in the celestial waiting room, located right outside the heavenly gates, for forty-six years by earthly count. Now he could hear the heavenly choir doing a run-through of the songs that would commence the upcoming Christmas Eve celebration.

"Hark, the herald angels sing . . . "

Sterling sighed. He'd always loved that song. He shifted in his seat and looked around. Rows of pews were filled with people who were waiting to be called before the Heavenly Council. People who had to answer for certain things they'd done—or not done—in life, before they received admission to heaven.

Sterling had been there longer than anyone. He felt like the kid whose mother forget to pick him up from school. He usually was able to keep up a cheerful front, but lately he'd been feeling more and more forlorn. From his seat by the window, he had watched over the years as so many people he had known on earth whizzed past, on a nonstop trip to heaven. Occasionally he was shocked and a little irritated when some of them were not made to do time in the celestial waiting room. Even the guy who had cheated on his income tax and lied about his golf score soared blissfully over the bridge that separated the celestial waiting room from the heavenly gates.

But it had been the sight of Annie that tore his heart. A couple of weeks ago, the woman he'd loved but hadn't married, the woman he'd kept dangling had wafted past, looking as pretty and young as the first day they'd met. He ran to the information desk and inquired about Annie Mansfield, the soul who had just flown by the observation window. The angel checked his computer, then raised his eyebrows. "She died a few minutes ago, on her eighty-seventh birthday. While blowing out the candles, she had a dizzy spell. What an exemplary life she led. Generous. Giving. Caring. Loving."

"Did she ever marry?" Sterling asked.

The angel pressed some keys and moved the cursor, much like a ticket agent at the airport, trying to find confirmation of a reservation. He frowned. "She was engaged for a long time to some jerk who strung her along, then was heartbroken when he died unexpectedly. He was beaned in the head by a golfball." The angel pressed the cursor again and looked up at Sterling. "Oh, sorry. That's you."

Sterling slunk back to his seat. Since then he'd done a lot of thinking. He admitted to himself that he had sailed through his fifty-one years on earth, never taking on any responsibility and always managing to stay away from the unpleasant and the worrisome. I adopted Scarlett O'Hara's motto, "I'll think about it tomorrow," he acknowledged to himself.

The only time Sterling remembered experiencing prolonged anxiety was when he was on the waiting list for Brown University. All his friends from prep school had received thick envelopes from the colleges of their choice, welcoming them into the fold and strongly encouraging them to send in their checks immediately. It was only a few days before school started that he got the call from an official in the admissions office at Brown confirming that there was room for him in the freshman class. It put an end to the longest four and a half months of his life.

He knew that the reason he had only squeaked into Brown was that, although he was blessed with a keen intelligence and excellent all-around athletic skills, he had simply coasted through high school.

A chill that was pure fear engulfed him. He'd finally gotten into the college he wanted, but maybe up here he wouldn't be so fortunate. Until right now he had been absolutely sure that he'd make it to heaven. Sterling had reminded the angel at the door to the Heavenly Council that some of the people who came in behind him had been called and suggested that perhaps he had been inadvertently overlooked. He had been told politely but firmly to return to his seat.

He so much wanted to be in heaven this Christmas Eve. The expression on the faces of the people who soared past the window, seeing the open gates ahead of them, had filled him with wonder. And now Annie was there.

The angel at the door signaled for everyone's attention. "I have glad tidings. Christmas amnesty has been granted to the following. You will not have to appear before the Heavenly Council. You will go straight through the exit door on the right that leads directly to the heavenly bridge. Stand and file through in an orderly fashion as your name is called . . . Walter Cummings . . ."

A few pews over, Walter, a sprightly ninety-year-old, jumped up and clicked his heels together. "Hallelujah!" he shouted as he ran to the front of the room.

"I said in an orderly fashion," the angel chided in a somewhat resigned voice. "Though I can't much blame you," he murmured as he called the next name. "Tito Ortiz . . ."

Tito whooped with joy and raced down the aisle, hot on Walter's heels.

"Jackie Mills, Dennis Pines, Veronica Murphy, Charlotte Green, Pasquale D'Amato, Winthrop Lloyd III, Charlie Potters, Jacob Weiss, Ten Eyck Elmendorf . . ."

Name after name after name was called as the pews emptied out.

The angel finished reading from the list and folded the paper. Sterling was the only one left. A tear formed in his eye. The celestial waiting room felt cavernous and lonely. I must have been a terrible person, he thought. I'm not going to make it to heaven after all.

The angel laid down the list and began to walk toward him. Oh no, Sterling thought frantically, don't tell me he's sending me to the other place. For the first time, he realized what it was like to feel completely helpless and hopeless.

"Sterling Brooks," the angel said. "You have been summoned to an extraordinary meeting of the Heavenly Council. Follow me, please."

A tiny whisper of hope flickered in Sterling's being. Maybe, just maybe, he still had a chance. Bracing himself, he stood up and followed the angel to the door of the chamber. The angel, his face and voice full of sympathy, whispered, "Good luck," as he opened the door and pushed Sterling inside.

The room was not large. It was bathed in a soft, exquisite light, the likes of which Sterling had never experienced. The floor-to-ceiling window gave an awesome view of the heavenly gates and he realized the light was reflecting off them.

Four men and four women were seated at a long table, facing him. From the halos shining around their heads, he realized immediately that they were all saints, even though he didn't recognize them from the stained-glass windows in cathedrals he had visited while on vacation. The outfits they were wearing varied from biblical robes to twentieth-century dress. With the instinctive knowledge that was now part of him, Sterling understood that they were wearing the typical garb of the periods in which they had lived. The man at the far end, a grave-faced monk, opened the proceedings.

"Sit down, Sterling. We've got a bone to pick with you."

Sterling took the seat, acutely aware that all eyes were fixed on him.

One of the women, dressed in an elegant red velvet gown

and wearing a tiara, said in a cultured voice, "You had an easy life, didn't you, Sterling?"

Looks like you did too, Sterling thought, but held his tongue. He nodded meekly. "Yes, ma'am."

The monk looked at him sternly. "Uneasy lies the head that wears a crown. Her majesty did great good for her subjects."

My God, they can read my thoughts, Sterling realized, and he began to tremble.

"But you never went out of your way for anybody," the queen continued.

"You were a fair-weather friend," said a man in shepherd's garb, seated second from the right.

"Passive-aggressive," declared a young matador, who was picking a thread off the end of his red cape.

"What does that mean?" Sterling asked, frightened.

"Oh, sorry. That earthly expression came into use after your time. It's a very popular one now, believe me."

"Covers a multitude of sins," muttered a beautiful woman who reminded Sterling of the pictures he'd seen of Pocahontas.

"Aggressive?" Sterling said. "I never lost my temper. Ever."

"Passive-aggressive is something different. You hurt people by *not* doing things. And by making promises you have no intention of keeping."

"You were self-absorbed," a sweet-faced nun on the end said. "You were a good estate lawyer, tidying up little problems for the ultrarich, but you never lent your expertise to the poor unfortunate who was unfairly losing his home or the lease on his store. What's worse, you actually considered helping out once in a while and then decided not to get involved." She shook her head. "You were too much of a good-time Charlie."

"The kind who jumped into the first lifeboat when the ship was going down," a saint in the uniform of a British admiral snapped. "A cad, by George. Why, you never once helped an old lady cross the street."

"I never once spotted an old lady who needed help!"

"That's it in a nutshell," they said in unison. "You were too smug and self-absorbed to really notice what was going on around you."

"I'm sorry," Sterling said humbly. "I thought I was a pretty nice guy. I never meant to hurt anybody. Is there anything I can do now to make it up?"

The members of the council looked at each other.

"How bad could I have been?" Sterling cried. He pointed toward the waiting room. "In all this time I've talked to a lot of the souls who have passed through there. None of them were saints! And by the way, I saw someone who cheated on his income tax go straight to heaven. You must have missed him!"

They all laughed. "You're absolutely right. We were on a coffee break. But on the other hand, he donated a lot of that money to charity."

"What about his golf game?" Sterling asked eagerly. "I never once cheated the way he did. And I got hit in the head by a golf ball. As I was dying, I forgave the guy who did it. Not everyone would be that nice."

They stared at him as his mind filled with images of all the times in his life when he'd let people down. Annie. He was too selfish to marry her, but he always let her keep hoping because he didn't want to lose her. After he died, it was too late for her to have the family she always wanted. And now she was in heaven. He had to see her again.

Sterling felt wretched. He had to know his fate. "What are you telling me?" he asked. "Will I ever get to heaven?"

"Funny you should ask," the monk replied. "We've discussed your case, and we've decided that you seem to be the appropriate candidate for an experiment we've been weighing for some time."

Sterling's ears pricked up. All was not lost.

"I love experiments," he said enthusiastically. "I'm your boy. Try me. When do we start?" He realized he was starting to sound like a jerk.

"Sterling, be quiet and listen. You are being sent back to earth. It is your job to recognize someone with a problem and help that person solve it."

"Sent back to earth!" Sterling was dumbfounded.

The eight heads nodded in unison.

"How long will I stay?"

"As long as it takes to solve the problem."

"Does that mean if I do a good job I'll be allowed to enter heaven? I'd love to be there for Christmas."

They all looked amused. "Not so fast," the monk said. "In the jargon of the day, you have a lot of frequent flier miles to earn before you achieve permanent residence inside those holy gates. However, if you complete your first mission to our satisfaction by Christmas Eve, you will be entitled to a visitor's pass for twenty-four hours."

Sterling's heart sank a little. Oh well, he thought. Every long journey begins with one small step.

"You'd do well to remember that," the queen cautioned.

Sterling blinked. He'd have to remember they were mind readers. "How will I know the person I'm supposed to help?" he asked.

"That's part of the point of this experiment. You have to learn to recognize people's needs and do something about them," a young black woman wearing a nurse's uniform told him.

"Will I have any help? I mean, anyone I can talk to if I'm not sure what to do? I'll do anything to get the job done properly, you understand."

I'm babbling again, he thought.

"You are free at any time to request a consultation with us," the admiral assured him.

"When do I start?"

The monk pressed a button on the council table. "Right now."

Sterling felt a trap door open beneath him. In an instant he was hurtling past the stars, around the moon, through the clouds, and then suddenly whisking past a tall, brilliantly lit Christmas tree. His feet touched the earth.

"My God," Sterling breathed. "I'm in Rockefeller Center."

*M*arissa's dark hair cascaded around her shoulders as she twirled around the rink in Rockefeller Center. She had started taking ice-skating lessons when she was three. Now that she was seven, skating was as natural to her as breathing, and lately it had been the only thing that eased the hurt that filled her chest and throat.

The music changed, and without thinking she adjusted to the new, softer rhythm, a waltz. For a moment she pretended she was with Daddy. She could almost feel his hand linked with hers, could almost see NorNor, her grandmother, smiling at her.

Then she remembered that she really didn't want to skate with Daddy or even talk to him, or to NorNor. They had gone away, hardly saying good-bye to her. The first bunch of times they phoned she had pleaded with them to come back or to let her come visit them, but they had said that was impossible. Now when they called, she wouldn't talk to them.

She didn't care, she told herself.

But still, she closed her eyes whenever a car she was in happened to drive past NorNor's restaurant; it hurt to remember how much fun it had been to go there with Daddy. The place was always crowded, sometimes NorNor played the piano, and people always asked Daddy to sing. Sometimes they'd bring over his CD and ask him to sign the cover.

Now she never went there. She had heard Mommy tell Roy—he was Mommy's husband now—that without NorNor, the restaurant was really struggling and would probably have to close soon.

What did Daddy and NorNor expect when they went away? Marissa wondered. NorNor always said that unless she was there every night the place would fall on its face. "It's my living room," she used to tell Marissa. "You don't invite people over to your house and not be there."

If NorNor loved her restaurant so much, why did she go away? And if Daddy and NorNor loved *her* like they said, why did they leave her behind?

She hadn't seen them in almost a whole year. Christmas Eve was her birthday. She would be eight years old, and even though she still was very angry with them, she had promised God that if the bell rang on Christmas Eve and they were standing at the door, she would never be mean to anyone as long as she lived and would help Mommy with the babies and stop acting bored when Roy told the same stupid stories over and over. If it would help, she'd even promise never to skate again as long as she lived, but she knew that was a promise Daddy wouldn't want her to make, because if he ever *did* come back, he'd want to take her skating.

The music stopped and the skating teacher, Miss Carr, who had brought twelve students to Rockefeller Center as a special treat, motioned that it was time to go. Marissa did one final pirouette before she coasted to the exit. The minute she started to untie her laces the hurt came back. She could feel it growing around her heart and filling her chest and then rising like a tide into her throat. But though it was a struggle, she managed to keep it from pressing against her eyes.

"You're a terrific skater," one of the attendants said. "You'll be a star like Tara Lipinsky when you grow up."

NorNor used to tell her that all the time. Before she could help herself, Marissa's eyes began to blur. Turning her head so that the attendant wouldn't see that she was almost crying, she looked straight into the eyes of a man who was standing at the fence around the rink. He was wearing a funny-looking hat and coat, but he had a nice face and he was sort of smiling at her.

"Come along, Marissa," Miss Carr called, and Marissa, hearing the slightly grouchy tone in her teacher's voice, began to run to catch up with the other kids.

"It seems familiar and yet so different," Sterling murmured to himself as he glanced around Rockefeller Center. For one thing it was far more crowded than the last time he was here. Every inch of space seemed to be filled with people. Some were carrying shopping bags laden with gifts, hurrying about, while others stood gazing up at the big tree.

This tree seemed taller than the last one he had seen here—forty-six years ago—and it had more lights on it than he remembered. It was magnificent, but so different from the otherworldly light he had experienced in the celestial conference room.

Even though he'd grown up on Seventieth Street off Fifth Avenue, and lived most of his life in Manhattan, a sudden wave of homesickness for the celestial life swept over him. He needed to find the person he was supposed to help so he could complete his mission.

Two young children came racing toward him. He stepped aside before they ran into him, then realized he had bumped into a woman who was admiring the tree.

"I beg your pardon," he said. "I hope I didn't hurt you?" She did not look at him or indicate that she had heard a single word he said, or even that she'd felt the bump.

She doesn't know I'm here, he realized. He had a moment of total dismay. How can I help someone if that person can't see or hear me? he wondered. The council really left me to sink or swim on my own.

Sterling looked into the faces of the passersby. They were talking to each other, laughing, carrying packages, pointing to the tree. No one seemed to be in any special distress. He thought of how the admiral said he never helped an old lady cross the street. Maybe he should try to find one now.

He walked quickly toward Fifth Avenue and was appalled at the volume of traffic he saw. He passed a shop window, then stopped, astonished when he saw his reflection gazing back at him. Other people couldn't see him, but he could see himself. He studied his image in the window. Not bad, old boy, he thought admiringly. It was the first time he'd seen his reflection since that fateful morning when he left for the golf course. He noted his salt-and-pepper hair, in the early stages of recession, his somewhat angular features, his lean, muscular body. He was wearing his winter outerwear: a dark blue chesterfield coat with a velvet collar, his favorite hat, a gray felt homburg, and gray kidskin gloves. Noticing the way other people were dressed, he realized that his clothing must have gone out of style.

If people could see me, they'd think I was heading for a costume party, he decided.

At Fifth Avenue, he looked uptown. His best friend used to

work at American President Lines. The office was gone. He was aware that many of the shops and firms that he remembered had been replaced. Well, it *has* been forty-six years, he thought. Now, where is the sweet old lady who requires assistance?

It was almost as though the council had heard him. An elderly woman with a cane began crossing the street as the light was turning red. That's too dangerous, he thought, even though the traffic was barely crawling.

Taking long strides, he rushed to assist her, but was chagrined to see that a young man had recognized her plight and was already grabbing her elbow.

"Leave me alone," she screamed. "I've gotten by for a long time without the likes of you trying to grab my pocketbook."

The young man muttered something under his breath, dropped her arm, and left her in the middle of the street. Horns blared, but the traffic stopped as, without any indication of haste, the old lady made her way to the curb.

Clearly the council didn't send me back to earth for her, Sterling decided.

There was a long line in front of the Saks Fifth Avenue windows. He wondered what they were looking at that was so special. Nothing but clothes was ever displayed in those windows, he thought. From the corner of his eye he could see the spires of Saint Patrick's Cathedral, and he felt his sense of urgency deepen.

Let's reason this out, he thought. I was sent to help someone, and I was placed in Rockefeller Center. That certainly suggests that I'm supposed to begin my task there. Sterling turned and retraced his steps.

With ever-increasing care he studied the faces of the people he was passing. A couple walked by, both wearing skintight, black leather outfits, both also appearing to have been scalped. Pierced noses and eyebrows completed the fashion statement. He tried not to stare. Times sure have changed, he thought.

As he moved through the crowd, he sensed he was being drawn back toward the majestic Christmas tree that was the heart of the holiday season at Rockefeller Center.

He found himself standing next to a more traditional looking young couple, holding hands and appearing to be very much in love. He felt like an eavesdropper, but he had to hear what they were saying. Something made him certain the young man was about to propose. Go for it, he thought. Before it's too late.

"I've decided it's time," the young man said.

"I'm ready too." The girl's eyes were shining.

Where's the ring? Sterling wondered.

"We'll move in together for six months and see how it works out."

The young woman looked blissful. "I'm so happy," she whispered.

Shaking his head, Sterling turned away. That was never an option in my time, he told himself. Somewhat discouraged, he walked to the railing overlooking the ice-skating rink and looked down. The music was just ending, and skaters were heading for the exit. He saw one little girl give a final twirl. She's very good, he thought admiringly.

A moment later she looked up, and he could see that she was trying to blink back tears. Their eyes locked. Does she see me? Sterling wondered. He couldn't be sure, but he was certain that she had sensed his presence, and that she needed him. As he watched her slowly skate off the ice, her shoulders drooping noticeably, he knew with certainty that she was the one he had been sent to help.

He watched as she changed into her shoes and then headed up the stairs from the rink. He momentarily lost her in the crowd, but then caught up with her just as she was boarding a van marked MADISON VILLAGE SCHOOLS that was waiting on Forty-ninth Street. So that's where they were going, he thought—Long Island. He heard the teacher call his new little charge Marissa. Obviously the youngest student in the group, she went straight to the back and sat alone in the last seat. Quickly becoming comfortable in the knowledge that no one could see him, he followed the little girl onto the van and slid into the seat across the aisle from her. She glanced in his direction several times, as if she somehow were aware that he was there.

Sterling settled back. He was on his way. He looked over at Marissa, who had leaned against the window and closed her eyes. What was weighing so heavily on that little girl's heart? Who was she thinking about?

He couldn't wait to see what was going on in her home.

"*I* can't believe it. Another Christmas with Mama so many miles away." Eddie Badgett was close to tears. "I miss my homeland. I miss my mama. I want to see her."

His ruddy face dissolved in grief. He ran his thick fingers through his plentiful grizzled hair.

The Yuletide season had thrown Eddie into a blue funk that all his worldly wealth, accumulated through loan-sharking and pyramid schemes, could not erase.

He was speaking to his brother Junior, who, at fifty-four, was three years younger. Junior had been named for their father, who had spent most of his sons' lives incarcerated in a dank prison cell in Wallonia, a tiny country bordering Albania.

The brothers were in the room their pricey decorator had grandly dubbed the library, and which he had filled with books that neither one of them had any intention of reading.

The Badgetts' mansion, set on twelve acres on Long Island's North Shore gold coast, was a tribute to the ability of the brothers to separate other human beings from their hard-earned assets.

Their lawyer, Charlie Santoli, was with them in the library, seated at the ornate marble table, his briefcase beside him, an open file in front of him.

Santoli, a small, neat, sixtyish man with the unfortunate tendency to complete his daily toilette with a substantial quantity of Manly Elegance cologne, eyed the brothers with his usual combination of disdain and fear.

It frequently occurred to him that in appearance the pair resembled a bowling ball and a baseball bat. Eddie was short, squat, rounded, hard. Junior was tall, lean, powerful. And sinister—he could chill a room with his smile or even the grin he considered ingratiating.

Charlie's mouth was dry. It was his unhappy duty to tell the brothers that he'd been unable to get another postponement of their trial for racketeering, loan-sharking, arson, and attempted murder. Which meant that Billy Campbell, the handsome, thirty-year-old, climbing-the-charts rock singer, and his glamorous mother, aging cabaret singer and popular restaurant owner Nor Kelly, would be whisked out of hiding and brought to federal court. Their testimony would put Eddie and Junior in prison cells that they could cover with pictures of Mama, because they'd never lay eyes on her again. But Santoli knew that, even from prison, they would manage to make sure that Billy Campbell never sang another note, and that his mother, Nor Kelly, never welcomed another patron to her restaurant.

"You're too scared to talk to us," Junior barked. "But you'd better start. We're all ears."

"Yeah," Eddie echoed, as he dabbed his eyes and blew his nose, "we're all ears."

$\mathcal{M}$adison Village was a few exits past Syosset on the Long Island Expressway.

At the school parking lot, Sterling followed Marissa off the van. Wet snowflakes swirled around them. A guy in his late thirties, with thinning sandy hair—tall, lanky, the kind Sterling's mother would describe as "a long drink of water"— called to Marissa and waved vigorously.

"Over here, honey pie. Hurry. No hat on? You'll catch a cold."

Sterling heard Marissa groan as she ran toward a beige sedan parked in the midst of a half-dozen vehicles that looked to Sterling more like trucks than cars. He had noticed a lot of this kind of vehicle on the highway. He shrugged. Just another change in the last forty-six years.

Marissa said, "Hi, Roy," as she hopped into the front seat. Sterling squeezed himself into the back between two tiny seats that were obviously for very small children. What will they think of next? Sterling wondered. When I was a toddler, my mother used to drive with me in her lap and let me help her steer.

"How's our little Olympic skater?" Roy asked Marissa. Sterling could tell he was trying his best to be pleasant, but Marissa wasn't having any of it.

"Good," she replied without a trace of enthusiasm.

Who is this guy? Sterling wondered. It can't be her father. Maybe an uncle? The mother's boyfriend?

"Fasten your seat belt, princess," Roy cautioned in a too-cheery voice.

Honey pie? Princess? Olympic skater? This guy is embarrassing, Sterling thought.

Give me a break, Marissa sighed.

Startled, Sterling looked for Roy's reaction. There was none. Roy was staring straight ahead, paying rapt attention to the road. His hands were wrapped tightly around the steering wheel, and he was driving ten miles below the speed limit.

I could skate home faster, Marissa moaned.

Sterling was inordinately pleased to realize that he not only had the power to make himself visible to her on demand, but when he tuned in, he could read her thoughts as well. The Heavenly Council was obviously making certain tools and powers available to him, but leaving it up to him to discover their extent. They certainly weren't going to make it easy for him.

He leaned back, aware that even though he was not there in the flesh, he nonetheless felt crowded and uncomfortable. He had had much the same reaction when he'd bumped into the woman at the skating rink.

The rest of the seven-minute ride home was spent mostly

in silence, except for the radio, which was tuned to a station playing particularly bland music.

Marissa remembered the time she had switched the station in Daddy's car to the one that played this stuff. He had said, "You're kidding! Haven't I given you any taste in music?"

"This is the station Roy listens to!" Marissa had cried triumphantly. They had laughed together.

"How your mother went from me to him I'll never know," Daddy had marveled.

So that's it, Sterling thought. Roy is her stepfather. But where's her father, and why, now that she's thought about him, is she both sad and angry?

"Roy went to pick her up. They should be here any minute, but I don't think she'll want to talk to you, Billy. I've tried to explain that it isn't your fault that you and Nor have to stay away for a while, but she isn't buying it." Denise Ward was on her cordless phone, talking to Marissa's father, her ex-husband, and trying to keep her two-year-old twin boys from pulling down the Christmas tree.

"I understand, but it's killing me that—"

"Roy Junior, let go of that tinsel!" Denise interrupted, her voice rising. "Robert, leave the baby Jesus alone. I said . . . Hold on, Billy."

Two thousand miles away, Billy Campbell's concerned expression cleared for a moment. He was holding up the receiver so that his mother, Nor Kelly, could hear the conversation. Now he raised his eyebrows. "I think the baby Jesus just went flying across the room," he whispered.

"Sorry, Billy," Denise said, back on the phone. "Look, it's pretty hectic here. The munchkins are all excited about Christmas. Maybe you'd better call back in fifteen minutes, even though it's going to be a waste of time. Marissa just doesn't want to talk to either you or Nor."

"Denise, I know you've got your hands full," Billy Campbell said quietly. "You have the packages we sent, but is there anything Marissa really needs? Maybe she's talked about something special I could still get for her."

He heard a loud crash and the sound of a wailing two-year-old.

"Oh my God, the Waterford angel," Denise Ward nearly sobbed. "Don't go near it, Robert. Do you hear me? You'll get cut." Her voice taut with anger, she snapped, "You want to know what Marissa needs, Billy? She needs you and Nor, and she needs both of you soon. I'm worried sick about her. Roy is too. He tries so hard with her, and she simply won't respond."

"How do you think I feel, Denise?" Billy asked, his voice rising. "I'd give my right arm to be with Marissa. My guts are torn out every day that I'm not with her. I'm grateful that Roy is there for her, but she's my kid and I miss her."

"I think of how lucky I am to have met a dependable man who has a nice steady job, who isn't out till all hours playing with a rock group, and doesn't get himself into situations where he has to hightail it out of town." Denise did not pause for breath. "Marissa is hurting. Have you got that, Billy? Her birthday is in four days. Christmas Eve. I don't know what she'll be like when you're not here for that. The child feels abandoned."

Nor Kelly saw the expression of pain that came over her son's face and watched as he clasped his hand over his forehead. Her ex-daughter-in-law was a good mother, but was nearing the end of her rope out of frustration with the situation. She wanted them back for Marissa's sake, but would be frantic with worry that Marissa might be in danger if they were around.

"So, Billy, I'll tell her you called. I've got to hang up. Oh, wait a minute. The car just pulled into the driveway. I'll see if she'll talk to you."

A nice house, Sterling thought as he followed Marissa and Roy up the steps. Tudor style. Evergreens covered with blue lights. A small sleigh with Santa and the eight reindeer on the lawn. Everything pristine. He was sure Roy was a neatnik.

Roy unlocked the door and flung it open. "Where are my munchkins?" he called playfully. "Roy Junior, Robert, your daddy's back."

Sterling jumped aside as two identical sandy-haired toddlers raced toward them. He could see into the living room where a pretty blond woman, looking extremely harried, was holding a phone with no cord (obviously another innovation since Sterling's departure). She gestured to Marissa. "Your dad and NorNor want to talk to you very, very much," she said.

Marissa walked into the living room, took the phone from her mother, and to Sterling's astonishment, replaced the receiver on the cradle, and, her eyes brimming with tears, ran upstairs.

Wow! Sterling thought.

He didn't yet know what the problem was, but he empathized with the helpless glance Marissa's mother exchanged with her husband. It looks as though I've got my work cut out for me, he decided. Marissa needs help *now*.

He followed Marissa up the stairs and knocked on the door of her room.

"Please leave me alone, Mom. I'm not hungry, and I don't want to eat."

"It's not Mom, Marissa," Sterling said.

He heard the lock turn, and the door opened slowly. Marissa's eyes widened, and her woebegone expression changed to one of astonishment. "I saw you when I was skating and then when I got in the van," she whispered. "But then I didn't see you anymore. Are you a ghost?"

Sterling smiled at her. "Not really a ghost. I'm more on the order of an angel, but I'm not really an angel. In fact that's why I'm here."

"You want to help me, don't you?"

Sterling felt a wrench of tenderness as he looked into Marissa's troubled blue eyes. "I want to help you more than anything in the world. For my sake as well as yours."

"Are you in trouble with God?"

"Let's just say he's not thrilled with me at the moment. He doesn't think I'm ready for heaven yet."

Marissa rolled her eyes. "I know lots of people who are never going to get to heaven."

Sterling laughed. "There were some people I was sure wouldn't make it, and now they're right up there with the best of them."

"Go figure," Marissa said. "Do you want to come in? I have a chair that was big enough for my dad when he came over to help me with my homework."

She's charming, Sterling thought as he followed her into the spacious room. What a little personality. He was glad that Marissa knew instinctively that he was a kindred spirit, one she could trust. She already looked a little happier.

He settled himself in the armchair she indicated and realized he was still wearing his hat. "Oh, sorry," he murmured, took it off, and placed it neatly on his lap.

Marissa pulled out her desk chair and sat down with the air of a polite hostess. "I wish I could offer you a soda and some cookies or something, but if I go downstairs they'll want me to eat dinner." She wrinkled her nose. "I just thought about something. Do you get hungry? Can you eat? Because it looks like you're there, but not really."

"I'm just trying to figure all that out myself," Sterling admitted. "This is my first shot at this sort of thing. Now tell me, why won't you talk to your dad?"

Marissa looked down as a shadow fell over her face. "He won't come and see me and he won't let me go and visit him and neither will NorNor—she's my grandmother. And if they don't want to see me, I don't want to see them."

"Where do they live?"

"I don't know," Marissa burst out. "They won't tell me, and Mom doesn't know. She said they're hiding out from bad people who want to hurt them and they can't come back until it's safe, but at school kids say they think Daddy and NorNor got in trouble and had to run away."

Which is it? Sterling wondered. "When was the last time you saw them?"

"Two days after Christmas last year was when I *really* saw them. Daddy and I went ice skating. Then we went back to NorNor's restaurant for lunch. We were supposed to go to Radio City Music Hall on New Year's Eve morning, but he and NorNor had to go away. They rushed in when I was hardly even awake and said good-bye. They didn't tell me when they were coming back, and it's been almost a whole year." She paused. "I have to see Daddy, I have to see NorNor."

Her heart is broken, Sterling thought. He understood that kind of ache. It was like the yearning he felt when he saw Annie go past the window to heaven.

"Marissa . . ." There was a knock at the bedroom door.

"Oh, I knew it," Marissa said. "Mom is going to make me go down and have dinner. I'm not hungry and I don't want you to leave."

"Marissa, I'm going to get to work on your problem. I'll be back to say good night."

"Promise?"

"Marissa." There was another knock at the door.

"Yes, but you promise me something in return," Sterling said hastily. "Your mom is really worried about you. Give her a break."

"Okay. I'll even give Roy a break, and anyhow, I like chicken. Mom, I'm coming," she called. She turned back to Sterling. "Give me a high five."

"What's that?" Sterling asked.

Marissa was incredulous. "You must be pretty old. Everybody knows what a high five is."

"I've been out of touch," Sterling admitted as, following her example, he raised his hand, palm flat, and held it open as she gave it an enthusiastic slap.

Precocious, he thought, smiling. "See you later," he whispered.

"Great. Don't forget your hat. I don't want to be mean, but it really looks dumb."

"Marissa, dinner's getting cold," her mother called.

"Dinner's always cold," Marissa whispered to Sterling as he walked her to the door. "Roy takes forever to say grace. Daddy says Mommy should stick to cold cuts."

Her hand was on the knob. "Mommy can't see you, can she?"

Sterling shook his head and disappeared.

*I*n the celestial conference room, the board had been following Sterling's movements with interest. "He's made contact immediately. Using the old noggin, I call it," the admiral said approvingly.

"That little girl is so unhappy," the nun said softly.

"And quite outspoken," the monk observed. "However, I do realize it was different in my day. Sterling is about to request a conference with us. I believe we should grant it."

"So be it," they chorused.

Deep in thought, Sterling stood for a brief time in the breezeway of Marissa's home, sheltered from the slowly falling snow. I could snoop around town and find out about her father and grandmother, he thought, but there's an easier way to get the full picture, one that would involve requesting permission from the council.

He closed his eyes. Before he even had time to make the request, he found himself in the conference room. Relieved, he saw from their faces that his saintly mentors seemed to be observing him with guarded favor.

"I see you tried to find an old lady in distress," the admiral chuckled. "The young fellow who beat you to her got quite a surprise. I say, she was a prickly one."

"At least Sterling didn't waste a minute when he reached earth," the nurse said approvingly.

Sterling glowed to hear the praise. "Thank you, thank you. As you can understand, I don't want to waste a minute now. I believe I can best help Marissa when I fully understand the cause of her problem.

"Marissa's father and grandmother were planning to take her to Radio City Music Hall last New Year's Eve morning. But something went wrong just before that. They came to see her very early that day and told her they had to go away for a while."

The monk nodded. "To get to the root of most problems you have to do some digging in the past."

The shepherd, who had been very quiet, suddenly spoke up. "Most people's problems go way back. You should have met my family. Why do you think I became a shepherd? The only place I got a little peace was out on the hill."

They all laughed. "Don't get me started," the queen said. "My family's problems were the talk of the kingdom."

The monk cleared his throat. "I think we all understand you, Sterling. We know why you're here. You are requesting permission to go back in time to learn why Marissa's father and grandmother needed to leave town."

"That's it, sir," Sterling said humbly. "Perhaps you feel

that by granting permission you'll make my job too easy, and of course, if that's the case, I don't expect special favors."

"When you see what this is all about you may need a few special favors," the matador said wryly. "Personally, it's my opinion that you'll be stepping in the ring with two bulls, not one, and—"

The monk shushed the matador. "It is Sterling's job to figure this out for himself." His hand reached for the button.

That was fast, Sterling thought as he felt himself once again hurtling through the solar system. They're sending me a different way. I guess because I'm going back in time.

The next thing he knew he was standing in the parking lot of an inviting-looking restaurant. Seems to be pretty popular, he observed. Through the windows he could see that there was a bustle of activity inside. To get his bearings, he walked to the end of the driveway and read the sign: NOR'S PLACE.

Very good, he thought. Marissa's grandmother's restaurant. He didn't need to be Sherlock Holmes to figure out that the next step would be to go inside and take a look around. He hurried back up the driveway, climbed the steps, crossed the porch, and started to open the door.

I can just go through it, he chided himself. No use wasting heat. A sharp breeze accompanied him inside, where a shapely woman of about sixty, with blond hair held up in a loose twist by a jeweled comb, was standing at a small desk, studying the reservations book.

She looked up. Tendrils of blond hair brushed her fore-head.

A most attractive woman in a showy kind of way, Sterling thought.

"I'd swear I shut that door tight," Nor Kelly murmured as with two quick strides she was beside him, giving the door a decisive pull.

"NorNor, sit down. Your coffee's here," a child's voice called.

A familiar voice. Sterling whirled around to face the din-ing room. Mahogany paneled walls, tables covered with crisp white cloths and topped with wide red candles created a cheery and welcoming atmosphere. A piano was at a right angle to the bar. Strings of Christmas lights twinkled on the walls and windows, and holiday music was playing softly in the background.

"NorNor," the child called again.

His eyes roamed the crowded room. A little girl was stand-ing at a corner table just to the right of the door. She was look-ing in his direction. It was Marissa! She was slightly younger looking, her hair a little shorter, but the most noticeable dif-ference was how happy she looked. Her eyes were sparkling, her lips were curved in a smile, she had on a bright red skat-ing outfit. With her was a strikingly handsome, blue-eyed, dark-haired man in his late twenties.

Billy Campbell, Sterling thought. He's got movie-star looks. I wish I'd looked like that when I was alive, he reflected. Not that I had anything to complain about.

Nor looked up. "I'll be right there, Rissa."

It was obvious Marissa had not seen him. Of course, Sterling thought. We're not due to meet until next year.

He strolled over to the table and took a seat opposite Marissa. What a difference in her, he thought tenderly.

She and her father were finishing lunch. The crusts of a grilled cheese sandwich were on Marissa's plate. I never liked crusts either, Sterling remembered.

"Daddy, can't I please go to the party with you?" Marissa asked as she played with the straw in her soda. "I love to hear you and NorNor sing, and I promise I won't be a pest."

"You're never a pest, Rissa," Billy said, giving her hair a tug. "But this party is not for kids, believe me."

"I want to see what that big house looks like inside."

"A lot of people do," Billy murmured, raising one eyebrow. "Listen, we're going to Radio City on New Year's Eve. That will be a lot more fun. Trust me."

"A kid at school said that the men who own that house are like the people in *The Sopranos*."

Billy laughed. "That's another reason not to bring you there, kiddo."

Sopranos? Sterling thought.

Nor Kelly slipped into the chair next to Marissa. "Don't forget your other grandma is coming to your mom's house in time for dinner tonight. You were looking forward to seeing her."

"She's staying for three days. I can see her tomorrow. I don't want to miss the chance to hear you two sing."

Billy's eyes twinkled. "You're too young to be a groupie."

Groupie? So many new words, Sterling thought.

"Daddy, everybody loves your new song. You're going to be so famous."

"You bet he is, Rissa," Nor confirmed.

I can see why Marissa has missed them so much, Sterling thought. She's in her element with them. Already, he thoroughly liked Nor Kelly and Billy Campbell. You could not mistake that they were mother and son, and that Marissa had inherited those blue eyes, fair skin, and good looks from them. Nor and Billy had the natural charisma of born performers, and Marissa was already showing signs of possessing that same quality.

The restaurant was beginning to empty, and people were stopping by the table to say good-bye. "See you on New Year's Eve," a number of them said. "We'd never miss your party, Nor."

"That party I'm coming to," Marissa said decisively, pointing her finger for emphasis.

"Until ten o'clock," Billy agreed, "then you're out of here."

"Don't try last year's trick of hiding behind the bar when it's time to go home," Nor warned, laughing. "And speaking of going home, your mother should be here any minute, and Daddy and I have to get moving. We're due at our job in an hour."

Billy stood up. "Here's Mom, Rissa."

Denise Ward was crossing the room to them. "Hi, Billy. Hi, Nor. I'm sorry I'm late," she apologized. "I had to pick up some groceries, and the line at the checkout counter practically went around the store. But I bought what we need to make cookies, Marissa."

Neither Denise nor Billy could be thirty yet, Sterling thought. They obviously had married young, and although divorced, seemed to have stayed friendly. Just looking at the two of them, she in her somewhat prim winter pantsuit and he in his black jeans and boots, you could tell they weren't on the same wavelength.

And God knows Billy Campbell hadn't followed the adage that every man marries his mother. No one would ever accuse Nor Kelly of looking prim. She was wearing a striking white cashmere pantsuit with a colorful print silk scarf, complemented by eye-catching costume jewelry.

"How are the babies?" Nor asked.

"Just starting to walk," Denise announced proudly. "When Roy Junior took his first step, Roy Senior stayed up half the night, installing gates all over the house."

Sterling thought he detected a slight roll of Billy's eyes. She's letting Billy know how helpful Roy is, Sterling decided. I bet he hears about some new accomplishment of Roy's every time he sees her.

Marissa stood up and hugged her father and grandmother. "Have fun with the Sopranos," she said.

Denise looked surprised. "The Sopranos?"

"She's joking," Nor said hastily. "Our job this evening is at the party the Badgett brothers are giving to benefit the senior citizens center."

"Don't they live in that big house—?" Denise began.

"Yes, they do," Marissa blurted, "and I hear they have an indoor pool and a bowling alley."

"We'll let you know every sorry detail," Billy promised. "Come on. Let's get your jacket."

As they started walking toward the coat check, Sterling took a moment to look at the framed photos along the walls. Many of them showed Nor posing with diners at the tables. Some were autographed by people who were probably present-day celebrities, he decided. There were pictures of a glamorous Nor onstage, singing with a band; Billy, guitar in hand, performing with a group; Nor and Billy together onstage; Billy and Nor with Marissa.

Sterling could see from the older pictures that Nor once must have been a cabaret singer. He came upon a number of photographs in which she was performing with a partner. The sign on the bandstand read NOR KELLY AND BILL CAMPBELL. Billy's father, Sterling thought. I wonder what happened to him, and how long has she had the restaurant? Then a poster for a New Year's Eve celebration at Nor's Place dating back twenty years made him realize that she had been in this business a long time.

Marissa left after a final kiss from Billy and Nor. Even though Sterling knew that Marissa couldn't see him, he felt left out that she hadn't somehow sensed his presence and maybe given him a high five.

You're being ridiculous, he chided himself. But when he saw Marissa with Billy it made him think of the child he might have had if he and Annie had married.

Agreeing to be ready to leave in fifteen minutes, Billy and Nor rushed to change. To kill time, Sterling wandered over to the bar, where a single patron was chatting with the bartender. He sat on a nearby stool. If I were still alive, I'd order a scotch, he thought. It's certainly been a long time since I had one. Next year Marissa will ask me if I get hungry or thirsty. Actually, I don't have any desire to eat or drink, he realized, even though I get cold when I'm outside and feel crowded in cars. As Marissa would say, "Go figure."

"Christmas was nice, Dennis," the patron was saying. "I never thought I'd get through it, the first one without Peggy. Honest to God, when I went downstairs that morning I was ready to shoot myself, but then when I came here it was like being with family."

Well, I'll be darned, Sterling thought. That's Chet Armstrong, the sportscaster. He was just starting out on Channel 11 when I got beaned. He was a skinny kid then, but the way he delivered the sports news, you'd think every play was crucial. Now he's broad shouldered, white haired, and has the craggy face of a man who spent a great deal of time outdoors.

"I felt almost guilty that Christmas Day turned out to be so pleasant," Armstrong continued, "but I knew Peggy was probably smiling down on me."

I wonder if Peggy ever did time in the celestial waiting room, Sterling thought. He wished Chet would open his wallet. Maybe he was carrying her picture.

"Peggy was a terrific gal," Dennis, a beefy redhead with large, agile hands, agreed as he polished beer glasses and filled orders from the slips of paper the waiters dropped in front of him. Sterling noticed that Armstrong's eyes darted to one of the framed pictures over the bar. He leaned forward to get a good look at it. It was a picture of Nor with Chet, whose arm was around the shoulders of a petite woman who had to be Peggy.

I *did* see her, Sterling thought. She was a couple of rows behind me in the waiting room. But she didn't stay there long enough to really settle in.

"Peggy was a lot of fun, but don't get on her bad side," Chet reminisced with a chuckle.

Oh, that's what delayed her, Sterling thought. She had a bit of a temper.

"Listen," Dennis said in the tone of a father confessor, "I know it seems impossible, but I bet that someday down the line you'll meet someone. You've still got plenty of time."

Just watch who you play golf with, Sterling reflected.

"Turned seventy last March, Dennis."

"Today that's young."

Sterling shook his head. I'd be ninety-six. No one would accuse me of being a spring chicken.

"How long have you been here anyhow, Dennis?" Chet asked.

Thank you, Chet, Sterling thought, hoping that Dennis's reply would be a big help in his getting the lay of the land.

"Nor opened this place twenty-three years ago. Bill died just when Billy was starting school. She didn't want to be on the road anymore. I knew her from one of the clubs in New York. After six months, she gave me a call. She'd caught her bartender with his hand in the till. Our kids were almost school age, and my wife wanted to get out of the city. I've been here ever since."

Out of the corner of his eye, Sterling saw that Billy and Nor were on the way out. I'm falling down on the job, he thought, hurrying to catch up with them as they walked across the parking lot.

He was not surprised to see that they had one of those little trucks. Must be the style these days. He smiled at the thought of Marissa getting into Roy's staid vehicle. Like any kid, she probably hated her friends to see her associated with anything boring.

He hoisted himself into the backseat as Billy was turning the key in the ignition, then glanced over his shoulder at the boxes of what appeared to be musical equipment. If only they knew they had a "groupie" in the backseat, Sterling chuckled to himself.

Settled in, he stretched his legs. I don't miss being crowded by baby seats, he thought. He realized he was looking forward to the party. At the party the night before his final golf game, they had been playing Buddy Holly and Doris Day records. It would be fun if Nor and Billy sang like them, he mused.

The car drove through the snow-covered streets of Madison Village. Reminds me of Currier and Ives, Sterling thought, looking at the well-kept houses, many of them tastefully adorned with holiday lights. Evergreen wreaths with holly berries graced front doors. Festive Christmas trees sparkled through parlor windows.

On one lawn, the sight of a beautiful crèche with exquisitely carved figures provoked a wistful smile.

Then they passed a house with a dozen lifesized plastic angels cavorting on the lawn. That bossy angel at the door of the Heavenly Council room should get a load of that monstrosity, he thought.

He caught a glimpse of Long Island Sound. I always liked the North Shore of the Island, he reflected, as he craned his neck for a better look at the water, but it's a lot more built up than it used to be.

In the front seat, Nor and Billy were chuckling about Marissa's attempts to be with them so she could see for herself the inside of the big house.

"She's some piece of goods," Billy said proudly. "She takes after you, Mom. Always with her ear to the ground, afraid she'll miss something."

Agreeing, Nor laughed. "I prefer to call it a healthy interest in her surroundings. Shows how smart she is."

As Sterling listened, his spirits fell. He knew that their lives were about to change and that they were soon to be separated from this child who was the center of their lives.

He only wished he had the power to prevent it.

*W*henever Junior and Eddie Badgett held an event in their mansion, Junior had an attack of nerves. Here we go, Charlie Santoli thought as he followed the baseball bat and the bowling ball brothers. Junior, the baseball bat, had small, cold eyes. Eddie, the bowling ball, was always in tears when he talked about Mama, hard as nails about everything else.

The usual flurry of activity before a party was going on. The florists were scurrying around, placing holiday arrangements throughout the house. The caterer's team was setting up the buffet. Jewel, Junior's airheaded twenty-two-year-old girlfriend, was tripping back and forth in stiletto heels, getting in everyone's way. Junior and Eddie's special confidential assistants, uneasy in jackets and ties, were standing together, looking like the thugs they were.

Before he left home, Charlie had been forced to listen to yet another sermon from his wife about the Badgett brothers.

"Charlie, those two are crooks," she told him. Everybody knows it. You should tell them you don't want to be their lawyer anymore. So what if they put a wing on the senior citizens home? It wasn't their money that did it. Listen, I told you not to get involved with them fifteen years ago. Did you listen? No. You'll be lucky if you don't end up in the trunk of a car, and I don't mean a rumble seat. Quit. You've got enough money. You're sixty-two years old, and you're so nervous you twitch in your sleep. I want the grandchildren to know you in the flesh and not have to kiss your picture good night."

It was no use trying to explain to Marge that he couldn't get out. He had intended to handle only the various legitimate businesses of the Badgett brothers. To his regret, however, he had learned that when you lie down with dogs, you get up with fleas, and a number of times he'd been coerced into suggesting to potential government witnesses that it would be worth their while financially—and physically—to forget about certain events. In that way he had managed to prevent the brothers from being indicted for a number of criminal activities, including loan-sharking, fixing basketball games, and illegal bookmaking. So to refuse to do anything they requested of him, or to try to quit working for them, was tantamount to committing suicide.

Today, because of the magnitude of their donation to the senior citizens center, a two million dollar wing given in honor of their mother, they'd managed to get an A-list of guests to come to celebrate their absent mother's eighty-fifth birthday. Both U.S. Senators from New York, the Commissioner of Health and Human Services, various mayors and dignitaries, and the entire board of governors of the senior citizens center would be there. The board alone included some of the most prominent names on Long Island.

In all, a total of about seventy-five people would be present, the kind of people who would give the brothers the aura of respectability they craved.

It was essential that the party go well.

The main event would be held in the grand salon, a room that combined various aspects of a French royal palace. Bright gold walls, spindly gilt chairs, ornate rosewood tables, satin draperies, tapestries, and hovering over all, the reproduction of a two-story-high fifteenth-century marble fireplace, replete with sculpted cherubs, unicorns, and pineapples. Junior had explained that pineapples "symbolized lots of good luck," and he'd instructed the decorator to make sure there were lots of pineapples on the reproduction and to forget about some of those other doohickeys.

The result was a room that was a monument to bad taste, Charlie thought, and he could only imagine the reaction of the social set.

The party was scheduled to begin at five and last until eight. Cocktails, hors d'oeuvres, and a sumptuous buffet would be served. The entertainment would be provided by Billy Campbell, the up-and-coming rock singer, and his mother, Nor Kelly, the former cabaret singer. They were very popular throughout the North Shore. The highlight of the evening would occur at 7:30 P.M. when, via satellite hookup from Wallonia, the mother of the Badgett brothers would be present to hear the assemblage sing "Happy Birthday Heddy-Anna."

"You sure you got enough food?" Junior was asking the caterer.

"Relax, Mr. Badgett, you've ordered enough food to feed an army." Conrad Vogel, the caterer, smiled dismissively.

"I didn't ask you to feed an army. I wanna know if you've got enough fancy food so that if somebody likes one thing and eats a ton of it, you won't be telling him there's none left."

Charlie Santoli watched as the caterer withered under Junior's icy glare. You don't dis Junior, pal, he thought.

The caterer got the message. "Mr. Badgett, I assure you that the food is extraordinary and your guests will be very pleased."

"They better be."

"How about Mama's cake?" Eddie asked. "It better be perfect."

A tiny bead of perspiration was forming over Conrad Vogel's upper lip. "It was specially made by the finest bakery in New York. Their cakes are so good that one of our most demanding clients used them for all four of her weddings. The pastry chef himself is here, just in case the cake requires any slight touch-up after it's unboxed."

Junior brushed past the caterer and went to study Mama Heddy-Anna's portrait, which would be formally presented to the senior center's trustees to be hung in the reception area of the center's new wing. It had been painted by a Wallonian artist and ornately framed by a New York gallery. Junior's phoned instructions to the artist had been precise: "Show Mama to be the beautiful lady she is."

Charlie had seen snapshots of Mama. The portrait of a

handsome matriarch in black velvet and pearls bore not the slightest resemblance to any of them, thank God. The artist had been handsomely rewarded for his services.

"She looks real nice," Junior conceded. Immediately his moment of satisfaction evaporated. "Where are those people I'm paying to sing? They're supposed to be here by now."

Jewel had come up behind him. Slipping an arm through his, she said, "I just saw them turn in to the driveway, sweetie pie. Don't worry about them. They're good, really good."

"They better be. You recommended them."

"You heard them sing, lovey. Remember I took you to Nor's Place for dinner?"

"Yeah, I forgot. They're okay. Good restaurant, good food. Good location. Wouldn't mind owning it myself. Let's take a look at the cake."

With Jewel still on his arm, her flaming red hair dancing around her shoulders, her microminiskirt barely reaching her thighs, Junior led the inspection tour into the kitchen. The pastry chef, his towering white hat regally settled on his head, was standing beside the five-layered birthday cake.

As he saw them approach, he beamed with pride. "Is it not magnificent?" he asked, kissing his fingertips. "A spun-sugar masterpiece. My finest, finest effort. A worthy tribute to your beloved mother. And the taste. The divine taste. Your guests will cherish every bite."

Junior and Eddie walked reverently to view the masterpiece. Then, as one, they began shouting.

"Stupid!"

"Jerk!"

"Dope!"

"It's HEDDY-ANNA, not BETTY-ANNA," Eddie snarled. "My mama's name is *Heddy*-Anna!"

The pastry chef looked incredulous as he wrinkled his nose and frowned. "*Heddy*-Anna???"

"Don't you dare make fun of my mama's name!" Eddie shouted as his eyes welled with tears.

Don't let anything else go wrong, Charlie Santoli prayed. They'll both lose it if anything else goes wrong.

*I*t was a supreme effort for Hans Kramer even to begin the fifteen-minute drive from his home in Syosset to the Badgett brothers' mansion on Long Island Sound. *Why did I ever borrow from them?* he asked himself for the thousandth time as he turned onto the Long Island Expressway. *Why didn't I just declare bankruptcy and have done with it?*

An electronics executive, forty-six-year-old Hans had quit his job two years earlier, taken his retirement fund and all his savings and mortgaged his home to open a dot-com company to sell software he had designed. After a promising start, with orders rushing in and the warehouse filled with inventory, the technology industry had crashed. Then the cancellations began. In desperate need of immediate cash, and in an effort to keep the business afloat, he had borrowed from the Badgett brothers. Unfortunately, his efforts so far hadn't paid off.

There's no way on God's earth I can raise the two hundred thousand dollars I borrowed from them, not to mention the fifty percent interest they've added, he despaired.

I must have been out of my mind to go near them. But I've

got a great line of products, he reasoned. If I can just hang in there, things will turn around. Only now I've got to convince the Badgetts to let me renew the note.

In the year since his financial troubles began, Hans had lost twenty pounds. His light brown hair had become streaked with gray. He knew his wife, Lee, was worried sick about him, although she had no idea how bad the situation was. He hadn't told her about the loan, opting instead to tell her only that they needed to cut back on their spending. Why, they'd even practically given up going out for dinner.

The next exit off the expressway led to the Badgett mansion. Hans felt his palms begin to sweat. I was so cocky, he thought as he flicked on the turn signal. Came over here from Switzerland when I was twelve years old and didn't speak a word of English. Graduated from M.I.T. with high honors and thought I'd set the world on fire. And I did for a while. I thought I was immune to failure.

Five minutes later he was approaching the Badgett estate. The gates were open. Cars were lined up, waiting to be admitted by a guard at the foot of the long and winding driveway. Obviously the Badgetts were having a party.

Hans was both relieved and disappointed. I'll phone and leave a message, he thought. Maybe, just maybe, they'll give me an extension.

As he made a U-turn, he tried to ignore the voice inside him that warned that people like the Badgetts never give extensions.

$\mathcal{S}$terling, Nor, and Billy entered the rear door of the Badgett mansion just in time to hear the insults being heaped on the hapless pastry chef. Sterling hastened into the kitchen to see what was going on and found the chef frantically adjusting something in the lettering on the cake.

Wrong age? Sterling wondered. He'd been at a party once where the twelve-year-old daughter had baked a birthday cake as a surprise for her mother. When she proudly carried out the cake, candles blazing, the mother had nearly fainted. The age she had so carefully concealed was starkly revealed in hot-pink lettering on the vanilla cake. *I remember thinking that anyone who couldn't read could always count,* Sterling thought. *That wasn't too charitable of me.*

Fortunately this chef's mistake was small. With a few twirls of his pastry tube, he changed Betty-Anna to Heddy-Anna. Nor and Billy had been drawn to the kitchen by the uproar. "Just make sure not to sing 'Happy Birthday, Betty-Anna,' " Nor whispered to Billy.

"I'm tempted, but I want to get out of here alive."

Sterling tagged along as they went into the salon. Nor ran her fingers over the piano; Billy took his guitar out of the case, and they tested the microphones and sound system.

Charlie Santoli had the responsibility of giving them a list of songs that were favorites of the brothers. "They don't want you blasting your music so loud that people can't think," he said nervously.

"We're musicians. We don't blast," Nor snapped.

"But when Mama is hooked up via satellite, you'll be leading the 'Happy Birthday' song, and then they want you to really project."

The bell rang and the first wave of guests were admitted.

Sterling had always liked being around people. He studied the guests as they came in, and as he listened, realized that there were some pretty important people present.

His general impression was that they were here purely because of the largesse of the donation to the senior citizens center, and that after the party they would be happy to forget the Badgett brothers. But a number of the guests stopped to admire the portrait that would be hanging in the new wing.

"Your mother is a beautiful woman," the president of the center's board of governors said sincerely, nodding at the portrait. "So elegant, so dignified. Does she come to visit you often?"

"My precious mother isn't a good traveler," Junior told her.

"Mama gets airsick and seasick," Eddie mourned.

"Then of course you visit her in Wallonia," she suggested.

Charlie Santoli had joined them. "Of course they do, as frequently as possible," he said smoothly.

Sterling shook his head. He's not telling the truth.

Billy and Nor started their first song and were immediately surrounded by an appreciative audience. Nor was a fine musician with an attractive, husky voice. Billy, however, was exceptional. Standing in the crowd, Sterling listened to the murmured comments.

"He's a young Billy Joel . . ."

"He's going to be a star . . ."

"And he's gorgeous," the daughter of one of the board members cooed.

"Billy, let's hear 'Be There When I Awake.' "

The request brought spontaneous applause.

His fingers moving lightly on the strings of the guitar, Billy began to sing, "I know what I want . . . I know what I need."

That must be his hit record, Sterling thought. Even to my out-of-date ears, it's great.

Thanks to the music, the atmosphere at the party loosened up. The guests began interacting, allowing their glasses to be refilled with the excellent wines, and piling their plates with the truly spectacular food.

By 7:15 the Badgett brothers were beaming. Their party was a success. They were a success.

At that point, Junior picked up the microphone and cleared his throat. "I wanna welcome all of you, and my brother and me hope you're enjoying yourselves very much. It is our pleasure to have you as our guests, and we are very, very happy to have given you the money, I mean donated the money, for the wing of the senior citizens center to be known as the Mama Heddy-Anna wing in honor of our saintly mother's eighty-fifth birthday. And now, by the miracle of satellite, from the historic village of Kizkek where my brother and me were raised, our mama will appear. Mama stayed up way past her bedtime to be with us 'cause she's so honored. Now I ask all of you to join in singing 'Happy Birthday' to her. Our wonderful Billy Campbell and his mother, that doll Nor Kelly, will lead us in song."

There was a faint smattering of applause. The birthday cake was rolled out, ablaze with eighty-six candles, one to grow on. The ten-foot screen dropped down from the ceiling, and Mama Heddy-Anna's dour face emerged to fill it.

She was seated in her rocking chair, sipping grappa.

Eddie's eyes streamed with tears, and Junior blew kisses at the screen as the guests dutifully sang "Happy Birthday, Heddy-Anna" in Wallonian, working from phonetically marked song sheets.

Her cheeks puffed like twin red balloons, Mama blew out the candles on the cake her sons had sent by chartered plane to Wallonia. That was when it became all too clear that she'd filled the hours past her usual bedtime by drinking more than her share of grappa. In broken English she started cursing and complaining loudly that her sons never came to see her and she wasn't feeling so hot.

Junior quickly turned down the volume but not before she had screamed, "How much bad things you two do, you can't come see your mama before she die? Not once you come in all these years."

Billy and Nor immediately started another vigorous round of "Happy Birthday, Heddy-Anna." This time no one joined in, however, and the telecast closed on the unforgettable sight of Mama thumbing her nose at her offspring and their guests, as she came down with a case of the hiccups.

Jewel's laugh was a high-pitched trill. "Doesn't Mama have a wonderful sense of humor? I just love her."

Junior brushed Jewel aside and stalked out of the room. Eddie followed close behind.

Nor quickly whispered to Billy, "This is a disaster. What should we do? He told us to sing 'For She's a Jolly Good Fellow' while people ate the cake.

"And then the medley of songs about mothers, starting with 'I always loved my mama, she's my favorite girl . . . ' "

How about "Little old lady, time for tea," Sterling thought. That was a hit in my day.

"We'd better check on what they want us to do now. I'm not taking any chances on second-guessing them," Nor said, glancing around the room at the stunned expressions on the faces of the guests.

As Sterling trotted after Nor and Billy, he sensed imminent disaster. Junior and Eddie were disappearing into a room at the end of the hall.

Billy and Nor raced to catch up with them, and Billy tapped on the now-closed door. When there was no response, he and Nor looked at each other. "Let's take a chance," Nor whispered.

Just go home, Sterling urged, but knew it was a year too late to even think that.

Billy turned the handle and cautiously opened the door. He and Nor stepped into what appeared to be a small reception room. It was empty.

"They're in there," Nor whispered, pointing to an inner room that could be seen through a partially open door. "Maybe we'd better . . ."

"Wait a minute. They're checking the answering machine."

An electronic voice was announcing, "You have one new message."

Nor and Billy hesitated, not sure whether to wait or to leave, but then the message they were overhearing froze them to the spot.

It was a plea from a man who sounded desperate, begging for "wery little extra time" to pay back a loan.

The answering machine clicked off, and they heard Junior shout, "Your time just ran out, buddy. Eddie, get on it. Tell the guys to burn his stinking warehouse down and do it now. I don't wanna hear that it's still standing tomorrow."

"There won't be nuthin' left," Eddie assured him, sounding much cheerier, his mind off Mama for the moment.

Billy put his finger to his lips. Silently he and Nor tiptoed from the room and hurried back to the salon. "Let's get our stuff," Billy whispered. "We're out of here."

What they did not notice, but Sterling did, was that Charlie Santoli, at the other end of the hall, had seen them come out of the office.

*T*he celestial waiting room was filled with newcomers gazing around and trying to adjust to their surroundings. The angel in charge had been ordered to hang a large DO NOT DISTURB sign on the door of the conference room. There had been several instances of former top executives, not used to being kept waiting, who had rushed in demanding a meeting when the angel's back was turned.

Inside the conference room, the Heavenly Council was following Sterling's activities with keen interest.

"Did you notice how chagrined he was when Marissa didn't even sense that he was present in the restaurant?" the nun asked. "He was truly taken aback."

"That was one of the first lessons we wanted him to learn," the monk stated. "During his lifetime, too many people were invisible to him. He'd look right past them."

"Do you think Mama Heddy-Anna will turn up in our waiting room soon?" the shepherd asked. "She told her sons she's dying."

The nurse smiled. "She used the oldest trick in the book to get her sons to visit her. She's as strong as a bull."

"I wouldn't want her in the ring with me," the matador commented wryly.

"That lawyer is in real trouble," said the saint who had reminded Sterling of Pocahontas. "Unless he does something drastic very soon, when his time comes, he won't be dealing with us."

"Poor Hans Kramer is desperate," the nun observed. "The Badgett brothers have absolutely no mercy."

"They belong in the brig," the admiral proclaimed sternly.

"Did you hear that?" the queen's tone was shocked. "They're going to set that poor man's warehouse on fire."

Shaking their heads, the saints fell silent, reflecting sadly on man's inhumanity to man.

$\mathcal{V}$alets frantically rushed to deliver the cars of the guests pouring out of the house. Sterling leaned against a column on the porch, bent on hearing the reactions of the departing merrymakers.

"Bizarre!"

"Give them their money back. *I'll* donate two million for that wing," a dowager snapped.

"Reminded me of the movie 'Throw Momma From the Train.' I bet that's what those two characters feel like doing now," a board member's husband snickered.

"At least the food was good," someone said charitably.

"I hope you caught that they haven't set foot in Wallonia since they left. Figure out why."

"You got a load of Mama, didn't you?"

Sterling noticed that the two U.S. Senators were screaming at their top aides as they were whisked away. They're probably worrying that they'll be written up in the tabloids for partying with mobsters, Sterling thought. They should know what Junior is going to do to some poor guy's warehouse. He couldn't wait to slip into Nor and Billy's car and hear what they had to say about everything that had happened.

A guest, who clearly had slurped as much vodka as Mama had grappa began to sing, "Happy Birthday, Heddy-Anna" in Wallonian, but didn't have his phonetically marked song sheet to consult. He switched to English and was joined by several other guests, who were also feeling no pain.

Sterling heard a valet ask one of the guests if his vehicle was an SUV. What's that? Sterling wondered. A moment later the valet pulled up in one of those little trucks. So that's what it is, Sterling thought. I wonder what SUV stands for.

Billy's SUV was parked in the back. Don't want to miss them, Sterling thought. Two minutes later, when Nor and Billy appeared, lugging their equipment, he was in the backseat.

It was obvious from the nervous expressions on both their faces that they were deeply worried.

Wordlessly, they loaded the car, jumped in, and joined the line of vehicles exiting the long driveway. They did not speak until they were out on the main road. Then Nor asked, the words rushing out, "Billy, do you think they were serious about burning down someone's warehouse?"

"Absolutely, and we're damn lucky they don't know we overheard them."

Uh-oh, Sterling thought. Their lawyer—what's his name? Charlie Santoli—saw you come out of the office. If he tells the Badgetts, your goose is cooked.

"I can't help thinking that I've heard that voice before, the one on the phone message," Nor said slowly. "Did you notice he said 'wery,' not 'very,' when he asked for more time?"

"Now that you say it, I guess I did," Billy agreed. "I just figured the poor guy was so nervous he was practically stuttering."

"No, it wasn't that. Maybe he has a slight lisp. I think he's had dinner at the restaurant. The thing is, if I could only remember who it was, then we could warn him."

"When we get to the restaurant, I'm going to call the police," Billy said. "I don't want to use the cell phone."

They rode the rest of the way in silence. In the backseat, Sterling shared their anxiety.

It was nearly nine o'clock when they entered Nor's Place. The holiday diners were in full force. Nor tried to greet people quickly. At the same moment, she and Billy spotted one of their old friends, Sean O'Brien, a retired detective, sitting at the bar.

They looked at each other. "I'll ask him to sit with us. He'll know what we should do," Billy said.

A smile plastered on her face, Nor went to her usual table at the front of the restaurant. From this vantage point she could oversee the operation, hold court, and easily greet her patrons. Sterling joined her, taking the seat he'd been occupying a few hours earlier.

Billy came to the table followed by Sean O'Brien, a solid-looking man of about fifty-five, with a full head of graying brown hair, alert brown eyes, and a genial smile.

"Season's greetings, Nor," he began, then immediately sensed something was wrong. "What's up?" he asked abruptly, as he and Billy sat down.

"We were hired for a party the Badgett brothers gave this afternoon," Nor began.

"The Badgett brothers?" O'Brien raised one eyebrow, then listened intently as they told him of the message on the answering machine and Junior Badgett's response to it.

"I know the voice," Nor finished. "I'm sure that man has been a customer here."

"Nor, the feds have been trying to pin something on those two for years. They're as slippery as fish in olive oil. They're crooks and they're vicious. If that was a local call, I wouldn't be surprised to be reading tomorrow about a warehouse that burned down overnight."

"Is there anything we can do to try to stop them?" Billy asked.

"I can alert the feds, but those guys have interests all over. We know for sure they have a presence in Vegas and Los Angeles. That message could have come from anywhere, but no matter where it came from, it doesn't mean the warehouse is in that vicinity."

"I never knew the Badgetts were that bad," Billy said. "You hear rumors, but they have those car and boat dealerships . . ."

"They've got a dozen legitimate businesses," O'Brien said.

"That's the way they launder their money. I'll make some calls. The feds will at least want to keep them under surveillance, but those guys never dirty their own hands."

Nor rubbed her forehead, her face troubled. "There's a reason I remember that voice. Wait a minute." She beckoned a waiter. "Sam, ask Dennis to join us. You cover the bar."

O'Brien looked at her. "It's better if nobody else knows you overheard that conversation."

"I trust Dennis with my life," Nor said.

The table is getting crowded, Sterling thought. I'll have to stand. He felt the chair being pulled out and jumped up quickly. He had no desire to have Dennis sitting on his lap.

" . . . and, Dennis, I'm sure I've heard that voice in this restaurant," Nor concluded a few minutes later. "He pronounced 'very' as 'wery.' Granted that could have been just nerves, but I thought maybe it's a guy who sits at the bar and talks with you sometimes."

Dennis shook his head. "I can't think of a soul, Nor. But I do know this—if that Badgett guy was on the level when he talked about burning down a warehouse, the fellow who called him will be 'wery upset.' "

"Wery, wery upset," Billy agreed.

They all laughed nervously.

They're trying to use humor to cover their very real anxieties, Sterling thought. If the Badgett brothers are as bad as Sean O'Brien believes they are, and if Nor and Billy have to testify about that call . . . Poor Marissa. She was so happy today.

O'Brien got up. "I've got to make some phone calls," he said. "Nor, can I use your office?"

"Of course."

"You and Billy come with me. I want to put you on the phone and have you repeat exactly what you heard."

"I'll be at the bar." Dennis pushed his chair back.

If I were still alive, that chair would have smashed my big toe, Sterling thought.

"Nor, I thought you and Billy were doing a holiday performance here at the restaurant tonight," a patron at a nearby table called. "We came specially to hear you two sing."

"You're going to." Nor smiled. "We'll be back in fifteen minutes."

In the office, O'Brien phoned his contact at the FBI, and Nor and Billy recounted what they had overheard. When the call ended, Nor shrugged her shoulders. "It is what it is. Unless I can remember whose voice that is, I'm no use to them."

Billy's cell phone rang. "It's Rissa," he said as he looked at the Caller ID. His troubled expression cleared. "Hi, baby . . . We just got back . . . No, we didn't see the swimming pool or the bowling alley . . . Well, I wouldn't say they were like the Sopranos."

"I would," Nor murmured.

"Uh-huh, we did our usual bit . . ." He laughed. ". . . Of course we were sensational. They couldn't get enough of us.

Listen, baby, NorNor will say a quick hello, then you get to bed. I'll see you tomorrow. Love you."

He handed the phone to Nor, then turned to O'Brien. "You've met my daughter, Marissa, haven't you?"

"Sure. I thought she owned this place."

"She thinks she does."

Nor said good night to Marissa and smiled ruefully as she snapped the phone closed and handed it to Billy. She looked at O'Brien. "I can't help wondering if that poor guy who was begging for more time to pay off a loan is supporting a family."

Billy put his arm around her shoulders and gave her a quick hug. "You look tired, Mom, so I hate to say it, but your public awaits . . ."

"I know. We've got to get out there. Give me a minute to do my face."

O'Brien reached in his pocket. "Here's my card. If you get a brainstorm, call me at any time. I'll give one to Dennis too."

By 9:30, when Nor and Billy began to perform, every table in the restaurant was filled. They did two half-hour shows, one at 9:30, then another at 11, for the late-night crowd.

They're troupers, Sterling thought. You'd never know they have a care in the world. The minute Nor finished the first show she slipped into her office, carrying the reservations books for the last two years under her arm. Sterling sat with her as she went through them, saying each name aloud as she went down the list.

Several times she stopped and repeated a name, then shook her head and continued to read. She's trying to see if the name of the guy whose voice they heard jumps out at her, Sterling thought.

The concern in Nor's face deepened as she spoke name after name. But then she glanced at her watch and jumped up, opened her bag and pulled out her compact. In seconds she had lightly powdered her face, touched up her eyes and lips. She pulled the jeweled comb out of her hair and shook her head. Sterling was amazed at how deftly she twisted the long tresses in her fingers, swept them up, and anchored them once again.

"I feel like Minnie off the pickle boat," she said aloud, "but I guess the show must go on."

You look wonderful, Sterling wanted to protest. You're a really beautiful woman. And who the heck is Minnie off the pickle boat?

At the door of the office, Nor let out a quick sigh, but a moment later she was wreathed in smiles as she stopped at table after table to exchange a few words with her patrons.

This place is full, Sterling noticed, and it's obvious from the way Nor talks to everyone that they're all regulars. They seem so glad to have a word with her. Well, she's good. He listened as she inquired about someone's mother, someone's son, another's planned vacation, then congratulated a couple who had just become engaged.

The Heavenly Council will never tell her that she didn't pay attention to other people, Sterling thought. That's for sure. Too bad I wasn't more like her.

Billy was deep in conversation with a man and woman at a corner table. Sterling decided to tune in. I hope nobody else joins us, he thought as he took the one empty chair. Then as he caught the gist of the conversation, he raised his eyebrows. These people were executives from Empire Recording Company, and they wanted to sign Billy to a contract.

The man was saying, "I don't have to tell you the kind of people we've launched. We've been scouting you for a while, and you've got it, Billy. We're offering you a two-album contract."

"I'm very flattered and it sounds great, but you'll have to talk to my agent," Billy said, smiling.

He's trying to hide that he's thrilled, Sterling realized. It's every young singer's dream to be signed up by a record company. What a crazy day.

The last stragglers left the restaurant at 12:30. Nor and Billy sat at the bar with Dennis as he finished cleaning up. Nor held up a glass. "I've heard it's bad luck to toast with water, but I'm going to take a chance. Here's to Billy and the new contract."

"Your dad would be so proud," Dennis said.

"You bet he would." Nor looked up. "Here's to you, Bill, wherever you are up there. Your kid's done good."

I definitely have to meet him, Sterling told himself. He saw the suspicious touch of moisture in the eyes of all three.

Billy was just about the age Marissa is now when he lost his dad. It must have been awfully tough on him and Nor.

"Let's keep our fingers crossed that it all goes through," Billy told them. "I don't want to get too excited yet. That'll wait until I have the offer in writing."

"You will," Nor assured him. "But you're still singing with me here at Christmastime next year."

"I know, Mom, and for free," Billy laughed.

"You'll have to hire a bouncer for crowd control," Dennis declared. He folded a towel. "Okay, that's it. Nor, you look aw-fully tired. Let me drive you home."

"Listen, if I lived fifteen minutes away, the way I feel now, I'd take you up on it. But for the three minutes it'll take me to get there, I'd rather have the car at the door in the morning. You can carry those reservations books out for me. I'm going to keep at them for a while."

She kissed Billy lightly on the cheek. "See you tomorrow."

"Okay. I'm heading upstairs. Don't try to go over those books tonight, Mom. Leave it for the morning."

They looked at each other. "I know," Billy said. "By then it may be too late."

So that's where Billy lives, Sterling thought. He must have an apartment up there. It would be interesting to see what Nor's home is like. She said it's only a three-minute drive away. That can't be too far for me to walk back. Once again he found himself hurrying across the parking lot, this time fol-lowing Nor and Dennis.

The temperature has really dropped in these few hours, he

thought. He looked up. Clouds were forming and beginning to obscure the moon and stars. He sniffed. There was a hint of snow in the air. I was one of those people who preferred winter to summer, he thought. Annie thought I was crazy. If there was anything she loved, it was a day at the seashore. I remember her family had a place in Spring Lake.

Nor's car was a handsome Mercedes sedan. I used to drive one of these, Sterling thought, and in a lot of ways this one doesn't look that much different from the one I had. As Dennis laid the reservations books on the floor in the back and held the driver's door open for Nor, Sterling got in the front seat. I never liked to ride in the back of the car, he thought. My legs always felt cramped.

Nor locked the door and fastened her seat belt. Everybody does that these days, Sterling mused. I wonder if there's a law about it.

He readjusted his homburg, smiling as he remembered that next year Marissa would poke fun at it.

As they pulled out of the driveway, he jumped when Nor muttered aloud, "Mama Heddy-Anna. God help us!"

Sterling felt a little guilty. Nor thinks she's alone, and she's one of those people who talks to herself. I used to do that too, and I'd have died if I learned that someone was eavesdropping on me.

But it's okay because I'm here to help them, he comforted himself. Fortunately she turned on the radio and listened to the news the rest of the way.

Nor's house was at the end of a cul-de-sac, situated on a generous piece of property. The minute he saw it he sensed that it was the perfect home for her. It looked to him like a renovated farmhouse. The exterior was white clapboard with black shutters. The porch light was on, casting a warm glow around the front door.

"Thank God to be home," Nor sighed.

I know what you mean, Sterling said aloud, then rolled his eyes. Thank God she can't hear me. I might have given her a heart attack.

I'm not going to stay long, he promised himself as Nor fished through her purse for her house key, got out of the car, and gathered the reservations books in her arms.

Sterling walked to the front door, admiring the attractive shrubbery that was lightly coated with snow.

As soon as Nor opened the door, shut off the alarm, and switched on the light, he realized that she also had great taste. The ground floor was a single, very large room with white walls and wooden floors. A raised-hearth fireplace defined the living room area. At a right angle to it stood a floor to-ceiling-Christmas tree, decorated with strings of candle-shaped bulbs. The bottom three tiers clearly bore Marissa's touch. Handmade paper ornaments, a quantity of tinsel, and a dozen candy canes demonstrated her idea of how a Christmas tree should look.

Overstuffed couches, Persian area rugs, fine antique furnishings, and first-class paintings filled the rest of the room. The effect was that of vivid serenity—if there is such a thing, Sterling thought.

"Cup of cocoa," Nor murmured as she kicked off her shoes. She walked to the kitchen area, dropped the reservations books on the table, and opened the refrigerator. Hating to rush, Sterling scurried from painting to painting. These are valuable, he thought. I wish I had a chance to really study them. An English hunting scene particularly intrigued him.

As the attorney for a number of family trusts when he was alive, he'd developed an eye for good art. They used to tell me I could have been an appraiser, he remembered.

A staircase to the second floor beckoned him. One quick look and then I'm off, he promised himself.

Nor's bedroom was the largest. Framed pictures were on the bureau, the dressing table, and the night tables. These were all personal and many of them were of a much younger Nor with Billy's father. There were at least a half-dozen of Billy with his parents, starting from the time he was an infant. He seemed to be about six years old in the last one that showed the three of them together.

Sterling poked his head into the first of the other two bedrooms. It was small but cozy, with the uncluttered look of a guest room.

The third door was closed. The small porcelain tile on it said MARISSA'S PLACE. As he opened the door, Sterling felt a lump in his throat. This child is about to lose out on so much in this upcoming year, he thought.

The room was enchanting. White wicker furniture. Blue-and-white wallpaper. White eyelet bedspread and curtains. Shelves of books on one wall. A desk with a bulletin board against another.

He heard Nor's footsteps on the stairs. It was time to go. Remembering the door had been closed, he quietly pulled it shut, then watched as Nor went into her room. A moment later, with the collar of his chesterfield turned up, his homburg pulled down as far as he could get it, Sterling walked briskly down the road.

I've got several hours to kill, he thought. Billy's probably asleep. Maybe I'll just drop by and look in on Marissa. But where exactly does she live? I never was too good at directions.

Until now there'd been plenty of activity to keep him occupied, but with everyone going to bed, he felt a little lonely as he trudged through the quiet streets.

Should I try to contact the Heavenly Council? he wondered. Or will they decide I can't do the job? And if so, what then?

Suddenly something caught his eye.

What's that?

A piece of paper was fluttering from the sky. It stopped falling when it was directly in front of him. Sterling plucked it out of the air, unfolded it, and walked to the next street lamp to read it.

It was a map of the village. Marissa's home and Nor's Place were clearly indicated. A dotted line started at a point marked "you are here" and gave specific directions—"four blocks east . . . turn left one block, then right"—showing him the way to Marissa's house. A second dotted line illustrated the way from there back to the restaurant.

Sterling looked up, past the moon, past the stars, into eternity. Thank you. I am very grateful, he whispered.

*N*o matter how late the hour, Dennis Madigan always read the *New York Post* before settling down to sleep. His wife, Joan, had long ago learned to sleep with his light on.

Tonight, however, he could not concentrate on the paper. He knew neither Nor nor Billy realized that their lives could be in serious danger. If the Badgetts were as bad as Sean O'Brien portrayed them . . . Dennis shook his head. When he worked in bars in Manhattan, he'd seen and heard a lot about their kind. None of it good.

Very. "Wery." What is this reminding me of? he asked himself as he irritably flipped through the pages of the newspaper. Nor thinks the man might be someone who comes into the restaurant. He can't be a regular, though, or I'd know him.

"Wery," he said aloud.

Joan opened her eyes and blinked. "What?"

"Nothing. Sorry, honey. Go back to sleep."

"Easy for you to say," she muttered as she turned her back to him.

Dennis skipped to the *Post*'s television section and smiled as he read Linda Stasi's funny review of a corny holiday special.

Still not remotely sleepy even though it was 3:30, he began to skim the restaurant pages. The write-up on a new midtown restaurant caught his eye. "We started with vichyssoise . . . ," the columnist began.

Sounds like a good joint, Dennis thought. Have to check it out. He and Joan enjoyed going into the city occasionally and trying new places.

He stared at the paper. Vichyssoise. He remembered a smart aleck waiter at Nor's—one who didn't last long—joking that a customer who ordered "wichyssoise" last time, now would like a cup of "wegetable" soup.

What's the customer's name? Dennis thought. I can see him. He and his wife always had a cocktail at the bar. Nice people. I didn't think of him right away because that's the only hint of an accent he had, and he hasn't been around in a long time . . .

In his mind, he could see a face. He's local, Dennis thought. And his name . . . his name . . . it sounds European . . .

Hans Kramer!

That's it! That's his name!

Dennis grabbed the phone. Nor answered on the first ring. "Nor, I've got it. The guy on the answering machine. Could it be Hans Kramer?"

"Hans Kramer," she said, slowly. "That doesn't ring a bell with me. I don't remember . . ."

"Think, Nor. He ordered 'wichyssoise' and 'wegetable' soup."

"Oh my God, of course . . . you're right." Nor leaned on one elbow and pulled herself up. Sean O'Brien's card was propped against the lamp on her night table. As she reached for it she could feel adrenaline surging through her body.

"I know Kramer has something to do with computers, Dennis. Maybe he has a warehouse. I'll call Sean O'Brien this minute. I just hope we're not too late."

As Sterling approached Marissa's house, everything looked quiet and peaceful. All was dark inside except for a faint light shining through an upstairs window.

My mother used to leave the hall light on for me, he remembered. And she'd leave my bedroom door open a crack so I could see it. I was chicken, he thought with a smile. Never mind the light, I slept with my teddy bear till I was ten.

Noting a small sign that indicated the house was wired against intruders, he slipped inside, not bothering to open the door just in case the alarm was on. He had the feeling that the Heavenly Council wanted him to move around like everybody else except when it prevented him from doing his job, but he was very sure they didn't want him setting off alarms.

He tiptoed up the stairs and stepped over Roy's safety gate, hoisting his leg high to clear it. How big does he think those kids are anyhow? Sterling wondered as he felt a tug on the cuff of his trousers. The next thing he knew he was tumbling onto the hallway floor.

Thank God I don't make any noise, he thought as he stared up at the ceiling. His hat had gone flying. He got up slowly, aware of a faint twinge in his back. Retrieving the homburg, he resumed his attempt to visit Marissa.

Her bedroom was the last one at the end of the hallway. All the bedroom doors were slightly ajar. A light snore was coming from inside the master bedroom. As he passed the munchkins' room, he could hear the sound of one of the boys stirring. Sterling hesitated and listened closely, but then the child seemed to settle down again.

Even though the night was beginning to cloud over, there was enough light from the heavens for him to see Marissa's face clearly. She was curled up in bed, her hair soft on her cheek, the covers tucked around her.

A pile of boxes in the corner were testimony to the fact that she had received an abundance of presents for Christmas and her birthday. Not surprising, Sterling thought. I'd love to be able to give her something myself.

He sat in the same chair he would sit in next year, when he would talk to Marissa for the first time. From there he could study her face. She looks like an angel, he thought tenderly. If only she didn't have to go through the change that is coming. If only I had the power to keep her world the way it is now. But I can't, so next year I'll do everything I can to put her world back together again. By hook or by crook, he resolved.

And not just because I want to go to heaven. I truly want to help her. She looks so small and vulnerable. Hard to believe she's the same kid who was trying to call the shots at the restaurant today, and who didn't waste any time phoning her father to get the lowdown on the party.

With a smile that ended in a sigh, Sterling got up and left the room. As he went down the hallway he heard one of the munchkins start to cry. Then the other one joined in.

Luckily, they don't need me, Sterling thought. An instant later Roy staggered out of the bedroom and into the nursery. "Daddy's here," he crooned. "Roy Junior, Robert, Daddy's here."

Denise has him well trained, Sterling thought. My friends used to turn a deaf ear when their kids started howling in the middle of the night. But times have changed.

I was an only child, he thought as he descended the stairs. My parents were in their forties when I was born. I became the center of their universe. They were in heaven long before I arrived in the celestial waiting room.

It will be so good to see Mother and Dad again, he thought, once more glancing skyward.

Sterling consulted the map before he left the house, then made his way to Nor's restaurant. As he walked through the quiet streets, he suddenly felt an acute sense of urgency. Even though it absolutely was not coming from anyplace nearby, he was beginning to smell smoke.

They did it! he thought. The warehouse fire has just been set.

$\mathcal{S}$ean O'Brien had put in twenty years with the Nassau County Police Department. During that time he had learned to expect predawn phone calls if there was an important development in a case he was working on.

When his phone rang at 3:40, Sean woke up immediately and grabbed it. As he hoped, it was Nor.

"Sean, I just heard from Dennis. He came up with the name of the guy on the answering machine, and he's right. I'm absolutely positive that he's right."

"Who is it?"

"His name is Hans Kramer. He lives in Syosset and has some kind of computer software company. He comes into the restaurant occasionally."

"Okay, Nor. I'll get right on it."

Thoroughly awake now, Sean sat on the side of the bed. He was alone in the room. His wife, Kate, a nurse, was working the night shift on the pediatrics floor of North Shore hospital.

His first call was to police headquarters in Syosset. There was a chance Kramer was known to them.

It proved to be a good bet. Nick Amaretto, the lieutenant

in charge, knew exactly who Kramer was. "Nice guy. He's lived in town twenty years. Was on the zoning board for a while. Ran the Red Cross drive a couple of years ago. Has his own software company."

"Does he have a warehouse?"

"Yeah. He bought property in the area off the expressway that had that string of crummy motels. He built a nice little complex with an office and warehouse."

"I have a tip that it may be torched. A matter of an overdue loan from the Badgett brothers."

"Oh, boy. We'll get over there right away. I'll contact the bomb squad and the fire department."

"I'm calling the feds. Talk to you later."

"Wait a minute, Sean," the lieutenant snapped. "Something big is coming in on the radio."

Sean O'Brien knew even before Amaretto got back on the phone that he was too late. The Kramer complex was already in flames.

*H*ans Kramer received the call from his security service at 3:43 A.M. The smoke detectors in the warehouse had been activated. The fire department was on the way.

In silent desperation, Hans and his wife, Lee, threw on clothes, stuffed their bare feet into sneakers, grabbed jackets, and ran to the car.

I dropped a lot of the insurance coverage, Hans thought desperately. I couldn't afford the premiums. If the fire department can't save the warehouse, what will I do?

He felt a tightening in his chest. Even though the car had not yet warmed up, he was dripping perspiration.

"Hans, you're trembling," Lee said, her voice sick with worry. "No matter how bad it is, we can handle it. I promise, we can handle it."

"Lee, you don't understand. I borrowed money, a lot of money. I thought I could pay it back. I was sure business would pick up." The road was almost empty. He pressed the accelerator and the car raced ahead.

"Hans, the doctor has been warning you. That last stress test you took wasn't good. Please calm down."

I owe them three hundred thousand dollars, Hans thought. The warehouse is worth three million, but I'm only insured enough to cover the mortgage. I won't have enough to pay off the loan.

As they turned onto the street that led to the complex, both Hans and Lee gasped. In the distance they could see flames shooting through the darkness, fierce angry flames surrounded by thick billowing smoke.

"Oh, dear God," Lee breathed.

Hans, in shock, said nothing. *They* did this, Hans thought. The Badgetts. This is their answer to my request for an extension on the loan.

When Hans and Lee reached the warehouse, it was surrounded by fire trucks. Gallons of water from high-powered hoses were pouring into the inferno, but it was obvious the blaze could not be contained.

As Hans pushed open the door of the car, a gigantic wave of pain washed over him, and he toppled onto the driveway.

Moments later he could feel something being clamped over his nostrils, a jolting in his chest, and strong hands lifting him. In a crazy way he felt relieved.

It was all beyond his control.

$\mathcal{S}$terling arrived back at the restaurant and was not surprised to see Nor getting out of her car in the parking lot. They must know about the fire already, he thought as he broke into a trot.

He followed Nor inside and up to Billy's apartment, which encompassed the entire second floor of the building. Dennis was already there, and Billy had made coffee.

"Sean is on his way over," Nor told Billy. She had no make-up on. Her hair was loosely caught up in a comb, but long tendrils were slipping around her neck and face. She was wearing a light blue sweat suit and a pair of sneakers.

Billy had on rumpled blue jeans, a wrinkled denim shirt, and old moccasins. His eyes looked tired, and he needed a shave.

Dennis was wearing a gray Madison Village sweatshirt over well-worn corduroy pants.

"Sean said it's important that he talk to us right away," Nor said as Billy poured coffee into mugs, and the three of them went to the table in the dining room.

From the chair he selected, Sterling could see into the liv-

94

ing room. Billy's place was a comfortable bachelor pad, slightly untidy, with sneakers under the coffee table and a pile of newspapers on top of it. The couch and chairs were basically nondescript but looked inviting.

It was clear that Billy worked on his music in the living room. There were a couple of guitars propped up against the piano, and sheet music was scattered on the couch.

As at Nor's home, many of the homemade ornaments on the Christmas tree looked as though they had Marissa's touch.

The ringing of the doorbell indicated that Sean O'Brien had arrived. Billy buzzed him in and waited as he climbed the stairs.

O'Brien's expression was grave. He nodded when Billy offered coffee, joined them at the table, and told them about the fire.

"How bad is it?" Nor asked.

"About as bad as it gets," O'Brien said. "Hans Kramer is in the hospital. He's had a pretty severe heart attack, but he should make it."

Nor inhaled sharply. "Oh, no."

"His place burned to the ground," O'Brien continued. "There's absolutely nothing left. It was one expert job."

"It was definitely set?" Nor asked flatly, already knowing the answer.

"Yes, it was."

"What happens now?" Billy asked.

"The FBI will be here soon. They need to take statements from you. Your testimony directly implicates the Badgetts.

When Kramer is well enough, we'll get his statement. Then the feds will go for an indictment. Since you overheard Junior's order to torch the warehouse, it looks like this time there will finally be a solid case against them. But I warn you, it's absolutely imperative that no one knows you two are witnesses."

Billy and Nor exchanged glances. "I think we both understand," Billy said.

"I certainly do," Dennis said grimly.

Sterling shook his head. The lawyer, he thought. The Badgetts' lawyer, Charlie Santoli. He saw Billy and Nor coming out of the office. Do the Badgetts know that yet?

On Monday morning at 7:30, Charlie Santoli went downstairs to the kitchen of his home in Little Neck, Long Island. His wife, Marge, was already there preparing breakfast.

Hands on her hips, a worried frown on her face, she took a good look at him. "You look like you've been up for a week, Charlie," she said bluntly.

Charlie raised his hand. "Marge, don't start. I'm okay."

Marge was an attractive, generously sized woman with short brown hair, a shade she preserved by regular visits to the local beauty salon. For years she had kept a standing appointment every Saturday for a wash, set, and manicure. Every fourth Saturday she had a seaweed facial and a color job.

Marge never allowed circumstances to quiet her lively tongue. She had a reputation for conducting conversations with fellow patrons of the salon while sitting under the dryer. Of course this meant that she had to shout to be heard, but, as Charlie had learned, Marge was born with her Irish ancestors' gift of gab. Nothing stood in the way of her having both the first *and* the last word.

Now she continued to scrutinize her husband, studying his face, taking in the lines of fatigue around his eyes, the tightness of his lips, the faint quiver of a muscle in his cheek, and then began a familiar refrain. "You look terrible, and it's all because those two are driving you crazy."

A buzzer went off. Marge turned, and with her mittened hand, removed a tray of freshly baked corn muffins from the oven. "Did you get any sleep at all last night?"

Did I? Charlie wondered. His head was aching, his stomach was knotted and churning. He shrugged his answer.

Yesterday evening, when he arrived home at nine o'clock, Marge had pounced on him for details about the party, but he had begged off. "Marge, give me time to get over it."

Mercifully she had done just that, helped by the fact that a vintage Christmas movie she'd always loved was about to start on an obscure cable station. A box of tissues next to the couch, a cup of tea on the table in front of her, Marge had cheerfully prepared herself for a good cry.

Immensely relieved to have a reprieve, Charlie fixed a strong scotch and buried himself in the Sunday papers.

It had nearly killed Marge to miss the Badgett party, especially with the delicious prospect of seeing Mama Badgett on satellite television. What kept her away was a long-planned, late-afternoon, holiday reunion of her classmates from St. Mary's Academy. As chairperson of the event, she had chosen the date for it and therefore simply could not miss it. As Charlie had pointed out, she was hoist on her own petard.

Now Marge put a muffin on a plate and placed it in front of

him. "Don't stand there," she said. "Sit down and eat like a normal human being."

It was useless to protest. Charlie dutifully pulled out the chair as she poured him a cup of coffee. His vitamins were already lined up next to a glass of freshly squeezed orange juice.

If only he could call up the Badgetts and tell them he wasn't ever going to walk into their home or office again. If only he could just sit here in this cozy kitchen with Marge and have a peaceful breakfast without ever having to think about the brothers again.

Marge poured her own coffee and slathered jam on a muffin. "Now tell me," she ordered. "What happened at the party? The way you dragged yourself in last night, it must have been awful. Didn't the satellite hookup work?"

"Unfortunately, it came through loud and clear."

Her eyes widened. "What do you mean, 'unfortunately?' "

"Mama Heddy-Anna was plastered." Charlie relayed the rest of the story, omitting nothing and finishing with a vivid description of Mama Heddy-Anna thumbing her nose at the North Shore social set.

Frustrated, Marge thumped the table with her clenched fist. "I can't believe I missed that. Why do I only go with you to the boring parties? And to think I was the one who said Thanksgiving weekend was a bad time to have our reunion. What did I ever do to deserve this?"

Charlie sipped the last of his coffee. "I wish I *had* missed it! Those two are going to be in one foul mood today." It was on the tip of his tongue to tell her that it was now obvious to everyone present at the party that the Badgett brothers had not been back to Wallonia since they left it, and to relate to her Mama's own words, "How much bad you do, you can't come visit your mama?"

Charlie had never had the courage to tell Marge that it was only after he was in too deep to get out that he had learned the full extent of the situation in Wallonia. Junior and Eddie had been sentenced, in absentia, to life imprisonment there, for a host of crimes Charlie didn't even want to think about. They could never go back, and he could never get away from them.

With something akin to despair, he got up, kissed the top of Marge's head, went to the closet, put on his overcoat, picked up his briefcase, and left.

The Badgett office building where Charlie worked was in Rosewood, about fifteen minutes away from the estate. Junior and Eddie were already there when Charlie arrived. They were in Junior's private office, and to Charlie's surprise both men were in remarkably good spirits. He had expected them to be in foul moods and to somehow manage to blame at least part of the Mama fiasco on him.

On the drive there from Little Neck he had been preparing his defense: "I suggested you make the donation for the wing, give the party, and present the portrait. The satellite hookup was your idea."

But, of course, Charlie knew that was the last thing he could say. Any hint that Mama's appearance had been less than a delight would be unforgivable. By now the brothers would have figured out another reason why the party had been a colossal flop.

The entertainment, Charlie thought. They'll decide that Nor Kelly and Billy Campbell didn't cut the mustard. They'll blame Jewel for suggesting them and me for hiring them. As he turned into the reserved parking area, he suddenly remembered how upset Kelly and Campbell had been when they came out of Junior's office yesterday.

The brothers must have found fault with the way they sang "Happy Birthday" in Wallonian, Charlie decided. Reluctantly he turned off the ignition, got out of the car, and pressed the "lock" symbol on his key ring. Dragging his feet, he walked to the building and took the elevator to the fourth floor, which was entirely dedicated to the Badgett brothers' quasi-legitimate enterprises.

The reason for the early meeting was that Junior was interested in purchasing a new car dealership in Syosset that was beginning to cut into the profits of his own operation. Junior's secretary was not yet in. As Charlie murmured a greeting to a receptionist and waited to be announced, he wondered how long it would be before the deal closed, before the new dealer got the message that he didn't have a choice not to sell to the Badgetts.

"Tell him to come on in," Junior's genial voice boomed on the intercom.

The office had been done by the same decorator who had lavished his excesses on the mansion. An ornately carved partner desk with a shiny finish, gold-striped wallpaper, a dark brown carpet emblazoned with the brothers' initials in gold, heavy brown satin draperies, and a glass-enclosed miniature village with a plaque inscribed OUR BOYHOOD HOME were only some of the points of interest.

To the left of the door, a couch and chairs upholstered in a zebra pattern were grouped around a forty-inch television screen hung on the wall.

The brothers were drinking coffee and watching the local station. Junior waved Charlie in, pointing to a chair. "The news is coming on, I wanna see it."

"After six hours, the warehouse fire in Syosset is still burning fiercely," the reporter at the news desk began. "Two firemen have been treated for smoke inhalation. The owner of the warehouse, Hans Kramer, suffered a heart attack at the site, and has been removed to St. Francis hospital, where he is now in intensive care . . ."

Vivid images of the blazing building appeared. On a split screen, a tape was rerun of a fireman administering CPR to Hans Kramer, who was stretched on the ground, an oxygen mask clamped over his face.

"That's enough, Eddie. Turn it off." Junior got up. "Still burning, huh? Must be some heck of a fire."

"Faulty wiring, I bet." Eddie shook his head. "Happens, huh, Junior?"

Hans Kramer. Charlie knew that name. He'd been to see

Junior at the mansion. He was one of the people who received "private loans" from the brothers. They did this to him. He didn't pay on time, Charlie thought with absolute certainty, so they burned down his business.

This scenario had been played out before. If the cops can prove Junior and Eddie had anything to do with this fire, they'll be facing another arson charge, Charlie thought, quickly assessing the situation. If Kramer dies, they could be facing a murder rap.

But of course, none of this would ever be traced back to the Badgetts. They were too careful. The loan Kramer signed with them probably had a normal interest rate on the face of the note. No one would know that the fifty percent interest rate had already been built into the principal. And of course the guy who actually set the fire would not be one of the thugs on their payroll. For that they would have contracted a free-lancer.

But if anything comes up to tie this fire to Junior and Eddie, I get the job of helping people to forget what they know or think they know, Charlie thought despairingly.

"Hey, Charlie, why so glum?" Junior asked. "It's a beautiful morning."

"Yeah, a really great morning," Eddie echoed, as he got up.

"And, like Jewel said, Mama was cute as a button on the satellite," Junior added. "She always loved her grappa. Like Jewel said, after Eddie and I went into the office yesterday, everyone kept saying that Mama was adorable."

"Yeah," Eddie agreed, his smile becoming nostalgic.

"And those entertainers were something else. Good. I mean really good."

Charlie had not seen Junior bubbling over with such fervent good humor in months. Jewel isn't the airhead I thought she was, he decided. If she managed to convince those two that everybody loved Mama, she ought to be made ambassador to Wallonia.

"I'm glad you liked Nor Kelly and Billy Campbell," he said. "They looked so upset when they came out of your office that I thought maybe you'd told them you weren't satisfied with their music."

Charlie was immediately aware of a drastic change in the atmosphere. Junior looked at him, his eyes cold slits, his cheekbones flushed, the muscles in his neck suddenly prominent. "What did you say?" he asked, his voice chips of ice.

Nervously, Charlie glanced at Eddie, whose bovine cheeks were now rigid. The sweet sentiment evoked by Mama's name had vanished from his eyes. His lips had become a thin, grayish-red gash across his face.

"I simply said that . . ." his voice trailed off . . . "that Nor Kelly and Billy Campbell seemed a little upset when they came out of your office after your mother's satellite visit."

"Why didn't you tell us they were there?"

"Junior, there was no reason. Why would I have told you? I thought you knew."

"Eddie, the door was open from the reception room, wasn't it?" Junior asked.

"Yeah."

"All right, Charlie. You should have told us they followed us in. You should have known it would be important for us to know. Now you're going to have to make a few calls to the songbirds." He paused deliberately. "I think you know what I'm talking about."

I guess that's the end of the questions and the depositions, Sterling thought as he watched the FBI personnel shaking hands with Nor, Billy, Dennis, and Sean. It was now eleven o'clock. For the past two hours, the FBI had been taking sworn statements from the four. They even had Nor and Billy draw a floor plan to show where they were standing when they heard Hans Kramer's voice on the answering machine and Junior's order to burn the warehouse.

"Ms. Kelly, you're sure the Badgetts didn't suspect that you were in the room right outside their office?" Rich Meyers, the head investigator, asked again as he picked up his briefcase. "As I explained, if they knew you overheard them, you'd need to be protected immediately."

"I don't think they knew. From what I understand about the brothers, if they had seen us they probably would have called off their plans for the fire." Nor readjusted the comb that was holding her hair in place. "There's an old expression, 'I feel like something the cat dragged in.' . . .

My mother used to say that, Sterling thought.

". . . and that's exactly the way I feel now. If you're done with me, I'm going to go home, climb in the Jacuzzi, and then get a couple of hours' sleep."

"A very good idea," Meyers said sympathetically. "All right. We'll be in touch with you. In the meantime go about your business as usual."

Sounds easy, Sterling thought. Unfortunately it's not going to work like that.

Sean O'Brien lingered only a minute after the federal officers left. "I'll keep you posted," he promised.

"Dennis, why don't you take the day off?" Nor suggested. "Pete can handle the bar."

"And lose all those holiday tips? I don't think so." Dennis yawned. "I better start setting up. We've got another holiday lunch group, Nor."

"I haven't forgotten. But they'll have to do without me. See you later."

When the door closed behind Dennis, Billy said, "Holiday tips? Forget it. He just wants to make sure that he's around if any trouble starts."

"I know. Are you going to try to get some sleep, Billy? Don't forget, we've got two more shows tonight."

"Right now I have to check my messages. I talked to a couple of the guys about getting together for lunch sometime this week."

Nor slipped her arm into her coat. "Hearing Hans Kramer's message was the reason we're in this mess. It would have been one thing if we could have stopped the fire, but now the prospect of being witnesses against those two scares me."

"Just remember they have no idea we overheard them." Billy pressed the playback button on the answering machine.

Sterling shook his head as he thought of Charlie Santoli. Maybe he won't mention that he saw Nor and Billy, he thought hopefully. But given the future events he already knew about, he was sure that wasn't the way things played out.

"You have two new messages," the electronic voice began.

The first was from a friend who was organizing a lunch for the next day. "You don't have to call back unless tomorrow doesn't work for you." The second was from the recording company executive who'd offered him the contract last night.

"Billy, this is short notice but Chip Holmes, one of our top guys, is coming into town unexpectedly. He would really like to meet with you today. He's staying at the St. Regis. Can you join us for a drink around 5:30? Let me know."

"Why do I think you can make it?" Nor asked when the message clicked off. "Chip Holmes. Billy, that's great. If Holmes likes you, the sky's the limit with that company. You won't just be another singer with potential. He'll put big money into building you up."

"Which is exactly what I need," Billy said, as he did a quick drumroll on the tabletop with his fingers. "I don't want to be a one-hit wonder. You know better than I do how many guys had a little success early on, and then ended up job hunting when they were thirty-five. Let's face it. In this business I'm already no kid."

"I know what you're talking about, but you're going to make it," Nor assured him. "Now I really will get out of here. Break a leg. I'll see you tonight."

At the door, she looked over her shoulder. "I always swear I won't give you advice, but I can't help myself. You'd better leave plenty of time to get into New York. The holiday traffic is still pretty heavy."

"I'll take the train," Billy said absently, as he picked up his guitar.

"That's smart."

When Nor left, Sterling settled back in the club chair, his legs stretched over the hassock. He listened as Billy began plucking at the strings and softly singing words he'd written on a crumpled sheet of paper.

He's trying out new lyrics, Sterling thought. Upbeat, but with a nice plaintive touch. Billy really is good. I always did have an ear for music, he recalled.

Forty-five minutes later, the phone rang. Billy picked it up, said, "Hello," listened, then said, nervously, "You're calling from Badgett Enterprises? What can I do for you?"

Sterling hoisted himself from the chair and in two quick strides was at Billy's side, his ear to the receiver.

At the other end of the line, Charlie Santoli stood in his office, hating himself more and more with every word he uttered. "I am a representative of the company. The reason I am calling is that, as you may know, the Badgett brothers are philanthropists who have a large scholarship program for children in the local area. They thoroughly enjoyed your performance last night, and they know you have a young daughter."

Sterling saw Billy's forehead tighten. "What has my daughter got to do with this?"

"Her future has a great deal to do with it. The Badgetts understand how uncertain your future as a performer may be. They would like to set up a trust fund to ensure that Marissa will be able to go to a fine college in another ten years."

"Why would they want to do that?" Billy asked, restrained anger in his voice.

"Because sometimes remarks made in jest are overheard and, if repeated, take on a life of their own. The Badgetts would be very upset if that happened."

"Are you threatening me?"

Of course I am, Charlie thought. It's my job. He cleared his throat. "What I am offering is to make your daughter one of the selected recipients of a one hundred thousand dollar trust fund. It would please Junior and Eddie Badgett very much if you'd accept. On the other hand, they would find it dismaying if you were to repeat lighthearted remarks that might be misconstrued."

Billy stood up. The receiver hit Sterling in the jaw, causing him to blink.

"Listen, you representative of Badgett Enterprises, whoever you are, you tell those two that my daughter doesn't need their trust fund. I'll take care of her education myself without any help from them . . . And as for their 'joking' or 'lighthearted' remarks, I don't have a clue what you're talking about."

He slammed down the phone, sank onto the couch, and clenched his hands into fists. "They know we heard them," he said aloud. "What are we going to do?"

*T*he Heavenly Council was watching the developments on Earth with rapt attention. Charlie Santoli's phone call to Billy Campbell brought instant response.

"Charlie Santoli had better watch out," the monk said sternly.

"He'd better not come crying to us when his time is up." The shepherd's eyes flashed fire.

"It wasn't what the sisters taught him at St. Francis Xavier," the nun said sadly.

The queen's expression was grave. "He'd better wake up before it's too late."

"He wants to be good," the nurse volunteered.

"Well then, madam, for goodness sake, Charles Santoli must mend his ways and get on with it," the admiral thundered.

"I think Sterling will be looking to confer with us again," the Native American saint reflected. "He has great humility. He wants to do his job, and he's not afraid to ask for help."

"He was always capable of deep caring and love," the shepherd observed, his tone now mollified. "I was pleased by the expression in his eyes as he sat watching Marissa when she was sleeping."

$\mathcal{S}$terling caught up with Marissa just as she was putting her ice skates in her carrying case and rushing out to the car. When he had realized that Billy was going to catch a few hours' sleep, he had trotted over to Marissa's house to see how she was doing.

He arrived in time to join Roy as he drove Marissa to the rink, bringing the munchkins along for the ride. Squashed between the twins, Sterling ducked flailing arms that attacked him from both sides. His jaw was still a little sore from being bopped with the receiver when he'd been listening in on Santoli's conversation with Billy, and, at one year of age, Roy Junior had a mean right cross.

But they are cute babies, he conceded with only a shade of reluctance. It's kind of fascinating to see how they're taking in everything they see. My problem was that I didn't have any brothers or sisters. Maybe I wouldn't have been so anxious to stay away from kids all my life if I'd had some experience with them.

He remembered the time he was godfather at a christening and the baby had drooled all over his pin-striped suit. It was the first time I wore it, too.

In the front seat, Roy was saying to Marissa, "I understand Grandma is going to teach you how to make apple strudel today."

What a thrill, Sterling thought, and realized Marissa was having exactly the same reaction. However, she said politely, "I know. Grandma's so nice."

Roy smiled benignly. "I want to have at least *two* pieces."

"Okay, but don't forget I have to save a piece for Daddy and one for NorNor."

It's not easy to be a stepparent, Sterling thought sympathetically. Marissa always keeps him at arm's length. If I'd known Roy better before I met him next year, I wouldn't have been so quick to dismiss him as a bore.

But he does drive like a snail with a bad back. Sterling concurred totally with Marissa's impatient thought, "Step on it. Practice will be over before I get there."

She's Nor to a tee, Sterling decided.

When they arrived at the rink, Marissa thanked Roy for driving her, kissed him on the cheek, and waved to the twins before rushing out of the car.

Sterling climbed over Roy Junior's car seat and saw the surprised expression on the baby's face. He senses me, he thought. They both are beginning to sense me. Babies have so much awareness of the metaphysical. Too bad it gets lost along the way.

He caught up with Marissa and listened as she chatted animatedly with her friends at the side of the rink.

Miss Carr was the teacher he would see next year at the skating rink in Rockefeller Center. She blew a whistle and ten children, all the others a couple of years older than Marissa, skated onto the ice.

Some of the children were very good, but Marissa was simply outstanding. What a little trouper, Sterling thought as he watched her take a couple of hard spills. She just gets up, shakes herself off, and tries the spin or jump again.

Later, when the children had changed back into their shoes or boots, one of the girls came over to Marissa. "My sister got your dad's single for Christmas. She wondered if he would mind signing it for her."

Marissa's beaming with pride, Sterling thought as he watched and noted with amusement that she tried to sound oh-so-casual when she said, "Oh, sure. My dad likes to sign autographs for my friends."

"Is he writing a new song now?" the girl asked.

"He's always writing a new song."

"Tell him to write a song about us!"

"He's writing one about me first!" Marissa giggled.

Seven going on twenty-five, and bursting with love for her dad. Sterling sighed. And so near to being separated from him for a long time. Well, I've got to be off. He took one last look at Marissa's glowing smile, then left the rink.

Adjusting his homburg, he started walking back to Billy's apartment. He was planning to accompany him to his meeting, and was looking forward to being in Manhattan again.

But I'm really getting to know my way around Madison Village, he thought, as his feet crunched in the snow, making a sound only he could hear. I must say it's a very nice place to live.

"So howd'ya make out when you talked to Johnny one note?" Eddie asked. He was standing behind Junior, who, like a judge about to pass sentence, was sitting upright at his desk.

"Not very well." Charlie's hands were drenched in perspiration. He wanted to keep his voice calm but could not. "I spoke to Billy Campbell and offered him the scholarship for his daughter and explained that you would be dismayed if any remarks made in jest were misconstrued."

"All right, all right, we know what you were gonna say," Eddie said impatiently. "So what did he say?"

There was no staving off the answer. "He said for me to tell you that he'd pay for his daughter's education himself, and that he doesn't know what you mean by joking or lighthearted remarks. Then he slammed down the phone."

Charlie knew he could not soften Billy's reaction to the call, that if he tried, the brothers would see through him. The fact that Eddie was asking the questions was a frightening sign that now the next step would be taken. Coercion. And if that didn't work . . .

"Get out of here, Charlie," Junior ordered. "You sicken me. You let this happen." He looked up at his brother and nodded.

Charlie slunk out of the office. By tonight, Billy Campbell and Nor Kelly would have a warning that might frighten them into silence. Please let them take that warning seriously, he prayed, then shook his head in misery.

Once again he cursed the day fifteen years ago that the Badgett brothers had come to his one-man law office in Queens and asked him to represent them in their purchase of a dry-cleaning chain. I needed the business, so I didn't ask enough questions about them, he thought. Truthfully, I didn't want to know the answers. Well, I know them now.

When she reached home, Nor relaxed in the Jacuzzi, washed and blow-dried her hair, and, planning on a nap, dressed in lounging pajamas. Then Billy's phone call destroyed all thought of sleep.

Her throat closing, she listened as Billy related his conversation with "a representative of Badgett Enterprises."

"I called that FBI agent, Rich Meyers, and left a message for him. Then I called Sean, but he's out too. I waited to call you, Mom, because I hate to upset you, but you have to know what's going on."

"Of course I have to know about it. Billy, somehow those people found out that we were in that outer office. Maybe they have hidden cameras."

"Maybe. Or maybe someone spotted us coming out of there."

Nor realized she was trembling. "Do you know who it was on the phone?"

"He didn't give his name, but I think it might have been that guy who told us what to sing when we got there yesterday."

"I remember him. Kind of nervous and weasely-looking."

"That's the one. Look, I'd better get moving. I'm taking the three o'clock train into Manhattan."

"Billy, be careful."

"You're supposed to say, 'Break a leg.' "

"I already did."

"That's right, you did. See you later, Mom."

Mechanically, Nor replaced the receiver on the cradle. Break a leg. She had worked in a nightclub where the owner was behind in his payments to someone like the Badgetts. A broken leg had been his first warning to pay up.

And what didn't seem to have occurred to Billy yet was that the caller had talked about Marissa. Will the Badgetts try to get to Billy and me through Marissa? Nor agonized.

She dialed Sean O'Brien's number, hoping against hope that she'd reach him. He knew a lot about the Badgetts. Maybe he could tell her what they were likely to do next. We've already given statements, she thought. Even if we wanted to, how could we possibly take them back?

She knew the answer. It wasn't that they *couldn't* take them back. It was that they *wouldn't*.

I always used to dress in a suit when I had a business meeting, Sterling thought as he followed Billy onto the three o'clock train to Manhattan.

For his appointment with the recording company executives, Billy had chosen vintage jeans, a loose-fitting dark blue shirt, boots, and a leather jacket.

I'll never get used to these new styles. But then again, in the 1880s, when Mother was a young woman, she wore laced corsets, high-button shoes, bonnets, and floor-length dresses. Sterling sighed, suddenly nostalgic for the serenity of the afterlife, where concerns about clothing simply didn't exist.

He took the aisle seat next to Billy, who had found a vacant window seat. I always wanted the window seat too when I traveled by train, Sterling remembered. When Annie and I went to visit our friends in Westport, I always grabbed the window seat, and Annie never complained. I wonder if that's what the Heavenly Council meant when they called me "passive-aggressive"?

He could see how deeply worried Billy was just by looking at the troubled expression in his eyes and on his face. He was glad when Billy closed his eyes. Maybe he can relax a little, Sterling hoped. He's going to need to be "on" when he meets that guy Chip Holmes.

The train was a local and took forty-five minutes to get to Jamaica, in Queens. From there they took the subway to Fifty-ninth Street in Manhattan.

We're an hour early, Sterling noted as they climbed the steps to the street. Darkness was just setting in. The traffic was heavy, and there were Christmas decorations in all the windows. I hope Billy kills the time by taking a walk. I haven't been in this part of Manhattan in forty-six years.

It looks the same and yet different. Bloomingdale's will never change. But I don't see Alexander's. I loved living here, he remembered as he took it all in. There's no place like it in the world.

He trailed behind Billy to Park Avenue. The trees on the center island were glowing with white lights. The air was cold but clear. Sterling inhaled appreciatively even though it wasn't necessary for him to breathe. The hint of evergreen in the air made his mind drift back to other Christmases.

They started downtown and passed the building at 475 Park Avenue. My boss used to live there, Sterling recalled. He always invited Annie and me to his New Year's Day open-house party. Whatever happened to him? I never noticed him in the celestial waiting room and I never saw him whizzing by the celestial window.

Just then, a very old man, cane in hand, hobbled out of the building and spoke to the doorman. "My driver's late. Get me a cab, sonny."

Sterling gasped. It's him, my boss. Josh Gaspero. He must be a hundred years old! I'd love to be able to say hello, but from the looks of things, I suspect I'll be seeing him soon enough.

Billy was half a block ahead of him, and Sterling hurried to catch up, glancing over his shoulder several times as he watched his boss impatiently tapping his cane on the sidewalk. He hasn't changed, Sterling thought fondly.

The St. Regis was on Fifty-fifth Street, but Billy kept going south on Park Avenue. At Fiftieth Street he turned right and walked a few blocks west to Rockefeller Center.

Here I am again, Sterling thought. It's such a great place to be at Christmastime. I bet I know just where Billy's headed. Five minutes later they were in front of the magnificent evergreen with its thousands of colorful lights, looking down at the skating rink.

This is where it all started. Sterling smiled to himself. Started next year. Together they watched the skaters and listened to the music floating up from the rink. I'll bet Billy has skated here with Marissa. Sterling looked at the expression on Billy's face. I can tell she's in his thoughts right now.

Billy turned to leave. Sterling tailed him across Fifth Avenue and up the steps of St. Patrick's Cathedral. He's stopping to say a prayer, Sterling thought. The moment they walked through the door and experienced the majestic beauty of the cathedral, Sterling felt an intense sense of longing. His mind became filled with the image of the joy and peace he had seen on the faces of the people approaching the open gates of heaven. Head bowed, he knelt beside Billy, who had lit a candle at a side altar.

He's praying for his future on earth. I'm praying for mine in eternity. To be in heaven even for an hour on Christmas Day . . . Sterling felt tears in his eyes and whispered, "Please, help me complete my mission on earth so that I may begin to be worthy of You."

When they left St. Patrick's a few minutes later, Sterling was filled with both gratitude and regret. He knew that at last he was beginning to truly appreciate the gift of life and the gift of life everlasting.

At the St. Regis Hotel, Billy went into the King Cole bar, sat at a small table, and ordered a Perrier.

Oh, they've changed it here, Sterling thought as he looked around. But the Maxfield Parrish mural behind the bar is the same. I always loved it.

It was almost five o'clock. The bar was suddenly filling up. I remember meeting friends here for a glass of wine after work, Sterling mused. Just as people are doing now, getting together with friends, enjoying each other's company—that at least is timeless.

A couple of young women at a nearby table cast smiling glances at Billy, who was too absorbed in his own concerns to even notice them.

At five-twenty, Sterling could see that Billy was gearing up for the meeting. He straightened his shoulders, began sipping the Perrier, and kept his eye on the door. Ten minutes later, when the recording executive who had been at Nor's

Place appeared with a fast-moving, balding man in tow, Billy was the picture of easy charm.

They moved to a bigger table. But there's always room for one more, Sterling thought as he took the unoccupied seat and began to sort out his companions. It only took a moment to figure out that Chip Holmes was the top executive of the recording company, while Eli Green headed the New York office.

Holmes was a no-nonsense, say-it-and-be-finished-with-it type. "You're good, Billy, you're very good. You've got a special quality to your singing that makes me confident you'll catch on big time."

That's what I said, Sterling thought.

"You've got good looks, too, which is a rarity among the male performers in this business . . ."

Sterling silently applauded Billy's demeanor throughout the half-hour meeting. He looked and sounded confident, and, while appreciative, he did not grovel when Holmes offered a substantial contract and promised that he would have the kind of backup support he needed.

"We're teaming you with one of our top producers. He wants to get to work with you as soon as possible. By this time next year you could be a star, Billy."

The meeting ended with handshakes and a fervent expression of gratitude from Billy.

Good move, Sterling thought. During the discussion, you impressed him with your composure, but it was time to let him know how happy you are. I know his type. He loves having the role of kingmaker.

In the lobby, Billy consulted his train schedule and looked at his watch. Looking over his shoulder Sterling could see that he was going to try to make the 6:50 from Jamaica. A little tight, Sterling worried, but it's an express train, and the next one is a local.

They covered the seven blocks back to Fifty-ninth Street in half the time it had taken them to get to the hotel. Billy must be walking on air, Sterling thought. For the moment, at least. I'm sure that instead of thinking about the Badgetts, he's reveling in what the recording contract means to his future.

They hurried down the subway steps and onto the crowded platform. Consulting his watch again, Billy made his way to the edge and leaned forward, hoping to see a headlight emerging from the tunnel.

It happened in an instant. Sterling saw a burly man suddenly materialize, and with a slam of his shoulder send Billy teetering over the tracks. Anguished, Sterling tried to grab Billy, knowing that he could not regain his balance on his own, but his arms went right through Billy's body.

The train was rushing into the station. He's going to fall, Sterling thought helplessly. A woman screamed as the same burly man suddenly pulled Billy back to safety, then disappeared into the crowd, headed toward the exit.

The doors of the train opened. Numbly, Billy stepped aside as exiting passengers rushed past him.

"Are you all right?" someone asked him anxiously as he boarded the train.

"Yes, I'm all right." Billy grabbed the center pole near the door and held on tight.

An elderly woman admonished him. "Do you know how lucky you are? You should never stand that close to the edge of the platform."

"I know. It was stupid," Billy agreed, then turned away, struggling quietly to normalize his rapid breathing.

It wasn't stupid, Sterling wanted to shout, dismayed that he could not warn Billy. Billy doesn't realize he was pushed. The platform was so filled with people, he must think that the press of the crowd caused him to lose his balance, and that somebody grabbed him in time.

Sterling hung onto the center post with Billy as the subway bounced and swayed down the tracks. They arrived in Jamaica just in time to make the 6:50 to Syosset.

All the way home, chilling thoughts kept running through Sterling's mind: What happened on the subway platform was no accident, and what will the Badgett brothers do next?

*L*ee Kramer sat alone in the small hospital waiting room reserved for the families of people in intensive care. Except for the few minutes at a time that she had been able to stand at the foot of Hans's bed, this was where she had been since before dawn, when she had followed the ambulance to the hospital.

A massive heart attack. The words echoed dully in her mind. Hans, who in the twenty-two years of their marriage had hardly ever had a cold.

She tried to remind herself that the doctor had said that Hans was stabilizing. He said that Hans had been lucky. The fact that the fire department was at the scene and had the equipment to shock his heart and start it beating again had saved his life.

He's been under too much stress, Lee thought. The sight of the fire put him over the edge.

She glanced up when the door opened, then turned away. A number of her friends had stopped in and sat with her during the day, but she did not know this sober-faced, dark-haired man.

FBI agent Rich Meyers had come to the hospital hoping that he would be allowed to speak to Hans Kramer for a few minutes. That was out of the question, the nurse had told him firmly, but then added that Mrs. Kramer was in the waiting room.

"Mrs. Kramer?"

Lee whirled around. "Yes. Is anything . . . ? "

The strain on Lee Kramer's face was obvious. She looked as though she'd been punched in the stomach. Her short, ash-blond hair, blue eyes, and fresh complexion told Meyers that, like her husband, she was probably of Swiss extraction.

Rich introduced himself and handed her his card. A look of alarm came over her face. "FBI?" she asked.

"We're investigating the possibility that the fire at your husband's warehouse was deliberately set."

"Deliberately set? Who would do that?" Her eyes widened.

Meyers sat down in the vinyl chair opposite her. "Do you know anything about loans your husband may have taken out?"

Lee put her hand to her mouth, and the thoughts that had tormented her all day tumbled out. "When everything turned and the business started to go bad, we took a second mortgage on the house for every cent the bank would lend us. There's a mortgage on the warehouse, but only as much as we could borrow on it. I know it's underinsured. Hans was so sure that if he could tough it through a little longer, the business would take off. He really is brilliant. The software program he designed can't miss." Her voice faltered. "And now what does all that matter? If only he makes it . . ."

"Mrs. Kramer, in addition to the mortgages, were there any other loans your husband may have taken?"

"I didn't know about any, but this morning, after we got the call about the fire, he said something like, 'I borrowed a lot of money . . . ' "

Meyers's face remained impassive. "Did he tell you who it was borrowed from?"

"No, that was all he said."

"Then you probably wouldn't have known if he made a phone call yesterday evening and left a message for someone about repaying a loan?"

"No, I don't know anything about that. But he was very agitated last night."

"Mrs. Kramer, does your husband have a cell phone?"

"Yes."

"We'd like to have your permission to check his cell phone account and home phone records to see if he made a call last night."

"Who would he have been calling?"

"People who don't give extensions on loans."

Her insides churning, Lee was afraid to ask the next question. "Is Hans in any trouble?"

"With the law? No. We just want to talk to him about that loan. The doctor will tell us when it's possible to see him."

"*If* it's possible," Lee whispered.

*C*harlie Santoli had left the Badgetts' office as quickly as possible after he'd been excoriated for not succeeding in his mission to buy Billy Campbell's silence, but at four o'clock Junior sent for him again.

He hastened down the corridor and around the corner to the executive suite shared by Junior and Eddie. Their long-time secretary was at her desk. Years ago, Charlie had decided that even as a baby, Lil must have had pugnacious features. Now that she had passed the fifty mark, they had settled into a permanent scowl. Still, he liked Lil, and she was probably the only person in the building who was not afraid of Junior.

She looked up, her eyes magnified by her oversized glasses, and jerked her thumb over her shoulder, always the sign to go right in. Then in a voice made hoarse by years of chain-smoking, she rasped, "The mood is slightly better." She paused. "Ask me if I care."

Charlie knew he didn't have to respond. He took a deep breath and pushed open the door.

Junior and Eddie were sitting on the zebra chairs, glasses

in their hands. Toward the end of the business day they often had a drink together before getting into their limo and heading home. If Charlie happened to be there, he was usually told to help himself from the bar.

Today was not one of those days. He was neither offered a drink, nor was he asked to sit down.

Junior looked over at him. "Just in case Campbell smartens up, we need to have this scholarship program on the level. Everyone knows we just gave big bucks to the old folks. Now we gotta take care of the little ones. You figure out the details. Find nine other outstanding kids from the area, all of 'em the age of Campbell's kid. We think it would be very nice of us to give them scholarships too."

They've got to be kidding, Charlie thought. Hesitantly, he suggested, "I think it would be wise if at least some of the children are older. How can you explain to the media that you want to give ten college scholarships to first-graders when there are high school boys and girls who need them now?"

"We don't wanna do that," Eddie barked. "We wanna build for the future. And if Campbell is smart enough to fall in line, we slide his kid's name in with the others."

"Marissa's marks are good and she's a nifty little ice-skater," Junior remarked offhandedly as he bit the end off a cigar. "Go find us other talented kiddies like her."

Charlie felt one more turn of the winch that twisted his digestive system. *Nifty little ice-skater.* How does Junior know so much about Marissa Campbell? he wondered bleakly.

"Of course, if you can't persuade Billy Campbell to retract anything he might have said about our little joke, there won't be any need for a fund," Junior said quietly. "Don't let us keep you, Charlie. I know how busy you are."

Back in his own office, Charlie tried to reassure himself that, bad as they were, people like Junior and Eddie never went after the children of their enemies.

But those two . . . He could not pursue the thought. Instead he found himself praying that Billy Campbell would wise up and accept the scholarship.

Shaking his head, he reached for a folder with the information about the car dealership the Badgetts wanted to buy. He had intended to spend his whole day on it, but had been too distracted to concentrate.

At 6:30 he closed the file and got up. He had his coat on and his briefcase in his hand when the phone rang. Reluctantly he picked it up.

A low, husky voice that he did not recognize said, "Charlie, the boss told me to pass the word that Billy Campbell almost took a dive in front of a subway train, but I managed to save him."

Before Charlie could answer, the connection was broken.

He replaced the receiver and stood at his desk for a long minute. In all the years he'd worked for the Badgetts, the worst he'd done was to speak to potential witnesses as he had spoken to Billy Campbell, and later arrange laundered payments to them. It had never gone beyond that. He could get the book thrown at him for tampering with witnesses, but this was different, and much more serious. They want me to be involved in whatever happens to Billy Campbell and Nor Kelly if I can't convince them to keep their mouths shut, he thought. I've never seen Junior and Eddie as foul tempered as they were today, and I know it's because they're worried.

He closed the door to his office and walked to the elevator. Even if Billy Campbell and Nor Kelly agreed to forget what they had overheard, would that be enough to ensure their safety?

Charlie doubted it.

$\mathcal{N}$or's Place was bustling when Billy and Sterling returned at eight o'clock. The dinner hour was in full swing and the bar was busy. Nor was talking to people at a table near the bar, but as though she had eyes in the back of her head, she turned around the instant Billy walked into the dining room. Her face brightened, and she hurried over to him.

"How did it go?"

Billy grinned. "Chip Holmes is crazy about the 'special quality to my singing.' "

He does a pretty good imitation of Chip Holmes, Sterling thought. He captures that nasal quality.

Nor threw her arms around him. "Oh, Billy, that's fantastic." She signaled to a nearby waiter. "Nick, we're celebrating. Bring us a bottle of Dom Perignon."

I wouldn't mind a glass of that, Sterling thought. As he took his usual seat at Nor's table, a host of memories rushed through his mind.

His mother and father opening a bottle of "Dom" on his twenty-first birthday . . .

Another "bit of the bubbly" shared with them when he passed the bar exam . . .

That wonderful crisp October day when he and Annie had driven with another couple to visit the Roosevelt home in Hyde Park. On the way back they stopped for a picnic lunch on the Palisades, and Annie had surprised everyone when she trotted out a chilled bottle of champagne and four glasses.

After I finished mine, I drank half of hers, he thought. Oh, Annie!

Sterling swallowed over a lump in his throat and realized he hadn't been paying attention to Billy and Nor. Obviously Billy had told her about the meeting, because she was saying, "Billy, that's wonderful! You're on your way."

None of them noticed that Sean O'Brien had come into the restaurant. They all looked up, surprised, when he joined them.

"Sorry I didn't get back to you earlier, Nor," he apologized. "Next time call me on my cell phone. Has anything else happened?"

"Tell Sean about the call from Badgett Enterprises, Billy," Nor said.

Sterling watched Sean O'Brien's expression darken as Billy related the scholarship offer.

When Billy shrugged his shoulders and said, "So that's it," Sean's first question was to ask if he had told the FBI about the call.

Billy nodded. "Rich Meyers wasn't in his office. I left a message."

"He called back here at about five o'clock," Nor said quietly. "My impression is that he thinks it was an iron fist in a velvet glove kind of warning."

O'Brien looked grim. "Listen, after being a detective for nearly thirty years, I know too much about these people. The iron fist will be front and center if you don't fall in line."

Billy, tell O'Brien about what happened in the subway, Sterling pleaded silently. You need protection.

"I guess we have no choice but to wait it out," Nor said. "Look, here's the champagne. On a happier note, we're drinking to Billy's future." She turned to him. "You'd better sip that fast. We have to go on pretty soon."

Billy got up. "I'll take it upstairs with me. I have to change, and I want to give Marissa a call. You know her. She wanted me to give her the scoop as soon as I got back."

I'll just wait here and keep Nor company, Sterling decided, when Dennis appeared from the bar.

"I wanted to congratulate Billy, but he's disappeared already."

"He went upstairs to change," Nor said.

Sterling listened as Nor happily filled the men in on Billy's meeting with the recording executives. Then she said, "The news about the contract is wonderful, but I can't tell you guys how tense I've been all day. Ever since Billy got that phone call, I've been so afraid of what the Badgetts might do next. . . . And right now I'd better get ready myself," Nor concluded. "We're on in fifteen minutes. Can you stay, Sean?"

"For a while. Kate's on duty tonight."

Dennis turned to Sean. "I've got to get back to work. Why don't you sit at the bar?"

As the group broke up, they all spotted Billy running down the stairs, a fire extinguisher under his arm.

"Mom, your car is on fire," he snapped. "I called 911."

Word of the fire spread through the dining room. Dennis grabbed a fire extinguisher from the bar. O'Brien and Sterling one step behind him, he raced outside to the blazing vehicle and, with Billy, tried to extinguish the flames.

Nor came out of the restaurant, surrounded by several diners whom she had been trying to calm.

Fire trucks came roaring into the parking lot, and immediately the firefighters ordered people to stand back.

It took only a few minutes for the fire to be extinguished. Nor's car had been in its usual spot near the kitchen entrance, well away from the general parking area.

Then Nor called, "Come on, everybody." She stood at the door, ushering people back into the restaurant.

When the hoses were turned off, the fire chief, Randy Coyne, accompanied by a Madison Village police officer, spoke to Nor, Billy, Sean, and Dennis privately in Nor's office.

"Nor, your car's a loss, but it could have been a lot worse. At least the fire didn't spread to any other vehicles, and I can tell you right now you're lucky it didn't spread to the restaurant."

"How did it start?" Nor asked quietly.

"We think it was doused with gasoline."

For a moment there was complete silence in the room, then Sean O'Brien said, "Randy, we have some idea of who's behind this, but it's a matter for the FBI. They're already investigating a telephoned threat Billy got this morning."

"Then call them immediately," the police officer said. "I'm going to make sure that we have a patrol car stationed here overnight."

"And one at Nor's house," Sean O'Brien said firmly.

"I'll be glad to know someone's keeping an eye out," Nor admitted.

Sean turned to Nor and Billy. "Nor, a piece of advice. The best thing you can do right now is for you and Billy to go out there and conduct business as usual."

"Wish I could stay for your show," the fire chief said with a half smile.

"I'll be outside until I can get someone posted here and at your home, Mrs. Kelly," the cop promised.

Billy waited until they were gone, then said slowly, "Something happened to me in the subway today. I really thought it was my own stupidity, but . . ."

Sterling watched the expressions on the faces of Nor, Dennis, and O'Brien become increasingly grave as Billy told them what had happened on the way home.

"The same guy who jostled you at the edge pulled you back," Sean said flatly. "That's an old trick with these people."

The phone rang. Billy answered it. He listened for an instant as the color drained from his face. Then, the receiver still in his hand, he said, "Someone just told me he's sorry he bumped into me on the platform, and maybe next time I should borrow my mother's car when I come in to New York."

*A*n instant later in eternity, but one week later by the earthly calendar, Sterling requested and received a meeting with the Heavenly Council.

He sat in the chair facing them.

"You look as though you have the weight of the world on your shoulders, Sterling," the monk observed.

"I feel as though I do, sir," Sterling agreed. "As you know, the events of the past week moved rapidly after the car fire. The police and FBI convinced Nor and Billy that it was necessary to go into protective custody until the Badgett brothers' trial. The expectation was that the trial would take place in a relatively short time."

"We all know *that* won't happen," the shepherd said.

"Do you have a battle plan?" the admiral asked imperiously.

"I do, sir. I'd like to move through this earthly year quickly. I'm most anxious to get to the point where I meet Marissa and can start doing something to help her. My hands are tied until then. I'd just like to have glimpses along the way of what

I will need to know to assist me in safely reuniting Marissa with her father and grandmother."

"So you don't want to spend another full year on earth?" The queen sounded amused.

"No, I do not," Sterling told her, his voice solemn. "My earthly time is behind me. I'm impatient to help Marissa. She said good-bye to Nor and Billy only a few days ago, and already she's desolate."

"We're aware of that," the nurse said softly.

"Tell us your plan," the Native American saint suggested.

"Give me the freedom and the power to move through the year as quickly as I feel necessary, plus the ability to transfer myself from location to location by a simple request to you."

"Who are you planning to visit?" the matador asked.

"Mama Heddy-Anna, for one."

The Heavenly Council stared at him in shock.

"Better you than me," the monk muttered.

"Mama Heddy-Anna has put up with a lot," the nun said.

"I dread the day she shows up here," the admiral said. "I commanded ships in battle, but a woman like that, I must say, might just turn me into a coward."

They all laughed. The monk raised his hand, palm outward. "Go forward, Sterling. Do what needs to be done. You have our support."

"Thank you, sir." Sterling looked into the face of each of the eight saints and then he turned his head toward the window. The gates of heaven were so close he felt as though he could reach out and touch them.

"It's time to go, Sterling," the monk said, kindly. "Where do you want to be placed?"

"Wallonia."

"To each his own," the monk said and pushed the button.

$\mathcal{A}$ light snow was falling, the wind was cold, and the village of Kizkek looked as though it had been unchanged for a thousand years. It was in a little valley, nestled at the foot of snow-covered mountains that seemed to form a protective shield against the outside world.

Sterling found himself on a narrow street at the edge of the village. A wagon drawn by a donkey was approaching, and he stepped aside. Then he got a good look at the face of the driver. It was Mama Heddy-Anna herself, and she was hauling a load of logs!

He followed the wagon around the side of the house to the backyard. She stopped there, jumped down, tied the donkey to a post, and began to unload the logs, chucking them vigorously against the house.

When the wagon was empty, she unhitched the donkey and pushed it into a fenced-off section of the yard.

Stunned, Sterling followed Mama into the stone cottage. It appeared to be one fair-sized room built around a central fireplace. A large pot hanging over the fire was sending out the delicious smell of beef stew.

The kitchen area had a wooden table and benches. Mama's rocking chair was facing a television set, which stuck out like a sore thumb in its surroundings. A couple of other well-worn chairs, a hooked rug, and a scarred wooden cabinet completed the decor.

The walls were covered with photographs of Heddy-Anna's two offspring and her incarcerated husband. The mantel over the fireplace held framed pictures of several saints, obviously Mama's favorites.

While Mama pulled off her heavy parka and scarf, Sterling climbed the narrow staircase to the second floor. It contained two small bedrooms and a tiny bathroom. One room was clearly Mama's. The other had two side-by-side cots—obviously where Junior and Eddie laid their innocent heads during their formative years, Sterling decided. A far cry from the gaudy mansion on the north shore of Long Island they now inhabited.

The cots were piled with women's designer clothes, all with the tags still on. Clearly these were gifts from the missing sons, all items that their mother found absolutely useless.

Sterling could hear the faint sound of a phone ringing and hurried downstairs, immediately realizing that the Heavenly Council had given him a gift he hadn't thought to request. I never thought I'd see the day I could understand Wallonian, he reflected, as he heard Mama tell a friend to pick up some extra wine. Apparently there'd be ten of them for lunch and she didn't want to run short.

Oh good, Sterling thought. Company's coming. It's a great way to find out what Mama Heddy-Anna is all about. Then his eyes widened. She was speaking on a wall phone in the kitchen area. Next to the phone, where most people keep emergency numbers, there was a blackboard with a numbered list.

Probably a shopping list, he decided until he saw the words written in bold lettering across the top of the board:

ACHES AND PAINS

Sterling's eyes raced down the list:

1. Bad feet
2. Pains around heart
3. Gas
4. Dizzy spell
5. Threw up twice
6. Can't taste food no more
7. Need operation
8. Broken heart
9. Never close an eye
10. Bad back
11. Swollen gums

Now, I've seen it all, Sterling thought, as he noticed checks after each complaint, with dates of the brothers' phone calls from America. She's got this down to a science, he thought. She doesn't use the same complaint twice in a row.

Mama Heddy-Anna had hung up the phone and was standing next to him, examining the list with a satisfied smile.

Then, moving with the decisiveness of a drill sergeant, she began slinging dishes, glasses, and cutlery onto the table.

A few minutes later, her friends started to arrive. Wreathed in a smile, she greeted them with bear hugs.

She had said there would be ten of them. They're all very prompt, Sterling observed. The tenth guest was the one carrying the wine.

He guessed that they were all in their seventies and eighties and looked as if they had spent many years working outdoors. Their leathery complexions and callused hands were testimony to a lifetime of hard physical labor, but their ready laughter and joy in socializing was not different from that of the groups of friends Sterling had observed gathered at the King Cole bar in Manhattan, or at Nor's Place on Long Island.

Mama Heddy-Anna produced a steaming loaf of fresh-baked bread from the oven and dished out the stew. The wine glasses were filled, and everyone gathered at the table. Frequent bursts of laughter followed the exchanges of stories about their fellow villagers, or about outings they had enjoyed together. There had been a dance at the church hall the week before, and Heddy-Anna had done the Wallonian national folk dance on a tabletop.

"Now I want to dance on a tabletop at the monastery when they have their grand opening as a hotel on New Year's Day," Heddy-Anna announced.

"I skied over and took a look," the baby of the crowd, a sturdy seventy-year-old, said. "Can't believe how nice it is. It's been closed for twenty years, since the last monk left. It's nice to see it all fixed up."

"My boys used to ski over there all the time." Heddy-Anna helped herself to more beef stew. "Too bad the monastery is over the border. We could use the tourists' money here."

The peal of the telephone made them all giggle. Heddy-Anna wiped her mouth with her napkin, winked at her friends, put her finger to her lips, and waited for the fifth ring before answering feebly. "Ha . . . lllllo."

She stood up to get a better look at the blackboard. "I can't hear. Talk louder. Wait, I gotta sit down. My foot's so bad today. It came out from under me. I laid on the floor all night. Finally managed to get up."

Her expression changed. "What'd'ye mean, 'Wrong number,' isn't this my Eddie?"

She slammed down the phone. "False alarm," she told her friends as she sat down and picked up her fork.

"It was good practice," the woman next to her said admiringly. "Heddy-Anna, believe me, you get better every time."

The phone rang again. This time Heddy-Anna made sure who she was talking to before she began to recite her list of complaints. She repeated almost verbatim the story she had told to the first caller. "And besides that . . ." she continued, tears in her voice.

The friend nearest the phone jumped up and pointed to item six on the list.

Heddy-Anna nodded. ". . . I can't taste a single bite of what I eat. The weight is dropping off me."

I guess I have the picture of what's going on in Wallonia,

Sterling thought wryly. *Now I'd like to jump ahead to the next season and look in on Marissa.*

He left the stone cottage, looked up at the mountains, then stared into the heavens.

May I please go back to Marissa's house? And let it be April, he requested, and then closed his eyes.

$\mathcal{S}$pring comes first to the willows, Sterling thought as he looked at the slender and graceful clump of willow trees on the lawn outside Marissa's home in Madison Village. There was a pinkish haze about them, a promise of the blossoms that would soon be visible.

It was early evening, and dusk was just beginning to settle as the lingering rays of the sun disappeared. He went inside and found the family at the dinner table.

He took a chair in the dining room as far away as possible from Roy Junior and Robert, who were vigorously thumping their high chairs with spoons.

Marissa was sitting opposite them, silently picking at a small slice of chicken.

Denise and Roy were at the ends of the table, each one with the chair pushed close enough to the side so that they could easily feed a twin.

"How was school today?" Roy asked Marissa, as he managed to get a spoonful of mashed potatoes into Robert's mouth.

"It was okay, I guess," Marissa said listlessly.

"Marissa, you're just pushing the food around on your plate. You've simply got to eat something," Denise pleaded, then abruptly closed her lips after receiving a warning glance from Roy.

Marissa put down her fork. "I'm really not hungry. May I be excused?"

Denise hesitated, then nodded. "Daddy and NorNor should be phoning in an hour."

"I know."

"I'll call up to you, and you can go into our room and talk to them there."

Sterling was tempted to follow her but decided he wanted to hear what Denise would say to Billy when he called.

Denise waited until Marissa had disappeared up the stairs before speaking. "Roy, I couldn't bring myself to talk to her about the progress reports. She just can't seem to focus on her classes. The teacher said that she believes Marissa is blaming herself for Billy and Nor leaving, that Marissa thinks that somehow she did something wrong."

"A lot of kids feel like that when something happens to their parents, whether it's death, or divorce, or separation," Roy said. "We just have to be understanding."

Roy's a good soul, Sterling thought. He's trying very hard.

"Down, down, down." Roy Junior had had enough of sitting at the table.

"Down, down," Robert echoed, bouncing in his high chair.

Roy took a final bite of salad and got up. "Coffee later. I'll get these two upstairs and their baths started."

Denise began to clear the table. The phone rang a few minutes later. "Oh, Billy, you're early," she began. "No, of course, Marissa isn't out. If she knows you're going to call, she doesn't budge from the house for fear of missing you. Any new developments?"

She listened, then said, "Well, when you talk to her, tell her how proud you are that she's always been such a good student. We both know she'd do anything to please you. All right, I'll put her on. Give my best to Nor."

She laid the receiver on the table and walked to the staircase. "Marissa," she called.

Marissa was already at the head of the stairs. "Is that Daddy on the phone?"

"Yes."

Sterling hurried up the steps and followed Marissa's flying feet to the master bedroom. She closed the door tightly behind her.

For the next few minutes, Sterling listened as Marissa pleaded with Billy to come back. She promised she wouldn't *ever* pester to go to the movies, or try to make him stay on the phone and talk to her when she knew he was busy, or . . .

Sterling went over and bent down to listen to what Billy was saying. "Baby, don't even *think* like that! This has nothing to do with anything *you* did. I loved it when you phoned me . . ."

"Then why won't you tell me your phone number right now?" Marissa asked tearfully.

"Rissa, it's just that I can't. I have to borrow a phone when

I talk to you. NorNor and I want nothing more than to get home to you as soon as possible. Once I'm back, I'll make this all up to you, I promise . . ."

After she had finally said a tearful good-bye, Marissa went back to her room, sat at her desk, and turned on her CD player.

The sound of Billy's hit single filled the room. "I know what I want . . . I know what I need . . ."

Sterling watched as she put her head down on her arms and began to sob. I'm going to get you what you want and need, Marissa, Sterling vowed. And I'll do it if I have to move heaven and earth. No, with the *help* of heaven, he corrected himself.

He closed his eyes and addressed the Heavenly Council. Would you please deliver me to wherever the Badgett brothers are at the moment?

When Sterling opened his eyes, he found himself inside a large, bustling, noisy restaurant on the water.

Unless the brothers are traveling, I guess that's Long Island Sound, he thought. He looked over at a woman studying the menu. The cover read SAL'S ON THE SOUND.

It was a steak-and-seafood place. People with bibs were happily breaking lobster claws; sirloin steak on sizzling platters was obviously popular. And, he noticed, many diners had chosen his favorite appetizer, crabmeat cocktail.

But where were Junior and Eddie? He was on his second tour of the tables when he noticed a secluded semicircular corner booth with a prime water view. Upon closer inspection he saw the three occupants were none other than Junior, Eddie, and a scantily clad Jewel.

Junior and Eddie had just had one of their telephone visits with Mama Heddy-Anna, and as usual both of them were in a tailspin worrying about her. Jewel had suggested they'd all feel much, much better if they went out for a nice, relaxing dinner.

They were already sipping cocktails, and the waiter was in the process of collecting the menus.

Sterling took a seat on the windowsill at a right angle to them. I wonder what they ordered? he thought.

"I don't think I can eat a bite," Eddie lamented. "When I think of how sick Mama is, I'm crying inside."

"You've been crying outside too, Eddie," Jewel said. "Your nose is all red." She patted Junior's hand. "Yours is red too, lambie."

Junior pushed her hand away. "I have a cold."

Jewel realized her mistake. "And your allergies, honey. The allergy season is terrible right now. This is the worst it's been in years."

"Yeah, yeah." Junior picked up his glass.

"She fell again," Eddie mourned. "Our poor mama's foot gave way again, and on top of that, her gums are swollen. She can hardly chew."

I guess she didn't use that one last time, Sterling thought.

"And her friends keep begging her to eat. Nothing tastes good to her anymore."

"She's been saying that ever since I met you guys three years ago," Jewel said earnestly. "She must be eating *something*."

Beef stew, Sterling thought. Lots of beef stew.

"She hasn't fallen since January," Eddie continued. "I was hoping her legs were getting better." He turned to Junior. "We gotta go see our mama. I'm telling you we gotta go see her."

"We can't and you know it," Junior snapped. "We sent her some nice new clothes to cheer her up."

"She's gonna love them," Jewel enthused. "I picked them out special. Two pairs of satin lounging pajamas, a cocktail dress, and a hat with lots of flowers to wear to church on Easter Sunday."

Eddie's expression soured. "Mama says the clothes we send her stink."

"That hurts my feelings," Jewel said, pouting. "If I met her, I'd be able to shop for her better. Every woman has figure problems. I mean it could be her hips, it could be her waist, her behind might have a funny shape—"

"Shut up, Jewel," Junior thundered. "I don't want no more anatomy lessons."

I was enjoying it, Sterling thought.

Obviously offended, Jewel got up. "Please, excuse me," she said with exaggerated emphasis.

"Where yuh goin'?" Eddie asked.

"To the lala." She flounced away.

"Is she mad because I said Mama don't like the clothes she picked out?"

"Forget the clothes," Junior barked. "Listen, I got a call when *you* were in the lala."

"When was I in the lala?"

"You're always in the lala."

"No, I'm not."

"Yes, you are. Every time I go look for you, you're in the lala. Now listen to me. Our guys can't track down Nor Kelly and Billy Campbell."

"They're a bunch of dopes," Eddie said.

"It takes one to know one. Keep your mouth shut and listen to me. The whole case against us falls apart if Kelly and Campbell don't take the stand. We gotta get rid of them."

"It's a big country. How do we get rid of them when we can't find them?"

"We gotta find them. I took the next step. I called a certain hit man."

Eddie looked at Junior. "Not Igor?"

"Yes, Igor," Junior said. "He's very good at what he does. I told him the only lead we have so far is that they're somewhere out West."

"Here I am," Jewel chirped as she slid into the banquette and kissed Junior's cheek. "I've forgiven you both for not appreciating all I do to make Mama Heddy-Anna happy and comfortable, and I have to tell you something. I think you should figure out a way to go visit your mama in person, and you should do it before it's too late."

Junior glared at her. "Drop it."

The waiter appeared with a tray of appetizers.

I've learned what I needed to know, Sterling thought. The Badgett brothers are determined to track down Nor and Billy and make sure they don't live to testify against them.

Sterling decided to take a long walk before he made a request to be transported somewhere else. An hour later, he had made his decision. He closed his eyes and whispered, I'd like it to be midsummer, and may I please get together with Nor and Billy?

*S*urely they're not staying *here,* Sterling thought, dismayed. He was standing on the second-floor balcony of a rundown motel directly off a busy highway. Although it was blazing hot, the area was beautiful. Like Mama Heddy-Anna's village, the landscape boasted magnificent mountain views.

Of the six vehicles parked outside the motel, four had Colorado plates.

He noticed a heavyset man with dark glasses sitting in an SUV. It seemed to Sterling that the man was staring at his rearview mirror, watching the door directly behind him.

Sterling turned and peeked in the window. Billy was standing inside the shabby room, hands in pockets. He was looking at Nor, who was sitting on the edge of the bed, a phone in her hand.

They looked different. Nor's blond hair was medium brown, and she wore it in a prim knot at the nape of her neck. Billy had a beard, and his dark hair was cut much shorter.

Maybe this is where they make their calls home, Sterling thought. If they're in the Witness Protection Program, they can only phone from secured lines. They both look worried sick.

He went inside, and taking off his homburg, put his ear to the receiver. I'm getting good at eavesdropping, he thought. He heard a familiar voice at the other end of the line and realized that Nor was talking to Dennis.

"Nor, I don't have to tell you that this place is all about you," Dennis was saying. "Sure, I can do drinks, and the guys are good waiters, and Al is the best chef we've ever had, but that's not good enough. When the customers come in, they want to see you at your table."

"I know. How big a loss this month?"

"Very big. We're not a quarter full for dinners, even on Saturdays."

"Which means, of course, that the waiters' tips are way down," Nor said, "Look, Dennis, this can't last much longer. The minute the trial is over and the Badgetts are in prison, we'll be able to come home. Figure out how much in tips the guys are losing, and let's make up half of it to them in their paychecks."

"Nor, maybe you didn't hear me. You're losing money hand over fist as it is."

"And maybe you didn't hear me," Nor flared. "I know the restaurant needs me to be there. But you and Al and the waiters and the kitchen help and the cleanup crew are all part of what make it work. It took me years to put together such a good team, and I'm not going to lose it now."

"Take it easy, Nor, I'm just trying to help you keep your head above water with this place."

He Sees You When You're Sleeping ✳ 159

"I'm sorry, Dennis," Nor said contritely. "This whole business is grinding me down."

"How's Billy?"

"How do you think? He just called Marissa and the recording company. Marissa absolutely refuses to talk to him—or to me either for that matter—and the recording company told him that unless this is over soon, they'll have to cancel his contract."

There was silence, then Nor said, "Dennis, you know that impressionist painting near the fireplace in my living room?"

"The pain-by-numbers one?"

It was an old joke between them.

"Yes. You have power of attorney. Go to my safe-deposit box and get the papers on it. Take everything to the Reuben Gallery. I know they'll make an offer on it. It should be worth at least sixty thousand dollars. That will help."

"You love that painting, Nor."

"Not as much as I love my restaurant. Okay, Dennis, I guess that's all the good news I can handle at one time. I'll talk to you in about two weeks."

"Sure, Nor. Hang in there."

Her next call was to Sean O'Brien to see if there was any word about the trial date. There wasn't.

They left the motel room in silence, went down the steps to the parking area, and got into the SUV in which the man in dark glasses was sitting. He's got to be the federal marshal who looks out for them, Sterling decided.

He rode in the backseat with Nor. Not a word was exchanged on the twenty-minute drive. He spotted a road sign that indicated Denver was thirty miles away. I know exactly where we are, he thought. The Air Force Academy is near here.

Billy and Nor were living in a run-of-the-mill bi-level house, the sole virtue of which, at least as far as Sterling could tell, was its location. It was set on a large piece of property, shaded by tall trees that afforded privacy.

When the car stopped, Billy turned to the marshal. "Frank, come inside please. I've got to talk to you."

"Sure."

The living room furniture looked as if it had been purchased at the auction of a bankrupt motel: Naugahyde sofa and chairs, mismatched Formica coffee and end tables, burnt-orange wall-to-wall carpeting. A groaning air conditioner labored to pump in cool air.

Sterling could pick out Nor's attempts to make the room livable. Tasteful framed prints drew the eye away from the hideous furnishings. A vase of black-eyed susans and several large green plants helped alleviate the depressing atmosphere.

The living room opened into what was meant to be a dining area. Billy had turned it into a music room, furnishing it with a scarred upright piano piled with sheet music, a CD player, and shelves of CDs. His guitar rested on a club chair near the piano.

"What can I do for you, Billy?" the marshal asked.

"You can help us pack. I'm not staying here another night. I've had it."

"Billy, this is not Frank's fault," Nor said, hoping to placate him.

"For all we know, this trial will never happen. Am I supposed to spend the rest of my life rotting in this house? Frank, let me explain something to you. I turned thirty years old last week. In the music business that's old, you understand? It's *old*. The ones who make it these days, start at seventeen, even younger."

"Billy, calm down," Nor begged.

"I can't calm down, Mom. Marissa is growing up without us. She's growing up *hating* me. Every time I talk to Denise she tells me how worried she is about Rissa, and she's right. I'm taking my chances. If anything happens to me, at least it will happen while I'm living my own life."

"Listen, Billy," the marshal interrupted. "I know how frustrating this is for you and for your mother. You're not the first one in this program who's gone crazy. But you *are* in real danger. We have ways of finding out things. There was no reason to tell you this before, but there's been a contract on you and your mother since January. And when the Badgetts' personal goons couldn't find you, they hired a hitman."

Nor paled. "When did they hire him?"

"Three months ago. We know who he is and our men are looking for him. Now, do you still want me to help you pack?"

The fire went out of Billy. "I guess not." He walked over and sat at the piano. "I guess I'll just keep writing music that somebody else will have the chance to sing."

The marshal nodded to Nor and left. After a few moments,

Nor went over to Billy and put her hands on his shoulders. "This really won't last forever, you know."

"It's hell on earth."

"I agree."

I do too, Sterling thought. But what do I do about it? The more he learned about the problem, the less he felt able to solve it.

With a sympathetic glance at Nor and Billy, he went outside. I'm used to the altitude in the heavens, but not in Colorado, he thought, feeling a little light-headed.

It's hard to believe that Nor and Billy will still be here in December. I can only imagine the emotional state they'll be in by then. Where else can I go? What can I do? Everything hinges on the trial. Maybe I should drop in on the Badgetts' legal counselor. After all, he was the one who saw Billy and Nor coming out of Junior's office.

I'll be glad to get out of this heat, Sterling decided as he closed his eyes. Summer was always my least favorite season.

Once more he addressed the Heavenly Council. May I please be transported into the presence of Charlie Santoli, and may it please be in early December? Amen, he added.

"We should have put the lights up at least a week ago," Marge commented as she unrolled another string of bulbs and handed them to Charlie, who was standing on a ladder outside their living room window.

"I've been too busy, Marge. I just couldn't get to it." Charlie managed to loop the string over the top of the evergreen, which had grown considerably taller since last year. "You know, there are people we can pay to do this. They have higher ladders, they're younger, they're stronger, and they could do a better job."

"Oh, but then we'd miss out on all the fun, Charlie. We've been doing this together for forty years. The time will come when you really can't do it, and then you'll wish you could. Admit it. You love this ritual."

Charlie smiled reluctantly. "If you say so."

Sterling sat on the steps observing the couple. He really is enjoying himself. He's a family man, he thought.

An hour later, chilled but pleased with themselves, Marge and Charlie went into the house, shed their coats and gloves, and gravitated to the kitchen for a cup of tea. When the teapot and freshly baked Christmas cookies were in front of them, Marge dropped her bombshell.

"I want you to quit that job with the Badgett brothers, Charlie, and I want you to quit it tomorrow morning."

"Marge, are you out of your mind? I can't do that."

"Yes, you can. We're not rich, God knows, but we've got enough to live on. If you want to keep working, put out your shingle again and do house closings and wills. But I'm not putting up with watching you build to a heart attack working for the Badgetts for another day."

"Marge, you don't understand—I can't quit," Charlie said desperately.

"Why not? If you drop dead, they'll get a new lawyer, won't they?"

"Marge, it's not that. It's . . . please, let's just forget it."

Marge stood up and placed both hands firmly on the table. "Then what is it?" she asked, her voice rising with every word. "Charlie, I want the truth. What's going on?"

Sterling listened as Charlie, at first hesitantly, then in a rush of words, confessed to his wife that over the years he had been sucked into making threats to people who stood in the way of the Badgetts. He watched Marge's reaction change from horrified shock to deep concern as she came to realize how emotionally tortured her husband had been for years.

"The trial I've been getting postponed has to do with the warehouse fire near Syosset last year. The singers hired for that Mama Heddy-Anna birthday party overheard Junior giving the order to have it torched. The word on the street is that the entertainers are working in Europe, but the truth is they're in protective custody."

So that's the story that's been circulated about Nor and Billy, Sterling thought.

"Why do you want the trial postponed?"

"We bribed experts who will swear the fire was caused by exposed wires. Hans Kramer, the guy who owned the warehouse, disappeared, but the brothers found out last month that he and his wife are living in Switzerland. They've got family there, and after what happened, Kramer doesn't want to tangle with the Badgetts."

"You haven't answered my question, Charlie."

"Marge, I'm not the one who wants the postponements. The Badgetts want them."

"Why?" She looked straight into his eyes.

"Because they don't want the trial to start until Nor Kelly and Billy Campbell are silenced for good."

"And you're going along with that?" she asked incredulously.

"They may not find them."

"And they *may* find them. Charlie, you can't let that happen!"

"I know I can't," he burst out. "But I don't know what to do. You must realize that the minute I go to the feds, the Badgetts will know it. They have a way of finding out those things."

Marge began to cry. "How did this happen? Charlie, no matter what the consequences for us, you have to do the right thing. Just wait a few more days until Christmas is over. Let's have one more Christmas when we know we'll all be to-gether." She wiped her eyes with the back of her hand. "I'll pray for a miracle."

Charlie stood up and wrapped his wife in his arms. "Well, when you say your prayers, be more specific," he said with a tired smile. "Pray for a way to make Junior and Eddie visit Mama Heddy-Anna in the old country. I can have the cops ready to nab them the minute they set foot on Wallonian soil. Then we'd all be in the clear."

Marge looked at him. "What are you talking about?"

"They've been tried in absentia for the crimes they com-mitted over there and both got life sentences. That's why they can never go back."

Life sentences! Sterling thought. At last he understood what he had to get done. The only question was how to do it.

Sterling went outside. Marge had turned on the Christmas lights as soon as Charlie finished hanging them. The weather was changing, and the late afternoon sun had disap-peared behind heavy clouds. The multicolored bulbs on the evergreen twinkled cheerily, helping to dispel the growing gloom of the winter day.

Suddenly, like a gift, Sterling remembered something he had overheard at Mama Heddy-Anna's lunch table. It's possi-ble, he thought, it's possible. A plan to get the brothers back to the old country began forming in his mind.

It was a long shot, but it just might work!

"Sterling, it looks as if you've been doing your homework," the nun said approvingly.

"You're quite the world traveler," the admiral boomed.

"We were surprised that you went back to Wallonia," the monk told him, "but then we got an inkling of what you were up to. That was my old monastery, you know. I lived there fourteen hundred years ago. Hard to believe it's being turned into a hotel. I can't imagine that place having room service."

"I can understand that, sir," Sterling agreed, "but for our purposes it may be most fortuitous. I think I have at last found a way to help Marissa and Nor and Billy, and maybe even Charlie. He needs my help as much as Marissa does, but in a different way."

He squared his shoulders and looked into one face after the other. "I request permission to appear to Charlie so that he can work with me on solving the problems."

"Do you mean to appear as you did to Marissa, who understood you were not of her world?" the shepherd inquired.

"Yes. I think that's necessary."

"Perhaps you'd better plan to become visible to Marge as

well," the queen suggested. "Something tells me she rules the roost in that family."

"I was afraid to push the envelope and ask to meet her," Sterling admitted with a smile. "It would be wonderful if I could communicate with both of them."

"Push the envelope?" The matador's eyebrows raised. "That expression wasn't in vogue when you were alive."

"I know. But I heard it somewhere. Maybe in Nor's restaurant. I kind of like it." He stood up. "According to the earthly calendar, tomorrow will be the day when I first met Marissa. I've come full circle."

"Don't forget, it was also the day you first appeared before us," the Native American saint teased.

"That, I assure you, I'll never forget."

"Go forward with our blessing," the monk told him. "But remember—Christmas Day, which you hope to celebrate in heaven, is drawing very near."

$\mathcal{M}$arissa opened the door of her room and was delighted to see Sterling sitting in the big chair by the desk. "I thought you were going away and would come back to say good night," she said.

"I did go away," he explained. "I took a look at the whole last year of your life when you were down at dinner and understand now why Daddy and NorNor had to leave."

"But I've only been downstairs for an hour!"

"Time is different for me," Sterling said.

"I kept thinking about you. I ate fast, then got stuck listening to Roy tell his boring story about Christmas when he was a little boy and was one of the shepherds in the school play. I got away as fast as I could. I'm so glad you're here."

"Well, I learned a lot while you were at dinner. I'm going to have to leave now because I'm going to be very busy trying to get your daddy and NorNor back for your birthday."

"That's Christmas Eve," she reminded him quickly. "I'll be eight years old."

"Yes, I know."

"That's only four days from now."

Sterling saw skepticism mixed with hope in Marissa's eyes. "You can help me," he told her.

"How?"

"Say a few prayers."

"I will. I promise."

"And be nice to Roy."

"It isn't easy." Her whole personna changed, and her voice deepened. " 'I remember the time when . . . blah, blah, blah.' "

"Marissa," Sterling cautioned, with a twinkle in his eye.

"I knowwwwww . . ." she said. "Roy's all right, I suppose."

Sterling stood, relishing the momentary lightheartedness he saw in Marissa's eyes. It was an instant reminder of the first time he had seen her with Billy and Nor. I cannot fail her, he thought. It was both a prayer and a vow.

"It's time for me to go now, Marissa."

"Christmas Eve—you promised!" she said.

$\mathcal{C}$harlie and Marge always piled the presents under the tree a few days before Christmas. Their three children all lived nearby on Long Island, a blessing for which Marge gave daily thanks.

"How many people's kids are scattered to the ends of the earth?" she would ask rhetorically from under the dryer. "We're so lucky."

Their six grandchildren were a source of joy, from the seventeen-year-old about to start college to the six-year-old in the first grade. "All good kids. Not a lemon in the lot," Marge often boasted.

But tonight, after she and Charlie had arranged the gifts, they did not feel their usual sense of satisfaction and anticipation. Dread of the inevitable outcome of Charlie going to the FBI had settled over them, and at 8:30 they were sitting quietly side by side in the living room, Charlie aimlessly flipping the channels on the television.

Marge stared at the Christmas tree, a sight that usually brought her great comfort and joy. Tonight it didn't have that effect on her. Not even the homemade ornaments her grandchildren had made over the years could bring a smile to her face.

Then, as she watched, one of the ornaments slid to the carpet, the paper-mâché angel with one wing shorter than the other, and wearing a hat instead of a halo. She got up to retrieve the angel, but before she could reach it, the ornament started to glow.

Her eyes widened. Her jaw dropped. For once, not a word came from her lips. In ten seconds the angel had been transformed into a pleasant-faced man, neatly dressed in a dark blue chesterfield coat and wearing a homburg, which he promptly removed.

"AAAAAAAAAHHHHHHHHHH," Marge screamed.

Charlie had started to doze on the couch. He jumped up, saw Sterling, and cried, "Junior sent you, I know he did."

"Jesus, Mary, and Joseph," Marge cried prayerfully. "The Badgetts didn't send him, Charlie. He's a ghost."

"Please don't be alarmed. I'm here to help solve your problems with the Badgetts," Sterling said calmly. "Do sit down."

They looked at each other and then obeyed. Marge blessed herself.

Sterling smiled. For a moment he said nothing, wanting them to get used to him and lose any lingering fear that he might do them harm.

"Mind if I sit down?" he asked.

Marge's eyes were still like saucers. "Please do, and help yourself to the Christmas cookies," she said, pointing to the dish on the coffee table.

"No, thank you." He smiled. "I don't eat anymore."

"I wish I had that problem," Charlie said, staring at Sterling, the remote control still in his hand.

"Turn off the TV, Charlie," Marge ordered.

Click. Sterling was amused, remembering the queen's remark that in this house, Marge ruled the roost. He could see them both begin to relax. They understand that I'm not here to harm them, he thought. It's time to explain myself to them.

"You know Nor Kelly and Billy Campbell, Charlie," he began. "And you know they are in the Witness Protection Program."

Charlie nodded.

"I was sent here to help Billy's little girl, Marissa, who longs to be with her father and grandmother. In order to accomplish that, it is necessary to remove the threat that hovers over them."

"Junior and Eddie," Charlie said flatly.

"Those two!" Marge said contemptuously.

"As I began investigating the best way to ensure Nor and Billy's safety, I realized that you are in grave danger from the Badgetts as well."

Marge reached for Charlie's hand.

"Understanding all the circumstances, I have come to the conclusion that the best and most effective way to solve the problem is to get the Badgetts to go back to Wallonia, where they will be incarcerated for the remainder of their lives."

"And I hope they throw away the key," Marge pronounced. "Those two are bad, bad, bad."

Ever the lawyer, Charlie said, "I assure you, there is no way that those two will ever willingly set a foot on Wallonian soil."

"Even for Mama Heddy-Anna?" Sterling asked.

"They've been crying in their beer for nearly fifteen years about not seeing her, but they still haven't paid her a visit," Charlie said.

"I have a plan that just might take them back to their mother's side," Sterling explained.

Their expressions suddenly hopeful, Charlie and Marge listened raptly.

he next morning, FBI agent Rich
Meyers, accompanied by his top assistant, agent Hank Schell,
arrived at the home of Charlie and Marge Santoli. Dressed as
repairmen, they carried in tool kits that held recording
equipment.

They sat at the kitchen table with the Santolis while Schell
set up and tested the microphone.

When Charlie had phoned Meyers the previous night,
Meyers warned him that he might want to have legal counsel
before going on the record with potentially self-incriminating
disclosures.

Charlie had dismissed the suggestion. I've got something
far better than a lawyer, he thought. I've got Sterling in my
corner.

"Ready, Mr. Santoli?" Meyers asked.

"Yes, I am. For the record, my name is Charles Santoli . . ."

For the next hour, Charlie described his connection with
the Badgetts, starting with their legitimate enterprises, then
detailing his growing knowledge of their criminal activities.
He concluded by saying that in his opinion the government

would never be able to convict Junior and Eddie Badgett of arson in the Kramer warehouse fire, and that Nor Kelly and Billy Campbell would always be in grave danger, whether or not they were in protective custody.

Meyers listened impassively.

Charlie took a deep breath. "With what I'm going to suggest to you, you may decide I need medication, not legal help, but at least hear me out."

Sterling made a face at Charlie and winked.

With a slight smile, Charlie calmly laid out the plan Sterling had outlined to him the night before. Every once in a while he glanced over at Sterling for approval and was rewarded with an encouraging nod.

Meyers' first reaction—"You want to do *what*?"—gradually changed to a grudging "It's not impossible," to an eventual "We've spent thousands of hours trying to get these guys and haven't been able to make anything stick. But if they're in prison for good, in Wallonia, their whole rotten operation will fall apart."

"That's my point," Charlie said eagerly. "It may take years to get a conviction here, and even in prison, they'd still be dangerous. But put them in prison halfway around the world, and those dopey goons of theirs would just disappear."

When the recorder was turned off, the two agents stood up, and Meyers said, "Obviously I've got to talk to the big guys at the office about this. I'll get back to you in a couple of hours."

"I'll be here," Charlie said. "My office is closed through Christmas."

When Meyers and Schell left, Marge commented, "Waiting is always the hardest part, isn't it?"

Sterling thought of his forty-six years in the celestial waiting room. "I absolutely agree," he said. "Hopefully the waiting will be over very soon for all of us."

At one o'clock, Rich Meyers phoned back. "It's a go. If you can do your part, we'll take care of the rest."

"The stores are always so busy at Christmastime," Jewel sighed as the limo pulled through the gates of the Badgett estate at three o'clock. "But doesn't it get you into the spirit, going to the mall and seeing everybody rushing around, doing their last-minute shopping?"

"It gets on my nerves," Junior said sourly. "I don't know how you talked me into going."

"Me too," Eddie echoed. "I'm not the type to eat lunch in the food court. That place was so noisy, I couldn't hear myself think."

"You never think anyway," Junior muttered.

"Very funny," Eddie growled. "Everybody says I take after you."

"But we got some good stuff," Jewel said brightly. "Those ski sweaters I treated you to look so nice. The trouble is we never go away, and there's not much skiing on Long Island." She shrugged her shoulders. "Oh, well. What're you gonna do?"

Inside the house, Jewel went straight to the salon to plug in the Christmas tree. "I can't say I'm crazy about all these purple lights," she murmured as she squatted, cord in hand, fishing for the outlet.

Junior was at the window. "You invite one of your ditzy friends over here, Jewel? There's a car down at the gate."

"My friends aren't ditzy, and no, they're all out shopping."

The intercom rang. Eddie went to the security panel on the wall and pushed the button. "Who is it?"

"It's Charlie, and I have my wife with me. Mind if we come up for a few minutes?"

Eddie rolled his eyes. "Sure, I guess it's okay."

"What the heck is Charlie bringing Marge over here for?" Junior asked irritably.

"It's the holidays," Jewel reminded them. "People drop in and visit each other. No big deal. Just nice and friendly. And caring."

"The holidays stink," Eddie said. "They make me feel bad."

"That's a very natural reaction," Jewel told him earnestly. "I was just reading an article written by a very smart psychologist. According to him, people get depressed because—"

"Because people like you drive them crazy," Eddie interrupted.

"Watch it, Eddie. Jewel is only trying to cheer us up."

"Oh, lambie pie, you're so right. That's all I want to do."

Eddie went to the door to admit the Santolis.

As the handle turned, Sterling whispered, "Don't be nervous, Marge."

Eddie's lame greeting, "Hi yah, come on in," made both Santolis know exactly how welcome they really were.

Marge braced herself and followed Eddie into the salon, trailed by Charlie and the ever-present Sterling.

"Welcome," Jewel trilled. "Happy holidays. What a nice surprise. We were thrilled to see your car drive in."

Oh my God, look at that tree, Marge thought. The few times she'd been in this house around Christmas, the trees had been reasonably traditional. Not this year.

She was holding a tin of cookies and handed it to Jewel. "I make these for all my friends every Christmas," she said.

"A sign of love," Jewel cooed.

"Sit down for a minute," Junior said. "We were on our way out."

"Sit, sit, sit," Jewel encouraged.

"We won't stay," Charlie promised as he and Marge sat together on a couch. "It's just that Marge had a dream last night that was so powerful, she felt she had to alert you."

"Alert us about what?" Junior asked, his tone measured.

"I had the most disturbing dream last night—about your mother," Marge began.

"MAMA!" Eddie bellowed. "Did something happen to her?"

Marge shook her head. "No, but does she suffer from dizzy spells?"

"Yeah," Junior's eyes bored into Marge's face.

"Pains around the heart?"

"Yeah."

"Gas?"

"Yeah."

"She can't taste her food?"

"Yeah."

"Never closes an eye?"

"Yeah."

"Throws up occasionally?"

"Yeah."

"Swollen gums?"

"I can't take it no more," Eddie shouted, his face crumbling into tears. "I gotta call her."

He ran to the phone.

Mama Heddy-Anna's annual Christmas party was in full swing. The wine and grappa were flowing. Everybody had brought a favorite dish, and the table was groaning with food. An old phonograph was scratching out Christmas carols, and a sing-along was in full swing.

When the phone rang, the person nearest to the phonograph yanked the needle from the record and screamed, "Pipe down, everybody!"

A few additions to Mama's list of ailments had been added by a couple of the partygoers, and someone obligingly pointed them out, as after waiting for the fifth ring, Mama Heddy-Anna picked up the phone.

"Ha . . . Ha . . . lllo."

"Mama, how are you? Someone had a dream you weren't feeling so good . . ."

"They dreamed right." Heddy-Anna winked at her friends

and motioned for her eyeglasses as she squinted at the new writing on the board.

"Mama, talk louder, I can't hear you. You sound so sick . . ."

Heddy-Anna read from the blackboard. "I think this is my last Christmas." She sighed, then improvised: "Did the person with the dream warn you that I'm a dying woman?"

"Mama, don't say that. It's not true. Grandmama lived to be one hundred and three, remember."

"She was a strong woman . . . not like me."

Junior picked up the extension. "Mama, is something worse?"

"I threw up this morning . . . because my gums are so swollen . . . dizzy, you should know how dizzy I am . . . can't see straight . . . wait a minute . . . I got the heart pain again . . . somedays it won't stop . . ."

Heddy-Anna's friends, impatient to resume partying, began to signal her to hang up the phone.

She nodded. "I can't talk anymore," she whined, "I'm short of breath. I need my rest. I can't believe you're calling so late. But what do I expect from sons who never come to see their mama?"

"Mama, you *know* how much we love you," Eddie sobbed.

A click in his ear was her response.

Jewel handed Eddie a fresh handkerchief. Junior blew his nose vigorously.

Marge and Charlie looked appropriately grave. Marge stood up. "I'm so sorry I said anything. I just thought it might be better to let you know, in case you wanted to go spend the holidays with her."

Charlie looked embarrassed. "Marge, would you wait in the car please? There's a little business I have to discuss with Junior and Eddie."

"Of course." Marge grabbed Junior's hand and pressed it. "I'm so sorry," she mouthed.

As she passed Eddie, she kissed him comfortingly on the cheek.

"Walk Marge to the car, Jewel, and then give us a few minutes," Junior ordered.

Jewel linked her arm with Marge. "Come on, honey. You were just trying to help."

When they were out of earshot, Charlie said hesitantly, "Of course, you understand that Marge is under the impression that you've visited Mama Heddy-Anna regularly over the years."

"It's a good thing she understands that," Junior snapped.

Charlie let it pass. "I felt so upset when Marge told me about her dream. Knowing the circumstances, something occurred to me. It may be a wild idea, but . . ." He paused and shrugged. "Well, at least I want you to know about it. It's a way that just might make it possible for you to safely visit your mother on Christmas Eve."

"What are you talking about?" Junior demanded.

"What does the St. Stephen of the Mountains monastery mean to you?"

"St. Stephen of the Mountains monastery? That was in the next town from us, just over the border. We used to ski there all the time when we were kids. It's been shut down since before we left."

"I thought you might have heard about it. They're reopening the monastery as a hotel on New Year's Day."

"No kidding." Eddie blinked. "Nobody was ever allowed in there. But what about it anyhow?"

"My cousin, who is a nun, usually joins us for Christmas dinner. She won't be with us this year because she's going on a pilgrimage. Sixty nuns and brothers and priests from all over the country will be staying at St. Stephen's during Christmas week, before it opens to the public."

They're getting the message, Charlie thought, as he saw the brothers exchange thoughtful glances. "They've chartered a plane that is leaving tomorrow evening from Teterboro Airport in New Jersey. They'll land at the new airstrip near the hotel, which, of course, is just over the border from your mother's home."

Charlie hesitated, wishing he could mop his brow, but he didn't want to seem nervous.

"I asked my cousin if there were any seats left on the charter, and as of this morning there still were four or five."

Junior and Eddie looked at each other. "We could ski from the monastery to Mama's house in no time at all," Eddie said.

Charlie swallowed, aware he either was about to hit a home run, or strike out. "I was thinking that if you two dressed as monks who had taken the vow of silence, there'd be no danger of anyone finding out who you are. I imagine you could easily arrange for the proper documentation."

"No problem," Junior said brusquely. There was a pause. He looked at his brother. "It always seemed too risky to go back home, but this could work."

"I'm going back," Eddie said, determination in his voice. "I'd never close an eye if anything happened to Mama before I got to see her again."

Charlie frowned. "We're going to have to act fast. The seats may already be gone."

"They better not be." Junior glowered. "When you heard about them, you shudda told us right away."

Charlie took out his cell phone.

"No, call from our phone. Put it on the speaker," Junior ordered.

"Of course."

"St. Mary's Convent," a woman's voice answered softly. "Sister Joseph speaking."

"Sister Joseph, this is Charles Santoli, Sister Margaret's cousin."

"Yes, how are you Mr. Santoli?"

"I'm well. Is Sister Margaret there?"

"No, I'm sorry, she's doing some last-minute shopping for her trip. We were advised to bring extra sweaters or wraps."

The brothers looked at Charlie. "Ask her," Junior said impatiently.

"Sister, do you happen to know if the flight to St. Stephen's is full?"

"I think it is, but let me take a look."

"There's *gotta* be room," Eddie whispered, clenching and unclenching his hands.

"I'm back, Mr. Santoli. I was right. We were full, but we just had two cancellations. One of our elderly sisters isn't well enough to make the long flight, so she and her companion are staying home."

"She better not have a quick recovery," Junior growled. "Book us those two seats."

On the other end of the phone, FBI agent Susan White, who had been sitting in the convent for several hours, waiting for the call, gave a thumbs-up to Rich Meyers.

Then she began to write, "Brother Stanislas and Brother Casper . . ."

Marge and Charlie were marvelous, Sterling thought, smiling from ear to ear as he realized that the first phase of the plan had worked perfectly.

Marissa, we're getting there, he thought.

"Good night, Marissa," Denise said, as she tucked her daughter in and bent down to give her a kiss.

"Good night, Mommy. I can't wait to wake up tomorrow. It's my birthday *and* it's Christmas Eve."

"We're going to have *lots* of fun," Denise promised as she turned out the light.

Downstairs, she joined Roy, who was drying the pots. "Everybody bedded down?" he asked cheerfully.

"Yes, but it's strange. I thought Marissa would be upset tonight, but she seems to be excited and happy, as though she's expecting a miracle, as though Billy and Nor will be here tomorrow."

"Then she's in for a terrible letdown," Roy said mournfully as he folded the dish towel.

"I got them everything they need," Charlie fretted. "The monks' habits, the sandals, the prayer books, the suitcases—real beat-up ones, like the brothers took the vow of poverty and meant it."

He and Marge and Sterling were sitting in the Santolis' living room, all of them tense with concern that the Badgett brothers would smell a rat before the pilgrimage charter plane took off.

"How about their passports?" Marge asked. "Any chance of a glitch with them?"

"First-rate forgeries," Charlie said. "They took care of that themselves."

"How were they getting to Teterboro?" Marge asked nervously. "I hope they didn't go in that showy limo."

"They were having the limo drive them to New York to one of their dry-cleaning shops that was closed. They were going to change there and take one of those cheap car services to the airport."

It was 11:55. The plane was due to take off at midnight.

"I don't know. Those two have a sixth sense," Charlie

moaned. "If at the last minute they figure out this was a setup, and don't get on that plane, I'm dead."

"Did you pick up any indication that they were suspicious when you saw them earlier today?" Marge asked, nervously shredding a cocktail napkin.

"None. I'm their new best friend. Don't forget, I'm the one who's getting them home to see Mama."

If this doesn't work, I'm the one who gets blamed for suggesting it, Sterling thought with a pang of guilt.

The ring of the phone made everyone jump.

Charlie grabbed the receiver. "Hello."

"Mr. Santoli?"

"Yes."

"This is Rich Meyers. You'll be glad to hear that a certain charter plane has just taken off, with Brothers Stanislas and Casper on board."

Charlie's relieved smile told Marge and Sterling what they needed to know.

"They should be landing in Wallonia in eight hours. The police there are waiting to arrest them. Our agents on board will shed their clerical robes and ride back home as soon as the plane refuels."

Charlie felt as though a two-ton weight had been lifted from his shoulders. "I imagine you'll want to be taking further statements from me."

"Next week. Enjoy your holiday. I know you'll cooperate with us." Meyers paused. "Don't worry too much, Mr. Santoli. I think you know what I mean."

"Thank you," Charlie said quietly.

Sterling stood up. "It's going to be okay," he said. "You're going to be fine, Charlie. You're a good man. And now I must leave you."

"Sterling, how can we ever thank you?" Marge asked.

"Don't even think about thanking me. Just use your time on earth wisely. Believe me, it goes very quickly."

Marge and Charlie entwined their hands. "We'll never forget you," Marge whispered.

"Never," Charlie echoed fervently.

"We'll meet again. I'm very sure of that," Sterling said as he disappeared.

"*H*ow much longer? This robe is making me itch," Eddie hissed, and was rewarded by an elbow in the ribs from Junior.

Junior fished a pad from his pocket and wrote, "Vow of silence. Shut up. Almost there."

At that moment the voice of the flight attendant came over the loudspeaker. "We are due to land at Monastery Airport in twenty minutes . . ." The usual instructions followed.

Eddie was twitching with excitement and beside himself with joy. Mama Heddy-Anna! I'm coming, Mama! he thought.

Junior didn't know the exact moment when the sinking feeling started. He looked out the window and narrowed his eyes. It was cloudy and, as the plane began to descend, light snow drifted against the windows.

He craned his neck and narrowed his eyes then spotted the monastery and the landing strip next to it. It's okay, he thought. For a minute I had a feeling that Santoli mighta skunked us.

Then the voice of the flight attendant came on again. "We have just been advised that due to extremely icy conditions, we will be unable to land at Monastery airport. Instead we will be landing at Wallonia City airport thirty miles away."

Junior and Eddie looked at each other. Eddie pushed back the hood of his robe. "Whaddaya think?"

SHUT UP, Junior scribbled furiously.

"You will be bussed immediately to St. Stephen's Monastery," the flight attendant chirped happily. "We do regret this inconvenience, but your safety is our first concern."

"How do we go through customs?" Eddie was trying unsuccessfully to whisper. "Are the passports okay if they really look at them under a special light or something?"

SHUT UP, Junior scrawled. Maybe it's okay, he thought. Maybe it's on the level. He looked around, searching out the faces of his fellow passengers. Most of them were deep in their prayer books.

THE PASSPORTS ARE OKAY, he wrote. IT'S YOUR BIG MOUTH I'M WORRYING ABOUT.

Eddie leaned over him to look out the window. "We're over the mountain. Look! There's the village. Look! I bet I can pick out Mama's house."

His voice was rising. To cover the sound, Junior began to cough violently. Immediately the hostess was at his side offering water.

I need a drink, he thought wildly. If we get back to Long Island, I'll tear Charlie Santoli apart limb from limb.

The plane landed, taxiing to a halt a good distance from

the terminal. What Junior and Eddie saw out on the tarmac rendered them both more speechless than any vow of silence could ever have accomplished.

In the midst of dozens of uniformed Wallonian policemen, a lone figure was jumping up and down and waving vigorously.

Mama Heddy-Anna.

Junior shook his head. "She don't look like she's dying to me."

Eddie's face was puzzled. "She looks so healthy. I can't believe it."

"We took this trip for nuthin', and now we're gonna spend the rest of our lives in jail."

The door of the plane opened and four policemen raced down the aisle. Junior and Eddie were encouraged to get out of their seats and put their hands behind their backs. As they were led away, their fellow passengers began removing roman collars and nun's veils, and burst into spontaneous applause.

At the foot of the stairs, they were enveloped in one of Mama Heddy-Anna's bear hugs.

"The nice policemen came for me. They said you were coming home as a surprise. I know you're in trouble, but good news! Papa was just made head trustee at the prison where you'll be staying from now on." She beamed, "All three of my boys together, nice and safe, where I can visit every week."

"Mama," Eddie sobbed as he laid his head on her shoulder. "I been so worried about you the whole time I was gone. How do you feel?"

Heddy-Anna patted him. "Never better."

Junior thought of the estate on Long Island, the limo, the money, the power, and Jewel, whom he knew would have a new boyfriend in two weeks. As Eddie's shoulders shook with emotion, all Junior could think was, How could I have been so stupid?

On Christmas Eve morning, Billy and Nor were lingering over the breakfast neither one of them had any interest in touching. The distracting reality that it was both Christmas Eve and Marissa's eighth birthday hung over them, a dense, oppressive blanket of pain.

The sudden steady ring of the doorbell startled both of them. Billy ran to answer it.

A beaming Marshall Frank Smith boomed, "Grab only what you need. You're booked on the 12:40 flight to New York, and if you want to catch it, you haven't got a minute to spare."

On Christmas Eve, Nor's Place usually enjoyed a pleasant flow of lunch customers. Some were last-minute shoppers, stopping for a quick bite. Others, more organized, came in for a quiet lunch before the religious and family celebrations began.

Today this place feels downright eerie, Dennis thought, as he surveyed the room from behind the bar. He shook his head. At least Nor had agreed that it was pointless to stay open on Christmas Day.

"I guess you're right, Dennis," she had admitted. "Only ten reservations! Those people would be better off at a place with a little life in it."

We're pretty much at the end of the line here, Dennis thought, as he was handed an order for a single beer.

Just then the bar phone rang. He picked it up.

"Dennis!" It was Nor's voice, buoyant and energetic. "We're at the airport, on our way home. We're in the clear. The Badgett brothers are gone, locked up for good," she exulted. "Get a birthday cake for Marissa for tonight, and phone our usual Christmas people. Tell them Nor's Place will be open for Christmas dinner and it's on the house. But don't let Marissa know! We want to surprise her."

*F*rom the moment she opened her eyes on Christmas Eve and whispered to herself, "Today I am eight years old," Marissa began to lose faith that Sterling would be able to bring Daddy and NorNor home. She had been sure they would be there when she woke up, but now she realized it was going to be like all the other times.

She had promised herself they would be back for Easter, but they weren't. Then she had been sure they'd be home when school closed for the summer . . . Then when it opened in September . . . Then for Thanksgiving . . .

It's going to be just like that again today, she thought, as she got up and put on her bathrobe. Tears kept trying to flow from her eyes, but she pressed them back with her hands. Trying to put a smile on her face, she went downstairs.

Her mother and Roy and the twins were already at the kitchen table. They all began to sing "Happy Birthday" when they saw her. There were presents next to her cereal bowl: a new watch; books and CDs from Mommy and Roy and the twins; a sweater from Grandma. Then she opened the last two boxes: ice skates from Daddy and a new skating outfit from NorNor.

Now she was absolutely, positively sure they wouldn't be

coming home today. If they were, wouldn't they wait to give her the presents when she saw them?

After breakfast Marissa carried all her gifts upstairs. When she reached her room, she dragged the chair from her desk over to the closet and stood up on it. She lifted the boxes with the new ice skates and the skating outfit and put them on the top shelf. Then, with the tips of her fingers, she pushed them back as far as she could, until they were out of sight.

She never wanted to look at them again.

At eleven o'clock she was in the living room, reading one of her new books, when the phone rang. Even though her heart stopped when she heard Mommy say, "Hello, Billy," she still didn't look up.

But then Mommy came rushing over to her. She didn't give her a chance to say, "I don't want to talk to Daddy," before the phone was at her ear and Daddy was shouting, "Rissa, want to go to Nor's Place for your birthday dinner? We're on the way home!"

Marissa whispered, "Oh, Daddy." She was bursting with so much happiness that she couldn't say anything more. And then she felt someone pat the top of her head. She looked up and there he was—her friend who wore the funny hat and who was not quite an angel, and he was smiling at her.

"Good-bye, Marissa," he said, and then he was gone.

In a daze, Marissa climbed the stairs to her room, closed the door, pulled over her chair, and stood on her tiptoes to retrieve the presents she had pushed away. But when she pulled the boxes down, something fell from the shelf and landed at her feet.

She sank to the floor and stared at the tiny Christmas ornament that she had never seen before. It was an angel dressed just like her friend.

"You've got the same funny hat," she whispered as she picked it up and kissed it. Holding it to her cheek, she looked out the window and up at the sky.

"You told me you weren't quite an angel," she said softly. "But I know that you are. Thank you for keeping your promise to help me. I love you."

$\mathcal{W}$hen Sterling entered the celestial conference room of the Heavenly Council and saw the approving looks on the faces of the saints, he knew he had completed his task to their satisfaction.

"I say, that was most touching," the admiral said with uncharacteristic tenderness.

"Did you see that child's face?" The nun sighed. "It shone with as perfect happiness as is possible on earth."

"I couldn't help staying until I saw Marissa in her father's arms," Sterling explained to the council. "Then I went back to Nor's Place with them. What a wonderful birthday party it was. As you know, the word that they'd returned flashed all over town, and everyone came in to welcome them home."

"I had tears in my eyes when Billy sang the song he wrote for Marissa," the queen observed.

"Talk about a sure-fire hit," the matador declared.

"As you know, he'll be recording it and the other songs he wrote while he was away," Sterling said. "It was a very painful year for him, but he used it well."

"As did you," the shepherd said quietly.

"Yes indeed. Absolutely," they all murmured, nodding.

"You not only found someone to help and used your head to work out a solution to her problem, but you also used your heart," the Native American saint said, clearly proud of Sterling.

"And you saved Charlie Santoli from the destructive life he was leading," the nun added.

There was a pause.

Then the monk stood up. "Sterling, the celebration of the birth of our Savior is about to begin. It is the judgment of the council that you have earned not only a visit to heaven, but your permanent place there. It is time for us to lead you through the gates." He turned toward the door.

"Wait a minute," Sterling said. "I have something to ask you."

The monk stared at him. "What could you possibly have to ask at this moment?"

"I am so grateful to all of you. As you know, I long to be in heaven. But I so enjoyed this experience that, by your leave, I would like to return to earth every Christmas and find someone who needs help. I never knew how good it could feel to really make a difference in other people's lives."

"Making other people happy is one of the great joys of the human condition," the monk told him. "You have learned your lesson even better than we realized. And now, come along."

*

As they approached, the heavenly gates opened wide before them, revealing a light brighter than a thousand suns, brighter than anything that Sterling had ever been able to imagine. A profound inner peace permeated his being. He was going toward the light; he was part of the light. The Heavenly Council stepped aside, and slowly and reverently he continued to walk forward. He was aware that there was one large group of people who were gathered together.

He felt a hand touch his. "Sterling, let me walk with you." It was Annie.

"The other newcomers are just ahead of you," she whispered. "They all came together. Their lives ended tragically, and although they themselves have found eternal joy, they are deeply concerned for the loved ones they left behind. But they will find their own ways to send help and comfort to them."

Annie paused. "Oh listen, the celebration is beginning."

Music filled the air, rose toward a crescendo. With the angels and saints and all the other souls in heaven, Sterling lifted his voice in song as they continued walking toward the light.

"Glory to the newborn King . . . "